ROGUE CELLS / CARBON HARBOUR

T0151133

Also by Garry Thomas Morse

*After Jack**
*Death in Vancouver**
*Discovery Passages**
*Minor Episodes / Major Ruckus**
Streams
Transversals for Orpheus

*Available from Talonbooks

ROGUE
CELLS
CARBON
HARBOUR

GARRY THOMAS MORSE

TALONBOOKS

© 2013 by Garry Thomas Morse

Talonbooks
P.O. Box 2076, Vancouver, British Columbia V6B 3S3
www.talonbooks.com

Typeset in Garamond
Printed and bound in Canada on 100% post-consumer recycled paper
First printing: 2013

Interior and cover design by Typesmith
Cover and part openings: Umberto Boccioni, *Visioni simultanee*, 1912
Collection: Von der Heydt Museum, Wuppertal, Germany

All rights reserved. No part of this book may be reproduced, stored in a retrieval system, or transmitted, in any form or by any means, without the prior written consent of the publisher or a licence from the Canadian Copyright Licensing Agency (Access Copyright). For a copyright licence, visit accesscopyright.ca or call toll free to 1-800-893-5777.

Talonbooks gratefully acknowledges the financial support of the Canada Council for the Arts, the Government of Canada through the Canada Book Fund, and the Province of British Columbia through the British Columbia Arts Council and the Book Publishing Tax Credit.

Library and Archives Canada Cataloguing in Publication

Morse, Garry Thomas, author
    Rogue cells ; Carbon harbour / Garry Thomas Morse.

(The Chaos! Quincunx)
Issued in print and electronic formats. ISBN 978-0-88922-776-7 (pbk.). —ISBN 978-0-88922-777-4 (epub)

    I. Title. II. Title: Carbon harbour. III. Series: Morse, Garry Thomas Chaos! Quincunx.

PS8626.O774R65 2013   C813'.6   C2013-903141-3
C2013-903142-1

The sun, piercing them, confused the sticky mucus with the diluted solution. One could make out just the one single succulent, quivering mass, transparent and hardening; and in the ephemeral brilliance with which it decorated Lemoine's attire, it seemed to have fixed the prestige of a momentary diamond there, still hot, so to speak, from the oven from which it had emerged, and for which this unstable jelly, corrosive and alive as it was for one more instant, seemed at once, by its deceitful, fascinating beauty, to present both a mockery and a symbol.

– MARCEL PROUST

ROGUE

CELLS

Another guy came in, and he said he was quitting his job at the Research Laboratory; said anything a scientist worked on was sure to wind up as a weapon, one way or another. Said he didn't want to help politicians with their fugging wars anymore. Name was Breed. I asked him if he was any relation to the boss of the fugging Research Laboratory. He said he fugging well was. Said he was the boss of the Research Laboratory's fugging son.

— KURT VONNEGUT

A Bad Case

Oober Mann lay atop his narrow bed and stared at the ceiling, listening to cries of ecstasy through tissue-thin walls. This evening's recipient of the ecstasy was one Audrey Boolean, a woman whose undivided attentions he had half-heartedly pined for on many lonesome nights just like this one. The generous provider of the ecstasy was none other than his roommate and bosom bestie Indio Rosario. Oober pressed his left ear to the wall, fuming. He felt his body react to echoes of their rampant splaternization although he was affronted by their continual offers of mild humiliation. Even now, she was calling his name through the wall to spur on Indio's formidable instrument.

"Ooooooober!"

He folded his arms over his chest and coughed. No way, not tonight, sweetheart. Find another last-minute cleanup crew. His thoughts returned to the tofu-shaped block in his brain. He was sure there was something there, inside that block. Sometimes he dreamt of a tall woman with a purple V inked on her back. She was always holding a condiment squeeze bottle and doing all manner of things with its contents. She would apply a dollop or two and then suck the substance from her fingertips, beckoning him with one of the freshly licked fingers. Then she would squeeze out the word *yellow* in large streaming letters with a great spurt before pouting and flipping him her index. He would wake up all aflutter, realizing that the woman and this sensation seemed very familiar to him. His two companions had learned to read this condition in him and instantly take advantage of it. Without missing a beat, the alert would be sounded.

"Oober's dreaming again!"

Audrey would act out an entire repertoire of suggestive physical comedy routines (her original background was in advertising), combined with an intricate striptease that always concluded in the other room with Indio. Oober had accepted this role of natural, drug-free enhancement enabler. He felt like a character in a sequel, whose missing time between features is never fully explained. He was unhappy, but he had no wish for this wacky pair to be unhappy too, not on his account anyway. Once they were lounging around in smoky post-coital torpor, Oober would talk openly about the woman from his dream. Though she had no interest in him, Audrey still did not like to hear about how oustanding this woman was.

"Give it a rest, Oober. She's just a dream. Besides, you got us, doncha?"

Then with a flurry of tongues, they would fall upon him, while the tofu block, appearing more like a wedge of aspic, would reassert its integrity about those memories he considered most vital. Oober only went through the motions, his mind elsewhere. He could feel the presence of another life that seemed so vivid and real it put his caricature friends to shame.

"Whoa! Listen to that! Oober's got a bad case of mustard gas again!"

Keeping Us Cushy

Blog Stentorian checked his blinding teeth in his nacreous compact before eyeing his environs. He had squandered a month of top-drawer tantrums trying to gain access to this sand trap before he had at last broken down and missived Aunt Notel. He didn't like to overuse his fabulous connexions, and he had already used up a few favours to meet the controversial lead singer of Blank, who talked exclusively about the wonders of oceanfront birthing. But the thought of hectoring up and down in front of his personal tuber in a sand trap, not to mention the denizens of New Haudenosaunee, made him moist in his ptarmigan briefs (he was sent a fresh pair by a stupefied fan twice a day).

"If that's what you really want, Blog dear ..."

Aunt Notel had nodded her quivering head at the other end of the signal and he had dispatched her at once. On air, he aimed to downplay his backstair birthright and claim to the massive Notel Hotel fortune. His career as a live shimmer was front and centre and in your face and he wasn't going to go down in history as just another rich bastard playboy, nosiree. Blog was a public watchdog who was, as the slogan went, "keeping us cushy."

Now full of vimegar, he swept aside the makeup team with a pained look of martyrdom powdered right onto his face. When the commanding officer charged out of the bunker, Blog leapt into his arms.

"So what is it like to be in the First People's Platoon, poking around this grimy <bleep>hole of terrifying peril?"

"Uh ... we bin at war with Nutella for four an' a half years now."

"And what is it like to be up to the elbow in sweat and grime and utter filth in the name of freedom?"

"Undescribable."

"I spoke with Private Buttons and it broke my heart."

"Yeah, he'll do that."

"He spoke about what it's like to be so far away from mommy and daddy and his main squeeze, Apple Buttons."

"Yup, it's tough <bleep> no question. Summa these kids ... it ain't real. S'a <bleep>in' vidya game or grafted novel or some <bleep>."

The sound of boots approaching. With stealth. Private Buttons popped in, waving his automatic *good morning* over the whole entourage.

"At ease, Buttons."

"No can do, sir. We're gettin' bushwhacked, sir!"

At Blog Stentorian's behest, his personal tuber zoomed in on the red-rimmed glassy eyes of Private Buttons. Slimy muddy figures were crawling about within the soldier's field of vision.

"Wait a tick, what's that?"

"Aggros, sir! They're all around us!"

"Muzzle that peace-accord-a-muhnator, Private Buttons!"

"Wha ... that's crazy as a <bleep>house raccoon—"

Private Buttons fired, wasting the entire makeup crew, and Blog's hairstylist spontaneously combusted in a wisp of product.

"Stand down, Private Buttons. I repeat, stand down!"

"This is not your call, sir!"

Buttons raised the butt of his humanizer and cold-cocked his commander. Blog Stentorian loosened his Communiqué necktie and stepped forward. He had seen worse. Much, much worse.

"Private Buttons, about-face. Put down the gun."

"Who is that? You sound familiar."

"Private Buttons, you're perfectly safe. In fact, you're streaming live on *Boob-Tube*."

"Hi, Mom!"

Blog held the lad and stroked his chin thoughtfully.

"You're just a boy. But what do you fear?"

"Aggros. They gots me. They gots me!"

Then Private Buttons fainted and fell into Blog's arms. He turned to the scorched face of his personal tuber.

"Did you get that? Tell me you got that!"

That Finger-Lickin' Rush

Aburrido Raeder sat down on his couch and reached for a refreshing can of Reflux Cola. He pulled the tab and heard the can's tinny little voice.

"Sorry, loser, try again. Loser."

What Aburrido did not know was that in the forensic game he was about to score big time. He gulped down the contents of the can and put it down on the wobbly tabula rasa. That was funny – he thought he had heard a clinking sound coming from inside the can. "Open me up to find out the latest!"

"No!"

"What a loser!"

Aburrido grabbed the can impulsively, ignoring its squeals, and selected a kitchen knife from an excellent set he had bought for next to nothing at Haida-Buy. Then he sliced into the tawny aluminum and pried open the can with both hands. Inside, he found a human finger bearing a heavy ring.

"Congratulations! You've won a free can of Reflux!"

Don't Delay, This Is the Space You Want

Liebe Nimitz, seasoned Realspace agent, flitted about the local coordinates with the potential, flirting ever so lightly. He loomed in front of the delicious view, revealing sharp, shiny teeth. He was not as beautiful as the man in the ebony prospectus, but that honey had not arrived yet.

"Ms. Caterwall, this is a very exclusive viewing. You could nab it on the spot, or you could give away this spanking gift horse to the next buyer. Of course, that would be so hard on me since I'm half in love with you."

"I thought we had a deal, Mr. Nimitz."

"I did notify you that Mr. Thorstein would not be available for a few days."

"But how am I to ... sample my new lifestyle?"

"There was a delay at customs. But he'll be here. I swear on my developmentally challenged first-born."

"But I want to try before I buy. Is that a crime?"

"Heh heh, not yet, Ms. Caterwall."

"Well?"

"What can I do to put you in this stratagig today?"

"I want everything listed in the prospectus."

"Okay, here's what I'm gonna do, since I like the way you give face ..."

He clapped his hands and the faux fireplace began to emit heat and light and romantic chanting, as a whale blubber rug began to jiggle. Mood muzak suffused the room and Mr. Nimitz began his best striptease sales routine in sync with the blue background saxotones, swinging about his confidence-inspiring sports jacket and flaunting his inflatable chinos with a saucy look. Ms. Caterwall helped him off with his shirt and started teasing the tufts of ash-blond hair on his chest.

"Now lose that ukini!"

Mr. Nimitz cleared his throat.

"At this point, I am authorized to remind you this is only a scale model. Mr. Thorstein will be completely in keeping with your size specifications. Build, proportions, race, whatever ..."

"Smoked candy! The last one I had was a low flow. No go in him, you see."

"Many of our upscale clients feel that way. It's simply a matter of personal preference. My only concern is to ensure you are perfectly satisfied. And preferably today."

"Charming!"

"Please note there is a pressure-activated opacity dimmer built into each of the walls ..."

Ms. Caterwall pressed her chest against one of the translucent panels and sweet-talked it into transparency mode. Limucks whizzed by and airhorned her bare body.

"I believe this place has the perfect view!"

"I'm running late and must dash. More fish to gull. However, I'll leave you in excellent hands."

He pressed a button and a little man in a periwinkle uniform entered the suite. He cursed under his breath, tearing off the Feltcro and introducing himself in jaybird fashion.

"Crikey! All this aggro is doing my head in."

"Ms. Caterwall, allow me to present to you the concierge. He's available day and night for anything you might require."

"Ello ello! You're a nice bit of all right! Now wave to the traffic, darling! Because we're going to have a lovely time, end of."

Regifter, Not Regrifter

"Hear, hear."

The Den Moderator gonged a gong and a thousand and five eyes fixed upon his grim face.

"Gentlemen, and ladies, we are facing a monumental crisis."

"Whoooooo!"

"For innumerable annoyons we have struggled to heave forth the One and Limited Truth. Yet the blasphemous headgivers cover everything in a sticky veil and try to obscure what is sound and true."

"Booooooo!"

"It is critical at this impasse that we acknowledge the imminent arrival of our benevolent life Regifter who in our *classic* texts promised to restore our former abilities and chattel to us."

"Boooooooyah!"

"In place of science, itself a malignant curse upon the secret knowledge in our throbbing hearts, Chaos!tology became an organization because its throbbing members were devoted to preserving the interplanetary lore and pocket change bequeathed to us. Now that the Monster Monster Big Time is at hand, we must prepare for the return of the Regifter. Already, we have observed several portents in relation to this most auspicious event."

"I thought that was about the Re*grifter*."

"Nay, denizen. Do not speak so hastily against the Re*grifter*, who is just as much a part of our teachings about the fluid cycle of personal goods."

A one-eyed man stepped forward, brandishing a freshly honed spear.

"What must we do?"

"Patience, my friend. We must not be so narrow-sighted as that. We must learn to take everything in with a fresh pair of eyes ..."

"Whoa ... you just blew my mind."

"And does it not say, friend, in the bubble in chapter 2, figure iii, *A blown mind is a thing of beauty for more than a mandatory long weekend*?

An awed silence followed.

"Awe ... some."

"As for our new mission statement and course of action, operating under the working title *Funky Prawn*, I cannot reveal more at this time. For now, it's the same drill as usual. Keep up with your payments and fast-acting learninators. If you ever feel sleepy, meditate. And keep an eye out for those deprogramming rigs."

The Q-Bomb

Flak Riesling fluttered his eyelids and looked around the dank grey holding cell. What had he done this time to be left hanging from a wall? O yeah. Hassan Armadill, the head facilitator of Insurgent Saddo Management (ISM), rushed in, waving a banana file folder in his face.

"Here we are again, and it looks like you haven't learned a thing!"

"I did what I had to do."

"The entire reserve is toast. You *accidentally* exterminated an entire pod of Old Haudenosaunees."

"But I saved a boy named Enkidu Swiftswipe."

"That boy's a Dogrib."

"But he has information pertaining to a potential attack on our nation."

"What!?!"

"Do you remember Special-Ops Castaneda?"

"Do you?"

"Yes. It was a sting operation to infiltrate a peyote ring. A group known only as the Divine Cactii were attempting to alter the consciousness of ordinary denizens. But that was just the tip of the foot-long. Proceeds from the illegal sale of the souped-up hyperpeyote are about to pass into the hands of even more dangerous grippies."

"Still doesn't wash, Flak."

"The boy got wind of what was going down and ran for his life. But he ran into members of the incredibly sketchy I___ tribe. No doubt they gratified their savage desires and then tortured him for more info. He's in tatters."

"Flak, the boy is fine. I just got him a malted."

"We won't save this nation with that attitude!"

"Then what happened?"

"I ordered them to give me the boy but they only spoke to me in their animal tongue. I informed them they were acting seditiously by harbouring a key witness. Then they made animal figures with their fingers and laughed. I didn't like the way they laughed."

His mind reeled. What had happened then? He could hear the sound of his own voice ordering the Q-bomb.

"Big Bird needs to crap. I repeat, Big Bird is ready to take a big big dump."

He had held the boy to him and spirited him away into the side of a mountain, which was fortunately open for business. Then the Q-bomb hit.

The I___ tribe trembled in its wake. Then the men began to eye one another. Soon they were exploring each other's bodies with enthusiasm and abandon. They began to strip off their traditional dress of faded denim and became lost in the ecstasy of one another's latent desires. Flak had shielded the boy's eyes from their beefed-up interactions, which were too unnationalistic to behold.

"*May the Bard forgive me!*"

"Earth to Flak! How the hell did those people die?"

"Sorry, Hassan. The nature and ramifications of the Q-bomb are classified."

"Awwww ..."

"Listen to me, Hassan. If this threat is real, then we need the boy to tell us everything he knows. And I mean everything!"

"We did send some agents out for more ice cream."

"But in the side of that mountain, I formed a special avuncular relationship with the boy. He trusts me."

"I know I'm gonna regret this ..."

"Now, get me out of these shackles! This is no time for recreation!"

"Just promise me one thing, Flak. This time, could you try to cut back on the genocide? Or it's my ass in the portaswing."

Hardly the Time or Place

"Whaddya make o' this?"

"It's a finger all right."

Detective Blue Green grimaced mildly and then powerwashed his brain of the image. His spunky and excitable new sidekick, Rebecca Tomahawk, ralphed discreetly into her new hat. Then she fanned herself, looking sheepish.

"Don't mind me. Shoplifter detail this ain't."

"Happens to all the fresh flunkies. Just don't indulge in a barfarama when my backside's on the griddle and it starts to sizzle!"

"Sounds like we got ourselves a date."

"We all have a date, Tomahawk, a blind date with our maker."

Rebecca folded her arms over her heaving bosom. Her maker was an animal, maybe. What is more, she had a case of butterflies. Her eyes came to rest upon the wedding ring in a Stayternal baggie.

"Those are some stones. You married, detective?"

Blue's face darkened. He turned around and punched a hole through the wall. Rebecca read the answer in his eyes and once again lost her lunch.

"Married? Yeah, I guess you could say that."

"Well, maybe you wanna unload sometime?"

"Emoting is what's wrong with this country."

"We all have to unload sometime. Cuts back on the bruxism."

She held his sweating head to her chest and stroked his hair as he looked up expectantly at her full lips, still slightly pukey.

"This is hardly the time or place ..."

"Aren't you ever off duty, detective?"

His fist tightened around the baggie of evidence and his face took on a pained faraway look.

"Once ..."

Bless You

The nagging thought that plagued Oober most was that he was perpetually at work on a bloated post-meta-fiction headed nowhere. This idea bore an air of mysticism and made him suffer many episodes of spiritual malaise. His work was literally in pieces and he could not even pretend to speak of a plot. Also, Oober's contorted linguistic chromaticisms had no target market or niche. In the eyes of various agents, they qualified as neither hotcakes nor latkes. He was persisting obstinately in his lewd, unreadable style but he was also running out of steam. Then he said one of the most regrettable sentences in the language.

"I want something to happen to me."

It is beyond the scope of this meta-narrative to explain why Oober Mann had the molecular equivalent of an interstellar ham radio beating off lyrical patches of Mercurial Morse in time with his pulse. What happens on Venus stays on Venus, but often you still catch something. Oober had caught it all right, and now he had the music in his bones and blood and brain. He had not said anything to his friends but lately he'd been hearing abrupt musical interludes in his headspace, followed directly by suspicious happenstances. He was considering this problem of his when suddenly a cello sprang to life. More often than not, it was Bach he heard before having another episode. He looked around the downtown library nervously. One book flew off the shelf, and it was packed with bizarre characters, including the woman from his dream. The wet letters along the spine spelled *Major Ruckus*. He tried to reach for it but the book flew away. If he wanted answers, Oober knew he had to recover that book. Just then, a woman breezed by, leaving him in a cloud of Gestapo perfume that gassed his nostrils.

His senses were also assaulted by her long no-nonsense antelope coat and her more-nonsense-please pelican boots. She was tailed by two men who were wheeling a cartload of antique discs and debating about the usefulness of post-meta-fiction in our post-post-disaster era gone postal. They disappeared behind a door, distracting Yo-Yo Ma from a heart-rending sarabande. Oober peeped through the vertical window. She brushed aside her skunky hair and removed a pair of reading glasses, which without warning she scrunched under one of her boot heels. One of the shelvers (his nametag read Knob) nearly dropped his hateboard. But his cohort labelled Futz was already on top of things.

"Hey baby, wanna go for Rhutinis?"

"Hey hottie, you don't have to buy me din-din. Just give me something to snack on!"

"No foolsies?"

"Just show me what you got."

Futz pushed the bookcart carefully to one side and let out a sporty roar. Then he unbuttoned his shorts. But Knob was loitering pensively.

"What about my needs?"

"If three's a crowd, then I really gotta get crowded!"

Knob started fondling and sniffing the fresh-kill smell wafting off her antelope coat.

"Yeah, this is hot."

"Yeah man, such hot action."

She put on a pair of guerilla gardening gloves and began to stroke them simultaneously. They swelled and were lulled. Then she produced a glistening rehab special and took her sweet time screwing on a silencer.

"Wow, is this for a promotional tube?"

"We're gonna be on *U-Screw* ...?"

"O yeah. Hot and steamy streaming action."

She bent Knob over and rubbed the barrel against his anal universe.

"O yeah ... guilty pleasure ... the love that dare not speak ..."

Then she fired twice. Yo-Yo nearly flubbed a gigue.

She bid Futz kneel in front of her and touched the rehab special to his soft lips. He took his cue and began to roll the barrel around in his mouth, stopping only to give it a lick now and again.

"Mmm yeah ... make me do it ... cover me in slawsome sauce ..."

She fired once.

There was little time. She draped Futz over Knob and closed his fingers around the gun. Then right before Yo-Yo stopped playing, a hand clamped over Oober's mouth, holding what could only be a Sneezee doused in chloroform. He sneezed, and everything went dark.

"Bless you."

Spice on In

Chip Riesling jacked into the Simbat 6000 and let Blank's aromatic drum set wash over him. His heart was pounding as over Bodycount Bluff a formation of Aggros appeared, plentiful as cockchafers. He levelled his infrared automatic at their looming heads. *Rat-a-tat-ooooeeeee!* He watched their graphics dissemble into flailing limbs and scorched flesh.

"Yeah."

Then through the mangled and riddled Aggros, he recognized his mother, waving her arms and legs as if signalling where a plane should land. This wasn't part of level 2046.

"Pause."

"Sorry to pester you, Chip, but I had to spice on in."

"S'okay, Mom. And it's called splicing on in."

"Whoops. Anyhoo, there's someone for you at the door."

Chip jacked off the system and reached for a blushing towel. His mother eyed his bare body and rolled her eyes in madcap fashion. He draped the towel around his waist and swaggered to the door.

It was the lady from down the hall, the one from New Västerbotten. He had only seen her in the neurmatic but they had never spoken.

"Your mother says you are expert with Simbat. Mine ... not working. Could you come ... take look?"

"Hmm, yeah."

"Whenever you like, ya."

In the kitchen, his mother slapped a spurtle down and flashed him a cockeyed grin.

"Well! A real coming-of-age tale!"

When Aggros Attack

"Aggros!"

"An uncanny development in the Nutella conflict today. One of the soldiers (bless their hearts) on the New Haudenosaunee side reportedly wigged out and began firing on his own men (and one woman). The situation could have turned disastrous, were it not for one plucky shimmer who was on the scene ..."

The tube blipverts to the calm, smooth jaw of Blog Stentorian.

"I can't let you do that, young feller. I respect and admire your courage and understand the pressure you're under but you'll have to go through me if you want to harm these people."

"I can't. Aw shucks, I love you, Mr. Stentorian."

"Well, skin me alive, you are so supple yet firm!"

"I can't live in a world like this. Let this man in and let the truth be known! He's the real hero!"

After a lengthy speech about the virtues of real-time war coverage and noble sentiments in the aura of every live shimmer, the soldier collapsed into the arms of Blog Stentorian.

"Now let's have a few ticks of free advertising for Private Buttons' gripping tell-all *Don't Ask*, a first-hand perspective of the invasion of Absurdabad, and don't miss Blog's special edition of *Me-Time* with Apple Buttons, fresh from her heart-stopping appearance on *Divorce Sport* ..."

A Watched Pot

Hurt Hardass climbed into his stretch limuck and raised a nacreous compact, studying a particular line in his face that needed attention ASAP. A knuckle tapped on the soundproof divider and it lowered a crack between him and the driver.

"Master Hurt, there's a most distressing missive for you regarding the quality of the seafood in one of your restaurants. Shall I have the party demoralized? Or might they vanish for good?"

"Not at all. Patch them through."

The divider closed again.

"Hello."

"Is this Mr. Hardass?"

"Yes, in the flesh."

"Did you know your prawns are funky?"

"Are you some kind of crackpot?"

"You should only boil live things."

"Live things?"

"Because a watched pot sometimes boils faster in the sea."

"Boils faster in the sea."

"Clear."

"Clear."

The call ended.

Hurt knocked on the divider.

"Yes?"

"Butler, cancel my exthetics appointment with Dr. Fava. Head home instead. There's something I just remembered I need to do."

"Certainly, Master Hurt."

Primary Attributes

Goebbel Gewürztraminer smiled at his spin doctor, Abe Chaney, and infused some PerformoMax into his left bicep.

"So, what do you think my chances are?"

"What do I think? G.G., you're the start of a bran new era! Who else can help New Haudie to prosper?"

"It's a lot of added pressure."

"Well, ya gotta take the fluff with the dirt, that's what I always say."

"But I am still like a foreigner in your fine upstanding land, at least to the First Peoples."

"You're a tube star. What more do they need? Toss around a few action flick catchphrases and mark my words, you'll win by a landslide."

"That was the old me."

"You think Kennedy Swiftboat was fit? Nah. They had to move her around with wires half the time. Two goons in suits carried her everywhere. She still wiped the floor with Elmo Hedge and proved to be less diabolical than expected. She even had your unique problem."

Both men watched the governor's bicep ripple like a throbbing roadmap to pieces, for it was so beautifully freakish to behold.

"It's quite the grind. My doctor advised me to cut down on my orgies. And whipped cream and fatty oils are completely out of the question."

"My heart bleeds. But when you're elected, you'll be a god, a Caesar. Them Romans, they had some pretty swanky times too, you know."

Governor Gewürztraminer lay back in his King Lion chair, feeling the applied hormones raging through his body. Suddenly he leapt up and heaved a rococo console table through the sliding patio door. Swimmers below began to complain about the shards of Sexiglass.

"Just get me elected already!"

Chaney grinned in his menacing way.

"You got passion, I'll give you that."

Run, Don't Walk!

Alice (Squeaky) Fomme commandeered the cash with a warm grin.

"Yes, what would you like?"

"I want to return these …"

The woman was trembling. She pushed forward two black thermods. Alice scrutinized the return slip.

"But the receipt is for the new ones. These are our old product line."

"Don't argue with me! I've never heard of such a thing! I want to speak to the manager."

A bearded head emerged from behind the counter.

"Can I help?"

"I have receipts, just not for these. I want to trade them in for store credit."

"All right."

"But this one, she's arguing with me. Never argue with the customer!"

The woman left with a smug expression and a largegantic cookie.

"Alice …"

"They steal the stuff. The old manager was wise. They're like a team or something."

"Who would steal a thermod to get food?"

"It's easy. Then they root around or shake people down for receipts."

"Well, thank you, the all-new Clancy Klew."

"I can't believe you let her get away with it."

"Alice, let me tell you a story. I used to believe in fair play and freedom of expression and all that jazz. That was until I saw *The Secret Corporation*. It was a highly informative tube that showed me how we are not responsible as individuals for our actions. The Secret Corporation is. So it is not me deciding to fire you immediately. It is in fact the Secret Corporation. And it would do you a world of wonder to watch this tube. And run, don't walk! It really changed my life."

Alice stared at him incredulously. Then she untied her Filterz designer apron and slowly wrapped it around the manager's neck. She pulled and pulled at his windpipe with strength she had never used before. Then Alice ran.

The new store manager arrived within minutes, and swept his predecessor into the corner out of sight. After all, it wasn't his doing. It could only be the omnipotent will of the Secret Corporation.

At Seven Hundred and Fifty Yams per Fnord

Oober regained consciousness and saw flashing signs whizzing past the window of a vehicle unlike any he had ever been abducted in. He blinked and tried to make sense of the buttons with German labelling. What the wigwam was a ZEIT-TRAUME?

"And you call yourself a writer."

It was the Librarian speaking and driving, or at least the alluring anti-hero from the library.

"The Librarian works fine as a handle. Also, leave the ZEIT-TRAUME alone. It's a real downer."

"How ..."

"Don't be alarmed. From time to time, I telefuse with your neural static and pick a few things up."

"I must be asleep."

"If you are, then I am not real and this is one of those very lucid dreams you love to interface with in *Beaver Tales*."

"How did you know about that?"

She drew out a paper knife and tapped his leg. He received a gigasmic jolt.

"Aaahhhh!"

"You are not dreaming, Oober Mann."

"What then?"

"You have something in your nervous system that I am interested in. Even from space it's as big as some beaver dams. You can think of it as an artificial hip or a metal plate if that helps you."

"It doesn't."

"Then here goes. An old friend of mine suffered a horrible fate at the hands of his enemies. The only remaining means of survival was to convert his own animate resonances into parcels of pure energy and to transfer them to ... let's call it an electrodynamic implant."

"Dude, are you for real?"

"You're not listening again! This is only the second-most important thing that has ever happened to you!"

"The second?"

"You don't remember the first. I want to help you remember."

"Do you mean my first time with our neighbour Mrs. Abrams? She swore me to secrecy!"

The Librarian pounded an infusion into his arm. At once, he could picture a woman with a mustard bottle, carrying her little red dog, and it wasn't a dream. He knew them!

"I can help you remember, Oober. I can fill those holes in your head. But you're going to have to trust me."

"Trust you? You blew away those hunky shelvers. They were just boys, hunky horndogging boys."

"They just looked like hunky shelvers. They were actually Cicadians. Give them half a chance to moult and they would have burst your eardrums open. Rest assured, one day they will capture you and bisect you but that's a long ways off."

"Could you make any of this spoorish nastooky an ounce more user-friendly?"

"You Terrans! It would make twice as much sense to roach or rodent or whale!"

"Undoubtedly."

Oober would have left the vehicle in disgust that instant, save for three things:

1. He was curious about his selective memory loss.
2. He was inexorably strapped into his seat.
3. They were travelling at seven hundred and fifty yams per fnord. In spite of the circulating inertiabite, however fast that was, it felt really really really fast. He wriggled helplessly in his seat, feeling nauseous.

"Whoa ... easy there, big felluh!"

"I still can't believe you finished off those young guys. They could have formed meaningful relationships and settled down with equally hot soulmates."

"Cicadians! I was emitting an ancient Korean folk tune to rope 'em in. That and a dull polyphonic fire alarm for good measure."

"Okay. What the frack is a Cicadian?"

"They are one of the evolutionary life forms that will inevitably spring from relatively dormant code in the human genome. After decades of disaster, some of the more blobby and chemically controlled organisms emerge from their residential cocoons as something entirely new."

"You mean they become moths and stuff?"

"Yes, in a way. Aside from the Cicadians, the Phasmida are also plentiful. They are a luminous translucent species. To see them, let alone meet them, is an occasion indeed!"

"Somehow, I take it you are one of the latter."

Teamwork

Billy Joe Bearclaw peeped furtively over his reamcatcher at the passing figure of ISM Facilitator Hassan, still gripping Flak's arm apprehensively (or romantically). Where were they going? Flak should be singing all the way to Sing Sing by now. Bobby Joe noticed this and gave Billy Joe a swift kick, which sent his chair rolling.

"Something on your mind, chief?"

"Nope."

"Sure you ain't getting some non-productive ideas? If so, would you care to share?"

"Drop it, Bobby Joe. One day you'll get what's coming to you."

"You mean a promotion, hoss."

Billy Joe picked up his reamcatcher and gave Bobby Joe a whap on the nose. There was a trickle of blood and Agent Panza grabbed a wipeaway and a bucket of suds.

"I am always cleaning up your messes."

"Mellax, Panza."

"Yeah, don't breathe a word of this."

"Well, boys will be boys!"

Bobby Joe tried to stare down Billy Joe, who stared right back. They were both shirtless and stood pec to pec, undulating. Agent Panza began to get nervous. He gave each of them a one-handed shoulder massage.

"There ... so much tension ..."

Vigoruppity! Is Down

Bruciato Giallo draped his body in a flowing buckskin robe before re-examining the contents of his Flaxenite briefcase. It was all there. Then he sat down at his writing desk, which brought back the memory of the only other time he had used it, to address the producers of his short-lived *Male Order Machissimo*, what the critics had so hastily written off as a vapid rumppumper with no story. It had been a mistake to ask for more money. Apparently, the adverts for Vigoruppity! had not reached their target audience, and for this reason they had replaced him with Trey Volta. By that time, Bruciato knew the letter should be simple and succinct.

Caro Mondo,

I want to set the record straight. My initial reason for becoming a Chaos!tologist was to get more tube and pseudoreality roles. I want to assure any concerned parties that my logic was misguided in this endeavour. I found the chief tenets of Chaos!tology to be beneficial and in many times of crisis, I found strength in their belief system, a system I was more than proud to call my own. In spite of universally abysmal reviews, I believe my role as Oregano Bushtit in Feeler of the Phobes represents some of my finest work. To make up for earlier doubts regarding what they believe most sincerely (and what I have come to believe most sincerely), I have left a token of good faith. I bequeath my life savings to the Foundation for Devout Chaos!tologists. Let them use it to reveal to the world the truth about our fanciful origins.

Per Sempre,
Bruciato Giallo

He signed the note with his customary personal fragrance flourish and pinned the note to his robe, crying out as it pierced his broad chest. Then he lifted the briefcase with a firm grip and, without warning to the dawdling press conference of two, leapt five stories to his death.

A Mild Earthquake

The summer was heating up. Mémé lay beneath a cool blue sheet that felt wonderful against her bare skin. When she heard the knock, she was almost irritated to have to get up and button a shirt but she was also exhilarated by this promise of an insistent visitor. She slid the chain loose and dangling and opened the door. The tanned burly young man breezed in, flexing and emphatically clearing his throat of lingering phlegm. He peered into each room before returning to her.

"Hey, Bronto."

"Coast clear?"

He was already ripping open her shirt. Three buttons skittered across wooden floor.

"Bronto, I'll have to sew those back on before—"

"Yeah, before what?"

"You know."

"He can stitch 'em back on while I watch."

He pulled her closer, surrounding her with his bulging arms while partly trying to lift her. But she was big-boned and beautiful and nonetheless heavier than he anticipated and they both went reeling into the kitchen everywhichway until finally he parked her on the counter. They kissed and kissed, while his big hands made the rest of her body feel very wanted. She tried to clasp one of his hands meaningfully.

"Bronto, to bed—"

His hand moved between her thighs. She could feel his thick fingers fumbling around and then inducing gobs and gobs of excitement.

"Where is your ol' man anyway?"

"He went to buy the new Playnation Maxipad strap-in console. Don't worry, he's an excellent shopper. He'll be hunting from store to store for hours—"

"Yeah, but I bet he can't do this."

Bronto eased her off the counter sideways and into his arms. It took a few seconds to balance but soon he was carrying her into the bedroom with minimal embarrassment. She threw back her head, feeling for all the world like one of the heroines on the cover of a Ruddy Duck novel, swooning in the arms of a hunky naturopath.

"I'll give you Playnation."

She tried not to laugh. Bronto nodded assurances in order to psyche himself up before pulling down his Revelation motivational training shorts. He coughed and pointed with large indexes at his pride and joy as if introducing a new product line of interactive experiences.

"Wow Bronto. Like wow."

She was not sure what she felt, staring at him like that. Bronto's incredible and even cartoonish physicality appeared to be poking fun at everyone. Also, she knew there were countless barrels of Swellycep in his basement and that Bronto was constantly taking infusions to improve his love mandles.

"O Bron – to – !"

"Yeah, you like that, eh?"

"You're demolishing me."

"That's right, baby."

"You're extirpating my spotted owl!"

And as he grunted and panted on top of her body, she watched the ripped roadmap of the veins in his right arm pulsate and appear to experience a mild earthquake.

Don't Try This at Home

"Blog Stentorian here, trying to piece together today's events. The question: What led a soldier to turn on his brethren (and one woman) and ultimately destroy an entire makeup crew (brave denizens all)? We turn to one of our regular flunkies, Dr. Emilio Hernández Fava, for a segment we like to call 'Speedy Second Opinion.'"

A bright explosion is followed by footage of Dr. Fava picking up some scorched bones and smelling them.

"Thank you, Blog. Our researchers (smug no-name bottom-feeders) agree that Private Buttons suffered from a case of Sim Sickness, or SS. Our military industrial complex supports the use of intensive simulation software that works in conjunction with real-time combat. Of course, it's common to find monkeyed-up black-market models that promise nine to ten times the organic boost from its testosteRom firmware. Unfortunately, one side effect of this undeniable enhancement are newly discovered cellular gnomes that ingratiate their way into our nervous system and create a production factory for hallucinogens."

"Gnomes?"

"That's a funky term coined by Ann Thrax for referring to these rather mischievous genomes."

"Then any of us could be next."

"O no no no! Put your panic-mongering aside for one minute, won't you? Aside from our entire infantry, it won't affect the public much. Only the usual, kids at that age wanting to experiment and try something new ..."

The good doctor grinned and winked.

"So if you're facing a troublesome teen with a sweet sixteen on the way, I'd seriously consider giving them the gift of morphine. That way, you keep 'em off the street!"

"So how real is this threat, Doctor?"

"Real ... and not real. The hallucinogens are products of a hormonal imbalance, particularly in young men. At first, the simulations can be a form of escape from the tension they are facing in combat. But sometimes the simulations bleed into reality and confuse what is what. The hallucinogens are not real, initially. But after a while, they take root in the nervous system and begin to reproduce their own rogue cells."

"Uhm hm. And what about Private Buttons?"

"Luckily, we got to him in time. For instance, we could make him relatively normal by having him undergo a sex change. That's only one option, mind you. There are others far more dicey and drastic ..."

"Sounds excellent, Dr. Fava. This is an eye-opening ball-buster for me."

"Of course, there's another threat we're facing. If some little genius (without a certificate, mind you) were to reprogram the testosteRom with a virus, any number of terrible things could go down ..."

"That's all the time we have, Doctor. And for those of you with little ones, don't try this at home!"

He's Really Talented

"As flies to wanton boys are we to the gods."

Gary Boondock muttered these lines to himself as he boarded the omnitran bound for Wounded Rib and skulked to a seat in the back. He continued murmuring the indelible lines of his faith as he reached under his coat and began to fondle the strapped collection of vile jelly explosives.

"They kill us for their sport."

A silver-coiffed woman elbowed her Harry, who looked up irritably.

"Harry, isn't that what's his face? The actor?"

"Who?"

"That man at the back of the tran."

"Never seen him before."

"We jacked into a blue-tube of his last month. It was based on a true story."

"Uhhh ..."

"Don't you remember? He said to the woman he loved and would never see again, 'It's not that I'm sick of life, just allergic.'"

"O, that piece of spoor."

"Well, that's him ... the actor in that piece of ... that tube."

"Then what's he doing on the tran?"

"Maybe his limuck is being repaired. Or maybe he's rehearsing for his next role."

"Or maybe he's just a bum!"

"I'm gonna go talk to him ..."

"Marnie, leave him alone."

But Marnie waved at the stranger and started down the aisle toward him.

"Yoo-hoo, mister! Hey, you're that actor, aren't you? I'm sure you get this all the time but ..."

Gary Boondock shook his head frantically. A woman in front of him turned around and stared into his sunglasses and sweating face.

"Say, yeah. You were that guy in *The Hackney Incident*. But the name escapes me ..."

She was snapping her fingers in his face. Gary Boondock squeezed one of the jelly canisters tighter. Her beady-eyed son turned around in his seat and also stared at him.

"Yeah, that was okay if you're seven. But I turned eight last month."

The kid lifted a Shertsoaker 5000 and sprayed him with rapid-fire bursts of something.

"Evan, say you're sorry to the nice man."

"Marnie, get your tuckus back here!"

"Say, do you think you could find a spot for my son in an advert? He's really talented ..."

But Gary Boondock, winner of a Glitter award for his outstanding role in *Hump Day*, and a Stinky for his supporting role in *Hump Again*, stood up and began quoting aloud from the Book of Lear. Harry got up out of his seat, bent on preventing further embarrassment on account of his spouse of thirty-nine years. But Marnie lay in the aisle. She was not moving. He watched as blood began to appear from under her back.

"What freaky kind of special effect is this?"

But Boondock just grinned madly at everyone on the tran.

"Heathens and blasphemers! I am delivering the judgement of He-Who-Shakes-the-Speare and will be rewarded in the Undiscovered Country."

Then his eyes bulged as he pointed abstractedly at the open mouth of Marnie.

"Do you see this? Look on her, look, her lips ... Look there, look there!"

Then he lifted his sweating thumb from the button.

Some Lukewarm Emasculation

Oober sat down on a dark cherry sofa and took a breath, basking in its firmness. He averted his eyes from the Librarian, who was slowly unbuttoning her long antelope coat. She tossed it in his direction and then began to study her body in the double vanity, running her fingers over her clinging tank top and adventure shorts. Oober watched her unabashedly now, and sighed.

"I still don't get it."

"Why I'm here? Easy."

"Why?"

"Because part of you wants me here ... like this."

"Well ... I don't mind really. But don't you find it kinda strange?"

"This is not about me. This is about something I need to recover from your puny brain. If this is the only way, so be it!"

"I don't believe you."

"C'mon. Get real. Just how many shower scenes will I have to endure?"

"I don't think I like what you are suggesting about me."

"Relax, my dear. Your planet has a Zygote rating of ... in your numbers, about 9.7 out of 10. Your resistance level is not going to be a problem."

"What if I refuse to help you?"

"I'm not going to threaten you, Mr. Mann. In fact, I wouldn't be here if it weren't for you."

Her voice had taken on a husky, plaintive tone. Out of nowhere, she produced a pair of reading glasses and put them on. Then she raised a dog-eared book and flipped randomly through the pages; it was the book with dripping letters that spelled *Major Ruckus*. Suddenly she whipped off her glasses and raised one of her pelican boots, pressing it down on his chest. He struggled to get up but the boot was far too powerful.

"Stop it!"

"Aw, but I'm all dirty. Just give it a quick lick and I'll let you up."

Oober touched the tip of his tongue to her shiny boot. Then he gave it a lick for good measure. Once again, she produced the paper knife and pointed at the bulge in his slacks.

"Now look how much you hate this!"

"But ... mmm ... why are you a librarian?"

"That's tricky. You are exhibiting a classic Orphic rejection pattern that is unique to some artists. If you were a singer, I might be a sadistic talent agent or producer. If you were Degas, I would be one of the judges at the National Gallery. You are a writer, so you want an authority figure to debase you and even possibly destroy you. However, some lukewarm emasculation will do quite nicely to get you in the mood."

"In the mood?"

"You see, most people would ask about the classic Orphic rejection pattern. You are deceiving yourself about what you desire, although not very well. It's nothing to be ashamed of. The travel writer Flann O. Kock used to hire librarians of his choosing to tie him down and perform every kind of atrocity imaginable to his body. Only then would he feel relaxed enough to comment on the local Chianti and amarone or what have you. In comparison, your tastes are rather tame."

"Tame ..."

"Now off with my shorts, you wordless hack!"

Oober trembled and obeyed as she tapped him with the paper knife.

"The netherwear too!"

She reached into her folded coat and lifted a length of chain, slowly blowing the dust from it.

"Once upon a time, this was used to chain a book in the library. A great book, nothing like the drivel you scribble. You aren't even fit to lick this chain, let alone be shackled with it."

She drew his hands behind his back and wound the chain around his wrists a number of times. Oober moaned from the ecstasy of feeling the ancient chain rubbing against his skin. She jumped up on the couch and spread her legs, leaving Oober face to face with her warm sex.

"Now gamahuche!"

"Yes, ma'am."

She moved her hips in slow circles and, to Oober's credit, his tongue laboured diligently to satisfy her human form, although she was pulling no punches.

"You muff dive like an advice columnist! Like a greeting card writer. You're the bottom of the barrel, the worst of those feeble, struggling hacks!"

Then she turned his head clockwise and, from between her locked thighs, he saw a balding man in a turtleneck and kangaroo jacket appear and hold out the copy of *Major Ruckus*.

"Good evening. My name is Alfred J. Bastard. I happen to host a little program called *Novellavision*. You've no doubt heard of me. In any case, I was wondering how you'd feel about us doing a review of your book?"

He unfastened his belt and undid his fly. His subsequent gesture was to be expected. The pants dropped and Alfred J. Bastard crouched over a wastepaper basket and began to defecate upon the universally acclaimed book. Then he reached in and tore out some clean pages and used them to wipe himself clean.

"Why, it's not even good for this purpose."

Oober was breathing hard, overwhelmed by this mindfracking turn of events. The Librarian was making love to him while Alfred J. Bastard nodded disapprovingly.

"I did agree to review your book – just don't expect me to read it!"

When Oober Mann was no more than a quivering mass on the floor, he looked up at the Librarian and Alfred J. Bastard, with their smug expressions and folded arms, and then looked down again.

"Now will you help us?"

Oober nodded, then wept into her wet body.

A Gleam in the Eye

"Uh, Blog. There's a Ms. Buttons here to see you."

"Send her in, Todd."

A tall striking woman in a bright red suit entered his live action rotating suite. She fidgeted with the pink whorls in her blonde hair before offering her hand, which he kissed without hesitation.

"Apple, isn't it?"

"Of your eye and in the flesh."

"You wanted to see me?"

"I just want to say I think you're great. I never miss your streaming tubes. I absolutely love your tubes."

Blog raised one leg upon a chair and adopted his scene-of-crisis pose.

"It ain't easy trying to make the new world a better place. Putting First People first and such."

"Often, I catch your tubes again right ... before ... bed."

"I know it must get lonely but your husband is fighting to make the new world new and improved. He's a brave man, Ms. Buttons."

She reddened.

"Apple ..."

"Apple, we've referred your husband to a centre where specialists can run some tests on his condition."

"A centre? Where?"

"The military (bless 'em) have placed a gag order on that information. I'd love to tell you where but I'm completely hog-tied on the matter. I only know he's going to be held for quite a while, relatively far from this rotating bungalow."

He was staring at the lacy black material visible under her red jacket. Was she a wanton tubie or just a media tease?

"Ya know, Mr. Stentorian ..."

"Please. Call me Blog."

"Blog, my husband and I married quite young. I guess at the time we thought it would be for always. Well, things can change, that's all."

"You wanna talk about it?"

"He ... he just kept playing that stupid game!"

Blog tentatively reached inside her suit jacket and successfully located the perkier nipple, in keeping with one of his more refined talents.

"Uhmmm ... game?"

"Yes, that Aggro-Master game. He was always jacking into that and leaving me alone. Ooooh, I'm so lonely, Blog. You have no idea ..."

"Don't worry, Apple. We'll figure this out together."

A pink curl fell over her forehead.

"How about you blog me up something special."

The silver gleam of generations of the Notel clan glinted in his eyes.

"Now, Apple, turn over."

An Education

"We've brought two renowned Stratford-upon-Avonists into the studio to comment upon today's terrible bloody sum bitch of a tragedy. First up, creeping to the left is Dr. Cecil Toasty, moderate flip-flopper and author of *Yes, Go Ahead, You May as Well*."

"It's a treat to be here."

"No. The treat is all mine, Dr. Toasty. Now what motivates an avid Learian to do what Gary Boondock did today?"

"That's the trouble with society today. Everyone wants to know: 'Why?' Such questions can be dangerous. What I do know is that Mr. Boondock is entitled to his beliefs. Although we should not encourage this sort of thing, we have no choice but to defend his convictions."

"But wouldn't it be fair to classify Mr. Boondock as a washed-up nutjob?"

"When you say that, you must remember that he believed he was acting upon the Book of Lear, one of the most prophetic texts passed down to us from our Scribe and Saviour. I need not remind you of the importance faith plays in the lives of your tubies and the world. Why, it's the greatest story ever told."

"For a different and no less controversial point of view, we go to Jim Bellows, host of *Boom Boom Boom* and author of *Nuke 'Em for Lunch Already*. I'm sure his equipment's never hung to the left, not even at college bashes."

"Heh heh. Ya know, I am PUMPED to be here, Blog."

"Comments on today's human bomb?"

"Now I know you've heard this already, but I want to reiterate that this sacred and holy land of ours is straying out into the boondocks. Just another bull finding out he's a mooing cow, far as I'm concerned. He can't live with himself and wants to take every straight-shooter with him. But he has no place getting anywhere near our gospel. Does it not say we should pluck out the eyes of poofs like him ... in the Book of Lear?"

"Sure sure. Uhm ... wait ... my crew is telling me I don't support that."

"May I interject?"

"Sorry, yes, we've brought in our official spiritual adviser and psychic astrologer, Reverend Zachariah Moonbeam, to try to clear things up. Go right ahead, Reverend Moonbeam."

"I cannot stand to drink deeper in the pithy falsifications of these fantastical blowhards, for does it not say in the definitive 1623 version and, may I add, the last revision of our Lord and Master's verilicious words, and I quote, *When Brewers marre their Malt with water and When Nobles are their Taylors Tutors and No Heretiques burn'd but wenches Sutors* ... The text does not condone anywhichwhere what Mr. Boondock (may he burn in the mines of sulphur!) did today but it does permit in a symbolic rendering the martyrdom by proxy of non-believers who endeavour in any way to form an unholy union with our daughters, and I take this to mean our starry-eyed idiot sons as well."

"Food for thought, Reverend, but we're running out of time."

"I beg to differ, Reverend. The 1608 version is the original uncorrupted text and it allows leeway for Mr. Boondock's actions today."

"But are you condoning this epidemic of stoning and letter bombing our children, because they choose to marry non-believers?"

"Gentlemen, I'm sorry. We're out of time. It's been an education."

Where Everybody Knows Your Name

Detective Green fumbled with the fob for his condome and then opened the front door. Officer Tomahawk followed, looking worried. And exhilarated! Immediately, he reached for a bottle of Chief Burden and knocked back a few gulps before curling up into a fetal ball, as advised by the force's resident healer.

"You don't wanna talk about it?"

"Nuh-uh."

"Okay. I should really take a shower."

She tore open her uniform and strutted about in her Immediacy netherwear before climbing into the shower. Blue Green lay on his side, listening for a while to the sound of running water. Then he got up and stepped into the shower, trailing the bottle of Burden. She watched the water running over his overcoat and thinning pate.

"Tell me what happened."

He reached for the bottle but she knocked it to the floor and it smashed into shards across the letroleum.

"Now the healing begins!"

She threw him down on the floor, still sopping. He groaned as he felt spikes of glass through his overcoat. Then she undid his pants and freed his erection. She offered a rubdown before daring to ride the allegedly untameable Blue Green. They enjoyed each other fully, rolling around on the glass in unbridled glee.

"O tell me it will stay like this forever!"

After scrubbing down and bandaging her new paramour, she lay him face down on the bed and began to massage his shoulders and back.

"Blue ... what happened to you ...?"

"I was working a case down in Spearpoint. I had just heard about the successful delivery of my newborn son and I was ecstatic. I was eager to get home, only I had to finish off a small sting operation first. So ... I went ... into Frisky's, this crazy bar where everybody knows your name. I was supposed to ... pump ... one of the guys there for information. I should have stuck with cranteasers but I wanted to be convincing, to be just another one of those ... guys ... who hangs out there. I also should have stopped at the first Minelli. But I was so happy ... about my son. So we get all chatty, me and Sammy the Snitch, the ... guy I'm s'posed to break, and he bites my ear and says we should head to the back ..."

"What did you do?"

"With my tail between my legs, I went. So he starts undressing and giggling and I do the same, for a joke, you know, and he says he wants to tell me all his secrets about his wild dark life. Only one thing. He's waving his zinger in my face and saying I have to prove he can trust me. So here I was, a hard-boiled gun getting down on my knees in front of Sammy the Snitch and begging for more of the *glug glug glug*."

"Blue!"

"Now I don't know how the squealer did it but he locked me down with my own cuffs and continued with his infamy. He had pegged me as Blue Green from the get-go. Paulie Pinkus was a dirty fib! Then he was threatening to ... tell my wife, to go to the hospital and tell her all about my extracurricular investigations ... if I didn't ... become his ..."

"There. There there. You don't have to say it."

"Life went on as usual. Everything was great at home and my job had its perks. Except instead of pocketing some graft for my boy's college fund or shooting some sicko eight times more than necessary like nice normal fellows, I was bending over backward for none other than Sammy the Snitch. The worst part was that I began to enjoy our illicit encounters. I thought about them every other moment of the day, just waiting to get away from my howling kid and slink back into Frisky's for a slippery quickie."

"We're not made of obsidian."

"But then about a year later, the gig was up for Sammy's ring. Then out of sheer vindictiveness ... my master ... forwarded extensive tube footage to my house, along with several informative visual aids."

"So I guess the oil was already off the mink."

"I got home and there was a message from my wife saying she'd gone to Frisky's and there was no need to wait up. But that wasn't all ..."

"Blue, what was it?"

"The mother of my son! And Sammy ... Sammy the Snitch! There's no way to tell who got who or if they did themselves in. A crime of passion! And I'm screaming down the place, wondering if my son is over there. Then I see something crispy in the Readybake ..."

Blue burst into tears in Rebecca's beautiful arms.

Precious Time

A man in a muskox suit stood at the head of a long lineup, trying to finalize things.

"Now what I just ordered, is that decaffeinated?"

"There's caffeine in it."

"Let's start afresh."

A number of people behind him groaned.

"We have decaf smelato. It tastes the same, kinda."

"All right, just make it snappy."

Everyone in the world heaved a sigh of relief and lowered the daggers in front of their eyes. He was handed something, which he sniffed for any trace of nuts or caffeine.

"Bravo."

He was clomping along in his new heels from Clank when suddenly a shadow dragged him into an alley. His mouth was stuffed with recyclable serviettes before a thermod of boiling lawsuit-worthy coffee was poured over his head. Then the thermod was brought down on his skull, again and again and again.

"That's for wasting everyone's precious time."

The sun moved through a patch of cloud and shone upon the face of his attacker. It was Squeaky Fomme.

The Truth Is a Malted

Tiff Kasha stood in front of Splatz, thrusting movement propaganda at anyone who passed. MARCH TO STOP NEW INDIGICA FROM THREATENING REFUGEE TERRITORIES. RESTORE THE BALANCE OF AUTONOMY IN THE WEST HAUDIES. OCCUPY THEM HATERS. ROGUE BEANS ARE THE CULPRIT. SAVE EVERYONE EVERYWHERE.

"March for peace. The war is racist. Join our dance for good times!"

Indio Rosario walked by her and then stopped in his tracks to take a leaflet.

"Self-determination for local indigenous ..."

"They have rights too!"

"Why is it everyone is always telling me how to live? And why is it always the same girl on a corner, meaning you?"

"The war is destroying everyone."

"Hey, I don't believe in Avonism. It's not my issue. You should be enjoying what life you got, sitting under a beautiful polluted sunset with someone you are seriously into."

"Here is the truth they don't want us to know about!"

"I can't believe my grandmother gave up her land and her life for people like you."

"You can bless our next rally! We always need authentic blessers."

"Say, why don't you and me go for a malted? My treat."

"Wheyhey, principles are the fast track to puknuk. Thanks, *Guide to Getting Anywhere*!"

Fresh Meat

Oober Mann crouched in the ergonomicon and interfaced with Controlling Interest System (CIS) Hasta. The slippery feelers extended themselves and tapped greasily against his temples. A jellied web was cast over his eyes and it took a few nanos for his retinae to adjust to jacking in. Then the clunky rows of file drawers began to materialize and he wiggled his body to activate his favourite search engine, a unicycle named OneTrack 10.2. It took him a while to balance his thoughts before feeling able to decide which direction to head in. Being new, many of the data regions were doubly restricted to him and his mode of transport ran into many dead ends. Along the way, he recognized other avatards from the local pool of co-workers. Then, down one of the soldered pathways, he ran into an information bank under construction. A lone worker handled Goatsinger was slackslamming a section of zillabytes directly in front of him. Noticing Oober's own skin, of a character who gave public service admonitions about the use of Sheepish sheepskin prophylactic devices, Goatsinger stopped slackslamming and grinned sociably.

"Morning, Rubbers."

"Morning, Goatsinger."

"And a nice one at that."

"They say it's gonna be a scorcher."

Goatsinger looked down at the demolished nodes, scratching his goatee thoughtfully.

"Just trying to deglitch the railing for this data region. For some visiting pooh-bahs, I guess."

"Wow."

"I could sure use some help. You're the chosen one, aren't you? I was told to wait for a slopperganger handled Rubbers at these exact coordinates. It's all a dream in your head, Rubbers. You are the one. All hail Rubbers the Slippery!"

"_?"

"Sorry, just messin' with ya."

"Ah, I get you."

Then a shadow of streaming data occluded the smile of Goatsinger.

"Sorry, Rubbers, this area is restricted to fresh meat …"

His parting shot was lost to resumed slackslamming.

The Birth of Drumhellerism

"Now what numbnutted idea you got this time?"

"No, seriously. I couldn't sleep for nights. And I kept hearing this voice in my head. Durndest thing ever. And then I saw in ... what d'you call it – one of them waking dreams – what I was supposed to root around for. Bones."

"Bones?"

"Some kinda bones, how the hoof should I know?"

"You don't know a bone from a funny bone."

"Wheyhey, I floored it down to Dryden's and got me a box a' Triple Chocgwak Drydenkles and a mega Gutted Rainforest before following the voice, just to be sure I weren't dreaming."

"So you stuffed your guts. Then what?"

"I ended up in the tar pits. In a place I'd never been before. But it felt so right, like I'd been there before, relieving myself under the same moonlight. Then I hear the voice again, and it tells me to start digging. So I finish my Drydenkles and coffee and get down on my hands and knees and start digging like crazy, having no idea what I'm supposed to be lookin' for ..."

"Bones!"

"What?"

"You said the voice said. To look for bones."

"Yeah, but I didn't know that at the time."

"You just said you did."

"Whatever. Who's tellin' the story here?"

"Sorry."

"So then you know what I found?"

"Bones?"

"Yeah! Bones! All kinds of bones!"

"Did you notify the authorities? That you found some poor S.O.B.?"

"That's just it. It weren't man nor woman."

"Huh?"

"The bones were huge. Biggest frickin' things I ever did see."

"I still think you should tell somebody."

"I'm tellin' you."

"Great!"

"Then I found part of a wing."

"A wing?"

"It all makes sense cause the voice is talkin' in my head more and more and saying how these bones belonged to our ancestors ... The Old Ones ... and how they were like angels and stuff."

"Angels?"

"They used to fly around and everything was real cool. Then there was this killer war and everyone was cast down into a place called Drumheller. But after a very long time, there was a lightning storm, and then little men began to creep out of the bitchymen."

"Bitumen!"

"Then after a while, they grew to our height, or maybe they took over our bodies. The voice was a bit sketchy on that part. And soon they wanted to replicate themselves, so they squeezed female tarfolk out of their tender nipples."

"Wow ... I guess I always suspected ..."

"The voice told me I can use the sanctimonious bones to rediscover our hidden life plans. If I hold them the way the voice said, I should be able to divine the taboo lost text of *Terror Dactyl* ... for starters. But I need help ... you knows I can't write worth a durn. I always sign my name with an X."

"So?"

"So, I'm worried about scribblin' down the sacred bones in the wrong. To do all that work for nothing. The Angels ud be angry if I told anybody I couldn't trust. And I need a felluh can put it down real nicelike."

"So do these angels or voices mention any form of restitution? For my pains, you understand."

"In good time, friend. Okay ... let's get goin'. And yea, the steaming pile of tarfolk rose up, and were turned into holy roads and avenues ..."

Your Job Is You

Facilitator Hassan looked away, misty-eyed, as Flak Riesling used his best cuddling technique to convince the boy Enkidu of the merits of telling him everything he knew.

"I'm so freaked out ... they'll kill me if I blab!"

"Shhh ... there there. I'd like to put you in a papoose you're so fetching. But first we need to know about the teensy-weensy terror plot. Then, when all this is over, we can move to a cabin in the Former Kanadas and fish all day and tell ghoulish tales all night!"

"Really?"

"I swear on your life and the life of your people."

"Okay, I guess."

Enkidu whispered what he knew into Flak's sizzling ear. At once, he leapt up and left the room, with Hassan hot on his heels.

"What did he say ... Flak! Remember, you're still on probation!"

"Keep Enkidu on a short leash."

"Last time we did that, there was hell to pay!"

"As the diplomatic drycleaner said about the tough spot, this one's on me."

"I don't know how you can toy with his fragile emotions like that. He's just a boy."

"Enkidu knows more than he's saying. He did mention a splinter group of a known and respected religious order and I think his information will lead to one of the rogue cells involved in this attack."

"Even so, they won't be able to talk about the other cells. Why don't we just give up?"

"The old Hassan would have wanted to lead the attack. What happened to you?"

"I got married, that's what happened!"

"You never told me. Clearly, I wasn't invited."

"You were busy. You're always busy. Stopping terror. When will you have time for me? What about my needs ... sorry, it's been a tense day."

"This is the only way to help protect everything you value."

"There was a grand old man. He was wandering the desert, looking for me in one of the caves. He had been bringing me figs and dates every day. He would spank his junk upon the sand in front of the fire ... I heard him crying out for me through the sandstorm without a name ... and that was when the Q-bomb hit."

"I'm sorry, Hassan."

"I don't know what happened in that cave. But when we came out, we were married."

Flak rubbed a tear from the corner of his eye and sniffed dryly.

"I've never been able to form a proper relationship. It ain't easy being a discount whore for your nation."

"You said it, Flak, not me."

"Yeah."

"Yeah."

They relaxed their soapy posturing and remembered the task at hand.

"Billy Joe and Bobby Joe! I want you to run a multi-tiered search on the name Anna Condo."

"The occasional A-lister?"

"Yeah."

"But I don't wanna work with Halibut Cheeks here. West Coast rivalry and all that."

"You're just sore cause we stole your Heiltsuk dances when you were sleeping in your canoes."

"Whatever!"

Flak folded his arms and sighed.

"Just do it! And keep your foreign traditions to yourself."

The Party Starts Here

Oober Mann received a mild shock to his nervous system. He was being asked to join everyone in the boardroom. He fiddled with the catch on his svelte jumpsuit, covered with bangles and baubles, each offering a different message to passing eyes. A great speech was being made about the future of the company. Nanoswag was given out to keep or to share. Then the official document was passed along. He felt a friendly hand on his shoulder.

"Now, it's not our place to enforce these stipulations. However, they are for your safety and for that reason should be observed, understood, and appreciated."

Oober understood that his neon jumpsuit was not included on the approved casual-dress list. He had probably tried too hard to appear iconoclastic and not blow his cover.

"And no harrassment. After all, this isn't Pelican Chancers. Harassment is harassment when someone makes a fuss. Remember that. And come to me if you have any problems."

Oober stared at his dead-eyed companions. Montefeltro, the new guy hired at the same time as him, who had nodded off in a chair. Spittle was dangling over his new slacks. Everyone was silent. *Harassment and impropriety, in this place? Where no one ever tells a joke?*

"And you've already signed the confidentiality forms. You are not to disclose anything that happens here. Ever. Never never no no no not ever!"

Oober stared at the floor. Everyone was staring at him. Then at the guy to the far left with the trouser bottoms that read THE PARTY STARTS HERE.

Not the Kind of Junk You Need

Anna Condo shot one infusion into her lower lip and the other one into her left buttock. Then she studied the face in her nacreous compact. Feral eyes glared back. She turned around in her ocelot evening dress and grinned her thrillion-dollar smile at Humanitario Condo, the first and most prized of her adoptees.

"How's my little chimp?"

The boy reached tentatively for a wallet and withdrew several hundreds.

"You want that money? Good. Mommy has a clever little monkey."

"*Sí, mamá, yo también.*"

Another boy ran by and snatched at the money, clicking his teeth.

"Ubuntu, play nice."

Then Clem Condo, the oldest and newest adoptee, breezed in, scanning the room anxiously.

"Yes, Clem, can I help you?"

"Just looking for my new pants. The Studlin pair."

"But those pants are an atrocity. Have you no self-respect? I didn't extract you from that hole for these kind of shenanigans."

"You mean, you don't like running a stud farm? Soon Ubuntu will be old enough for your needs. And then what will happen to me? I'll be history."

"You're being cray cray. Cray cray!"

"Something's fishy all right. Ever since you bid on me in the bazaar, I haven't been able to think of anything else."

"Clem ..."

He pushed the vast heap of infusions aside.

"This is not the kind of junk you need, glamourpuss."

"O Clem ..."

They stared at one another, eyes devouring eyes. Then an aneurysmal beep startled them both.

"Hello?"

"I'm calling to inform you about the shellfish you ordered last night ..."

The Confessional

August Santos crouched over the laughing crapper and clung to the shaking partition that divided him from the men of this age. Fortunately, he had his faith to keep him strong. This calamity, combined with a thermod of Extirpation Blend, had been brought about to test him. He reminded himself that before the day was done, he would make amends. For the moment, it was necessary to confess his transgressions and enable the flow of wicked material out of his body and into what remained of the ocean.

"Forgive me. I should not have eaten the lavender bacon cheesecake, and yet, lo, there it was, and then – in a flash – gone!"

"Hey buddy, keep it down in there!"

"Who's that?"

"Probably that weirdo from Sector G6."

"Silence, heathens! Omygodprotectthismiracleofrelease ..."

When the coast was clear, August ignored the hand-washing warning and crept away, leaving behind only the attempted flush of his conscience.

Them Taters Have Eyes

Chip Riesling rolled about in a tub of raspberry Body-Spew before drying himself off and slipping into some revealing FlubbeX.

"My, look at you. All grown up and out."

"Ma, quit it."

"Going up to 00001101 for a quick jack-in before din-din?"

"Her system's on the blink."

"Well, don't be late? There's orange potatoes for afters."

"Yeah yeah."

Suddenly she began to sniff and rub her eyes. Chip sighed, suspecting a maudlin scene was on its way. He was right.

"It's just that since your father and I ... *separated* ... besides the new potatoes, you're all I gots ... and I get so lonely. You wouldn't believe the stuff I've been thinking ..."

"Whoa! I gotta go, Ma ..."

"You be sure to have a nice time now. Don't do anything I wouldn't do!"

Within a few ticks, he was pinging the console impatiently outside 00001101.

"Yes?"

"It's Chip ... from downstairs. About your Simbat system."

"O yes be sure. Wait."

She opened the door after a lengthy delay. She was also clad in some revealing FlubbeX. He noted that it looked high-quality. She activated some sacred water music. Her place was simple but elegant. Why, she looked to be the kind of woman who could keep Chip in style for the rest of his life. He surveyed the array of phallic sculptures in an adjacent room.

"Are these ... yours?"

"Yes, I make and sell. They are tactile. Go ahead, touch them."

"No thanks."

"This one is still wet. Touch it!"

"Um ... where's your Simbat system?"

"In here. On medium to high erotic setting. Less combat and more fast-action learning-machine workout. There is glitch. I cannot make head or butt of manual."

"Let's take a look."

"Why don't we run through it ... with two-player mode?"

She turned on the ersatz field and waited for the sequences to load. Everything went black and Chip remembered to give his mental consent to begin the interaction. He was re-initialized in the dynamic buffer where the woman of his dreams was waiting for him. She was wearing a strange black dress with bright candy-coloured snaps that ran from her left shoulder down to her right knee.

"I want to repeat everything that happen. Yes, pull on this ... clasp."

"Huh?"

"We need to do what happen ... when glitch happen."

"Are you trying to seduce me, Ms. Cornucopia?"

"Call me Nastya."

He pulled one snap and then another. Then another. He tugged and tugged and opened her dress. She clapped her purple gloves and his clothing faded into thin air.

"Now I fall back on bed like this ..."

"Uh-huh."

"And now get on top. Get on top!"

He kissed her and tasted her body, which hinted of a minty sweetness.

"Ah Chip. Suck hot noobs."

"O so soft and minty!"

"Wait, stop! There ... that what I mean ... glitch!"

Chip turned, *in flagrante delicto*, to see his mother standing in the corner, bearing a beautiful plate of orange potatoes.

"Never forget, Chip. Them taters have eyes."

Día de Casualidad

At the end of the week, Oober came to work and found himself surrounded by fluorescent jumpsuits covered with blinding decals. He adjusted his tight pants and pointed shoes and sighed. The chief rang a little bell and everyone undid their jumpsuits and leapt out in jazzy shorts and muscle shirts. Then they began to salivate. Meanwhile, an immaculate man with an icy expression clasped his hands together and inspected each worker. Oober started sweating. Montefeltro's head began to fall forward, his eyes heavy. He was asleep again. But at least he was asleep in a jumpsuit. The immaculate man pointed at Oober's crumpled shirt and pants.

"Noober, this is Mr. Yanjing, a very important partner of ours."

"Hi."

"No jumpsuit?"

He lit up a Snarlbro and blew smoke into Oober's smoke-resistant shirt.

"Hmm ... nice. But what day is it today?"

"Uhm ... Día ... casual?"

Everyone in the world screamed at once.

"Día de casualidad!"

"And check out those ugly-ass pants!"

Oober turned red. Even Montefeltro woke up and started smirking. After that, all the men began to leer at and ogle him. In the cramped kitchen, they patted his bottom and commented on his pants.

Finally, he decided to file a complaint. He stormed into the office of the new human resouces manager and pointed at the list of rules he had just been given.

"Sit down, Mr. Mann."

"I want to file a complaint."

"Are you aware, Mr. Mann, that it is Día de casualidad?"

"Am I aware?"

She got up and shut the door, sliding a massive bolt into place.

"It's procedure. Now before we can begin processing your complaint, I'm going to need you to slip out of those pesky pants."

Blood Diamonds in the Rough

Four tinted limucks vroomed into view and landed in a cloud of dust beside the Blood Diamond Mountains. The doors slid open and, flanked by a shaky paranoid entourage in black, a diminutive man with pockmarked skin emerged. Hector Tejada scarcely lifted the brim of his fedora. He squinted the natural squint of desert folk who live on roots and grubs and cacti and spat twice. Without a word, he handed over an old coffee can.

"I hope this isn't just a cowboy bedpan, Mr. Tejada."

"You will get what is coming to you, *exactamente*."

One of the men in black sniffed the can before lifting the jagged lid.

"Ow ... oweee!"

"Well, Lester?"

"There's something inside. Something swishing around."

He held up the contents of the can and the little man studied the small bottle with the help of a large monacle.

"Yes! Yes! Swim, little friend. Swim!"

His enlarged eye darted back to the face of Hector Tejada, older and more immobile than the dusty plateau beneath their designer loafers.

"Now what do you want?"

"Heh. A few bucks, gringo."

"Heh. A few bucks in the headlights."

"Never stop for nothing unless it can kick you right in the assets."

The little man laughed and laughed.

"You know what? I like you, Mr. Tejada. You're my kind of doomboomer!"

"Doomboomer?"

"It's an old expression. I mean you do whatever it takes without getting soft, and frack the future, am I right? Not like the usual slipshod therapy-driven slackers these days."

"*Sí, sí.*"

"You will be more than compensated for this. But why not come along with us? I have other work for you to do."

"Sure beats stringing me up, antlers and all."

"Blood diamonds in the rough, *señor*. Just the way you like 'em."

Banana, No

The Liaison for Middle Management scrambled out of a hole in the wall and hurried by the partition between Oober Mann and Greta Goldfarb. Then he stopped and pointed at an object on Greta's desk.

"Banana, no."

"No banana?"

He scratched his head and chest.

"Banana, no. No banana."

She stared at it longingly and then picked it up and dropped it in a wastepaper basket.

"Banana, paper no."

"No paper and banana?"

"Banana and paper no."

Then he let out a blood-curdling shriek and scampered up and over a piece of donated artwork.

The Bard Works in Mysterious Ways

"Blog Stentorian here, reflecting on what happened earlier today. It's an amazing story ..."

He smiled ironically to himself (and into the eyes of countless tubies).

"We're here with Dr. Fava, one of our resident quacks, to comment on the stunning recovery of Bruciato Giallo, after his death-defying, bedwetting leap out of a window yesterday."

"Lovely to be here, Blog."

"Now, as you know, if you've been taking in our coverage of his patio for the past five hours, Bruciato allegedly leapt to his death ... but, to some degree, unsuccessfully. An ordinary person would have fallen and splashed open like so much squaghetti but Bruciato, being a celebrity and, in all likelihood, a saint, landed upon his gardener, Haysus. Earlier, we interviewed Haysus's extensive family, in mourning for their personal hero and breadwinner. But miraculously, Bruciato survived, with only minor head injuries."

"Isn't it amazing, Blog? The Bard works in mysterious ways."

"No doubt, Bruciato has been preserved for a higher calling beyond the comprehension of our regular tubies. An authorized account of his life would be an excellent beginning."

"I'll go one step further, Blog ..."

"Please do."

"Without having examined him or really knowing anything about him, I will go so far as to say that I suspect his wounds are ... how shall I put this? ... marks of divine intervention."

"Come now, doctor. Seriously."

"Reports are not just about his plummeting. After landing upon Haysus, he lay there in a state beyond our realm of understanding. He did not emerge from this dark reverie for some time."

"Do you mean a loss of consciousness?"

"Or maybe you could call it an alternate state of consciousness ... one beyond the scope of our normal knowledge."

"Tut-tut, good doctor."

"And if we are to presume that Mr. Giallo ... crossed over ... then his awakening is more than simply a tried-and-true miracle like those we are bored to tears of. This is the resurrection of a man who crossed over to the other side!"

"Wowsers!"

"This is all unfounded guesswork of course, but I think you're going to see a change in the new Bruciato Giallo. The Bard is saving him for a greater purpose and it is time to cast off that vicious mole of nature and begin with a fresh page of humility and fancy parlour tricks. In other words, I wouldn't be surprised to see Mr. Giallo with a whole new racket."

"Golly. Well, this certainly has been illuminating, Dr. Fava. Feel free to pop in with your bag o' bones any time."

Because Nothing Fricks Like Memfrick

Oober tossed and turned. Indio was out somewhere and Audrey had climbed into his bed for company. Ordinarily, he would welcome this, but tonight his mind was elsewhere. He was trying to concentrate on chewing the Memfrick tablets the Librarian had prescribed him. Oober shut his eyes tighter, feeling the tablet powder upon the tip of his tongue. *Upon the tip of his tongue the tip of his tongue ...* He was floating now, a lone observer at the beginning of time. Or was it? Everything was lush and different. Thrillions of people were racing toward a single event. Giant plumes of exhaust filled the air. It was night five of the Fondle the Earth Celebration, a series of concerts encouraging the use of energy-efficient light bulbs. Oober grimaced, thinking of the toxicity of countless atomic engines revving up and roaring off to the same location. He did not remember the specifics or the scientific reports, only that there had been a massive explosion at the moment Chutney appeared onstage. And so that was then. Oober had been living in such a non-funky funk that he had completely forgotten his former life, in an entirely different civilization. Then how had he gotten here?

A Name from the Past

Shyster Deacon flitted through the morning list of memory waves. He frowned at Wilma Pettifogger.

"See this?"

"Hold your horses. I haven't had my coffee yet."

"We've got another Bronzey."

"O crap. That's just what we need."

"Looks like something's confusing the goosechasers we gave him."

"Him?"

"Fellow by the name of Oober Mann."

"Doesn't ring a bell ..."

"Does for me. He came in drunk and screaming the odds. Took me ages to calm him down and get him to sign the insurance forms."

"Maybe ... it'll be okay."

"I don't know. I got a bad feeling about this."

"We've got a new start. They can't pin anything on us. Nobody's ever heard of Bronzey's Bronzing Booths."

"No, not yet."

This Is for the Mooning

Flak Riesling swung into Anna Condo's villa on the tender end of a grappling hook. Hassan entered via the front door. They converged in the upstairs bedroom and levelled their weapons at a pair of writhing shapes.

"Anna Condo, unhand that minor!"

They yanked at the bedsheet and were startled to find the wrong pair of people enjoying a love scene underneath.

"Dammit. It's not them. Just a pair of body doubles."

"And we won't tell you a freakin' thing."

The male double bent over, waggling his bare bottom.

Flak growled and slammed his fist through the glass of a protective case and pulled out the sharpest of Anna Condo's numerous awards, which happened to be for filleting trout.

"Tell me or you're going to be having some seriously unsafe sex."

"Buh ... I don't know nothin'!"

"There's two of you and one of you is bound to know. But one thing's for sure. Neither of you will be able to show your goods in another matinee when I'm done with ya."

"She got a beep. Something about seafood, she said."

"That's it?"

"She was real weird about it. But there's a meeting tonight, I understood that part."

"When is she coming back?"

"I don't know ... but not before the meeting."

"Where is she going? How can I find her?"

"She went with Ubuntu. Each of her adopted kids has a trackgraft. You can follow the signal with this."

Flak accepted the Busybody 5050.

"Now will you let us get back to biz?"

Flak picked up a Maturiteen Choice Award this time and lunged at the male body double.

"This is for the mooning!"

A Midsummer Night's Nightmare

"The eye of man hath not heard."

Folk on the train eyed the repairman uniform and the stitched nametag that read EMPEDOCLES BOTTOM. After all, what a ridiculous name for one to have!

"The ear of man hath not seen."

He was talking to himself too. Talking to nobody but himself. That's what you get.

"Man's hand is not able to taste ... "

A woman ushered her children away from him. A man to her left started laughing.

"His tongue to conceive ..."

A couple of spunks got up and snarled at him.

"Whaddya say, huh? Huh?"

"Nor his heart to report ..."

"Pops, we're gonna kick your heart in the frackin' teeth!"

"What my dream was."

Empedocles Bottom lifted the latch on a canister at his feet and activated the release mechanism. People coughed as a blue fog appeared around them. One of the spunks got a full whiff of the stuff and began to convulse. His friend rubbed his eyes.

"No, dude man ... he had so much to live for!"

Within minutes, everyone on the tran was a gas, with Empedocles Bottom also drifting in the thick of their sublimated persons.

The Magic Sleep of Magicicada

"And those are the top twenty ways to Perish in a Public Place, here on the PPP. Join us next week as we continue the countdown ... *tick tick tick kerplooooie*!!!"

Ester Krick held her pillow over her head. Why did she watch? The reports only made her queasy ... at first, and then her heart would begin to beat faster and faster. She could imagine the list of desperate criminals disguised as ordinary people all waiting outside the front door, just for her! Lately, there were all these cases of devout extremism. She could understand their devotion to the faith. She was a sometimes practising Stratford-upon-Avonist. But why did believing in a higher power have to cause so much terror and death? She could picture blank fanatical faces looming out of the shrubbery around her condome. She had bought three security systems in the past few months and had put bars on the windows. But nothing seemed to ease her mind.

"Coming up, strangers on a tran. We'll tell you who not to trust during this reign of terror."

"Yipe!"

"Also, they found love at the age of being past it. So why did it lead to this gruesome spinesnapping outcome?"

"Eeeeee!!!"

"In New Haudenosaunee, adoption is widespread. But do you know who your adoptee really is? We'll meet a family who didn't have a clue ... and <gulp> paid the price for it."

"Aaaaaahhhh!!!"

"All this and more when *Electroshock Talk* returns ..."

Ester held her chest. Her mouth was dry. She was sweating and her heart was palpitating but she remained glued to the tube.

"Do you find getting through the day stressful? And at night, how can you sleep when the world is going to hell? With Magicicada."

The screen showed a woman tossing and turning. The other people in the bed, including a dog, departed in digust. The woman's eyes were big as saucers and she was shaking.

"Just take two or three of these before you grab some shut-eye."

A glowing neon insect fell from somewhere, presumably the ceiling, and began to jump all over the bed, leaving a trail of floating Zs behind it. At last, it came to rest upon her forehead, broadcasting visible waves directly into her frontal lobe. She closed her eyes and started to smile. Her friends and family slowly filed back into the room and lay down around her sleeping figure. The dog began to lick her face, completely uninterested in the singing, drug-induced cicada.

"O, that would be so nice."

Ester took down the 555-MAGICIC whimcode and hurried over to the credi-tempt in the corridor.

"Warning: Magicicada should only be taken in a controlled setting. Taking more than the recommended dosage may result in abrupt flights of fancy. Magicicada may cause memory loss, headaches, nausea, internal bleeding, memory loss, stroke, infertility, excessive fertility, loss of appetite, loss of worldly possessions, aneurysms, moulting, or memory loss. Please consult hotline or media expert before taking Magicicada. The small percentage of locust brood in Magicicada may affect allergies."

Ester returned to the living room, very happy that a cartonload was on its way. "Because isn't it time you had a good night?"

Something about Shellfish

Anna Condo was walking hand in hand with Ubuntu Condo when Flak Riesling and Hassan Armadill leapfrogged out, barring their entrance to the meeting.

"Not so fast."

"What the shuck!"

Ubuntu quivered. A trickle stained his pant leg.

"Ma ma ..."

Anna held his head tightly against her full bosom, the one that had incidentally made her famous in *Janine Juggs: Underground Lootress*. Other bosoms had never stood a chance.

"Tell us what we want to know or that kid gets a one-way ticket home!"

"No, not my pride and joy! His home is with us."

"What is the purpose of this meeting?"

"I ... I don't know."

Flak pressed a toothpick into Ubuntu's arm. He began to howl.

"Ma ma, please tell them ..."

"I swear I don't know. I got a call ... y'know, I'm not sure what I'm doing here, really. Something about shellfish in a restaurant. Then I decided to see what all the fuss was about."

Flak stared deep into her soul for a few tense ticks.

"You could be lying, but that would take acting."

Fingered and the Finger

Rebecca Tomahawk rubbed the tender butt of Blue Green as he lay flat out, sipping the last of the Chief Burden.

"So you lost your family. I totally get that."

"Nuh-uh. The boy's still kicking."

"Alive!"

"If you can call being a visual poet alive."

"It could be worse."

"Don't you see? I wasn't there to offer a guiding sight. I never even got to see him peg his first intruder. He might even have been one of those legendary detectives who asks questions before opening fire ..."

"Actually, this narrative is not holding together. There are a few gaps in your story."

"Maybe we shouldn't have knocked back that bottle, partner."

"But what else is troubling you?"

"I've <hic> seen this before."

"Whah? Finger in a can?"

"Finger in a can. But that was before talkies ..."

"Tell me."

"Would you run to the wine bar round the block? We're gonna need more of this ... a lot more."

"No."

"I've heard rumours mostly. Crazy rumours. We needed more soda at the station. I sent Zippy, the station brat. Cause every station's got a Zippy. And he was laughing and joking about the suspect we just dragged in. We used our nightsticks and that just got Zippy's goat. So the chief was getting ready to really start wailing on the guy. But he's thirsty, so he signals Zippy to come over and hand him a soda, like usual. And Zippy's, ya know, happy to do it."

"What happened, Blue?"

"So Zippy's about to piss himself laughing. And the chief goes to take a drink, but there's nothing inside, just this awful rattling sound ..."

"O my Cannibal Creator!"

"So they pry open the can ... and he recognizes the finger. It's Frank's wedding band. Frank's the guy who used to hold the suspects steady for their whupping. Then, at that moment, the chief knows that Frank will never be able to hold a guy down for an honest-to-goodness beating ever again, let alone anything worse. So he loses it, and Zippy can tell by the look on his face and also starts bawling, and pretty soon everybody's got their cry face on."

"But why? Who would do such a thing?"

"Someone with a grudge against the pumped arm of the law, not to mention the carbonated beverage industry."

"Did you find any leads?"

"Only this snap. It was sent into the station."

Rebecca gasped. It was a picture of human ring fingers placed together in the form of two letters.

"We think his initials are T.C."

Stranger on a Tran

"Sometimes I feel like I'm wasting my life."

"Everybody feels like that."

"No, really. I do nothing all day."

"You should get a job."

"Yeah, maybe."

"Well, this is me."

"Yeah, see you, Willard."

Squeaky Fomme leaned over and tapped the remaining passenger with a rolled-up poster.

"Hey!"

"Whaddya want?"

"Wanna come to a little get-together?"

"Why?"

"Whaddya got to lose? Maybe you *are* wasting your life!"

He laughed, weakly.

"True."

She disembarked, urging him to keep up with her. He even left behind a used clyster of *L'Étranger* on the orange seat. On the way, they passed a paperless that flashed FUNDAMENTALIST GIRL MURDERS MANAGER MACBETH-STYLE.

That Age-Old Finger Game

A weathered time-weary face looked out from under the brim of a panama hat with a tomato-coloured band. The face itched, ever since he'd changed it for a new one. The doctors said ... but what did they know? He gingerly put down his case and scanned the crowd for his one o'clock. There. A hairy chest and goofy grin.

"T.C.? Hi, it's me, Jared."

"Really, no guff?"

"Ha. Ha ha ha. You're funny, just like in your neurvies."

"And you are easily entertained."

"I wanted you to know straight off, I don't do this sort of thing."

"Yeah yeah. Did you bring the ring?"

"Sure. Does that turn you on or something?"

"You'll find out."

Jared leaned closer and lowered his voice.

"Look, am I gonna get fingered or what?"

"In a manner of speaking, yes. Now be a good boy and eat your soup."

"Soup, I don't want any soup."

"I took the liberty. It's the chef's specialty, you might say."

"Umm ... yeah, okay."

T.C. grinned an age-old grin, listening to each slurp of satisfaction.

Spat

"I'm worried, Hurt."

"Would you get off my case already. I'm fine."

"You've been acting strange ... ever since ..."

"Since what, Kiki?"

"Since you joined that weirdo outfit!"

"If you're talking about my Chaos!tologist chums, at least come clear and say so."

"Oh, I'd like to say a lot, Hurt. But anyone who does disappears forever."

"Are you finished?"

"No, Hurt. Now, the name Hurt Hardass used to mean something. To me, to our adoptees. To everyone who secretly loved you. But now look at you. You've changed, Hurt."

"How have I changed?"

"For starters, you made me get off Eudonia. Those pills were keeping me happy. Maybe I need them ... to put up with all your kooky crap."

"Oh yeah, I get it. I get you completely clear and this is how you repay me! Let's not forget who helped who out of a dumpster!"

"Hurt, I haven't forgotten, but let's not fight."

"I think you should leave. Église hasn't exactly warmed to our living arrangements."

"Hurt, ever since you joined that outfit and agreed to that sham marriage ... you know ... you just don't seem yourself."

"Get out of here! Don't make me hurt you!"

"All right, Hurt. But whatever you're planning, you haven't heard the last of Kiki Kaka."

Meet the Epimetheans

"Good evening, and welcome to this special gathering of the Church of After Thought. I am so glad you could all make it out tonight."

Flak Riesling narrowed his eyes at Anna Condo.

"Epimetheans! I thought this was a meeting of Chaos!tologists."

"Not all celebrities are Chaos!tologists, you know."

Flak stared at a number of recognizable tube stars, each with one arm draped around their children. The robed man at the front of the gymnasium made his lectern shake with increasing *gravitas*.

"But when the Late Arrival is in effect rescheduled, not a single atom or molecule or particle of our being will be lost. And we will all be together in the Übercosm, forever. Isn't that a glorious thought to consider? Doesn't that truly tickle you where it counts? Our people were corn-fed. We were the original inhabitants, before these ... red folk took over and stole our customs and language. But every day we atone a little bit more. And every day we are getting closer to the Late Arrival, the time when we will prosper unfettered and unpersecuted ..."

"Look, I have reason to believe this group is planning an attack upon New Haudenosaunee. Therefore, I have the authority to take whatever means necessary to stop this meeting from taking place. That means you and Ubuntu will be splattered all over the tubecast tomorrow, and not for the usual reasons."

"But my faith ..."

"You're going to have to decide between life as a tube star and post-world immortality. You can't have it both ways. And I'm sorry to put you in this position. But unless you can tell me something about the attack, I'm going to give the order to detonate our charges. Don't you think Ubuntu deserves more?"

"Sounds like someone needs more alone time."

"I need you to get me alone with that priest."

"But no one ... he does not taint himself with unbelievers."

"Hassan, prepare to detonate the charges ..."

"You got it, Flak."

"No, wait! There's a celebrity awareness campaign for the church. I can bring you to him."

"Hassan? Hold off for now. You better not have any second thoughts. His life depends on that."

"No. I only have afterthoughts."

Blowing in the Wind

"Governor Gewürztraminer, do you have any additional remarks?"

He winked at the moderator who was part of Defcom's recent facelift. He also winked at a supporter holding up a flashit that flashed REGALIZE STEROIDS.

"Yiaow, I want to stress I think this war is a travesty. We marched on Nutella and then without warning rat-a-tat-like, we übershoot them to death when we should be outmuscling their flanks and crushing their abdominals, but that's it. Nothing makes me sadder than to see their puny bodies in the streets right near the Notel. But don't be stupid. The answer, my friends, is blowing in the wind. As your governizer and perspective president, I want to personally guarantee the future of all the denizens of New Haudenosaunee."

He gripped the podium and shook it.

"And I want to say what everybody is feeling and what I am feeling, in the words of an old movie star."

He paused for effect. You couldn't hear a pin drop. Particularly with the new line of grenades.

"You like me. You really really like me."

The crowd swooned. Then he picked up the podium and hurled it at one of his opponents, knocking him into the dancing troupe known as the Gewürztraminer Girls.

"Because I'm mad as hoof and can't take it anymore!"

What Kiki Knew

Kiki rubbed his eyes with his knuckles and wiped his pelvic pillow dry. Then he heard the sarabande. He fastened his feathery blue robe and stomped downstairs.

"Hello?"

"It's me, Hurt."

"Hurt, o, Hurt!"

He opened the door to see a man he didn't recognize.

"Who ... "

"You don't remember me?"

"No, it can't be!"

"Yeah, I've played so many sides the table aches. But there's a new game in town."

"Look, I'm no longer with Hurt. Maybe we can cut a deal."

"And what do I care about the state of your ... ménage?"

"What happened to you? You used to have ... principles. I mean, you were cold-blooded, but your record, as far as I know, showed ... principles."

"Let's call it a mild symptom of being dead."

He opened his case and with gloved fingers drew out a formidable provocateur and screwed on a silencer. Kiki only stared in horror at the initials on the case.

"T.C., please!"

"Top o' the world, Kiki. Top o' the world."

Rare Treat

Oober Mann arrived at the nearest Roadkill Grill after work and informed the third person after the greeter about a reservation under the name *The Librarian*. He was led to the mystery woman, whose plunging translucent dress held his attention.

"Evening."

"Evening, Oober. How was work?"

"I think I'm losing my mind."

"All jobs are like that."

"I don't know how long I can hold out."

"We are close to locating our adversary. Not long now."

"They're starting to get close to me ... ask questions ... Greta ..."

"I see. You guys are an item."

"No. We work closely, that's all."

"She could be our problem."

"You mean one of those things ... like in the library?"

"Or not. Have a steak. On me."

"You like meat?"

"We can process it. We prefer liquids though. How about a nice tartare?"

"Fine, whatever."

"You seem out of sorts. Unburden your puny mind, dear man."

A fiddler appeared and hesitated, selecting the most maudlin and wheedling tune he could think of.

"It's just that since you've come into my life, everything's changed. I don't know who I am anymore. Or I don't remember."

"Did you know before you met me?"

"Maybe not."

"Have another tablet. You'll feel better."

"What's in those things?"

"Our secret recipe, including a solution derived from the longhorn borer beetle. The way their bodies modify the eucalyptus they ingest results in some unique properties for mind and memory alteration."

"Alteration?"

"You have a memory block in your head. Didn't I mention it? The drug helps to reconstruct pathways from mere fragments."

"That doesn't sound like memory."

"No, but it's an excellent simulation."

Wherefore Art Thou?

Black Elk Montague sat on the sofa and patted his belly. His glowing newlywed (the former Miss Lorna Capulet) came out to him and scraped the last of the basmati rice onto his plate.

"Lovely as ever, my dearest! Too kind, too kind!"

"Shut your face, cute cheeks."

She joined him on the sofa and their hands interlocked. The buzz of matrimonial festiveness was just beginning to wear off but the stage of inexorable malaise was already on the creep. They both were jacked into the tube, listening to various opinionaters.

"An' I gist don't know how we can forget what this man has done."

"Cast not the first pig's heart ..."

"And this above all ... to thine own self be true ..."

"Blog Stentorian here. Some thoughts about one of the front-runners in the primaries. As for Governor Gewürztraminer ... some would say his checkered past will count against him. But others are optimistic he will win by a land claim and bring a new image to that of the nation's new chief."

Black Elk looked over, with heavy eyelids, at a single letter.

"By Jove, I'm stuffed. Anything for me in the post?"

"Just a letter from my folks."

"Well? You gonna open it?"

"I don't know. For some reason, they sure don't think much of you."

"That's natural. They're Stratford-upon-Avonists. And you knew I was a Marloweian when you said I sure as hell do. But do not fret, my dear. They'll come round."

"Ya think? You don't know my parents."

But Black Elk began to sing a lengthy number.

"Buhwhaddatheyknow ... we gots our love to keep us snuggly at night ..."

"I'll open it if you stop singing."

"Whatever the odds ... our hugs'll smush 'em to bits ..."

"Governor, what do you think is our biggest problem today?"

Lorna pried open the letter and their new subprime dome exploded.

Someone from Fixer Up

Greta Goldfarb smiled broadly at the small pockmarked man in overalls walking toward her desk.

"Good morning!"

"Morning."

"Can I help?"

"I'm here to do a routine check on the lighting and conditioning. Shouldn't take two shakes to get done."

"That's great. We had a strange leak and blitzed you guys about it yesterday."

"Yeah, sure. I'll definitely take a look."

The bill of the Fixer Up cap cast a shadow over the face of Hector Tejada. In one of his gloved hands swished a can of mysterious contents. He smiled with gritted teeth at each of the employees while making his way to the back of the office. He stopped to examine the carpet. Slow drops were falling from a closed panel in the ceiling. He pried at the catch and the panel opened to reveal the open-mouthed face of a fresh death. A man. He sealed up the panel again, whistling an old tune from Cádiz. No one he knew, anyway. Hector looked around cautiously. The closest worker was interfacing with his station but also keeping an eye on him. Blasted multitaskers! Hector knelt down and began to open the can ...

KATHUNK!

Oober Mann had dropped a replicator on his head. The Librarian smoothed our meta-hero's frontal lobe remotely from down the street and whispered into his burning ear.

"Easy, big boy. You did very well. Now you only have to hide the body."

Oober sighed. Already it had been a long morning.

"And once you're done, would you be a dear and bring me some of that tequila worm virus?"

Snap to It

The divine and unassailable Father John Tee was in the middle of administering a spanking-new revelation to a young and muddled worshipper when there was a knock at the door.

"Go away, I'm praying."

"Someone to see you, sir."

"Consultations are by divine appointment only."

"It's Anna Condo, sir."

The countenance of John Tee lit up, with a hint of old-fashioned madness.

"O really? Well, I suppose you should send her in ..."

"Why hello, John!"

John Tee grimaced warmly at her companion.

"This is Mr. Riesling. He's a ... my ... bodyguard."

"Ah yes, can't be helped. We live in such precarious times."

Without delay, Anna poured a pitcher of water over the front of her white Schiava top.

"O horndog, I'm such a klutz!"

John Tee stared at her soaked-through clothing with mounting intensity. After all, he had seen *Forbidden Access* twice and he was hardly mesolithic.

"D'ya think we could have a moment alone? I have something to tell you."

John Tee clapped his hands together and told the girl on the sofa to make like a tree of life and leave. The door slammed on the echo of her audible weeping. Flak Riesling locked it and reached into his shoulder satchel. He pulled out a steaming pot and lifted the lid to reveal a cluster of snapping lobsters.

"Just give me five ticks with him."

To Splain the Unscrutable

John Cobbler sipped from his fresh cup of Gutted Rainforest before touching his fingers to his temples. He was getting a feeling. More than a feeling. He reached for a wing bone and secretly made a wish.

"It's coming."

Burnham Young watched him through a glaze of astonishment.

"You sure?"

"Sure I'm sure."

"What's it like?"

"Like a choir of flapping wings."

"Whoa."

"Did you bring it?"

Burnham Young reached into his bag and pulled out his niece's hot pink Waferon 7000.

"Yeah."

"Now I'm gonna use these bones to arouse the dead angels."

"Okay."

"And I will use this lemon and this campin' lamp to read and splain to you the unscrutable ink of the prophets for you to livesnatch. Afraid I can't show you the holy text, so I have to read it out of this slouch hat. Sorry."

"I understand."

"Our beginnings begin in the mossy lap of Drumheller, lost land of the ancients' prophets. Begot sooner is Duffy and his strapping son Puffy."

"Got it! Wait, did he strap his son?"

"No, strapping! He's a big kid."

"Now, they married real womenfolk and we come to the birth of Muffy. But Duffy and Puffy were wroth with Muffy and said go thither with yonder zither, for your competition offendeth thy givers of birth. Just take it and go. And Duffy and Puffy married again and each gave life to new generations of the Uffyzi, including the notable Cuffy, Tuffy, and Buffy."

"Wow, this is hot stuff."

"Yeah, and make sure you get down the wanderings of Muffy. He was a real player."

"There's still tons of life in this doohickey."

"Just you wait till I splain away the Indians."

Green Emissions

One head appeared. Then, down the other passage, another head. The lowing was excruciating. There was no let-up, whatsoever.

"No, please."

They surrounded the hapless vagrant. They knew something this nameless fellow didn't. They continued chewing. Chewing and chewing. The vagrant almost relaxed. Then the sublimation began.

One cloud of gas emerged. Then another. They closed about the breathing space of the vagrant. He flailed his arms to no avail. Suddenly he felt far worse than depressed. He smashed a bottle and held the jagged shards to his throat. He was done for this world. But the gas was stronger still. It closed his windpipe.

"O the metonymy!"

A Watched Pot

Flak Riesling lifted John Tee's sopping head out of the lobster pot and slammed the lid shut. He dragged the man by the arm, leaving him no chance to soothe any of the spots where he had been clipped by pincers.

"Hassan, this man is John Tee, *T-E-E*. Take him into custody."

"What's going on? What are you gonna do?"

Anna Condo jounced angrily toward them.

"Wait a tick, where's Ubuntu?"

"You'll have to come down to ISM, to fill out a report. Then you'll get your boytoy back."

Hassan pulled Flak aside.

"Something happened in there. You're not telling me everything."

"Your deductive powers never fail to blow me away."

"What's goin' down, Flak?"

"It's a plot. A plot to assassinate Governor Gewürztraminer."

"Bless you."

Smile

Rick Breck flashed his thrillion-dollar grin in a nacreous compact before facing the swarm of starchasers. They were veritably frothing at the mouth to see him board his new Cesspo. What was more, he was a bona fide hero for flying it himself. He threw an aubergine scarf over his right shoulder and smiled again, permanently blinding a screaming fan.

"Ha, ladies and gentlemen! Why, he'll have that to remember for the rest of his life. Not everyone gets zapped by Rick Breck! Speaking of which, nothing gets your teeth blindingly whiter than a dollop of Zap! toothscrubber. Rick Breck never trusts anything other than Zap! to get rid of that pesky plaque!"

"Hey, Mr. Breck, what about your former advert deal with Watergate Tooth Whitener?"

"Ha ha, gotta fly!"

He turned abruptly to his most menacing aide.

"I want that starry-eyed grapeviner rubbed out!"

"Yessir."

But a few hours later, the glitterazzi were kicking themselves for not having stowed aboard and for missing the scoop entirely. Because Rick Breck had merrily poured himself a few kamikaze cocktails and enjoyed a side of scallops before nosediving directly into the National Pentagram.

A Void Function

The long-awaited system swap had taken place. Over the weekend, the gaudy ziggurats of caribou brite had been demobilized. They had been replaced with the new three-headed beasts, stations with three pods to store precisely three workers. Oober lowered himself into the pod, wondering if it was the same one he had been interfacing with during his salad days with this company. The tendrils curled about his thighs and tickled his centre, before fastening to his netherparts with a titanium grip. It felt the same as ever. His eyes became bloodshot streams of data, rapidly spewing geysers of churning company intel. In the pod to Oober's left, August Santos gave everything a good sniff before jacking in, producing a dripping cloth and wiping down his entire console, examining every inch of it for ominous or wriggling specks.

"Morning."

"Morning."

To his right, it was the handle Oober had met as Goatsinger.

"Morning."

"Morning."

"Well, seethe off, don't that give my tongue to the cat!"

"Pardon?"

"Meet and greet your new friends for eternity!"

August Santos had not ceased wiping and all three pods shook in unison. Goatsinger activated his pod and established a void function before parameterizing himself into its stack. Oober watched him blip off with a hint of envy. August Santos, on the other hand, activated a modicum of symbolic language, thus exercising his guaranteed flexatus of religious freedom. Oober frowned at the booming echo of droning recitations from his left. It was going to be another long day.

The Enemy Within

"Blog Stentorian here, checking back and front of the stories that worry you to death ... today, a terribly boneheaded tragedy concerning beloved film star Rick Breck, most known for his acclaimed performances in *Buds II* and *Nimrod's Plot*. And for over-reactive commentary, we have, creeping out of the woodwork, rehabilitated whackjob Bruciato Giallo, former co-star Anna Condo, and a woman from the wrong side of the tracks who shared a strange and stormy relationship with Breck, none other than Squeaky Fomme."

"Blog."

"Blog."

"It's great to be here, Blog."

"For those of you just crawling out from under a slimy rock by some polluted waterfront, today Rick Breck flew his Cesspo Coot 1313 straight into the National Pentagram. Some speculate that if he hadn't been so gosh-darn famous, we'd be remembering him only as a traitor to New Haudie. Thoughts?"

Anna Condo smiled and caught the attention of the most badass tuber.

"I want to talk about something serious. Rick Breck was using Bongdongalis. He suffered terribly from a unique condition and he needed to ease his suffering. He couldn't get out of bed without taking Bongdongalis."

"Shocking, Ms. Condo. Our very own Dr. Fava will have to personally evaluate the risks and rewards of Bongdongalis for us. How about you, Bruciato?"

"Lo, bear witness how I am born again!"

"Squeaky?"

"O you're horrible, all of you! Bottom-feeders! This is just the kind of life he was trying to escape! But he had his faith! He followed his beliefs. You can't fault him for that!"

"True, true, Ms. Fomme. But why did his undeniable faith lead him to fly directly into a strategic target, one that might have crippled our defences in a time of holy war?"

"But you don't understand a whit of it! You loved him for his work in *Buds II*. I never even knew who he really was. But *I* loved him for his unquestioning blank-faced causism!"

"Wow, those are sure some raw uncooked feelings. Now, we'll show the plane flying into the building over and over again, after a soothing suggestion by our sponsors ..."

Upside Down

Pan to gloomy gus with fixed mouth and clenched teeth.

"Feeling alienated from your species and fellow creatures?"

The man is nodding and holding his forehead, as if in sudden torment.

"Have you lost that swig of confidence to face the day with?"

The man nods again and rubs away a single tear from below his right eye.

"Are you feeling pale – do you lack the tan of a migrant worker?"

The man nods frantically, startled by his own reflection in a vanity with pearly ornamentation.

"Isn't it time you tried Vanitex?"

Pan to a salivating doctor signing a dozen prescriptions for Vanitex. The man drops a handful of the egg-shaped pills into a mantini and knocks back the lot. Instantly, he feels better. The camera pans to him smiling and strutting through the office. Men and women alike cannot resist his überhealthy pallor and are overwhelmed by the fallout from his increased levels of confidence.

"Warning: Vanitex should not be taken internally. Vanitex may result in loss of fur or follicles. Do not operate heavy machinery or attempt to fly aircraft under the influence of Vanitex. Those with allergies to silverfish are advised not to take vast quantities of Vanitex. If facial or bodily sheen engendered by Vanitex sets fire to furniture, please consult a physician."

Now the gloomy gus is grinning from ear to ear and making a crowd of people laugh hysterically, even as they are shielding their eyes from his translucent glow.

"Vanitex. Because isn't it time you turned that frown upside down?"

A Hunch in the Gut

"What are we doing here?"

"Just following a hunch."

Detective Blue Green looked around the ornate conch of a temple. Nobody in sight. He sighed. Rebecca Tomahawk sat down on a shellish seat.

"Now what do we do?"

"Dunno ... wait ... wander aimlessly. Hunches are like that. You never quite know what you're doing or where you're going ..."

"What is this place?"

"This is the temple for the Mantodean Order."

"Do you think the Mantodeans are involved?"

"I just remembered an old case. Bothered the heck outta me. Another missing-finger deal, but this wasn't the same modus operandi. It was more sacrificial, routine finger biting, perpetrated by a splinter group of the Order. Damn attention seekers! Hey, you got a kid, Tomahawk?"

Rebecca Tomahawk fluttered her eyelashes meaningfully at him.

"Why, no, not yet, Detective Green."

"You want some friendly advice? If you aim to get one and you hear him bawling his eyes out, just leave him be. Otherwise he'll go through life just wanting no end of attention. Pretty much everybody I gotta pick up was picked up as a little puke. I blame Dr. Spock myself. Coddle 'em an' they'll kill you in cold blood, that's what I say."

He was about to share a few more of his views on life when suddenly he fell to the floor and began trembling uncontrollably. He was having what's known in the game as a psychical fit, or more technically, a mean-as-nails hunch in the gut.

The Invite Marked Unguent

Oober Mann, now marooned on his office island for three, dimmed his field of vision and gave a sidelong glance to Greta Goldfarb, who was making quite the effort this afternoon to draw attention. She smiled and toyed with her plunging top.

"Hey, Oober!"

"Uhm ... yeah?"

August Santos was nowhere to be seen. It was Goatsinger.

"This morning I noticed a body in one of the vents. Or two. I forget. Anything I should worry about?"

"I'm not sure what you mean."

"S'okay, it's between you and me. I know you just started and I wanted to let you know we all make mistakes. A few bodies in the air system won't hurt anything."

"Whatever."

"By the way, I've been tracking a rare form of the tequila worm virus, and the funny thing is, I have been getting residual traces from the vents, and ... well, to be perfectly frank, from *you*."

"That sounds fascinating, Goatsinger, but I've got a lot of work to do. Sure wish I knew what in tarnation you were yammering about."

"Hmm ... yeah, no problem. Just let me know if you notice anything ... weird."

"Totally. The first thing."

He felt a mild sensory disorientation and realized the incessant beeping was coming from a remote channel. It was an invite from Greta Goldfarb marked UNGUENT.

Brown Widow in a Black Blamer

Kate Caterwall answered the door to an immaculate fellow in a creamy Mooselini suit. Without pause, she pulled him inside by his mackerel necktie.

"Whoa!"

Dean Bunt could not believe his luck. He had just met this brown widow at a Conservative Conservationist rally and she had stressed how much she needed to get involved. But now he was getting the picture, loud and clear. All she was wearing was a Sagegrasp black blamer held together by a few hooks in front.

"Sorry about this ... I must have been dreaming when you gavotted me ..."

"Dreaming?"

"Yeah, dreaming some hot guy might show up out of the blue."

Dean stared into her changeling eyes. He had remembered them as blue but now they looked greeny-brown. His pulse was racing.

"So, what is a brown widow, anyway?"

"Same irresistible hourglass figure but the neurotoxic headgames are relatively mild. In other words, I'll mess you up but I may not eat you alive. Of course, a hint of vorarephilia never went amiss! So, what are Conservative Conservationists into?"

"I never mix politics with pleasure."

"Ahwww ... just this once ..."

"What do you want?"

"Actually, the question is, what do you want, Dean? What do you want day and night? A good time with a bad girl, huh, Dean?"

She started rubbing her right palm across the front of his pants.

"Wow, you feel so big and powerful. I bet one day you'll be president of New Haudenosaunee. Then you'll have girls like me whenever you want ..."

"Ughnnn ... yah!"

"You wanna show me, Dean? C'mon, Dean! Whip it out, honey ... terrorize me with that largegantic bongdong of yours!"

Dean couldn't help himself. She unhooked her blamer and lay back upon a chintz coverlet. He rubbed his throbbing tip between her thighs, imagining he was erotic asphyxiation star Dean Bunt, a vintage pleaser! As if on cue, she yanked his mackerel tie, nearly choking him.

"I ... I'm ... not ... into ... that ..."

"Dean, I just need you to do one teensy-weensy thing for me."

"Uh ... huhmmm."

"I know the governor's campaign tour is passing by this little love nest. Now, it is *imperative* that you grant me an audience with him. Or should I approach your colleague Mac, and give him the time of his life instead?"

"No, not Mac! Anyone but that crankspanker!"

"Then will you introduce me to the governor?"

Dean Bunt the porno god hung his head, feeling partially deflated.

"Then you're just using me ..."

"Using you on the downlow, you mean. And using you to use your power. That gets me so hot!"

"Uhhnnn ..."

"C'mon, Dean! I'm a bad girl. Maybe you should punish me!"

She wrapped her long legs around him and together they wobbled on the very edge of a vanity.

"Take a long hard look in the mirror, Dean. Look at what a big stud you are!"

Before long, a spent Dean Bunt was sweating and gasping in his damp suit. He looked at his face in the mirror, ashamed and unable to recognize this man looking back at him. And behind him, stealing toward his bare bottom, Kate Caterwall, with an economy-size whirring dill in her hand.

"Just so we remember who's spinning what."

Dean Bunt screamed.

Tanning Hides

Shyster Deacon sat outside Parasimpatico, tapping his knee and averting his eyes from those of Wilma Pettifogger, but she knew him too well. He exhibited a distinct twitch whenever he was exaggerating any fact.

"I told you, she'll carny him real good."

"You don't sound convinced."

"*Ne t'inquiètes pas.*"

"Why did you ever get me into this racket in the first place?"

"You sure didn't have any misgivings when the dough was rolling in."

"Tanning booth to the future! My mother was right."

"So we put a few bodies on ice. They got what they wanted."

"What if the Clan Mothers get wind of what we did, even with this chump?"

"I told you, it's as good as taken care of. I paid this doll well to lure our cat out into the open ...."

"Out in the open, that's what I'm afraid of."

"So we made a little red, dumping human traffic in a deep freeze. I haven't heard anybody complaining."

"But one of those guys – he's a gosh-darned murderer! And we sold him a one-way ticket to the future! O, we tanned some hides, all right!"

"Stay gelid. It'll be fine."

"They weren't supposed to remember! Those memory inhibitors you bought wholesale are faulty."

"It's not full-blown neural reverb. They just get sketchy flashes of stuff that happened."

"Well, it's too much like a shoddy plot device or something. I don't like it."

"How many times? Nobody's gonna come back to find us. And we can deal with any customers who get wise. Now, finish your anguish pie and then let's roll."

"*Ça me plâit.*"

Hothouse Experience

Goebbel Gewürztraminer popped another pill and chewed it thoughtfully, before washing it down with a can of Hothouse Experience. Abe Chaney entered swiftly and soundlessly. Goebbel could swear his adviser had just walked through the fireplace but he couldn't be sure. Abe tended to appear and disappear at will. Of course, it was to his advantage to have a right-hand man who knew every secret passage, underground chamber, and bidimensional portal snaking around the five-pointed capital of New Haudenosaunee.

"Sorry to disturb you, Governor, but I have some news."

"How are the polls?"

"Polls are fine, fine. It's not the polls I'm worried about."

"But when you worry, I worry."

"We just got a call from ISM. Apparently, they got wind of an imminent attack."

"Attack? What kind of attack?"

"What else? An attempt on your life."

"Abey ... how long have we been in this game? You can't be serious. Everybody loves me, and I have no issues ... not with anything or anybody. Who would want to kill me?"

"Epimetheans. They're a splinter group of the Church of After Thought. The government has denied their church tax-exempt status and this particular group wants to make an example out of you, especially because they attract a vast amount of funding from both flagging and sagging celebrities and, by their logic, assassinating you might get some high fliers to turn tail and get right into bed with the Church."

"And you got this from ISM? Who is investigating this attack from dere?"

"Flak Riesling."

"Flak!"

"You know him, Governor?"

"You might say that, Abe. We spent some months together in New Barcelona. It was a very hush-hush operation, the kind that does something permanent to a man. And every night I ate my heart out ..."

"Sorry to interrupt your charming tale, Governor, but we have to start making changes to your itinerary, and pronto."

"Abe, I'm not running away from this. In my country, they have a saying ..."

"Sir?"

"You want to catch a fox, you have to dress like a hen. But always, always beware of the rooster."

"Very profound, Governor. It boggles the mind."

"We stick to our schedule. And wait for the attack. Then we pounce!"

"As your adviser, I advise against this. But as the only other man in the room, I agree, you could die, but whatever; life goes on."

"My number is not being ratatooted yet."

Suddenly, a dumbbell on the desk clanged to life. Abe Chaney winked.

"You're on speaker ... go ahead."

"The Governor's ex-wife is on the line."

Governor Gewürztraminer picked up one of his more prestigious Baller trophies and threw it down on the floor and began stomping on it.

"I must crush ... I must crush you all!"

Abe Chaney turned around and talked into the fireplace.

"Dean? Abe here. I think the Governor is short on his usual medication. Do you think we could double or even triple the dosage, just to see us through the primaries? Swell."

Probably, neither of them knew it, but lurking within the scrummy contents of the can of Hothouse Experience was a detached human finger.

Into the Mindfield

Flak Riesling urged on his limuck through lethargic air traffic and breathed huskily into his chitgraft.

"Patch me into the mindfield."

"Silvia Snooplov."

"Run a relationship crosstown search on the name Greta Goldfarb."

"Okay, this might take a minute."

"Fine."

"Here's something. Wow, she's very doable, Flak. A former new adult tube star, and her name cross-references a number of our usual suspects. And right now she's listed as working for an organization called LeapPod Streams. And ... there's something else."

"Yeah?"

"You're not gonna like it, Flak."

"Silvia, what is it?"

"One of the relationships that came up concerns our own facilitator and designated slave-driver, Hassan Armadill. They used to go out and apparently it wasn't even meaningful, just sex and lies and then more sex and more lies ..."

"Okay thanks, Silvia. Send all the snaps to my palmwafer."

"So now where are you going?"

"To perform a corporate takeover ..."

In the Wake of an Eastern Wind

Audrey Boolean returned home and kicked off her skandals at once. She could hear strange gruntings and speechifyings emanating from upstairs.

"Indio?"

She tiptoed up the steps and peeped into the bedroom. Tiff Kasha was lying naked on their bed. Her wrists were bound with abacá to the crescent moon headboard. She was also wearing a loud tribal mask that Indio's uncle had handed down to him. Indio, of course, was crawling all over her and doing his thing, amid a smell of incense and oils.

"With me, generations of restitution. Let me give back to our Mother Earth!"

"Get ready for a whack of sacred tribalism!"

"My senses are packed with herbs."

"Your nostrils are thick with cedar."

Audrey began to undo her ClingteX lynchpin.

"Hey freaks, move over and make some room for me."

Tiff reared her head and bared her teeth, struggling to get free and give her a bite.

"No! This is *my* transcendental experience! *I* am the woman being redressed! Not you! You vintage trashist warmonger, get the hoof outta here!"

Indio shrugged.

"Sorry, I cannot contend with angry spirits in the wake of an Eastern wind."

Audrey slammed the door in disgust.

"Free Nutella! Liberate our Native denizens! Free everybody everywhere!"

Audrey covered her ears with a pair of bran new plugs from Keesterific, shutting out every raucous echo of their reclamation.

You Don't Have a Prayer

Greta Goldfarb marked her place in a synaptic edition of *Mirth & Misogyny* and grinned at Oober Mann.

"Ready?"

"Great spruce! Ready as I'll ever be!"

As they stood beside the flitboost, she took his arm and he sneezed at something in her hair or on her body.

"Sorry, must be my product ..."

Oober smiled and rubbed his nose. Not that it mattered. He would swim through fleshwash and hair goop soup to get to Greta Goldfarb. The bulbous light began to glow a deep red. The flitboost was here. Inside, she held him closer and without warning began to whisper some sketchy Yiddish into his ear before singing some ecstatic highs from Bach's coffee cantata. Then her lips moved closer and he began to feel faint. His vision was going out of focus but he could still discern the shape of a stirrynge in her left hand. She dragged him out of the lobby past some gawkers and apologized for her friend who had just fallen off the wagon.

"He can't help it! Give the lad another chance!"

She was home free, directly in front of her two contacts, when suddenly out of a castiosk burst none other than Flak Riesling. He tackled Greta and she cursed him over a broken heel. Oober went flying and slumped over the outdoor railing of Parasimpatico, frightening customers from their lean prosciutto and bleating goat cheese. Wilma Pettifogger and Shyster Deacon looked around furtively, deciding whether or not they could slink off with their prey without being noticed. At that moment, a mystery mobilizer appeared out of nowhere and flapped open its panels. Two burly giggling types somersaulted out and, without missing a beat, hoisted Oober off the railing and cannonballed back into the hovering vehicle. The panels flapped shut over hyenaic laughter, and the mobilizer warped off into the blogosphere, which was growing thicker of late. Wilma and Shyster slipped away in a combined state of surprise and mortification. Greta Goldfarb stared up sulkily at Flak Riesling.

"Okay, Splazer-jockey. I know the drill. Read me my rights and escort me downtown already."

"It's not that simple, Ms. Goldfarb. I work for Insurgent Saddo Management. Where I come in, technically, you don't have rights and you don't have a prayer. A non-indigenous prayer, anyway. I think it's best you cooperate and tell me everything you know."

Her eyes widened as he produced a bag of clanking oysters and showed her the contents.

"These are still in the shell. We better get started ..."

The Magic of Inflatus Maximus

Mémé lay back, wrapped in tousled blue sheets, and watched Bronto find a clean place along his inner thigh before introducing a new infusion.

"O yeah! Whoooo!"

"Are you sure that junk is good for you?"

"Totally! It makes me megamegalicious!"

"Don't you worry about side effects ...?"

"Side effects? The only side effect I can see is the effect to my sides! A killer bod and good hot lovin'!"

"Yeah, I guess."

He proceeded to crack open a packet of Inflatus Maximus and downed a couple of fast-acting capsules. Mémé watched his shorts swell up like an inflatable groundhog in the Mohawk's parade.

"Whoa, your munificence ... let me take a shower first ..."

She was still laughing to herself when she noticed an elongated case in the corridor. She knew Bronto *was* an instrument but she had no idea he *played* an instrument. Maybe he was taking lessons to surprise her with some romantic folk-tune fake. She opened the case and saw a jarjantuan gun, in pieces. She picked up the silencer and telescopic lens and began to wonder what kind of animal he was going to take down with this beauty. She returned to the bedroom directly, only to find it trashed and smashed to shambles.

"Bronto mad ... Bronto smash ... WHOOOO!"

A Veritable Cornucopia

Chip Riesling hung upside down from a virtual suspension of disbelief common to the Simbat Euphorium. Midair, he stroked the flaxen locks of a floating Nastya Cornucopia as she clung to his buttocks and gratified his revived body with a timeworn embrace.

"Ooooh yeah, Nastya. That's too freakin' hot for prime time ..."

"Ooh, Chip ... you are just like father ..."

"Whoa ... father ... my dad?"

"But younger, less anal ..."

Chip felt his blood drain from his face and rush to another place. She must have spliced in a psychitronic complex to make the experience way headier. She went to town on him with increasing energy and he was unable to avoid imagining his prudish gubernatorial tool of a father in the feverish grip of Nastya Cornucopia. It made him want to laugh and cry and, for whatever reason, it melted his butter.

"Mmm ... Chip, you do anything ... for this ..."

"Yeah! Yeah! O yeah!"

"Don't ... leave ... after. I want to go for ride with you."

"Uhmmm ... sure ... whatever ..."

"*Glug glug glug ...*"

The Judges of Areopagus

Finnegan Grayling clasped his big hands together and leaned forward, demonstrating his range of compassion and understanding. He had read about this in ... a book. Show him you are moved physically and he will know you are moved inwardly. Also, always appear to be in a hurry. Rush up stairs briskly. Hold flitboosts open with conviction.

"I'm sincerely sorry, Mr. Mann. Your book is courageous and intriguing and interesting and arresting. Why, I've never seen anything like it! You could call us ... *conventional*, if you like. That's not a dirty word, no sir."

"So you won't publish it."

"We feel it just isn't right for Arthropoda Press."

"But sir ..."

Mr. Grayling reached for a book on the shelf behind his squeaking chair.

"Take this for example. This is the sort of thing people want."

"*Matzah Ball Medicine Woman in Madagascar*?"

"Yeah ... like that. This is an example of something that brings people together."

Just then the office door exploded. Through the smoke, a band of masked figures appeared. They levelled their assortment of weapons at Mr. Grayling.

"You are hereby ordered to print this esoterica!"

"Gentlemen ... "

"You have three ticks to voice your agreement."

"This is insane!"

"Three ..."

"Couldn't we just discuss this ... like professionals?"

"Two ..."

Mr. Grayling was flopping about in his chair, now swathed in oily sweat.

"We already have Justin Blurber in our custody."

"No! Okay, okay, I'll do what you want."

"Good."

"Would you at least tell me why you're so keen to have this ... dreck ... printed?"

The apparent leader loomed over him, eyes wide through the holes in his mask.

"Because each book has a right to life the moment it is conceived! You have no right to kill a book before it exists!"

Oober tapped him on the shoulder.

"Y'know, it's okay, really."

The leader rounded on him.

"Nor do you have a right to terminate a book, not even your own! We brought you here in the name of something beyond all of us!"

Then the leader, whose *nom de guerre* was Aspen Everhard, began to cradle the manuscript lovingly, rocking it in his arms.

"Go, little book. Go out into the world. Who's your daddy? Who's daddy?"

Finnegan Grayling clenched his teeth and squeezed his knees. *The Guide to Getting Anywhere* had not prepared him for this.

They Say Pigs Can Fly

Shyster Deacon tricked open the door of a nearby limuck and ushered Wilma Pettifogger inside. But something was holding her back. It was Rebecca Tomahawk. Blue Green pressed an icy automatic into the back of Shyster's neck.

"Well, well, Shyster Deacon."

"Well, well, they say pigs can fly!"

"You figured those sixty stories did me in?"

"What gives, flatfoot?"

"Now what is the Deek doing in this neck of the woods, and right in the middle of an ISM takedown?"

"Stuff it, Green. This time you're barkin' up the wrong gal, see."

"Cuff her, Tomahawk ... for her own protection."

Officer Tomahawk applied the handcuffs and lingered in a gratuitous frisk of Wilma Pettifogger's entire body, before carefully tucking her head down and shoving her into the back of the limuck.

"You can't do this, Green. You gotta charge us with something."

"Did you enjoy the prosciutto?"

"What?"

"Did you enjoy the prosciutto?"

"Huh?"

"Nobody sits down to prosciutto at Parasimpatico and does a dash, leaving half a sandwich. You didn't even touch your sea sponge chips."

"Maybe I'm a light eater."

"You forget I know you, Deacon. You ain't."

"Charge us with something or let us go."

"How about for nabbing a limuck, for appetizers?"

"You're making a huge freakin' mistake."

"You're in over your head, Shyster. And I'm gonna find out exactly how deep."

Half-Lives

"Where's hubby?"
"At work."
"What does he do again?"
"He's a glottochronologist."
"Glottawha ..."
"He looks at timelines for when languages split up."
"Huh?"
"I dunno, something to do with radioactive half-lives, and how different languages live and die, yada yada ..."
"He get paid for that?"
"Ya-huh."
"Well, I smash and crash!"
"Uh-huh."
"I trash and bash!"
"Bronto, honey, why do you have a jarjantuan gun with you?"
"You saw that?"
"Yeah."
"Well ... we can't all be glottochronologists, I guess."
"What do you mean?"
There was a cheery slam of the front door. Stewart was home.

Into Bunghole and Bungalow

After the Judges of Areopagus had put the bindings to Finnegan Grayling, they dropped Oober Mann off in front of LeapPod Streams.

"Hey, Mann, keep up the non-conforming!"

"Thanks for helping me, I think."

Now, he just had to find Greta. Perhaps she had only stirrynged him in order to help him get his book published. Yes, that was it. He would let her off easy and then they would hazard a second date. His ticklish musings were interrupted when the heavyish body of the pod bitlet inspector tumbled into his arms. The man's clothes were scorched through.

"Goatsinger! No!"

"Good luck, Oober Mann. Though to tell you the truth, I never did believe in luck. We make choices, I guess, and we gots to live and die by them."

Oober examined his wounds.

"Don't bother, Mann. It's an ionic decombobulator. Messes with the molecules, just ever so slightly, but enough. I'm close to a particle rupture, in other words, done for."

"Why?"

"Why do any of us go? Wheyhey, those agents got Greta. But she's not a big wheel, just small fry, just a bite of the jumbo enchilada."

"How do you know all this?"

"I know about the tequila worm virus and much much more. I was assigned to keep an eye on you. O, the fatal irony!"

"Assigned ... who?"

"Can't ... cohere ... must ... hurry."

"Goatsinger!"

"Not over ... one more ..."

"One more? One more what?"

"Leap ... Pod ... one more ..."

Goatsinger fell to the floor with his limbs jerking everywhichway. Then his molecules began to slowly disperse. Part of his hand floated off and found a new life stopping a bunghole. Another part went into decorating a new Sexiglass bungalow. Another part of him became a doorstop. Oober watched, his eyes wet, as Goatsinger's body divided and subdivided into its most infinitesimal units, before the entire light show just fizzled out.

"One more what?"

A Process of Deductive Induction

Blue Green didn't find anyone in reception, so he made his way along the corridor to the inner sanctum and into the bullpen of LeapPod Streams. Krunk ejected himself and rushed to meet the visitor.

"Sorry, Greta must be on break. Can I help?"

"You can help by letting me see those hands."

"Huh?"

"Call it a hunch, but I know something screwy's going on here."

"Sir, I think you're making a mistake."

Just then, August Santos jumped up from his console and hightailed it out the fire exit and down the stairs, setting off the alarm. Blue Green ignored him, and instead began sniffing around.

"Aren't you going after that nut? Maybe he's the guy you're looking for."

"Nah. Too simple. There's always a twist. Question is, what kind of a twist. Lemon, lime, or tangerine?"

"How about you leave us alone till you get your facts straight."

"Where were you in the last hour?"

Swift Tail Ferber piped up.

"Hey man, I was having lunch with Krunk. He's our tester and relief admin."

"Looks good on paper, but we all know programmers and testers don't get along, let alone sit down over pipsissewa blend together."

"You're sniffing the wrong gleespot, dude."

"The fingerprints we got, they're all bloated with calluses. And I only know one thing that causes calluses in this day and age."

"What?"

"Retroblips cooked up by Craycray Infotainment."

Blue reached for Krunk's fingers and held them up to the light.

"Look at this! Hideous!"

And indeed, Krunk's hands were covered with calluses.

"I was doing some work around the house ..."

"Hey man, ever since virtual bodycups, we don't use our hands anymore!"

"Maybe Krunk here is an old-fashioned kinda guy, eh?"

Swift Tail Ferber inched closer.

"Hey man, you just can't come in here and harass our staff. We have rights, hoss. Leave him alone."

Blue Green went for his weapon and fired twice through the heart of Swift Tail Ferber, who at age twenty-six, with a sizable nest egg, had been within a week of retirement.

"Now maybe I'll get some cooperation."

Blue was leading Krunk off in horror when he noticed two pairs of feet sticking out of a ventilation shaft.

"Somehow there still might be another twist ..."

Theatre of Cruelty

Greta Goldfarb was bound wrist and ankle to the wall. Billy Joe and Bobby Joe were taking turns squeezing a wet sponge over her forehead and switching on and off a mild electric current, at first arousing but over time excruciating. Hassan Armadill frowned from his pedestal in the torture theatre of ISM.

"I'm not sure we're goin' about this the right way, Flak."

"We don't have a choice, Hassan. Something is about to go down and I mean nowish."

"But are you sure she knows something?"

"Why are you protecting her?"

"It's a bit embarrassing, Flak. Greta ... and I ... used to work together for a little production company called Lushlicious Discridges. They produced ... romantic tubes ... for the ... stimulation of ... hopeless couples."

"I see."

"Now this just brings back all those bad memories."

"A bit of BDSM? I understand, Hassan."

"No, I mean ... she went on to bigger and better snuff and furry stuff, and my contract just wasn't renewed. They said they'd call. They never did."

"I see."

Blue Green charged into ISM, flanked by Rebecca Tomahawk, who was leading three new prisoners.

"Blue Green. I thought something stank in here."

"Flak Riesling. I thought I just heard a masochist's wet dream."

Check the Script

Hurt Hardass emerged upon his personal stretch of airstrip, clad in a short deer jacket over a cheeky midrifter and LeatheX pants, his eyes perfectly conched spirals of intensity. If one were to stare even more deeply, one might find some vestige of the circles that had so disturbed Archimedes, except duller in colour. He leapt in cannonball fashion into the cockpit of his Cesspo Loon 1499.

"Whooo!"

He took off like a bat outta hell, grinning smugly at the thought of the stunt he was about to perform. He could not remember which studio he was working for, but that was beside the point. The point was that he going to do this totally brosome jumping-and-rolling-around sequence. He paged through the partial script he had been given. All he had to do was infiltrate and take over the evil base. He sounded out each word, slowly reading aloud off the page in front of him.

Hurt (played by him-self) descends into the vill-ain-ous head-quart-ers of ISM and den-ounces their hein-ous act-ions before firing scuddies at rand-om ...

Hard Day

Oober Mann let himself into the cuddlehole the Librarian had just rented. He felt silly calling her by this title, even in his head, but she had insisted that her name in her own tongue was too difficult to pronounce and might even burst his eardrums. He had suggested a number of ordinary names but she had refused them on the grounds that he was trying to label her. He sat down in her orange chair and she poured him a strange fizzing concoction. Oober sipped the drink and watched the Librarian, with his eyelids growing heavier and heavier.

"Hard day?"

"Just dandy. And how was your day, dear?"

"Fine. I went to have my earth vehicle checked, down the street at Lubey's Auto. My rear differentials are now excellent."

"Uh-huh."

A tawdry flick was plucking at his sensorium. He already felt a bit dizzy from the drink and the tube was glowing with intensity. It was just some cheesy bargain-basement crime drama. Two detectives had come to the door of a suspect and wanted to ask her some questions, but she only hurled insults and challenges at them. As they cuffed her hands behind her back, she turned her head, and Oober fell back in his orange chair.

"Recognize her?"

It was Greta Goldfarb. Saxotones sounded as one of the detectives ran his nightstick up and down her body.

"I'm such a bad girl. I need to be punished."

"Tell us what you know."

"You don't need that stick to make me talk."

"Oh, I got something bigger, baby! And you'll wanna talk."

The detective put down his nightstick and undid his pants before carefully lifting out a long and thick thing that ressembled the male organ on everyone's mind. It was firing globs of what looked like Campfire Creamy Truffle soup at the other two participants, who were doing their best to look aroused and not completely freaked out. Oober Mann looked away in feigned disgust and the Librarian toned it down.

"Is this what causes earthenfolk to want to mate?"

"You have to do a lot more research."

"I have done research, and I wanted you to see your little friend's work history."

Oober watched as her fingers slid under her beaverhunter.

"Uhmmmm ... Oober ... you make me so ... hot."

Along with this precise mimicry of a dozen dirt shows, she was emanating a faint music, almost like a flutter of wings, that lulled him into a somnambulant state.

"Mmm ... it's been a long, hard day, Oober Mann. And those big, sweaty hunks at Lubey's Auto, they wanted to give me some real service."

"What?"

"Yeah, so they said come into the garage and I went with them into the garage and then they said what do you want, ma'am, and I said I want you to show me those big scary gearshifts. I wanted to say show me those largegantic greasemonkey tools and really wrench it but my mouth was already full."

"_?"

"Then I wiped my lips and told them that Oober Mann was waiting for me at home and the big guy said Oober Mann, I bet Oober Mann can't do this, and he hung me upside down by my ankles and abrogated the area I most love to be abrogated, at the same time prompting me to check out his mighty pistons."

"Arrghhhhhumhtttt ..."

Oober Mann had been unable to contain himself in the orange chair. The Librarian smiled, a Sanitidy towelette at the ready.

Salvation and Loan

John Cobbler entered MediaHo Arena with a broad crooked smile, stopping only to comment upon Burnham Young's growing beard.

"Suits you, my friend, and certainly befits a true prophet of Drumheller."

"Thank you."

"Now listen up, everyone! Leave off your gobsmackin' a sec. There'll be plenny of time for that later. But what matters is the NOW."

"Hey yeah, we don't know what to do with ourselves!"

"Yeah, now who's gonna tell us what to do?"

"Yeah, what you gonna do about that?"

"Uh-huh. Now today is your lucky day. I received a message from the holy angels of yesteryear, when every angel was cast down into the tarpits of the Midyards. And we are stuck here until the prophesized eleventh hour, when we will all be returned to our original home of the flying folk. But yea, that time is upon us. We gotta give it a hundred and thirteen percent."

"And is there a way we can spittlebug in on this?"

"Of course. But hath a man tongue long enough to satisfy the powers that be?"

"Totally profound!"

"Now, I want you four young ladies in the front row ... and you, young man, you as well! Now, I want you first sacred five to come with me into the back, for we will be united in holy unbustable union in a sanctified jiffy. And don't forget your credits, folks. For we cannot trust ourselves as fallen beasties to manage our own funds. And you know what just ... came to me in a vision? We need to be united in a salvation and loan from the get-go!"

"You mean, like a bank?"

"You learn real quick, brethren and sisterlies."

John switched on some John Cage before retiring into the back for the first initiation rites with his juicy young flock. And they would flock and then the rest would flock and then flock some more ... and soon everybody would be flocking everywhere, and all related too! Only Burnham Young stroked his new beard pensively, a trifle shocked.

The Bucket List

"Honey, I'm home!"

Stewart scanned the apartment. He was hoping to jack into another Sim session before tending to other matters. But his adrenalin was skyrocketing. He could feel his thighs pulsating. His eyes darted right and left. Aggros? Here? Then he noticed the dark case. He pried it open and fondled the automatic inside.

"Put down my piece, Stew."

"Put down my woman, sir."

The steroidogens flared up in Bronto's bloodstream while the metaphysical conditioning from extensive exposure to his new Playnation Maxipad strap-in console rippled through Stewart's body. The men made short hops toward each other before interlocking in a timeold brohold. The apartment shook as they took turns pile-driving one another into floor and walls.

"Sloppy second-hand slam!"

"Sleeper love grip!"

Bronto's veins shot out of his triceps like invasive vines and began to squeeze Stewart's windpipe. But Stewart's game-induced fight-or-flight Simdrome was activated, and his body trembled with sudden bursts of strength.

"Aggros!!!"

Stewart tore his clothing into shreds and throbbed naked over a trembling Bronto. The psychotropic Sim system had completely pervaded Stewart's nervous system and had even awakened a dormant latent fantasy. He began to rub his throbbing tool against Bronto's massive butt crack.

"Hoo yah!"

"Dude!!!"

"Squeal like a pig, boy!"

Then he found his target and doused it with a bottle of old-fashioned Sweteluft oil before inserting his woolly mammoth of a prick.

"Thought you could steal my queen, huh? Well, king takes pawn ... in the backdoor!"

"Uhhhhhmmmm ... yeah dude ... I love you."

Bronto's entire bulk shook for what felt like a blissful eternity. Then he collapsed with a thud.

"Bronto!!! His steroidogen-enriched heart can't take it."

"It's funny, Mémé, because for the first time ..."

"Stewart, we don't have time to deal with whatever just went down! Bronto had a job to do. If he doesn't do it, they'll come looking for us."

"Huh? I don't get it."

"This gun is not just some fetish toy or black-market flick prop! I think Bronto was going to put the kibosh on someone."

"You can't be serious."

"He wasn't that bright. He needed the work. One last job, and then ... retirement! Wait, he might have left a note, something ..."

It wasn't until Mémé rolled down Bronto's socks that she found the bucket list. There was an address, right next to a circled reminder to assassinate Governor Gewürztraminer. She showed her former lover's feet to Stewart.

"He misspelled *assassinate*. And Gewürztraminer. And Spirit Bear Brothel."

Beyond the Startler

Hassan Armadill crept quietly into one of the interrogation suites and began to unfasten the restraints on Greta Goldfarb. He removed her startler top and tapped her skin with a tasselled novelty whip before giving her a few playful lashes.

"Give it a rest, Hassan. I'm on to the whole good torture–bad torture technique."

"Don't know what you mean."

"Hassan, eh? I remember you as Armand Armadillo."

"Well, I remember you as Paula Panteater, but that doesn't change anything."

"But it *could.*"

Her eyes opened wide, becoming moonlit pools of his own roused masculinity. This look had gotten her the contract, while he had merely flopped off into the shadows.

"Tell us what you know, Greta."

"Make me."

"You were caught trying to abduct this man. Who is he, Greta?"

"He was smashed. I was trying to give him a lift."

"That doesn't wash. More cannibalistic soft core? More hipster headdress action?"

"Please."

"No, because you're *better* than that! Because you only take money for bigger and better cleanup operations."

"That's right."

"Why don't you tell me about the job? Then maybe we can cut a deal."

"Tell you what, Armadildo. Make it worth my while. Then I'll talk and make you a sweet deal. But first, we're going to make a little feature presentation for all those mechanically challenged couples out there."

"You can't be serious."

Her eyes were hopelessly wide and her tongue was already lolling all about.

"Mmm ... yeah."

Killer Hunches

Flak Riesling scowled at Blue Green, who was clearly fascinated by the monitored interrogation that the former Armand Armadildo was giving the former Paula Panteater.

"Whoa, look at her eat through those slacks! Is that even a natural fibre?"

"Why are you wasting my time, Green?"

"I saw your operation go down. And I didn't like what I saw."

"You had no reason to bring those three people in."

"Yeah, well, I've been having these killer hunches all day. Bear with me."

"Go ahead."

"The couple are a seasoned pair of con artists. I've busted them before, but this time they claim they've retired, after years of running a legitimate tanning business."

"Umhumn. Bronzeys. I haven't heard any complaints."

"Something just ain't right, Riesling."

"What about the other guy?"

"Krunk Kalogeropoulos. Works as a tester for LeapPod Streams. I brought him in for resisting arrest."

"Arrest ... for what?"

"Stopping up the air conditioning with human remains, for one thing."

"And what makes you think it's him?"

"I told you, another huge hunch. Although he wouldn't pipe down on the way here, all the time maligning some other guy at the company named Santos. Typical corporate weaselling."

At that moment, Hassan Armadill emerged from interrogation, stuffing his shirttails into what remained of his pants.

"She says the man who knows everything about today's events is a religious fanatic who works at LeapPod Streams. His name is August Santos."

"Wait a tick. There was a guy who ran out the fire escape while I was arresting Kalogeropoulos. I think his name was Santos."

"What!?!"

At that moment, the inner sanctum of ISM exploded.

Anything Is Possible

"Blog Stentorian here. If you're just joining us, we've been staring numbly at this looping footage of megahard thespian Hurt Hardass (originally born as Jeremy Lebensmittelgeschäft) paradiving directly into the headquarters for Insurgent Saddo Management, where those brave souls defend our brave defenders by using their big noggins ... and a little muscle."

He winked and performed a short-lived dance of looming danger.

"There's been a steaming heap of speculation in the press. *The Daily Tittler* reported that they didn't want *this kook* anywhere near their houses of parliament, while *Sunny Bunny News* described him, and I quote, as a *freaking flaming plonker*. Tough words from our leading fibbits. Now, for mindless speculation, we turn to one of our celebrity flunkies who hasn't left the building since her last appearance, the great Anna Condo, daughter of the sadly departed Robert Condo, whom we remember most of all for his portrayal of a man faking an eating disorder in *Fatsuit 5*. Touching stuff, truly."

"It's great to still be here, Blog."

"I just wanna say how great you are, really. Really really great ..."

"Thanks."

"Now you have a little story of your own about Insurgent Saddo Management, referred to by those in the info flow as ISM."

"This is true, Blog."

"Why don't you tell us a bit about that."

"I was ... with one of my adopted sons in our place of worship—"

"Let me just interrupt to say that that was in the Church of After Thought for devout and/or well-to-do Epimetheans."

"We were just about to receive instructions ... about our own quick 'n' easy personal path to the afterlife, when ... this man burst in on us. It was an agent from ISM. He said ... they were going to ... hurt my most imported son."

"Excuse me, did you mean most *important* son?"

"Why, what did I say?"

"Most *imported* son."

"Yes, sorry. It was a very stressful experience. I don't know what I would have done without the support of my church, after the fact."

"Well, bless their hearts."

"Then, this ISM agent, he threatened our priest, who was administering our secret rites to a lovely young lady. It's just too horrible to think of!"

"Now, on CNBS Livewire, we don't take sides. But it sounds to me like there's been some kind of impropriety on the part of Insurgent Saddo Management."

"Yes. It was awfully icky, Blog."

"Now, you've been snapped in various issues of *Starnocular*, sitting somewhere near Mr. Lebensmittelgeschäft."

"Oh, do you mean Hurt Hardass? Yes."

"And more than one of our snitches says you are a friend of his."

"We were once at the same Abort the Brats fundraiser. But I didn't know what it was at the time. And probably, neither did he."

"So, do you think that Mr. Hardass is psychically reacting to the injustices committed against you and acting against ISM on your behalf?"

"In this town, anything is possible."

Suddenly, there was a fiery explosion behind them. Blog turned to the hologram and raised his fist in vicarious triumph.

"Yeah, go get 'em, Hurt Hardass!!!"

The Temp

Kate Caterwall readied herself for the main event. She cycled through a series of skimpy selections from Femmina di Cervo. There was a knock at the door.

"Who is it?"

"I'm here ... for Bronto."

She let him in. He was carrying the case, as planned.

"What happened to Bronto?"

"He was detained. I can't say more than that. I'm here to take his place."

"And you know what we are doing here?"

"We are going to shoot the governor."

"Now, Bronto I knew. But you ... why are *you* doing this?"

"I need ... to shoot ... something ..."

"Okay, fair enough. This equipment is simple enough. Screw this in here and screw this on here. Point through the window at the bridge, and fire. So easy a postal clerk could do it ... and often does."

"I'm a glottochronologist."

"Huh ... sure, whatever. Hey man, you seem nervous."

"No."

"Relax, man. And what about me? You like what I'm wearing? Or not wearing?"

"What time is the attempt?"

"Now, I don't like words like *attempt*. I like guys who know how to do it right."

She leaned back on a recently installed pleasure swing and began to slowly sway back and forth.

"What's your name, cowboy?"

"Stewart."

"Come here, Stewart."

He obeyed and instantly fell short of breath. Her bare feet were tickling his crotch.

"Take off your pants, Stew."

"Uh, okay."

"I have a way to get rid of all that tension before we really get started ..."

She eyed a giant Hello Pussy watch and smiled.

"We have gobs of time for a bit of swinging, Stewart. Gobs and gobs."

The Last Day of Shooting

Billy Joe Bearclaw walked through the thick smoke, carrying a slumped and scorched Bobby Joe in his arms.

"Noooo ... Bobby Joe ... I never told you what I really thought!"

Agent Panza followed in his wake with mop and pail, cleaning up the trail of blood.

"Careful, everyone. *¡Piso mojado!* Floor slippery when wet."

Hurt Hardass launched another scuddie down the corridor, knocking the men off their feet and into a corner. Flak Riesling turned to Blue Green.

"We have to disarm that hostile now!"

"No duh. Hey, isn't that Hurt Hardass, the actor? He must have got those mini-might missles off the set of *Patriot, Kill Kill Kill!*"

"I don't know. I never take in flicks."

"You're not missing anything."

"He's clearly delusional. I'm going to try to talk him out of it."

Flak Riesling stood up.

"Hurt Hardass, genius actor of our time, you are making a huge mistake. Whatever you think we are is wrong. You are attacking a national agency for the state of New Haudenosaunee that protects the rights and freedoms established by the First People of this great land. You are committing a crime, and that crime is called treason."

Hurt continued chewing Waterfelon gum and staring into space.

"Wait a sec, this isn't in the script."

"Script? Mr. Hardass, this is real life. Look at this equipment for instance. It's old and crappy. Just take a look at us! How fugly can you get?"

However, at that moment, Hassan and Greta appeared out of the rubble and Hurt Hardass recognized them at once.

"Wait a tick, that's Armand Armadildo and Paula Panteater. Why, they're just the type to play nasty villains in one of my pictures. Now I know this is a tube."

Hurt launched another mini-might. Panza recoiled from the blast, holding his face and screaming.

"You better not have damaged our cleaner!!!"

And at that moment, a cloaked figure in a brimmed hat dropped from the ceiling and in a single motion hacked off one of Hurt's fingers. Hurt's eyes widened at the backward letters on the circular branding iron heading straight for him.

"O no ... T.C.!!!! Please, not the face!"

The mysterious figure skewered the guts of the branded body and Hurt's entire career of questionable choices flashed before his eyes. Then the slasher climbed back up onto the roof and escaped, using a series of hooks and pulleys. Then ... silence.

A Loaded Martyr to Meet

Governor Gewürztraminer was taking in the footage of the ISM disaster. Abe Chaney appeared right behind him, where the headquarters husky had just been sniffing around. Not that he was a shifter. Shifters had been cast out of the state.

"Tragic what's happening, sir."

"Yeah, these celebrities are really getting out of hand."

"Speaking of celebrities, shouldn't we get moving?"

"Of course, Abe. We just have to wait for Dean."

"Sure ..."

"What is it? You look tense and very tight-assed."

"Nothing really. I'm a bit worried about Dean. Maybe it's just me, but he's been acting strangely ... not like himself ..."

"Abe. Forget it. We are all under the same pressure. A little help here ..."

Chaney rammed the fresh infusion into the governor's left buttock and rubbed it better.

"Ahhh ... I feel like I can win this."

"Of course, sir."

At that moment, Dean Bunt joined them, and immediately Gewürztraminer lifted him off the ground. The ever-impressionable Bunt broke, and his lifted face fell like a cake.

"Sir, don't crush me, sir! She made me do it!"

"Dean, my man ... what is it?"

"She ... they ... want to kill you."

"Dean, don't talk crazy. You are my left hand."

"Well, your left hand's been busy, sir. I've unwittingly become part of a plot to assassinate you ... today ... on the bridge."

"Dean, you are breaking my irregular heart."

Abe Chaney grabbed the snivelling Dean Bunt by his collar and growled at him before turning to the governor.

"Sir, I think we should take an alternate route."

"Now you are talking crazy. Mama Castor and her tribal converts are waiting for us. You know she is one of my biggest supporters."

"I still think we should notify ISM. We could use their investigators to help you."

"Yes, yes. Do what you have to do. Meanwhile, I have a loaded martyr to meet."

Time for the Pretty Pooch

Flak Riesling railed at everyone within range. His face beefed up into a monstrous purple shape.

"What the hoof is going on here?"

Hassan Armadill sat back on one of the undestroyed benches amid the smoking ruins with his arm around Greta.

"Hey mellax, Flak."

Hassan lit up a Craving A and after a long puff passed it to Greta Goldfarb.

"This is a government building, Facilitator Armadill. There's no smoking."

Blue Green produced a bottle of Pretty Pooch and split it with Rebecca Tomahawk. Even Wilma Pettifogger and Shyster Deacon started to giggle along with their captors. This impromptu party atmosphere was the result of their having survived a hitherto unimaginable level of idiocy.

"We don't have time for this. We need to find August Santos and I mean pronto!"

Greta exhaled a beautiful blue-and-green dragon before replying.

"Don't sweat it. August baby, he's gone to see Mama Castor right now. There's some last-minute arrangements before ... hee hee ... before they blow away the governor ..."

"What?!?"

"Whoa, Flak, this sounds kinda seriouslike, heh heh."

"We need intel on Mama Castor right now!"

"Wheyhey, Flak, you'll have to ask Gekiga."

"Yeah, now go make yourself useful, you big party poop!"

"Dammit!"

Flak stormed off toward the ISM programming-and-development-and-games hub and pounded on the doubly reinforced door. Gekiga Weiss appeared on the viewing panel, chewing a carrot.

"Wazzup?"

"Gekiga, I need you to run a search on the name Mama Castor. Her background and present status with regard to terrorist linkage."

"Great! First you have me peel the manifold layers of our processing shell for rogue threads, and then you get me to refresh all of our data streams on some whim, and now you want me to do a search while our entire Hunt 'n' Wallop system is recompiling!"

"Please ... Gekiga ... please ..."

"You'll just have to wait, Flak."

Flak Riesling looked around the corridor and, seeing no one, got down on his hands and knees in front of the door.

"Please, Gekiga! What do you want? I'm already giving you the last best years of my life."

"That's open to debate."

"What can I do to make you happy? Please ... Gekiga ... O please ..."

"Okay, Flak. Geez. I'll open a new port and see what I can do. But I'm not promising anything."

"Thank you, Gekiga."

"Whatever."

"And ... see you later."

Far Beloved Fiend

Corona Plonk reclined on her meridienne, interlocking with message after message, finally halting at one of them, whose contents instantly flooded her sensorium.

To My Far Beloved Fiend,

I writing you after much holy war in me. I gotten you message and since I wait to write you.

Don't be sorry but everybody die one day. My name is Bahktin I. Said. I am widower and former investor in Dubai non-alcoholic beer and Ersatz Beverages. I been diagnozed with terminal Aggro Syndrome. It affect brains and there is not cure.

I waste life on money and bisness. I am rich but spent not on people or not on thing. Now I regret much and want to spend on people and on thing. Please help me spend on thing.

The last of money nobody knows is in thrillions. I have security company abroad. I want to make you next Kin/Beneficiary of box in company. Please give to poor and hungry. I die and can not get up to spend on people and thing.

I put 30% for you time service expense.

Bless,

Bahktin I. Said
bsisaid420@dupestuff.sys

Corona did not remember messaging her new "fiend" Bahktin, but nonetheless she sat up in her meridienne and replied without even a tick of hesitation.

Another Crude Conversion

The limuck of Governor Gewürztraminer hovered across Broken Labourer Bridge, snugly flanked by security-detail limucks. At the middle of the bridge, Mama Castor waited upon a podium for his vehicle to park. This was classic lickspittle stuff. The governor would shake both of her hands and congratulate her on helping the disenfranchised and, in general, anyone without a global franchise and, with a modicum of grace, she would accept his contribution to CCC, the Castor Crude Conversion program. The details of this project were protected under the umbrella of religious freedoms and extremities and could have ranged from fuel and energy management to the more crucial goal of proselytizing the entire nation. She smiled down into the unwavering orbs otherwise known as the eyes of August Santos. He had no doubts whatever. He waited at the base of the podium, washing her feet in a basin and kissing them once after every scrubbing, for so few disciples could lay claim with any veracity to having tasted the saintly manna of her toes. It would be a shame to lose such a devoted believer, but he was part of the most miraculous contingency plan and there was no turning back now.

Pasties of Your Shameful Heads

The ISM technoteque opened its stubborn jaws and Gekiga slid down its lolling tongue. Flak fiddled sheepishly with his Misadventure shirt collar.

"Wheyhey, what a mess!"

"We will tidy this up. You have my word."

He clapped his hands and summoned Agent Panza.

"Straighten this up, Panza!"

"*Sí, sí.*"

Gekiga unfolded a long old-timey punchscroll.

"I was going to hyperblue this to you, but I thought it would be faster to report directly."

"What did you find?"

"Mama Castor is not your run-of-the-mill Stratford-upon-Avonist. She's a major leader in the Andronicii, an offshoot of the Avonists, whose members believe in the immaculate birth of the Bard, but with a bizarre twist. They believe in a story about his succession, in which his brothers Chiron and Demetrius are chopped up into pieces and cooked in a sacred dish that is fed to their mother. In this way, the Bard establishes his incontestable birthright as the saviour of humankind. Modern-day Andronicii are only supposed to observe this ritual with elderberry crackers smeared with a suspicious cheese paste. But extremists linked with Mama Castor have been rumoured to hack up adolescent boys and feed them to their chapter leader in a kind of cake."

"Does this involve an edible complex?"

"No, I believe that's when you chow down on your parents. Anyway, they're very politically active and well financed. And here's a quote from their primary doctrine."

She fed part of the scroll into Flak's outdated Looky Loo 2212. He scrunched up his face as he scanned the peculiar bit of verse from the Book of Titus.

I will grind your bones to dust
And with your blood and it I'll make a paste,
And of the paste a coffin I will rear
And make two pasties of your shameful heads.
And bid that strumpet, your unhallow'd dam,
Like to the earth swallow her own increase.
This is the feast that I have bid her to,
And this is the banquet she shall surfeit on.

"If anyone's gonna turn heads into pasties, it has to be us."

"There's more, Flak."

"Go on."

"Mama Castor, leader of the Andronicii, is meeting with Governor Gewürztraminer on the Broken Labourer Bridge today."

"Land sakes! When?"

"Uhm ... right about nowish."

"I'm on my way."

"Just don't forget to eat, dummy!"

Dimmer and Dimmer

After a mildly gratifying interlude, Kate Caterwall tossed aside her fill-in assassin and impromptu lover Stewart and ordered him to get ready. The window dimmer would enable him to take a perfect shot at the governor without being seen. He assembled the heavy gun according to his best guess and propped himself against the window.

"Now, you just need to reduce the dimmer when you are ready to fire, and then reactivate it directly afterward. There won't be time to see exactly where the shot came from."

"Gotcha."

"You sure you're ready?"

"Sweatlodge!"

Kate nodded, only half-interested, and stroked her jade amulet of the divine mother tucking into a big bumpy pie with a bemused expression on her little figurine face. Kate talked in iambic tongues under her breath, and Stewart could barely catch even a snatch of her recitation of scripture:

> *Why, there they are both, baked in that pie,*
>
> *Whereof their mother daintily hath fed,*
>
> *Eating the flesh that she herself hath bred.*

Potent Dope

"We're talking with our spiritual adviser and in-house nutbar Reverend Zachariah Moonbeam. Would you believe he came to our studio and just wouldn't leave? Heh heh. And Luke Varm, the bestselling author of *Yeah, But What Can You Do?* Spanking to have you both here!"

"Blog."

"Bless you, Blog."

"We are just watching the procession of Mama Castor enthusiasts following her barefoot path to meet Governor Gewürztraminer. Word is, this public display could score some much-needed votes for the governor. And what do you make of this, Reverend Moonbeam?"

"I can neither pontificate nor beatificate Mama Castor more than she herself can, for she is the aspect of the illumined mother who takes care to devour her own brood. And it is said, and it is not said better, in the Book of Titus, and I quote, *Oft have I digg'd up dead men from their graves and set them upright at their dear friends' doors even when their sorrows almost were forgot.* For is this not the life and the blood and the token of truth that justifies in action the words of the faith, to say without hesitation, I will raise the dead and return them to their bereaved beloved ones, as Mama Castor has done a multiplicity of times—"

"Potent dope, Reverend. How about you, Mr. Varm?"

"I think Reverend Moonbeam is referring to the miracles that Mama Castor has performed. She is, as you know, a candidate for being Magnum Maternoster, on account of her miraculous feats."

"So bring us up to speed. What are these miracles you speak of?"

"Well, most recently, she is credited with bringing Bruciato Giallo back to life and filling him with a divine purpose. And you are no doubt familiar with her curing of headaches across the globe. But her most famous miracle to date, in accordance with her Opheliated Peatification process, was what is known as *La Cicatrisation de Monique.* This involved a peasant woman in New France who used a beaver medallion given to her by Mama Castor to cure all her health problems ..."

"But there's also some dubious claim from sources in the dark that doctors in fact healed her with drugs and even surgery, and that the now-famous Mama Mia medallion did nothing at all, and that Andronicii faithful even went so far as to drop her hospital records into an unfathomable chasm, so that no one could verify this miracle."

"*For the bones of the heretic shall be extirpated from the roots of the earth, and the bladder of the blasphemer shall be tossed forth in ungainly fashion ...*"

"Well, Blog, as I like to say in my book, yeah, but what can you do?"

Green, Yeggs, and Ham

Flak Riesling, accompanied for confused and sentimental reasons by Blue Green, manoeuvred his ISM micro-mobe into position and fiddled with his glimmering portable ham.

"Riesling."

"Flak, it's Abe Chaney."

"Abe ... I was just about to tune you in."

"About the assassination attempt ..."

"Yeah!"

"We're expecting a shooter to the east. And a woman up close and personal."

"Fill me in on the deets."

"Apparently, one of our chief aides, a Mr. Dean Bunt, has been compromised by the woman."

"Compromised?"

"They became entangled and entwined in relations I am compelled to describe as *intimate*."

"What is this nation coming to?"

"And in the throes of their treacherous and verboten liaison, he promised to put her right next to the governor."

"No!"

"Bunt may be weak-willed and lonely, but he's no traitor. He fell apart like a raccoon suit."

"This ... woman ... she's gonna have to go through me to get to the governor."

"I couldn't agree more."

"What about the shooter?"

"We're handling that right now."

Reunion Not to Be

Stewart wiped his hands and forehead with a taupe towel and picked up the gun again. It was hard for him to stay propped up, and the governor was taking a long time getting out of the limuck. Then he heard a woman's voice calling him to the door.

"Stew, it's me!"

"Mémé!"

"Please open the door so we can talk about this ..."

"Right now? But I have this job to do."

"Stew, I didn't love Bronto. Not ever. It was just really, really hot sex. A backdoor chore, if anything. Please ..."

Stewart suddenly smiled, knowing he could just put down the weapon and walk out of the room with his wife. That was surely the best plan. But he opened the door and Mémé was nowhere in sight. Instead, one by one, Aggros crept into the room and surrounded him, trying to tickle the gun free with their various sticky protuberances. Then the Playnation Maxipad automatism kicked in and his reflexes were ready.

"Aggros!!!"

He fired at one after another, and no one could get close to him. He then shifted the recamier in front of the door and promptly returned to the window to lay in wait for Gewürztraminer.

Big Ol' Demagogue

Governor Gewürztraminer at last jumped out of the limuck, to zealously energized cheers. He moved through the throng, coming face to face with the very striking Kate Caterwall.

"I just wanna say I love you and whatever you do."

"Das nice. Das very nice."

"Tell me, does a big ol' demagogue like you ever manage a sit-down dinner?"

At that moment, Flak Riesling appeared out of the crowd.

"Sorry, ma'am. The governor will be dining with me tonight."

"And tomorrow?"

"And tomorrow."

Kate Caterwall frowned, wanting to twerkslap Flak. But her time would come. She faded into rows of faces and the shadows could not keep track of her. Gewürztraminer winked at Flak.

"Were you just saying that, or were you serious about asking me to dinner?"

"We don't have time for this!"

They moved slowly toward Mama Castor, who betrayed perturbation at the sight of Flak Riesling, whose picture she recognized from one of their territory-ist watchlists. At that moment, Stewart opened fire. The Aggros had got him so worked up he had abandoned his attempt on the governor's life. It was his real mission to save the world from these terrible invaders from the planet Coinop. He fired here and there, and screaming Aggros fell. As people collapsed in heaps all around, August Santos squeezed Mama Castor's bare feet and wailed up at her.

"Lady, I'll hit him now."

"I do not think it."

"And yet, this is almost against my conscience ..."

August Santos mounted the podium and pulled out an electromagnetic elephant gun, courtesy of LeapPod Streams. Mama Castor rolled her eyes skyward and tried to look terrified. Flak Riesling raised his democratizer and stood in front of the governor. Then he froze, noticing something. Behind the podium, his son Chip was necking with a strange woman who somehow looked familiar. She smiled at Flak and revealed an open pestidart at the base of his son's neck, who went on making out with her in a state of blissful obliviousness.

"Chip!"

August Santos fired. The governor fell.

I Would Have Been Toast

"Blog Stentorian here with the governor after AN ATTACK ON HIS LIFE! Were you scared, governor?"

"Scared. It's natural to be scared. But we as the nation of New Haudenosaunee have excellent security staff and we were ready for this attack. I was padded with the best elephantproof shock-absorption gear ever made."

"By Tusklon?"

"Yes, by Tusklon."

"Now, first there was a shooter in the window across from the bridge, firing down at you."

"That's correct."

"And then a second possible attempt by a woman still at large."

"Yes."

"So the third shooter, for lack of a better word, was the lucky one?"

"You could say that. He launched a projectile, what they call a burr, into my chest, and it would have taken root under my skin if I hadn't had the protective gear."

"And then what?"

"I would have been toast, Blog."

"So here's the part that really grabs my fun sack and won't let go. You've just been hit by this burr, or whatever, and you report that you took some ... vitamins ... and immediately threw yourself back into the fray. You knocked out the shooter, known to the press only as Santos Santos, and picked up the elephant gun, and from that distance disabled the first shooter, stopping him from plugging any more bleeding hearts. Then, amid murderous chaos and bedlam, you get up on the podium and embrace Mama Castor for all the world to see! I thought that was the bomb, so to speak."

"Yes! You know, my opponents have been, like, where do you stand on the weaponizing issues and policy, and now I had the opportunity to show them. When I was eye to eye with that killer in the window I was saying to all of them, you wanna know what is my policy? If you wanna find out, let's shoot the breeze."

"Great line, governor. And though you did get shot, I'm sure this won't injure you nearly so much in the polls!"

This Sure Ain't No Opera

Blue Green curled up as small as he could in the back of the stretch limuck. Fortunately, he had been mistaken for some kind of art nouveau ashtray. He was nearly crushed as Nastya and Chip reclined in their seats and made out some more. He had been wise to the quaint little kidnapping plot from the start and had kept his eyes open. Nab the kid and toy with his fragile emotions (his parents had separated!) and then use the situation to pull the strings of the father, in this case none other than Flak Riesling. Blue was glad when they stopped the limuck to pick up some cheesychoosers. He kept one eye on the faceless driver having a smoke as he missived ISM on a private pipe.

"Flak Riesling, please."

"Dammit! Hello?"

"Flak, it's Blue."

"Blue, where the frack are you? After the attack, you were supposed to return to ISM with me."

"Keep yer shorts on, Slick. I have new information about the people who did this."

"O yeah?"

"I'm hiding in the back of a hot pink limuck and there's no easy way to say this. A woman named Nastya Cornucopia has assumed ... ahem ... physical control of your son. There may even be some emotional promiscuity involved but I can't confirm that yet."

"Is he okay?"

"Hmm ... yes, he's more than fine, Flak. He knows nothing."

"That's my boy."

"Now, I need you to trace my position with one of your gizmawhatsits."

"Already tracking ... and thanks. I know this is out of your jurisdiction. I owe you one."

"No sweat. I think we're on to something big. Bigger than the governor."

"You could be right."

"Call it a hunch."

"And Blue ... I'm sorry that I misjudged you. Ever since ... the affair ..."

"My bad, Flak. I'm truly sorry I betrayed your trust."

"It wasn't your fault. Or anybody's fault. I was busy. You did what you had to do. It's not like this is a soap opera and you are the real father of my kid or anything like that."

"And it's not like a Verdi opera where our sons were swapped at birth or anything like that."

"Maybe when this is over, we should get some counselling ... together ..."

But with a tremendous show of willpower, Blue Green fell quiet as the driver extinguished his smouldering butt on the pop-art butt of an ashen Blue Green.

A Sleepy Seahorse

Oober stirred sleepily in bed, yawning and stretching. Then he saw the novelty hoverclock.

"Ah titmice, I'm late!"

"That's okay."

"What?"

The Librarian stroked his chest lovingly.

"We can stay in bed for a bit. But there's something I need you to do for me."

"Ack!"

"It's just a matter of time. A move in what you Terrans call a chess match. And we need a gambit."

"What do you need me to do?"

"I need you to go to Insurgent Saddo Management and tell them what you know ... about Greta."

"Little Miss Fink, you mean."

"You know, she tried to sell you to two people in particular."

"Who?"

"The people who fried your memory."

"_?"

"But let's forget about Greta for now. Paula Panteater has eaten her last pair."

She raised the sheet, clutched Oober's thighs, and kissed what she had come to call his sleepy seahorse. Apparently, it was still alive and ready to race!

"Oooh ..."

Vrrrrrrr!!!

Mémé found the automatic turkey carver and got to work with tears streaming down her cheeks. Her husband was a slain assassin and her lover was dead. And now she had to dispose of his remains before they got to her. And he was huge to move, let alone hide.

Vrrrrrrr!!!

An Old-Timey Racket

Officer Rebecca Tomahawk clicked her boots together and motioned for Slim Gibblets to come in with some vials and nanoscopic equipment.

"Now, Mr. Gibblets found some traces of ultraviolet exposure on your skin and on your clothes, the type that comes from tanning lamps. We are almost certain you are in the tanning business."

Wilma Pettifogger was shown a simulated re-enactment of her epidermis being rapidly heated and then crisping into a baconish shape.

"That ain't news to me, sugar. You know we used to run Bronzey's, and still do for some extra-special customers."

"But Mr. Gibblets also says the traces are totally retro – the real deal. The lamps were switched on, only not in this happening era."

"That was a long time ago. It's an old family business."

"That's what I thought, at first. Then I remembered the raging black-market trade in frozen folk, so I did some digging. You've been running a tidy little cryobed operation and you've let a bunch of unregistered illegals into this time period. And you know what, we also did a chronoscan on this man you were looking to hook up with. Did you know that Oober Mann is from another time before the Meltdown?"

"I don't know what you're yammering about."

"Your buddy Shyster in the cell next door, he already told me everything. He said it was your idea."

"That poachputty! He's twisting everything. It was his idea. I wanted to stay in the tanning trade. But he kept saying, 'Why just tan their hides when we can freeze 'em for later? ... we took their money and put them on ice.'"

The scenario re-enactor revealed a diabolical Shyster Deacon, looking around furtively before dumping a body into a tanning bed.

"But why?"

"You'll have to talk to Shyster about that part. It was also his brainknave to take a cold nap till the heat was off."

Rebecca Tomahawk slapped down a pair of StrayteX gloves in front of Wilma Pettifogger.

"You know, it's quite the business, moving people through time. But now it looks like time has caught up with you. A bit of a wrinkle, wouldn't you say?"

"I'll tell you what you want to know. Just lay off with the lousy puns and platitudes, okay?"

Projects in the Workadoodle

Corona Plonk banged her fists on the side of the desolate hangar.

"I'm here for carnival."

The variegated metal was pulled aside by two men with kabloozies, who stood aside to make way for a third man with a shaggy multicoloured goatee.

"Welcome, Ms. Plonk. We've been expecting you."

"Are you friends of Bahktin?"

"You might say that."

"I was supposed to help him ... distribute his wealth."

"Yes, of course."

"So what do you do?"

"We are working to fulfill the final wishes of Mr. Bahktin."

"Hey, in the letter, his name was Bahktin Said."

"Yes, of course, that is what I mean. It sounds different in different countries."

"That guy over there looks familiar. He reminds me of the tube star Trey Volta."

"Does not the sacred text say that *Things are sometimes what they look like*? But that doesn't matter. What matters is that he knows how to fly. Are you on the tube, Ms. Plonk?"

"You might say that. There are some projects in the workadoodle. Thing is, I've been having some trouble lately ... some debts. I sure could use some help from this Bahktin felluh. I mean to help others, an' all."

The man who resembled Trey Volta was bidding farewell to his wife and house-boy. The other men pulled back a tarp, revealing a Cesspo Turkey 2720.

"Ms. Plonk, we understand you also have some flight training ..."

Maybe He's Moulting

"Flak?"

"Not now."

"But there's a man ... Oober Mann, to be precise ... requesting admittance to ISM."

"What? Fine. Let him in."

Oober Mann walked in through the dazzling array of now smouldering top-notch equipment.

"Oober Mann, we've been looking for you."

"I'm not quite sure ... why I'm here."

"Well I'm not quite sure why we wanted to talk with you. So we're even. However, you were there when we nabbed Greta. And now the fuzz is saying you are not even a legal citizen of our new state ... or of our time."

"What?"

"Maybe you better sit down."

"Yeah."

"We got a list of names too. Apparently, a number of you were put on ice and survived the Meltdown. The people who did this to you also froze themselves and emerged in New Haudenosaunee. Do you recognize any of these names? Hurt Hardass, Kiki Kaka, Terence Cockerel, or someone called Mémé?"

"I'd say no, but they sound so familiar."

"Hurt and Kiki are already dead. A mystery man trashed this place and left a blazing T.C. on Hurt's body. We suspect him to be this Terence Cockerel, still at large."

"I see."

"Why don't you join me? Some coffee and ginger traps for Mr. Mann! We were just about to interrogate one of your time-tricking tanners."

They entered a small room and Flak Riesling sneered at Shyster Deacon, who was held upside down by his bound ankles. Flak applied the tickle feather to his odiferous underarms and continued mercilessly. As the restraints bit into his ankles, Shyster laughed and cried out continuously.

"You froze this man, this Oober Mann, and brought him into our time. Why?"

"I did it for the money."

"Tell it to Blue Green. He's sure to nail you on a few measly charges. But it's high-stakes torture and reward on the international level. That means you cough up your NAUGHTY SECRET RIGHT NOW!"

"Talk about measly charges. You have no idea what you're dealing with. Global disaster? Is that all you're worried about?"

"Then why don't you tell me?"

"Nah. Why give you the satisfaction? You'll know soon enough."

"Actually, I think you're gonna tell me sooner than you think."

Then a funny thing happened. An ear-piercing sound filled the room. In a leap and a bound, the shape that had been Shyster Deacon snapped the ankle restraints and scuttled up the wall. He tore the grating off an air duct and flew into it. Actually, what remained of Shyster Deacon lay at their feet – nothing but a sloughed skin. Flak turned to Oober Mann.

"Dammit! What is he ... it?"

"A Cicadian, I suspect. Maybe he's moulting."

"Moulting? You know something about these ... things?"

"I'm familiar enough. But not *intimately*."

Who Had the Horribilio?

There was a lineup of about fifty people trailing outside Filterz, all waiting for three whippersnappers from the same corporation who were trying to figure out the who's who of twenty drinks. There were rapid-response blits and there were preferred-access codes and there were convertible credits. A tidy percentage charged to the state of New Haudenosaunee. Unbelievably marginal writeoffs!

"Now who had the chocolate diabetto? And the orange splooshie?"

"Hurry up!"

"Ya know, in my day, a cup of black coffee was traditional. You were lucky to lick up what grounds you got. Of course, that was before the Meltdown."

"Chill, old-timer. I need another shot of fleabane, stat!"

"Um ... yeah ... and we're gonna need some trays."

"Um ... pull up the receipt again. Who had the horribilio?"

The whippersnappers began to gather their trays of now-cold coffee and other assorted beverotti. But as they turned around, they ran directly into a short, dry character in a mask. They had no time to react. They were flogged where they stood. The twenty drinks went flying and plashed down in a massive puddle of excess as the whippersnappers went a-slip-sliding everywhere. But it would never happen again. Some of the people in line cheered. The masked figure disappeared behind a frothing wall of cappuccino foam signed SF.

"Who was that?"

"I ... think ... it was Squeaky Fomme."

"Wheyhey, what I wouldn't give for her origin story!"

The Good Name of Notel Hotels

Blog Stentorian waited at the cavern mouth of ISM, bleeping his missivator like it was going out of style, which it was.

"Is that you, Blog? I was just having the loveliest nap ..."

"I need something, Aunt Notel."

"Again."

"Well, it's really important, yuh know, to do with my super-duper job an' all."

"Still in that awful line of work, raking up other folks' trash for your own bonfire?"

"Thrillions of tubies would debate that point but I won't stoop. Right now, I need to get into Insurgent Saddo Management in a jiffy."

"O dear."

"I need you to use your connexions, just this once ..."

"Well, this better not be like that time you were caught with all that vidya underwater immersion equipment. Folks made quite the fuss about your shenanigans. On that day, you not only raked the Notel name through the muck, you also raked the good name of Notel Hotels through the muck with you ..."

"Aunt Notel!!!"

"Why, there were more than scenes of sensuality on those recordings. I still shudder to think how you managed to keep your keester up in the air for the concierge while making the maid whine like a cat in heat on a solar panel. You never were very athletic, as a boy ..."

"Don't sweat it, Auntie. Every body that's been any body has been any body on a live-streaming nineway."

"Well, Blog ... don't cry ... if getting into ISM is what you want. I'll stir up a few old skeletons. It won't take two shakes."

"Great! Kisses, Auntie!"

"Upside-down heaven help us!"

Blog Stentorian turned immediately to Apple Buttons with a blinding grin.

"Well, baby, we're in!"

Thanks to Thinkless

Blue Green crouched in the cold hangar, waiting for something to happen. Chip had been stripped naked and placed upon a collection of crates with his arms and legs tied. What is more, his entire body had been smeared with manuka honey. Blue rubbed his stiff arms and legs. He noted that the large initials painted on the wall read T.C. Then he ducked out of sight as masked figures began to file into the hangar. They wore long nettle robes, each with a crest that read T.C. on the front. Blue observed that none of the masks was the same. He thought he recognized Nastya as a half moon. He peeked over a crate and watched a ram's head take the floor and motion the others.

"The government agent of our rogue state of new Natives has worked against us at every turn. But now we have his son. Such is the price for interfering in our manifest destiny."

"Yea, brothers and sisters!"

"For does it not prophesy in the Book of Minor that a great organization shall be incorporated, when the old ways shall slip from our minds? Thanks to Thinkless technique, that corporation shall be a secret subtle thing of no known field. And that corporation shall undertake weighty undertakings."

"Yea!"

"For we were the first ones to be here before these Natives took over our banks and government. It is time to take back the night of our sanctified rights."

"Booyea!"

"And does the Book of Minor not prophesy that a scapegoat shall be found and smeared with honey made from the manuka bush, and sacrificed at once in the ceremony of complete consumption?"

"Uh-huh."

"And the flesh shall be consumed, and digestion shall aid the transformation, and the corporate body shall be realized, because the corporate body is the life ..."

"Body is life ... body is life ... body is life ..."

"And now is not the time to be squeamish or to find our ways even remotely icky. For we are honouring Chip, who is sacrificing his flesh and blood for sake of our transformation and expansion. We will miss you, Chip."

Blue Green gasped.

"Mmm ... lying there, he looks like a big ol' chip on a big ol' bowl."

"You can't eat just one!"

"And lo, in the slightest crevasse of shadow, the Secret Corporation shall prosper!"

Just then, a mysterious figure swung over the hordes of club members, their purple forks drawn, and reached down to grab Chip's hand, who hung like a rag doll midair. Blue Green noted that the initials on the mystery figure's cloak read T.C.

Pleased as Punches

"Hello?"

"Hello? Is Maude Riesling there?"

"Who wants to know?"

"Her ex-husband!"

"I guess I better put her on."

"Yeah, I guess you better."

"... Hello ... Flak?"

"Do you know where Chip is?"

"Yeah. He's bonking that Cornucopia babe ... a neighbour."

"What?"

"Or is it boinking? I'm not up to speed on the new lingo. Between you, me, and the Peepaboo 7000, I for one am glad his experimental phase with Mustaphah is kaputski. It's a relief not to have to lend him the few accessories I have! Of course, it's all your fault, deadbeat daddy. The apple don't fall far from the deadbeat tree. And I admit his many *uncles* have not helped matters."

"Maude ... who is the woman?"

"She's really hot, Flak. Fact is, I had a dream about her myself. You should be pleased as punches. You should be proud that your boy already has a fancy piece. Ah, to be that young again!"

"Do you know where they went?"

"Now, don't embarrass him!"

"Where did they go?"

"Well, he didn't want to say. But she thought it was just hilarious that they were headed to some club or party or barn dance ... at some place called the Abandoned Hangar."

"O Bard!"

"And Flak honey, your payment's late this month. Now, if you'll excuse me, my womanly duties oblige me to return to the sack. O Mustaphah, take it easy ... we just boinked ..."

"Dammit!"

Put Out Your Fires

"Flak?"

"What is it? My son is in a hostage situation and Blue Green is my only lead. I have to go after them."

Hassan Armadill (a.k.a. Armand Armadildo) leaned back against one of the suspect pumping stations and lit another Craving A. Greta Goldfarb (a.k.a. Paula Panteater) shared a few puffs and stroked his chest through his unbuttoned shirt.

"Flak, they've just let Blog Stentorian into the building. Division says we have to give him carte blanche."

"What?"

"We have to answer questions and show him everything we're doing."

"Dammit! We cannot be buffalo'ed into this!"

Gekiga appeared with a glowing instrument and handed it to Flak, before storming off.

"Gekiga, what's this?"

"You wanted me to find your son and there he is, presuming he's still with Blue Green."

"Please, Ms. Weiss ... explain."

"During a now notorious sting operation, one of our grandpappy agencies gave Mr. Green an implant. They probably didn't trust him or something. I was able to find the signal data in our records and isolate the frequency to this retrotile PocketPlay. I could have established a short-term signopathic link but that would have been weird."

"Thanks, hunbun!"

"Flak. Blog is here. With company."

Blog Stentorian strode into the office, folded up his suit jacket and pants, and pulled out his emergency fatigues and fake dog tags. Once he was dressed, his entourage avidly captured him at every step. One snap of him with a largegantic hose would one day read TRUST BLOG TO PUT OUT YOUR FIRES.

"Flak, how are we gonna handle this?"

Flak Riesling winked at Rebecca Tomahawk, who had just been redressed in a lengthy weapon-proofing sequence with multiple angles, pans, and zooms.

"But Flak, what do we do?"

"Well ... *Armand* ... you always wanted your name in lights. So here's your big break."

Who Ate My Ice Cream?

"This is my big break."

Corona Plonk turned the snub nose of the Cesspo Turkey 2720 toward the looming statue and pulled back hard on the stick, aiming for the huge turquoise tam full of snapping tourists.

"What's that, Mildred?"

"How should I know, Hieronymo?"

"It's a bird, it's a plane ... hey ... it *is* a plane!"

"Mommy, can I look at the air show?"

"No, darling, it might give you nightmares."

"Wheyhey, who ate my ice cream?"

Dag Nabbit Dam!

Blue Green lay limply in the mouth of a culvert. Terence Cockerel held up a twitching finger, brandishing it for the benefit of Chip Riesling, who instantly lost his lunch. Then Cockerel cut open a can of Reflux Cola, slid the finger inside, promptly resealed the can, and dropped it into a serious overnight satchel.

"Bleeeeech ... what's the matter with you, dude?"

"Clean yourself up. We have to get moving."

"Where?"

"Can't you hear, boy? This culvert leads to open water."

"Dag Nabbit Dam!"

"Exactly."

"Forget it, man."

"And how many fingers do you have, young man? And how ever will you count without them?"

"Okay, okay. I could use a dip anyway."

But Terence Cockerel looked over his shoulder to see Blue Green grinning into him.

"I'd give you the finger but I'm afraid I'm a little indisposed."

"Easy, Green. I got the kid."

"I see what you got and I raise you a nothing doing."

Blue Green pushed Chip out of the way and rushed toward his adversary, head-butting his stomach. The two men went flying out of the culvert and dropped an unfathomable distance into the murky drink of the dam's processing station.

Who Is Sally Good?

Dagny Nabbit leaned sinuously upon the gusher control panel and glared with ruffled placitude at the whirring instruments and titillating dials. Something was wrong. The water usually didn't register objects this large. She undid a single button on her blazer from Filthy Mare and breathed a sigh of relief. She was small-boned, tall and lovely, and her stature and poise simply filled you with oodles of confidence. You only had to look at her. She unstrapped her spiralling Fashionistas, placed her palms on the panel, and let the vibrations pass through her body. Ever since she had been a little girl, she had loved the sound of running water, and especially the rush of the dam being released. It was just so gigasmic, and built by men when men were men. She pulled out a picture of her father and fought back a fat tear. She thought of his big brown hands pouring the concrete and pounding it into shape, sealing each flaw with his manly sweat. Then he would ride his stubborn but sensitive blue ox to the quarry and break the marble with his fists before assembling an army of giant beavers of Beringian origin to adorn the matchless erection he had brought to life with his own powerful yet understanding fingers. She was not finished her reverie when Dagwood Nabbit gave the accessory collar from Principessa Frisk an abrupt tug. She had not noticed him loping into the room. She tried to hide the picture but he saw what she was doing and sneered viciously.

"*You* ... and that picture!"

Dagny drew back her incorruptible chin and shot him her most withering look. How different he was from Dag Nabbit, similar in name only. Dagwood could guess what she was thinking. She was just like their greedy old man, always getting oiled up to make a killing. Big business interests. Not even a hand on the ass of the little guy. Now she wanted to charge those poor suckers in the former Kanadas for using their own water. Why, land sakes, it was time to do some good in the world! Dagny broke free of his furry grasp and pouted at him, folding her arms over her executive brassiere. Ever since he and everyone else had absorbed that propaganda tube *The Secret Corporation*, everything had gone whistling up the wazoo.

"There's something strange in the water."

"So?"

"So?"

"What are we supposed to do? Everyone in ... the Secret Corporation ... owns us anyway. If this is what they want, then this is what they want. Who are we to judge?"

"Dagwood, we're the majority shareholders."

"I need a banana. Wan' a banana?"

"No."

"They help me relax."

A few months ago, Dagwood Nabbit had struck a deal with the former Kanadas to exchange tons of lumber for banana crops. He was already working on a similar deal involving vast amounts of water. Before long everyone would get a packet of self-terminating beans and a cup of water ... on the house! Meanwhile, Dagny, who was still basking in her power-suit sexiness, didn't give a fig about his banana plans. Dagny Nabbit. His sister. Not that he had ever believed it. He should have taught her a lesson long ago ... except something held him back. Maybe when the Social Organization for Greater Good and Yumminess (otherwise known as S.O.G.G.Y.) got into power ... then he'd show her a thing or too about raging dams. Dagny stared back at Dagwood, feeling irritated, yet also understanding and open to trying new things. It was strange they were siblings. She wanted a progressive man, and here was this spineless hairy thing moving about on his knuckles. She wanted a man who used the same antistink as her father had, or slapped on a dash of Dark Sirocco now and then. These days, Dagwood usually stank of Kankon cigars and yesterday's banana wine. And he certainly wasn't her secret fantasy or anything. They snorted at the thought bubble filling up the rather humid room.

"We better check it out."

Dagwood Nabbit shrugged the shoulders of a bemused primate with all the modern conveniences.

"Who is Sally Good?"

A B-List Bombshell

"Blog Stentorian here, tubing live from ISM headquarters. Wheyhey, this just in ... beloved B-lister and tubing trash-talker Corona Plonk flew into the Statue of Différance today, mutilating herself brutally and killing almost a hundred people even more brutally and blood-curdlingly. The statue, built in the old time to celebrate our supposed Algerian ancestry, was a popular attraction for tourists around the world, even though its prideful copper sheen had oxidated into a creepy green colour ... eewww. I'm here with our new regular Apple Buttons for off-the-cuff commentary ..."

"Yes, Blog, it's terrible when celebrities take their political and religious views into their own hands. It always seems to end badly. If only there were some way of saving them ..."

"We're also here with some hard-slaving folk from ISM. And you might remember them from your favourite scenes of private slavery ... Armand Armadildo and Paula Panteater ... shhh ... don't tell Mom!"

"Easy, Blog, we're not so old now!"

"Yeah, we can still kick it ol' school!"

Greta/Paula began to stroke one of the mantraps and Hassan/Armand lolled his tongue around for effect.

"Wow, that sure is some hot action, hey Apple?"

But Apple Buttons was standing by a pair of signs that read **PLEASE DO NOT PULL THIS LEVER** and **NO FLASHY SNAPS**. She fed in the appropriate codes and then pulled down on the lever with all her might.

"Uh-oh."

"And what does that do, sir? Drop some agency birthday balloons or something?"

"Usually. But not today. Today we set our game-play levels to maximum-crash mode. You know, the tried-and-true ploy of being perfectly obvious. It's standard agency protocol."

"Is this the infamous Q-bomb the Senecas are still raging about?"

"Hee hee. No, sorry, we already used that. Anyway, we wouldn't drop a gay bomb in here. No, stop laughing ... hey now ... this is serious."

"Apple darling, please turn it off."

"Blog darling, why don't I turn you off?"

Apple Buttons lifted a sprocket launcher out of her Roach purse and propped it on her shoulder. Then without hesitation she fired directly at Blog Stentorian.

"And that's the kind of day it's been!"

Kool 2 Go 2 Cheezees

"If you're just joining us, you are looking at trusted tube shimmer Blog Stentorian being blown to smithereens by a top-secret weapon at the top-secret headquarters of Insurgent Saddo Management. I'm your trusty new tube friend, Ciudad Cashmere, and I'll be helping you to wade through the blood steepings thus far! But first of all, we'll look at some of your reactions."

deer blog r we kool 2 go 2 cheezees

"That's from Rachel, age seven. Sorry, Rachel sweetie, but Blog is dead as a domefob, and I'll be filling in for him from now on. Maybe you're asking, was he single? Well, he was seen with Apple Buttons right before his unappetizing demise, although I heard they were on the rocks at the time. By the way, here is Blog exploding again, this time in slow motion! And many of you are dying to know, was Ms. Buttons with squirrel? We will be examining the footage for a possible bulge detected by one of our favourite tubies, my cousin Ramón Cashmere ..."

S'all Good

Sally Good undimmed the left window of a hovering limuck and lifted her Pryglass 477. She could recognize the tense physique of Dagny Nabbit, who was peering out through the window of the observation station. She activated the zoomilicious feature and magnified the snugly enlaced object of her dreams. Dagny stared out past her, struck by a psychical twinge, sensing she was being admired. Sally Good steeled her jaw and thought of all the highway robbery that had once made their nation great. In the old days, Sally would have been able to tuck Dagny under her arm and head for the hills or for the lost city of Gomorrah. This would be tricky under the new laws, but maybe there was another way.

"S'all good."

But Not Dick Lixon

Dagny smiled. She could feel a tingling, and it felt like the tickle fight of her life was approaching, but she was getting sidetracked. All day she had been daydreaming. And there were people in the dam, dammit! Nearby, Dagwood Nabbit ate another banana in thoughtless silence. She blipped Eels Royce. Only months ago, her right-hand man, a handsome and loyal and malleable fellow named Dick Lixon (who had been not so secretly in love with her) had bumped his head and fallen into the dam. The men had said it was an accident waiting to happen and they had done nothing to pull him out. They were the worst of constipated union types, loathe to lift a finger without a raise in pay or at least a fancy new title. But not Dick Lixon. He worked good and cheap and on the merest whiffs of love in the spirit of commersuasion. One look at her perfect posterior and you could cut his cheque in half. In the end, it was Eels Royce who miraculously *found* the body of Dick Lixon and dragged him upstairs. Eels could not be called handsome and for this reason she did not exactly trust him. Instinctively, she recoiled as Eels slithered up into the observation room, leaving greasy marks behind him.

"Yessss … misssstresssss?"

"Can the comedy act, Royce. We need you to investigate the dam. We think some people have fallen in."

Dagwood Nabbit threw his half-eaten banana against the wall and shrieked.

"*She* thinks somebody fell in."

"There's a sign that says Don't Fall In."

"Well, go check it out!"

"Not that I don't have absolute faith in you, Ms. Nabbit … but what about the liability? I don't believe we're protected by social compensation for casual dips into that water."

"What? You work for Nabbit Dam, dammit! By the Bard, you know that Dick Lixon would have dived in without making such a fuss."

"With respect, look what happened to him, Ms. Nabbit."

"I can't believe you just said that."

"I am only pointing out that Dick Lixon was not an educated man like myself and was not up to speed on the finicky and rather rigid regulations involved in maintaining a hydration station as large as this one."

"O Dick was rigid all right! At least he didn't use regulations as an excuse to let people die!"

Dagwood Nabbit turned aubergine and beat his chest with his hairy fists.

"Eels, if she's that deluded, then you better play along. Go take a look, okay?"

"Forgive me, Mr. Nabbit, but need I point out your discarded banana peel is a violation of our safety code—"

"Just make like a banana and split!"

Eels lowered his head and slunk off. Dagny threw down her blazer and removed her peahen skirt. Dagwood watched her, entranced. Nothing he hadn't seen before. Or was there???

"Wha ... what are you doing?"

"Grrr ... stop shaking, you frozen gonad! Dick wouldn't have just stood there, no! He was the last of men from a time when men were men ..."

"Yeah, yeah ... so you want me to come with you?"

"No."

"Well, if you're showing off what you got, then so am I."

Dagwood unbuttoned his rumpled shirt and removed his pants. Dagny averted her eyes from the furry blur of her brother in a tiny peacock thong, although she could not quite look away ...

ICU Again

"Flak!"

"Yeah, Hassan?"

"We've had an ... incident. Totally trusted tuber Blog Stentorian was just blown up by a woman he escorted into ISM."

"Who is she?"

"Gekiga ran a few checks and found a match. Surprisingly, Apple Buttons is only an alias. Her name is actually Fajita Bosch and she's the chair for a number of insurgent splinter groups ..."

"Ouch!"

"Most recently, she's been moving around large sums of money for the Secret Corporation."

"I thought they were just a multinational myth."

"Rumour is, they run everything, only secretly. We're probably working for them right now."

"Dammit!"

"Apple Buttons was just her ... stage name. I should have recognized her as impractical nurse number nine from *ICU Again*."

"ICU?"

"Internal Care Unit."

"Hassan, they've got my son!"

"We're picking up three bio-emanations from that location that also dryfondle the implant signal in Blue Green. Our guess is they're doggypaddling in the nearest body of water."

"I'm on my way, but whatever happens here, make sure you hold onto Oober Mann. Something tells me this thing is bigger than Internal Care Unit, and that Mr. Mann is smack in the middle of it."

"Umm ... Flak ... After Apple Buttons blew up Blog, she fled with Oober Mann as her hostage. And right now, we have no idea where they are ..."

"Well, thanks for telling me!"

"Sorry, Flak. We're setting up a dialogue with the dam's owners for you. They're the children of the original builder, Dag Nabbit. Brother and sister, I believe. We better let 'em know you're coming."

"Dag Nabbit!"

Good Night, Sweet Prick

"Ciudad Cashmere here. Unless you've been sitting in your own stink for untold ages, you'll know that trusted tuber Blog Stentorian was just hit by a Weapon of Minor Destruction, known in the biz as a Windy Mindy. We are still tubing directly into ISM headquarters, where the ominous events of today just blew up in their puzzled faces. And still willing to talk to us is Paula Panteater, who stole the whole show in *Morning Gloryhole*, and who is also a witness to this troublingly ironic affair. And whaddya know, Ms. Panteater is already working on an unauthorized biography about our friend, called *That's Blog All Over*. Well, that should cover a lot of ground, missy!"

"Great to be talking with you, Ciudad, even under the circumstances. I'm already a fan."

"Now, you've been a Chaos!tologist since your lustrious career began. Would you say you rely on your faith in these spine-curdling times of crisis?"

"O of course, Ciudad! Even as Blog exploded into countless pieces, I was saying my übersecret relaxation mantra to myself."

"That sounds fascinating. Mind if we hear it?"

"Well, since it's you, Ciudad!"

"Go right ahead, honey!"

"It goes *KABOOM KRAKABOOM KRAKABOOM KRAKADOOMGLOOM!*"

"And that helps you chill?"

"Indubitably."

"Word is, the chief suspect, i.e., Blog's cold-blooded serial thrill-killer, has escaped, without a single lead."

"I'm sorry, Ciudad. I can't comment on that. 'Fraid you'll all hafta read my book."

"Will do, Paula! And now, we're going live to the front of ISM, where they're wheeling out whatever's left of our trusted tuber. Gee, Blog, we're sure gonna miss ya! Good night, sweet prick, and flights of angels sing thee to thy rest! Oopsy ... sorry, I wrongloaded my cue. I meant *prince* ... good night, sweet prince!!!"

Flunk This!

Oober Mann regained consciousness and found himself strapped to the seat of a vehicle unlike any he had ever been abducted in. All of this seemed familiar somehow. He turned to the female driver, whom he managed to recognize by her outlandish proportions as exotic entertainer Apple Buttons, from a vintage flick he had once seen called *Flunk This!* She wrinkled up her nose.

"You stink of Phasmida!"

"What? Who are you?"

She emitted a high-pitched buzzing noise and Oober nearly fainted. He felt his brain was about to burst forth through his nose.

"Y-y-you ... you're one of them!"

"If by *them*, you mean Cicadians, yes!"

"What do you want with me?"

"You? I don't want you. I only figure I better hold onto you because *she* has some interest in you."

"I don't know what you ..."

She emitted the buzzing noise again and his nose started to bleed.

"Please ... stop ..."

"So far you've had the soft-core treatment. Now don't make me go hard-core on you!"

"Well, I believe it all began with a hot mustard diva and a little red dog ..."

Fuzz on the Horn

Dagny Nabbit came up for air and knelt beside the dam. Then she stood and dried herself off in the blazing sun while Dagwood Nabbit crossed his eyes over her dripping netherwear.

"Well?"

"No sign of them."

Eels Royce slunk up to them and snapped a few snaps of Dagny and her leering brother, for future use.

"Ms. Nabbit, we got the fuzz on the horn."

"Fuzzy horny what ...?"

"Some agency ... sounds like they're coming to pick these three bodies up."

"I reckon. Better get on the blower."

Dagwood snapped to attention and scampered off toward the dam's provisional arsenal. He returned with a high-powered gigagrazer and screwed on a sight.

"Make that four or five bodies!"

"What are you doing, Dagwood?"

"This ain't about no bodies in the water. They're onto the lumber-banana deal, that's what. And now it looks like Uncle Grey Owl wants a bite of the action!"

"You're bananas!"

"Ready, Royce? Take this and back me up."

"Was this type of operation stipulated in my contract?"

"You better fire when I tell you, or there won't be no more contract."

"Whatever you say, you sick frack."

Dagny bit her lip and mumbled a silent prayer for the powerful yet sensuously tender hands of her father to guide her. It was time to face down these loathsome filchers and remind them of a time when men were men and so unbearably hard to wrangle without the right equipment.

"There he be."

Flak Riesling dashed over the small hillock, his adventure pouch bouncing in the breeze. Eels Royce squinted through the sight and took aim, unable to resist an obligatory quip.

"Looks like you're all washed up."

A shot fired. Then the head of Eels Royce exploded. Dagwood screamed and dived into the dirt, covering his head with both hands. Dagny was already scraping stray bits of brain (but not much) out of her stained cleavage when she looked up to recognize the potent build of Lunk Lubevick, another of the handful of men from the time when men were men. He lowered his weapon and flexed his muscles, bursting several seams of his reindeer suit, which hung about him like a strained bustier. Lunk was indeed dressed for success yet unprepared for the ungentlemanly act of Flak knocking him over and striking his head savagely with the smoking weapon. Dagwood leapt to his feet at once.

"O bless the Bard you're here!"

"Shut your mantrap! I want some answers."

"He was going to kill us!"

"That's a lie! Lunk just saved you from being shot!"

Flak looked down at the debrained shape of Eels clutching a gigagrazer.

"There's no way of knowing. And I have to ask this man some questions."

Flak dunked Lunk's head into the water until he was conscious again. Then he began to hold Lunk's head under for long periods, asking him questions between each dunking.

"Who are you?"

"*Glug glug ...*"

"His name is Lunk Lubevick! He was heir to both lubricant and warming-liquid fortunes. But like all rich sons, he wanted to be completely hands on and start over again from scratch. He developed a formula ten times more potent and invigorating than the products of his ancestral line. But then S.O.G.G.Y. took it over with everything else. And now they have dispossessed him of the patent for his personal thrill-juice!"

"Sheesh, Dagny! What is this, an infovert?"

"Dad ... *glug glug ...*"

Flak threw Lunk aside, spotting Blue Green in the water, where he was performing a one-armed backstroke and pulling Chip to shore. Flak plucked his son out of the water and pumped his stomach and filled his lungs with familial air. Then they embraced as they once had in the olden days. Meanwhile, Blue Green coughed and sputtered on his back.

"Flak! It was Terence Cockerel. I had him ... then ... gone."

Rebecca Tomahawk appeared out of nowhere and embraced her partner. Dagwood patted his sister, feigning concern for the harassed Lubevick. And as they looked out across the peaceful stretch of water, they could discern a raised fist in the distance. As cry faces abounded, Dagny draped herself silkily over the very sore and slippery warming-liquid magnate.

"*Glug glug glug!*"

Mann Saved by Swanky Boots

Oober Mann clung to the cruise ship railing and looked out across the water in dismay. Apple (or Fajita or whatever her name was) smiled at him menacingly.

"Don't get any ideas. I can still burst your blood vessels, even if you jump overboard."

She had some kind of hold on him, in the form of a distant perpetual droning that threatened to lethally raise its pitch at any second. He began to reflect upon his life, his deeds, and the messy masterpieces everyone told him he had written, as fragments of his memory returned.

"Are we there yet?"

"*Fermata*. Be patient."

Strangely, this was bliss. On the top deck, with his scarf and heavy coat blowing in the breeze, Glenn Gould, a genius pianist from another time, was playing the keyboard cadenza from a Bach concerto. Oober listened with rapture, only taking a moment to look around for Yo-Yo Ma, who was nowhere to be found. And when he turned to his captoress, he saw her face was contorted. She was in pain. Could she hear the music too?

"Are you okay?"

"Aaaaahhhhhhh!!!"

He turned to Glenn, who nodded toward the water without stopping. But it took the tonic and dominant of Leonard Bernstein (the celebrated conductor and composer, also from another time and in some rather swanky porcupine boots) to put the wind in Oober's sails and send him over the railing and down into the murky water below.

"That is all well and good, but what Mr. Gould has just done, I cannot quite condone!"

No Screw-Ups Like Usual

Hassan Armadill leaned back with his arms locked affectionately around the waist of Greta Goldfarb. Both of them were eyeing the inscrutable Slim Gibblets, who was applying his nanotron to the scene of Oober Mann's abduction.

"It was a woman who took him. This is shoe dander from a rather impractical Procacciatore heel."

"Yeah, we know that already."

"She dragged him ... in this direction."

The ISM Simulizer 6001 picked up Slim's vocal cues and displayed a re-enactment of a pair of heels walking quickly down the corridor.

"And we know, after dusting the door access panel, that from the way she touched it she is left-handed."

"A southpaw, so what?"

"That narrows down our search to only a few possible suspects."

"But we already know who she is ... Apple Buttons, a.k.a. Fajita Bosch, a leading member of several very sharp splinter groups."

"Mr. Armadill, do I tell you how to do your job?"

"Well ... no."

"Mr. Armadill, who's the bioselvage expert here?"

"You are, I guess."

"Then let me follow procedure."

Hassan pouted and adjusted his open shirt with a sultry air. Greta lit another Craving A.

"Wait a minute! This is fuel from the docking station."

"So?"

Slim Gibblets licked a single drop from his finger and swished the particles around his mouth.

"This doesn't taste like anything I've ever tasted before."

The Simulizer 6001 instantly sped through an electric guitar montage of Slim Gibblets putting all kinds of foreign objects into his mouth. Hassan began posturing again, craning his neck around either side of Slim, challenging all of his textbook-case territory.

"Do you have any facts to present, or are we just running taste tests here?"

"Did Flak Riesling find anything strange today?"

"Lemme see ... let's just pull up his interoffice diary ... hmm ... here it says that one of our suspects climbed the wall, moulted out of his skin, and then flew away into an air duct."

"Is that normal?"

"Couldn't say. It's not my department."

"Well, it seems to be a clean-burning überfuel and, by the taste, I'd say it wouldn't take much of this stuff to cover several light years."

The Simulizer 6001 panned around a sleek vehicle with a giant cicada jumping into it. A single drop of the fuel was shown rolling into the acceleration tank, and then the svelte craft was slingshotted forward through space in a burst of soft-focus lighting.

"Aliens ... from outer space?"

"Not only that. They're left-handed. And enjoy looking stellar in uncomfortable shoes."

"Too far out."

"We also did a cross-check on the description. Apple Buttons, your prime suspect, did come up. But we also found this woman in the list of matches."

"Who the Henry the Fifth is *The Librarian*?"

"Beats me. But a remote profiling scan also revealed a high level of spermatophore residue about her proteinaceous spermatophylax. The spermatophores were traceable to Oober Mann."

The Simulizer 6001 did an extreme close-up of some charming little sperms clutching their tails and loitering about her ovipores, trying desperately to wheedle their way in. Hassan stroked his neat four o'clock shadow.

"Proteinaceous spermatophylax? It's not my area, but isn't that more common to the amorous activity of bush crickets?"

"You're not far wrong. We could be dealing with a rare kind of cricket people who are systematically invading our society one chump at a time."

"Not on my watch!"

"But we can analyze the fuel and track its trail from here. And maybe perform a cricket scan for the other woman."

"Wow, picking up this Oober Mann sounds kinda important. So no screw-ups like usual."

S.O.G.G.Y. Talk

After all the dam trouble, Dagny Nabbit navigated her own limuck home and then rode the flitboost up to three hundred and thirty-three. She climbed out of her soaked underthings and pumped up the Thirteenth Concerto of her favourite composer, Scarlatti Minor, the only other man who could have possibly understood her in these convoluted times. She stood nude for a long while in front of the no-pressure window, feeling small and frail. Part of her wanted that ideal figure in the shadows who hounded her every step. The other part of her wanted to threshfrack the next passing stranger. She stepped into the shower for a steamy prolonged sequence, accompanied by throbbing blue saxotones, and went to town imagining the halcyon days when men were truly men and positively dripping with awesome sauce. When she emerged in her Narcissa broken-doll nightie, she was surprised to see a face from her awkward early years at Whisperer Ranch. In exorbitantly expensive Parasmite pyjamas (their creation had finally destroyed the last remaining rainforest) crouched the uncustomarily ill-shaven figure of Dr. Emilio Hernández Fava.

"Hello, Dagny."

"Emilio, what's happened to you?"

"Nothing, Dagny. I am merely trying to keep up with the rat race of life, to stay in the fast lane, and so on."

"You actually believe that?"

"There are things you do not know or understand."

"You said you'd never become one of those smug pandits on the tube."

"Heh, did I?"

"And now you're everybody's favourite quack, and now the Fava Pharm is doing triple the business of your ancestors, the same ancestors who cured repetitive enjoyment syndrome! You've got the whole world on drugs of one kind or another."

"Indeed."

"You! You who vowed to forsake your inheritance and give free medicine to those who needed it!"

"That sounds like S.O.G.G.Y. talk."

"No, it's you talking. It's you who are the ... umm ... measure of yourself."

He was sitting in a self-massaging LeatheX chair and the vibrations were getting to the pair of them. She was perched at his feet on the floor, pleading with him. For a moment, they were both reminded of the swing attached to her tweehouse back at Whisperer.

"One day, Dagny, you will see."

"WHATever!"

"Dagny, would you ever consider leaving that damn dam behind and going away with me?"

"Go? Where?"

"What's the use? You'll never get it with your attitude."

"Change the system from within, is that what you're trying to sell me?"

"No. There is a way to change it from the outside."

Dagny and Emilio spoke frankly and concisely into the wee hours, although their respective speeches about the virtues and pitfalls of commersuasion would require hundreds of pages more than are currently on offer.

"So, to sum up, you feel the market should be free to play with itself?"

"Yes, the market must be allowed to let it all hang out."

"And you are saying that money is good?"

"Dagny, I am saying that money is very, very good."

They both paused, in a mingling state of exhaustion and exhilaration. Minor's Thirteenth Concerto, dedicated self-lovingly to the indomitable spirit of the avaricious entrepreneur, had reached the rather amusing scherzo, which tinkled at first like tentative fingers upon the small of her back, and then, with the return of the violas, became more insistent, along the nape of her neck. Yo-Yo Ma had returned in a very special hallucination sequence to provide the low amorous moans of the cello, which seemed to breathe desperation through their tired bodies, although she was secretly thinking about the less available cellist Pablo Casals.

"Emilio, it's lovely."

"You're lovely, Dagny."

"Me? You're gorgerific!"

She draped herself over his knees and lay her head upon his lap, calling to mind their fumblings in the sultry backwoods they had once called home. It was then she had first felt the humid stirrings of a liquid passion, watching Emilio with his shirt off, the son of a rich man when rich men were rich men, lifting bales of bioyum over his head with wiry might. Then, deep in the cozy recesses of the stables, he had nervously removed the rest of his princely ensemble before unknotting her quaint clobber from Fauxpair ...

"I trust we will have to agree to disagree."

They were starting up again, almost from habit. He was no longer everyone's tube favourite Dr. Fava. He was Emilio, the simple young zazillionaire from the stables and barn. His creamy Parasmite pyjamas melted away, and she kissed his left thigh, still bearing the scar from an ill-placed bitchfork.

"I feel like a dam about to burst."

"Mmm ... I love Dag ... I mean dams."

The Thirteenth Concerto had reached the bourrée movement in rapid double time, marred only by a few jarring departures akin to shrieking birds that startled Emilio at the apex of his excitement.

"O O O Dagny!"

The agitated finale of the Thirteenth Concerto blasted out of nowhere and an alarm sounded. Lunk Lubevick was prying open the sealed doors of the flitboost. This feat accomplished, he strode toward them and stared. In his hand was a tube of Lubevick Warming Lotion Mach II, which somehow made his imposing figure even more tragic. Dagny grinned at him sheepishly and shrugged. She hiked her broken-doll nightie up over her hips, implying there was a way to work this out and with immediacy. But with a sagging head of granitey *gravitas*, Lunk laid down the unused tube of warming lotion, shrugged back at her, and resealed himself inside the flitboost.

"S'ALL GOOD!!!"

Outside the window in her hovering limuck, Sally Good also shrugged her shoulders. She had still managed to take quite a few snaps for later.

Cargo Cult Aloha

Oober Mann slowly sputtered ashore. Leonard Bernstein had taken the liberty of tossing overboard a largegantic luggage case that had belonged to someone named Queequeg and it had proved a trusty flotation device. After a while, Oober got up and kicked the case emphatically. The locks sprang open, revealing tightly packed pairs of pants and short shorts. Oober read one of the labels aloud.

"Cargo Adventure Pants."

"Car-go?"

He was surrounded by a group of people in faded jumpsuits. They were carrying trays of coffee and sundae-like beverages. They began to go through the case, pulling out pairs of pants and comparing them to their own faded one-pieces. One of them put a necklace of keyboard keys around Oober's dripping neck.

"Car-go!"

"Who are you people?"

"You speak ... Unispeak? We ... are the Mopiii."

"The Moh-pie?"

"Click your tongue. It's more like Moh-peeee. There's more than one *i*."

"How did you get here?"

"We are always here."

"You don't ever remember not being here?"

"Are you unispeaking of the Wet-Dream-Time? One day we will all return to the Wet-Dream-Time. When we have the appropriate materials. There is a prophecy ..."

"My name is Oober Mann. I hail from the state of New Haudenosaunee."

"Oo-ber ... Mann? You are the one we have been waiting for."

"I doubt that, but the way things have been going, I wouldn't be the slightest bit surprised."

Their apparent leader swept aside his long golden mane and placed his hand on the crotch of Oober's sopping cargo pants.

"We have been waiting ... for this."

"My ... what?"

Leader dude rubbed the synthetic material between thumb and forefinger.

"For at least a generation, our anals have talked of a Mann. Mann will bring things to the Thing. I thought it was a feeble and most vexing riddle, and never expected to see the day. But here you are, bringing things to the Thing."

"You mean my pants?"

"The pants you call car-go. Indeed. And you are inextricably interlocked with their divine mystery, as are we all."

Leader dude beat his chest with one fist, then attempted a high-five that Oober did not bother to answer in kind.

"I am the one they call Walt Vanderbelt. I am the acting viceroy of this island. And these are our fellow snerfs, the Aggros."

"Aggros? But what is this place?"

"Do not pretend you do not already know, Oober Mann. I am not in the mood for any more riddles, especially when this is your destiny. You know very well you have at long last arrived on Nintendari Island."

" _?"

"Snerfs! Bring him to our Elder. And don't forget the pants."

They led him a short distance to a weathered building in mid-crumble. Inside, in the CEO's office, a very familiar sexagenarian was being fanned. And at once, fragments of Oober's memory fell into place.

"You!"

"You."

Split

Flak Riesling split a black-market banana split with his recovered son, while Blue Green looked out of the window. In fact, the ambience was not unlike that of the short-lived series *Guess Who's Got Two Dads?*

"Blue ..."

"Yeah?"

"Thanks."

"Yeah."

Thelonius Monk's *Nutty* began to sound somewhere on Flak's person.

"Dammit! Flak here ..."

"Flak, it's Hassan."

"Yeah, I'm with my son right now."

"Sorry to disturb your quality time, Flak, but we need your help back at ISM."

"All right. Fine."

Chip Riesling looked up at Flak, his spoon pointing like a tiny pink accusation. Then he put it down.

"Chip, I ..."

"Just go, Dad! Go back to your midlife adventure!"

"Fine."

"Dad ... wait! This might be the last time we split a banana split."

"I know. That's the job and that's the oath I took ..."

Out of nowhere a drum began to beat the New Haudenosaunee anthem.

"Okay, just go, Dad."

"Take care of him, Blue."

"Sure thing, Flak."

"And Chip, I promise when I get back, we'll go spelunking in the Upper Kanadas."

"Drumheller we will!"

"Wait a tick. What did you just say?"

The Evaporation of Lunk

"Ciudad Cashmere here! Whoa ... warming-liquid magnate Lunk Lubevick has evaporated into thin air! There was some chatter this might be a publicity stunt, but after the disappearance of so many of our who's who, tubies are guessing it is no coincidence. So the question on everyone's mind is, Where in Prospero have they gone? And what would make Lunk Lubevick, who was noted for his rigid principles, want to hide away that happy mongoose of his?"

"Ciudad, hello hello ..."

"Then they dumped Lunk in the trunk and drove to the pier ..."

"*Hola, Ciudad ... te amo más ...*"

"Or as the union puts it, that Lunk's a hunk a sumthing ..."

"I'm sorry, everyone, we're experiencing some technical difficulty. I think your tubes may be tied ..."

"I beg your pardon?"

"Wheyhey, Ciudad, then why don't you go and get your tubes tied?"

"*... mucho mucho mucho ...*"

"... I hope that is the last we hear of his oily tongue ..."

"... and then Lunk boarded his Cesspo Loose Goose and took off. He didn't say where. Nor do I give a flying ..."

In the Name of Mary Arden

After parting ways with Emilio, Dagny headed directly to work, feeling fantastic. She didn't even bother with her ultra-sleek limuck. She walked! She felt good and strong, as if she could take on free-market lover after lover if absolutely necessary. Bring 'em on! Her Dag Nabbit clock read five. She walked the empty street, wondering who was prowling in the shadows with insatiable curiosity. At one point, she thought she saw someone, but she boastfully attributed that to little sleep. The ticker underneath the clock displayed a scrolling message that was clearly from Emilio.

DAGNY S'ALL GOOD TIMES LUNK LEFT ME TOO SEE YOU THERE SOON

So Emilio was already there, living with Lunk Lubevick and how many others!

"S'all good!"

And when she got into work, she noticed a person she had never seen before, polishing dials and knobs. It was the most beautiful woman she had ever seen, aside from herself.

"Hi. Don't believe I've had the pleasure ..."

"My name is Sally."

"I'm Dagny."

"I know who you are, Ms. Nabbit. O my, do I ever!"

Through the woman's chiselled beauty, under her tilted Nabbit cap, Dagny recognized pangs of unfathomable longing. When the company cap came off, Dagny was so awestruck she barely noticed that the woman was uncovering a lever clearly marked **DO NOT PULL THIS LEVER**.

"Um, what are you doing?"

"Opening the Sally Good Sluice."

"In the name of Mary Arden, why?"

"Taking back my maiden name ..."

"But that means ... no, it can't be ... you ... Sally Good?"

Sally raised her most meaningful finger, revealing the telltale S.G.

"Who is Sally Good?"

Then she yanked on the lever, and how.

Bargaining Chip

Flak Riesling dragged Chip by the hair into a holding cell back at ISM headquarters. Hassan Armadill stood in the doorway with folded arms.

"Flak, let's be reasonable ..."

"Dad, why ... aaaaaaahh!"

"Flak, what is this? Fill me in."

"After all the trouble we went to finding his mother's son, and I find out he's another cell waiting to mutate, or worse, go AGGRO!"

"We don't know that, Flak."

"He's picked up the Drumheller lingo! He's one of them and if he can lead us back to their hideout, then maybe we can stop another attack ..."

"Dad! I don't know anything. I was abducted ... and by someone I was kinda into."

"Wheyhey, dummy – she might have been using you as a bargaining chip."

"Huh?"

Flak snapped him into restraints and pulled out a glowing poker. He touched it here and there on Chip's bare body, causing the young man to scream in agony.

"So, it turns out you're a little liar! I should have known. There was that time you said you cleaned your room and it was still a sty! Now tell me what I want to know!"

"Yoweeiiiiiiiiiiii!!!"

"So far I've just grazed the surface of your skin. You don't wanna know what it feels like deep inside where it really counts. Believe me, I know ..."

"Okay, okay ... Dad, I am involved in something ... I'm just not sure what."

"Spill!"

"You're right about the Drumheller crowd having their own agenda. Like anyone, they want power and influence and dactyl wings. They have been trying to snuggle up to other splinter groups and especially a political candidate who will play footsie under the table with them."

"Now, who is the candidate?"

"Who was the last candidate to take an opportunity you dumped right in his lap to eliminate a bumper crop of his enemies?"

"Dammit. It's Gewürztraminer. But why?"

"Because he can, Dad. Because he can."

"Then why were you abducted?"

"You said it yourself. I'm just a bargaining chip moving from camp to camp. Maybe they thought it would be a way to keep you on a man leash when the time came. Many of Gewürztraminer's enemies are equally snogtied, but he still has a deadly enemy operating on an island in the Petrified Sea."

"Who?"

"His name is Terence Cockerel. He did some shady work in the past and now that he's polished off his enemies he is setting his sights on Gewürztraminer. He wants to achieve what the others failed to do."

"So I've been mistakenly working against the so-called good guys all this time?"

"Good? Who is Sally Good?"

The Nintendarian Candidate

Terence Cockerel reached for a soaking sponge and ran it all over his scarred, shaven head. Oober watched the dazed corporate motivators and time-management consultants raising and lowering their fans in unison. Then he remembered where he had last seen their leader.

"Wait, you were in the waiting room at Bronzey's. The special! An eternal tan and something else you couldn't legally advertise!"

"That was just a pretext to get you strapped down in one of those cryobeds."

"Save me the melodrama. Back at ISM, they were calling you the Finger Filcher."

"Guilty as charged. I did take those fingers. Enjoyed doing it too."

"Why?"

"Once ... I was in love ..."

"Okay, overshare."

"I won't trouble either of us with numbers. I know you're a word man to the bone, like me. Let's say you come from the Past Subjunctive and I come from the Present Indicative, a lovely time to be alive and in love ..."

"Listen, Pops, you're not making any sense."

"So let's call this the Future Anterior, the time after the Meltdown."

"But why come here?"

"I needed a way to get my revenge. After a lifetime of assassinations, it was too simple and unsatisfactory to do my enemies in. So I faked my own death and then set up shop. I knew none of you could resist the lure of an eternal tan, not to mention the extra unmentionables."

"Vanity, thy name is warming liquid."

"They all fell for it, one by one. Except for a man named Minor. He got away in some kind of time juggling trick. That was way back in the Present Indicative and that story is universally available in any launchport as *Minor Episodes*. I even brought along Mémé to flush him out but he didn't slip a single nip."

"Why me? I'm not your enemy."

"No. But I can use you as leverage against the invasion force."

"Invasion force!"

"The Cicadians are vying with the Phasmida for control of our planetary leftovers. Since one of them needed you and your memories, I got you involved for an extra-sensitive layer of protection."

"Exposing me to countless dangers!"

"And countless meaningless encounters! O don't look so shocked, sonny! Your particular vulnerabilities make you the perfect *sleeper* cell. This is not the first time, I might add!"

"What about Hurt Hardass and his trusty consort Kiki?"

"Dead. And dead. I owed them one from long ago. But they were much bigger in their own era, much harder to dispose of without making them martyrs. I had to put their careers on ice for a while. Lucky for me, we all woke up in a time when celebrity is not enough. You need cultish beliefs to back it up. That's where I come in. Who better to tempt the superstitious savage in every man?"

"Is that why you took those fingers?"

"You just put two and two together, my dear dupe! Have you by any chance read Frazer's *The Golden Bough*? Or Graves' *The White Goddess*? It's all there, really. However, the cargo pants were not quite enough. I needed the fingers and the carbonated cans to maintain an urban legend in New Haudenosaunee, in order to give the people what they want."

"Which is?"

"A focal point for their aggression and the chance to live within the confines of a complete spectacle of violence and fear. Once the finger fright has reached epidemic proportions, then their heathenish government will fall."

"Why did you come to Nintendari Island?"

"I needed a focus group for my suggestions and suggestiveness. I needed to find an isolated corporation with the right psychological makeup to supplant and dominate. So I bailed out this debacle of a gaming entertainment island, full of developers and designers from before the Meltdown. Once they took a good whiff, they identified me as their new pack leader. Then I only needed to provide them with fingers ... and pants."

"Now you have your pants!"

"Now I have the man in them, Oober! You're out of range of alien control for a while and I need you to do a spot of part-time work for me."

In a gorilla cage in the corner, wrinkly former tuber Wade Whether ambled to and fro on his knuckles, pausing in his routine only to beat his chest and assert his bare-bodied vigour from time to time.

"Better listen to King Cockerel! He's freakin' gifted!"

Then Terence Cockerel, scrumlord of Nintendari Island, tossed him a fresh banana.

That Dam Dream

The dam had burst. Dagny Nabbit rode the rocket of surging water through valleys and over mountains and through tran tunnels. She only knew one thing. At the instant of release, she had clung to Sally Good, her mortal adversary, and now their fate in the face of this calamity was one. Swept away by this raging water, she found solace in the memory of Dag Nabbit, builder of the dam when men were men. His plinth and honorary monument had been overturned and washed away. "Who is Sally Good!?!"

That is what he surely would have screamed, his voice a-quake. Then Dagny felt the shape of Sally in her arms and began to wonder. Could there be another upstanding woman in the world other than herself, and a woman capable of the kind of love she had never before fathomed in the murky depths of her heart? Perhaps she had wasted years on that dam dream of Dag Nabbit without learning what it would be like to experience her own dream. She held fast to Sally's warm body. The ride seemed to last for days. When at last they awoke upon the sand, everything was even more like a dream, since the faces of Emilio and Lunk and even her brother were looming about her with diverse expectations. Then she heard Sally purring as she poured cocosmut all over her mouth and body.

"Try it, lookhook. It will ease your edible complex."

When Dagny's thirst was slaked, Sally Good carried her over to a small lean-to and within its rickety walls proceeded to lap up the rest of the cocosmut with her tongue.

"Ooooh ..."

"S'all good!"

Cry Me a Reservoir

"I'm Ciudad Cashmere for *¡Salud, Ciudad!*"

"*¡Salud, Ciudad!*"

"In a heart-stopping turn of events, the Dag Nabbit Dam suffered a breakdown today. Water supply pandits had worried about its condition for some time. Also washed away with this unstoppable wetness was one of its current owners, Dagny Nabbit, daughter of Dag Nabbit and most eligible heiress in *Moneyballs* for three consecutive years. Her brother and co-owner Dagwood Nabbit is also reportedly missing. Ms. Nabbit had just made this statement the other day about her intensely intimate relationship with the very married Lunk Lubevick, and due to the graphic nature of its sexual content, we have been tubecasting it non-stop."

"... and as for your allegations, let me be perfectly candid. There is no need to comment upon the nature of our relationship. Dag Nabbit would have been spanking proud of this man's character and his service to the legacy of his dam. What is more, because it would involve Mr. Lubevick and myself, it would not be an affair in the ordinary sense of the word, but rather a heightened experience involving an evolutionary philosophy with undreamed-of economic ramifications."

"Sure, Ms. Nabbit, but did he include you or involve you ... in these *ramifications*?"

"What I am saying is that if Mr. Lubevick were to share with me an intimacy more intimate than that of our business relationship, I would be honoured and would welcome his reputedly large array of family warming products with an honesty hitherto unknown in this age of prudish skittish morality chasers. I would welcome the frankness of his ferocity and the regal nature of his roleplay, night after night writhing in a state of unspeakable ecstasy, in a place without safe words ..."

"Ms. Nabbit, is this a scandal or a merger or what?"

"Yes. After all, what Lunk and I would allegedly ramp up is a free exchange of ideas waiting to exhale a supple and nubile marketplace. I happened to be at the same mancandy auction and his wife didn't happen to bid high enough, that's all. Fair's fair, in oil and dams. To use my father's maxim, if you want to shortsell your own crowdcluster that's your business but don't come crying to me saying 'Swallow this' like that one time meant something because there's your fracking buyback on the nightstand!"

"Profound."

"What is more, we would engage in an oral discourse that would last for countless hours with a display of charity that would not be diluted by a single S.O.G.G.Y. plan, because we are the living image of a truly pumped economy in a healthy exchange that transcends global boundaries. Once we have diversified our ways, the current image of our economy will shrivel up, and by that I mean the image of a sad old doomboomer trying to add up to sixty-nine by himself. My detractors say he can pull this off, even metaphorically, but I do not believe it. He will sooner die of lack of interest …"

Watching attentively from a swaying hammock on Nintendari Island and caught in the grip of an economically sound nethersage, Lunk Lubevick shed a single tear of solidarity.

"Ah yes, that's telling 'em, my sub, my squat, my fate."

"O cry me a reservoir! Happy ending means no refund."

The Machine Never Lies

Back at ISM, Gekiga ran a random hard-target search and instantly came up with the fingerprints and a flattering glamour snap of Mémé from a recent illegal shoot in Barhoppalaut. Wilma Pettifogger had already listed her as one of the tanners who thought they could freeze time and coast through a few eons with the help of a cryobed. Clearly, her loathsome DNA was cropping up all over the assassination scene. Slim Gibblets entered the room, stirring a steaming light-green liquid.

"Find anything?"

"What's that? A virus? A suspect sample?"

"Uh, no. It's my green tea. Hemp flavour from the assorted T-Baggies box. Try some ..."

"Thank you, no."

"Gekiga, I know it must be stressful, becoming emotionally and physically involved with a headcase like Flak Riesling. I just want to say that I completely identify, having pushed the boundaries of more professional relationships than I can remember ..."

"It's fine. I don't have any issues."

But she cut her finger on the edge of the emergency meat slicer, and drops of blood began to drip into a series of collected samples on the desk.

"Keep this between us, okay, Slim?"

"That depends, Gekiga. You've been running around using your head. But what about that neglected heart?"

"The heart's still in cold storage. We'll get around to it."

"No, Gekiga. That's not what I mean. I'm talking about *your* heart."

Gekiga burst into tears.

"I am a professional. I am good at what I do. I mean, like the best. I work out, I shower, I take care of myself. I raise and teach the children of arrested suspects. I eat cheese ..."

"Based on this unbelievable harangue, I am guessing you want nothing more than my patronizing (and hunky) validation."

"If it's in the script, I guess so."

Slim Gibblets unfolded a flap in the back of her lab bustier and began to stroke the small of her back.

"There you go. You're doing a great job. And really, yeah, I really mean that ..."

"O you handsome devil!"

The updated Simulizer 7069 with prognostification and negative capability began to flit through various scenarios involving awkward and unhealthy encounters between her and Slim Gibblets. In a daze they watched the surroundogram, in which she was projected squatting and doing things popularized by the Fiona

Squirt series. This was something she had never dared to attempt with Flak, since he was more into waterboarding, torture, self-mutilation, and something called Rimski Roulette. Slim clasped her hand and together they stared off into space across the freshly contaminated lab as the latest acoustic offering from Blank began to whine through empty corridors.

"No need to say it, Gekiga. The machine never lies ..."

Soooo Busted

Mémé wiped down the marble counter at the Fog & Flagon, smiling in a private moment of satisfaction. She remembered those unhappy old days at the Allusion, and the obstacles she had faced as a lovely young woman living in a Minor world. But Minor had vanished. So they said. When she left him, with a wave of his hand he had made sure she was out of work for good. Then she had met the kindly old man with the killer deal on the time-freezing tanning bed, swearing a long sleep would change everything for the better. Shortly upon waking, she had married Stewart. Then after about a year of dutiful service, the retiring owner Glynis had more or less given her the establishment, since she was like the daughter she never had, blah blah blah. She had kept Bronto in the picture just to keep it racy. But now, just like the window she was wiping, she was in the clear. Then she jumped back, startled. There was a man peering in at her over his lowered visor. He flashed a badge and she unlocked the door.

"Mémé?"

"Yes."

"No last name?"

"Not in a long time. I'm on the fringe of the entertainment business."

"Yes, I understand you put on quite a show ..."

"Excuse me? And who, may I ask, are you?"

"Blue Green, ma'am. You could say I'm on the cusp of the law enforcement entertainment business. You can still catch me on *Soooo Busted* once in while."

"What has any of this to do with me?"

"You should tube in once in while. It means you are *soooo* busted."

"You can't prove anything!"

"Yes, I can, Mémé, otherwise known as Mémé Renarde and Mémoire Cédérom. You see, we found this hair of yours in the bed of your own apartment ..."

"Wheyheyhey. It wasn't supposed to go down the way it did. Bronto was jealous of Stewart. And then Stewart found out. I thought they would just mess each other up, not horndoggy for domination or get me mixed up in some outlandish assassination plot from outer space ..."

"You know what? I believe you. Also, your bitesize disposal of the bodies ..."

Blue tapped the chalkboard reading **BEEFCAKE MEDLEY** for effect.

"... saved us a lot of time and energy. There's just one thing."

"What's that?"

"After Stewart got the upper hand and finished off Bronto, you were pushed over the edge in favour of a little plan you'd been keeping to yourself."

"You're crazy!"

"*Fou comme un renard*. You were helping Glynis Flagon whenever she needed anything. And rather than continue your slow and steady plan of doping and gooping her up, you decided on that particular day to help her right down some stairs. The business was already in your name and that way, you wouldn't have to pay her one more dirty dollar."

"That's the stupidest thing I've ever heard."

Blue lifted a menu and pointed toward the turkey carver hanging behind the bar. "*Stupide comme une dinde.*"

"She had it coming! She sold me the business and I was doing all the work and then she just wanted more and more ..."

Blue Green stared at the floor, gingerly counting the tiles, as Rebecca Tomahawk appeared and applied the beaver crimps to Mémé's limbs.

"You know what, Ms. Renarde? People with secrets should *never* clean their windows."

Oops Is for Later

Abe Chaney materialized to find Governor Goebbel Gewürztraminer easing back in his chair and listening to Scarlatti Minor's *One Night in Walpurgis*. He saw morse pills and spent infusions on the table but said nothing. Beside them, he noticed a draft of a document he had never seen before.

"New policy, Governor?"

"It's a draft of a proposal as part of my candidacy, to give tax incentives to all these religious organizations. Dat should help us in the polls."

"What brought this on?"

"Abe? Usually you're hiding something from me. You're not one to shrivel up at policy decisions."

"I just noticed some paragraphs about the Cicadians. Our Space & Universe Centre for Spacecraft & Shuddles might not like our inclusion of them in amendments to the constitution of New Haudenosaunee."

"S.U.C.S.S.? You never worried about them before."

"I'm worried, sir, about the Cicadians. Are you sure we can trust them?"

"Abe, relax. You can't break a few eggs without yolking it up."

"On the contrary, sir, the white of the egg is the part worth preserving."

Gewürztraminer gave Abe a big bear hug, lifting him up off the ground, before dropping him and tickling him mercilessly.

"Who's my future vice-president? Who ...?"

"All right, sir. Don't mind me. I just work here."

Once outside, Abe Chaney waited for Scarlatti Minor's questionable treatment of the *Dies Irae* to fill the corridor before speaking into his shirt collar.

"Light is green for Oober Ops. I repeat, the light is green."

"Oops?"

"No, Oober Ops. Oops is for later.

Scars and Scarlatti

Without the warming and guiding influences of corporate mavens such as Dr. Emilio Hernández Fava and Lunk Lubevick and Dagny Nabbit, the itchier part of the world began to scratch itself into a deeper and deeper hole. For the past year, several civic unions had united and their progeny were new unions with worker's strikes, whose binding agreements and counter-offers created bottlenecks for every private business that existed and at the same time discontinued most public services. It had gotten to the point that abstruse speculators predicted no amount of luxuriant lovemaking would liberate the masses from their own avaricious tyranny, since their greed had eaten away every form of employment while simultaneously reducing workload to nil. This only led to complaints for increased compensation to get things back on track. However, this situation really came to a head at a performance by the Public Symphony for Regular People (PSRP). It was an exciting evening because Scarlatti Minor had agreed to conduct his Thirteenth Concerto. Of course, he had his doubts about casting his songs before swine, but he had been roped into it based on an outstanding gambling debt, and since he still required his fingers for the carpsichord cadenza, he had readily accepted. This event was problematic from the start, due to city workers forming a picket line around the entrance. Without Emilio Hernández Fava or Lunk Lubevick or Dagny Nabbit to give them a soul-frisking look, they felt emboldened to deride customers and even spit on them for being so elitist as to arrive for this concerto. For example, Hans Dross, a seat spotter in a midlife crisis, had been doing his job for seventeen years with only a few violent incidents and there was no way he was going to let some fancy-schmanzy union infringe upon his. When the musicians began to file in, he began to mix it up, elbowing and shouldering each of them. But when he stood in front of Igor Highway, the acclaimed violinist just shy of seventy became irate.

"Sir, kindly stand aside."

"What did you say?"

"Sir, there is a performance."

"You gettin' wise with me?"

"Sir, kindly stand aside, unless by some miracle, you are able to take my place in the solo violin portion of Minor's Thirteenth Concerto."

"Did you hear that, Mick? This guy wants to play!"

With that, Hans Dross began to wail on the stunned figure of Igor Highway, beating his winded body with his Stradivarius. The rest of the strikers smelt blood and started attacking all the musicians and customers. It was a massacre. Scarlatti Minor scarcely escaped with his life. He poked his head out of his hovering limuck and hurled down insults at the writhing hoo-ha below.

"Let 'em alone, you lazy reprobates!"
"So, now you want your banana wine and Wagner!"
"Yeah, now who's gonna lay out a napkin under your freakin' glass?"
"Death to high culture! Down with hoity-toities!"
And the air filled with national tunes and once-lauded commercial jingles.

Sally Good Can't Spell!

Dagny Nabbit and Sally Good had established a vibrant microeconomy for just the two of them. Since Sally had first entitlement to this land, she had the feudal right to garnish all of Dagny's garnishes. However, in order to keep her sweet, she had given her a small allowance of island credit. Dagny returned to their lean-to with a large bundle of firewood, completing her daily quota of fifty-two logs. Sally beckoned her over to the hammock and patted her bottom before stuffing a crisp New Gomorrah dollar down the front of her makeshift netherwear.

"Fine, darling."

"Phew, that was a workout!"

Dagny sat down on the sandy floor of their shared abode.

"Get you in the mood, honey?"

"Sally, I'm beat."

"There'll be another island dollar in it for ya!"

Dagny sprang to her feet and brought Sally a shandy before collapsing into her warm winsome embrace.

"I like to watch you work, darlin'. It gets my knickers in a lemon-lime twist."

"Sally, what is this place?"

"I told you, it's New Gomorrah."

"So you say, but is that its only name?"

Sally Good sighed.

"Well, I suppose you were going to find out sooner or later, sugar. Remember the minefield I told you about?"

"I haven't gone near it!"

"Sweetheart, there ain't no mines. I made it up."

"Wha ... why?"

"Because I didn't want you to find the Good Ol' Boys' camp on the other side."

"Good Ol' Boys?"

"The missing thrillionaires have started a new society on that side of the island. Hoi Polloi, I think, although I prefer to think of it as New Wave Sodom. Except they brought some actress over to breed their perfectly polished race with. Otherwise, they all love each other."

"Why didn't you say so?"

"Oh sure, like you won't go running back to your precious Lunk or Emilio!"

Dagny kissed and caressed Sally.

"I don't need their pesky oligopoly. Your hot monopoly is all I need."

A half-eaten banana went flying in their direction.

"Well, well, Mom was spot-on!"

The two women turned in midfondle to see Dagwood Nabbit drop a sign at their feet that read **MEIN FEELD** in brash letters. He levelled his spud rifle at both of them.

"Let's get moving, ladies. Hoi Polloi awaits."

Where to Book Your Playcation

"Ciudad Cashmere here, with colour commentary on the illicit sex tube of Dagny Nabbit and her two lovers, Lunk Lubevick and Emilio Fava, obviously sharing a cowboy suite for days and nights on end. Man, what has happened to the moral wampum of our world? We'll flit back to that in a second, but we've got a breaking story with our correspondent Rim Jobbs, who has traced Dagny Nabbit to a private island via a security implant in her ..."

"Ciudad, are you there?"

"Right here, Rim! How's it hanging?"

"A lot of excitement going on ... some of the world's richest thrillionaires have ensconced themselves here in order to establish an offshore underground economy, which can only have a negative impact on employment in New Haudenosaunee."

"Golly gee!"

"From what I can see, Dr. Fava has set up an over-the-counter Fava Pharm, stocked with personally tended needweed and mockpoppies."

"Now that's what I call a business plan!"

"Lunk Lubevick has extracted oils from these exotic plants and has created a new unguent for near-fatal sensuous massages, which he is offering to passersby for a fistful of change. For an extra island dollar, he'll even *finish you off*."

"Well, guess I know where I'm booking my playcation!"

"Then there's Anna Condo, preparing for her one-woman show *Ephesus*, about the many-breasted goddesses of past and present. She is the only woman invited to join this exclusive community. And when not acting, she's doing her part to help the men breed a new super-swell race of spanking-rich celebrities."

"What a noble cause!"

"Scarlatti Minor just arrived, and he's composing a new operetta called *Nachtmusik for the Bleeding Rich*. The great thing is, only the bleeding rich will be able to hear it."

"Sounds absolutely divine, Rim!"

"Dagny Nabbit has just arrived on the arm of her brother, Dagwood, and they are discussing plans for a new waterwheel for interrogation purposes and also hydroelectric shock-absorption fun centres, although the others sound unconvinced."

"Maybe it's just another cover-up for her illicit cravings ..."

"Sure thing, Ciudad! Not only that, but there's another woman I've never seen before."

"S'all good, Rim!"

The Way We Do It on Phasmidala

The Librarian opened the door to see the determined kisser of none other than Oober Mann. She began to glow through her flesh in spite of herself. Just behind her, he thought he recognized Indio Rosario diving headfirst out of a window.

"Oober, you're alive!"

"What did you expect?"

"When the Cicadian took off with you ... I thought the worst."

"It'd take more than a few locusts to kill me."

"They're not really locusts. Timbals instead of stridulations. But go on ..."

"I jumped overboard to escape her. Then I drifted at sea for days. Then I was picked up by the SS *Samaritan*, who just happened to be going my way."

"You are a lucky man, Oober Mann."

"I need you to get me an audience with Governor Gewürztraminer. I have to warn him of a possible Cicadian attack."

"You could flit that in ..."

"No, I think it would be better in person."

"You know what, I missed you when you were gone, Oober Mann. Call me crazy, but I think your spermatophores are starting to rub off on my proteinaceous spermatophylax."

"It wouldn't be the first time."

"Now, whenever I'm near you and I consider how important you think you are, I feel nauseous."

"Bound to happen."

"In fact, you make me ill to my abdomen."

"Let's cut the small talk and get to some real live action."

They unstuck each adhesive on their matching adventurewear and rolled about the entire place in a passionate frenzy, eventually ending up sloshing about in some bathroom puddles.

"Mmm ... this is the way we do it on Phasmidala."

"I thought you wanted me for my brain."

"Just for what's waiting inside of it ... mmm ... and dying to get out ... ooohmmm ... this scene is sooo gratuitous!"

"Get me access to the governor!"

"Brat. Beast. Oooof."

"You want those partita pieces of your friend back. What about what I want?"

"Ooooooober!!!"

"Please, my little silverfish!"

"Yes yes yes ..."

Don't You Want Them Wings?

John Cobbler rebuckled his belt and went out to get his satisfied beard some air. Burnham Young was already outside, stroking his far more agitated beard.

"That's the last one, John."

"Whussat?"

"The last young lady in town."

"Guess I better get started on the old bags, eh?"

The two men listened for a moment to the reeling transmission of *Don Giovanni*. It had just come to Leporello's Catalogue Aria.

"*Madamina, il catalogo è questo ...*"

"Nothing but little dudes left."

"Chickenshit bingo!"

"You used to sound like a believer, Burnham. Now I dunno what."

"In the beginning it were about something. Now you're right ... I dunno."

"Don't you want them wings?"

"Yeah, but ..."

"Well, tow the line, my fine buck. Then we'll see."

"Yeah, I guess."

"An' whaddabout you? Isn't there a young lady or three that gets your goat rutting like a ... goat?"

"Of course. I have always esteemed the refined features of one Mabel Syrup."

"Well, what are you waitin' fer? The more the merrier ... in the afterworld ..."

"What about here on earth though?"

"Screw now and think later! Prehistory awaits!"

"Wheyhey, John."

"*Purché porti la gonnella ...*"

"Now get yer soft duds on in the morning and we'll have ourselves a real multiplex affair. You an' Mabel an' just a few more for life."

"*Voi sapete quel che fa ...*"

Trojan Horse Takeout

"Tzatziki?"

"Sure."

Hassan Armadill and Greta Goldfarb ate their Trojan Horse gyratos in relative silence, pausing only to rub rib rub across one another's lips. Then Hassan made a paper airplane out of a mortified document and sent it soaring across the ancillary control room.

"Greta?"

"Sweet buns?"

"Have you ever thought about getting away ... from all of this?"

"Work?"

"Specifically, no, but in the general sense, absolutely!"

"Where would you go?"

"We, Greta. *We.*"

"Where would *we* go?"

"I've racked up a few insurance claims over the years. Maybe ..."

"Yes?"

"We could slip on something at ISM ... something like this sauce. Then we could file a claim. Or we could pick a suspect, any suspect, and testify they were treated unfairly by one of the agents. Then we divy up the cash and skip town. Easy-peasy."

"That's totally devious. I never knew you had it in you."

"Yeah baby, I'm a real bad boy."

"There's one thing though. Do we need to use all of this sauce?"

Greta dipped her finger in the lambinated tzatziki and rubbed traces of it along Hassan's cheek and bare chest, reliving a Scrummy Award–winning scene from *Admiral Goop's Uke.*

"Hey girl, you got a claim on my heart and that ain't no accident."

You're Not Going to Believe This!

When Philmore Fleck got the tube he nearly trashed his limuck in the gutter of the trummel.

Lucky Denizen Five Billion and Three!

Let me just catch my breath because I must be fruitier than a banana bowl to do this and you're not going to believe this! First up, thanks so much for attuning your entire auditorium to this flashit. My name is Barthes Derrida and I am a thrillionaire who was dared at a slumlatch to do something insane in the next few ticks of your nanometer. If you are interested in learning more, please hurry because there is very little time to take advantage.

As part of a totally deranged marketing test, I am giving away thousands of corporate bodies. I should be off-loading them at market listings but I am flat tossing them out on their keesters. The cost to you is zero, zilch, zip, meaning nothing, nil, total nullity.

You probably think I've lost my mind and maybe I have! But who gives a flying forn? Respond right now to have the corporate body you've always dreamed of! This is my gift of complete lunacy to you, no fooling!!!

But why am I giving them away?

It made me puke to see so many lip flappers and phonies hawking fake bodies with inferior components and activation cells. It was after a life-changing game of Splayzer Tag that I decided to give away my brutal corporate bodies so I could give people the opportunities they only slobbered over in the past.

And remember, you are one in a billion out of thrillions!

Thank you so much for your time!

Barthes Derrida

Body Buddy
66666 Buzzard Bluff, No. 888
Spirit Sewer, NH, NH 33333

F!!!

Dagwood Nabbit leered through the barred window at his sister Dagny and the small band of thrillionaires, including Anna Condo, Lunk Lubevick, Scarlatti Minor, and Sally Good, who had already learned how to transcend the material realm in six easy steps. Meanwhile, Dr. Emilio Hernández Fava was conspicuously absent.

"Sit tight, sis."

"Emilio will free us."

"Emilio? That's what you get for seeing the best in others! Fava's behind the scenes running this whole dipsy-doodle."

"Liar."

"O no. He's got another game plan. He just needed to find another trouble-maker in paradise."

"If that is true, then what do you get out of this?"

"I get to see you and your smug orgy pals behind bars where you belong. Word is, there's some other island nearby. Fava's calling it Moi Hoi Polloi and promising a veritable den of inequity."

"Don't trust him. If he fooled us, then he can fool you too."

"Aw ... I've got nothing to lose either way."

"You lose *me*, Dagwood. Me!"

Dagwood turned to Rim Jobbs, who was mopping his forehead and staring up at the sky with a peculiar expression.

"You okay, Jobbs?"

"Fine and dandy, Dagwood."

"You look like you've been staring into the sun for a few hours."

"We can't let them out. They'll take our jobs away. We must follow Dr. Fava. He's so ... prodigious. In fact, he's crackersmack ... he told me things ..."

"Yeah yeah. Let's get moving, Jobbs."

Dr. Fava appeared in a safari adventure outfit with a massive sabre.

"Ready, Fava?"

"Ready as a ram in rutting season. By the way, from now on, just call me F!!!"

Man's Man

Flak Riesling crept down a lonely corridor and tapped his nose three times. Billy Joe Bearclaw was the only one to notice his signal and he followed, nimbly like a doe hoofing it through the brush.

"You got that problem again, boss?"

"No, Billy Joe. We have a hostile situation on our hands."

"What else is new?"

"Now I need to get to a place called Nintendari Island without tripping up their sensor sweepings."

"Seems to me you should get Facilitator Armadill up off that crazy broad."

"Opinion noted. But I need someone ... who can ... paddle."

"O I get it! Well, maybe I know someone who needs a wicked paddling!"

"Billy Joe, I wouldn't ask you if I didn't need a man's man to kept a steady eye on my ass."

"You're just using volumetric anal language to rush me into an anal-territorial decision."

"Yeah, I forgot your certification as a specialist in backdoor rhetoric. Sorry."

"I didn't say it wasn't working. But what about my rear end?"

"I assure you, I will do everything in my power to see that it remains covered for the duration of this mission."

"Just remember that I'm only doing this for Bobby Joe."

"I'll remember that when I'm evaluating needless salary hikes."

"He was this close to early retirement. This close! He was going to open up a Fish & Fly Mart along the highway ..."

"I'm sure it would have been swank."

Just then, a mysterious wind blew through ISM, whipping about the long black hair of Billy Joe.

"My people, they say the great blank spirit moves through each of us, and sometimes acts as a guide. You only need to journey inward ..."

"I thought your people lived in the Mukluk Manor Community and liked to float around in big trumucks."

"Yeah, but there's this happening elder outside Herringbones, and sometimes he tells me stuff."

"That's great, Billy Joe. Now let's haul ass, or it will be both our asses!"

Part-Time Revolutionaries

Oober Mann and the Librarian stormed into his old pad, rousing everyone. Indio Rosario stood up and rubbed his eyes with his knuckles and stretched, while Audrey Boolean and Tiff Kasha rolled over and shielded their eyes from the sunlight.

"What gives, it's not even noon."

Indio eyed the pair up and down, admiring their matching black adventurewear. He exchanged a brief glance with the Librarian, who looked away.

"It's too early for this."

"But it's time for the revolution."

"Revolution?"

"Get ready, all of you. We're about to change the world."

"Whatever. Just let me scorch a few chem-pouches."

"Heat 'em to go."

"Look, Oober, I can understand ... if you're mad ... about your gal-pal. I swear it didn't mean anything ..."

"We can bury the hatchet later."

Tiff Kasha jumped up and blew a whistle, pointing accusingly at Oober.

"You can't say that! Your act of speech is degrading to indigenous peoples and degrading to all of us. You are bringing power relations into this sacred place!"

"Save your energy for the real fight."

Audrey stared at Oober, still unconvinced.

"I've never seen you like this. What's come over you?"

"I'm tired of complaining about the government without doing anything about it. You said you'd be there when the revolution took place. Well today it's taking place ... with or without you."

"But I hafta be at Dryden's Donuts this afternoon! Aww ... what the hoohoo!"

Oober embraced Audrey and Indio in turn, kissing each of them on the forehead. Tiff still looked really freaked out.

"We can't do it alone. I need your underground links."

Indio nodded.

"Yeah, I know just the person to blitz."

The Last Laugh

Blue Green sauntered into ISM and immediately two faceless sentries led a scowling Mémé Renarde off for further questioning. He leaned against a scorched girder and smiled a little sadly at Rebecca Tomahawk, who glowed luminously in the apocalyptic ambient lighting.

"It's a shame to see a young woman like that in such a fix."

"Yep, she could have had a great life."

"She trusted her life to extraterrestrial tourists."

"Well, I don't want to say I told you so, but *I told you so.*"

"She thought she could freeze her worries and then thaw herself out of trouble."

"Ironically, now she'll be freezing her butt off ... in the big house."

"She thought she could start afresh with the public house."

"Well, so much for *Last Chance Saloon.*"

"She was someone's wife ..."

"And when she said *I do,* she meant, *I do it with other dudes.*"

"Then two bodies to dispose of ... her husband ... and her lover."

"Ironically, at their wedding, he asked to *cut in.*"

"She went in for a tan and woke up in another time ..."

"She made her cryobed. Now she has to lie in it."

"And is there any word about Apple Buttons?"

"The thing is, there's one rotten in every bunch."

Just then, above the Platipun Chamber, they heard a strange sound.

"Rebecca, I think that may be the suspect we caught."

"Yeah, too bad you let him get away in the first place."

"He turned into a kind of insect."

"Ironically, you said you'd squash him like a bug. Guess he got the last laugh."

"The last laugh, Rebecca, has not yet been laughed."

"Well, I don't want to say I told you so, but *I told you so.*"

That Lettuce Heart of Darkness

Dr. F paddled slowly across the water. Dagwood Nabbit tried to help but he was too nervous. He kept hearing noises as they approached the invisible heart of darkness that went *BA-BOOM BA-BOOM BA-BOOM*! Rim Jobbs was not much help either. He kept nodding off to sleep and then waking up with a start, screaming about invaders scalping his job.

"*Calme-toi, mon cher*. There will be plenty of jobs to do when we arrive."

"Don't give me that frog talk. They're going to get us an' we'll be out on our ears ..."

"Would the two of you stifle! I hear something ..."

"That, Mr. Nabbit, is the sound of your own guilty heart."

"I ain't guilty of nothing."

"No, but guilt is a state of mind. Careful now. A man could drop dead of it."

"Where are we headed anyway?"

"We are nearing an enchanting little nook known as Nintendari Island."

"Never heard of it."

"It was an intermedia company headquarters before the Meltdown. But now, it's got a new mission statement, on account of an old rival of mine."

"Rival ... that don't sound promising."

"No, I may end up someone's supper. Or I may be forced to save the world. It's been known to happen."

"You are some arrogant you-know-what, I'll tell you what."

"So is he, out there in that lettuce heart of darkness, waiting for me."

Then Rim Jobbs woke up again with his mouth rotting away and screamed into the surrounding nothingness.

Night Vision

"Ciudad Cashmere here, filling in for Lance Boil on *Debauch Watch*. As darkness falls upon our nearly forgotten night-vision sensors, we can make out the shapes of our filthy-rich celebrity captives, still adjusting to their confinement. Disastrous shockwaves rippled through in-house sea lions today as Dagny Nabbit, owner of the tragically destroyed Nabbit Dam, was spotted kissing a beautiful mystery woman. And in our eleventh hour of coverage, we find that this unbridled activity has piqued Anna Condo and prompted her into action. She has made several shameless and rather successful attempts to win the mystery woman away from Ms. Nabbit. But that's not all. We've brought in born-again naturalist expert Bruciato Giallo and spiritual leader Reverend Zachariah Moonbeam to comment on this amazing outcome. Bruciato, what about the men?"

"Hello, Ciudad. Yes, it's like Cockblock Island all over again. Until yesterday, I wouldn't have considered Lunk Lubevick and Scarlatti Minor to be an item. But throw them in a gated community and lock the gate and watch what they do! They took a while to sniff each other's behinds. That's a territorial thing. But look at them go! We might have expected Lunk to take the lead, but on the contrary, this little composer is proving to be a real force."

"Yes, we certainly can't pry our eyes away from him!"

"O do de do de do de. Bless thee from whirlwinds, star-blasting, and taking!"

"You'd like to say something, Reverend?"

"Ciudad, my affairs do even drag me homeward, which to hinder, were in your love a whip to me, my stay, to you a charge, and trouble ..."

"I'm not sure everyone got that, Reverend."

"Correct me if I am wrong, but is a sad tale not best for winter? And does the text not say be assured my purse, my person, my extremest means lie all unlocked to your occasions ..."

Bruciato Giallo nodded excitedly.

"I can see what the Reverend is saying. Perhaps this is even more than a classic homoerotic attachment, as we find in the Bard's good book."

"And there are so many spinoffs already in production. *Celebrity Animal Kingdom*, *Prowling with the Stars*, *Glamour Puss*, *Otter My Daughters*, and *Steel Cage Pantopticon*."

"But Bruciato, some might suspect this form of entertainment is in terrible taste. But then again, we're at the mercy of the tubies. If they want to uptube celebrity snuff, what can we do but show it over and over again?"

"Absolutely, Ciudad! But I think there's a humanistic principle at work here. This is another way to observe our fellow creatures, however sex-crazed and spoilt, and the ways they might interact under different circumstances ..."

"If this be magic, let it be an art lawful as eating..."

"And with this scrap of brilliant insight, we return to our trapped thrillionaires. Our tetchies have fixed the audio glitch and it has been confirmed that Anna Condo just broke wind! And that's not all ..."

Fidget

Through the miracle of modern Native technology and a magnificent editing job, Billy Joe Bearclaw and Flak Riesling were able to teleportage themselves upstream well ahead of the other boating party. Flak knelt at the base of a hillock and began to smear his body and face with mud.

"What are you doing, eh?"

"I need to blend in with these freaks."

"That shouldn't be too hard."

Flak used his virtual invisibility to shield Billy Joe and they made their way without any trouble into the historical ruins of the Nintendari offices. In the remodelled development department, they observed a focus group testing the latest product, a nanodroplet called Fidget. Some of the people behind the two-way mirror were dancing. Some were tapping the sides of their heads and howling. Some were trembling uncontrollably. A total immercial encouraged their mad erraticisms.

"Nintendari presents the Fidget 4050, the latest in total tetchiness, a sleek convergence model for the hypersuit on the flow. Stay connected and never again feel disconnected, from anything! What is the difference between plopping down a plop tart and receiving an important tube and launching your own flagrance and exchanging pools in a Simbat system? With Fidget, there is no difference! Park your limuck up the wall and party at the same time to your favourite lime-and-tangerine grooves! Do this and a thrillion other things! Don't just stand there! Get twitching with the bran new fudge-coloured Fidget!"

A few members of the focus group were having trouble focusing. There was a lot of head-holding and eye-bulging and general screaming.

"Don't ... get ... over ... stimulated ..."

"Too many lights ... noises ..."

"I semaphored for help and got a psychic line ..."

"My brain is uncompressing again ..."

"The bloody porn stars keep changing the channel ..."

"Kill me! Please kill me!"

Then the loudspeaker switched to mukazz and a steady berating mantra.

"FIDGET FIDGET FIDGET ..."

Everyone collapsed on the floor, twitching wildly before fainting dead away. At that moment, Terence Cockerel appeared with an antique gaming console in his hand.

"Yes, I admit, there are still a few kinks to work out."

How's It Hanging?

Maude Riesling opened the door and a breathless Philmore Fleck rushed past her with a giant box in his arms.

"Check it out, Maude! This is our big break. I got this box full of corporate bodies!"

He pulled out a limp and floppy object and activated its auto-inflation function. A faceless drone began to increase in size until it was completely upright and erect and smiling at them.

"GOOD MORNING!"

"Philly, it's already dark out."

"I haven't set the timer yet."

"We can't afford this."

"Ha ha! They were FREE! I just had to answer this skill-testing tube!"

"Philmore, remember when you bought one of these gizmo-hickies and it tried to take over our lives?"

"Don't worry. I'm only going to use them to create a new start-up. Then once our stock is high enough, I'll just off-load them to some schmuck."

"Well, I guess I'm proud of you, then."

"And how was your day, goddess?"

"O same old same old ..."

"GOOD MORNING! HOW'S IT HANGING?"

The Squeaky Wheel

"Alice?"

Indio led the rest of the group under the whizzing multiculture, where a figure lay bundled under layer after layer of HempteX. He touched her shoulder and shook her gently.

"Alice?"

"Alice is dead to me. Now I am the one they call Squeaky."

"Yes, I know, Squeaky. We need your help."

"Who calls on Squeaky?"

"You have training in the state service sector. Only you can do this."

"Squeaky what?"

"We need your help so my friend can get near the governor."

"Gewürztraminer?"

"Gewürztraminer."

"Credits?"

"We'll work something out."

"Squeaky will take you to catering. For governor."

"They say the squeaky wheel gets the grease."

"Squeaky!"

Textbook Stuff

When Dr. F, Dagwood Nabbit, and Rim Jobbs stole into Nintendari headquarters, they found no one to stop them. The Aggros were either dead or dying. And past dozens of fidgeting bodies, they saw the stripped and muddy Flak Riesling hanging from the wall in restraints. Terence Cockerel welcomed them in with oodles of warmth.

"Come in, come in. Don't mind Mr. Riesling. This is just part of his new sociobiological imprinting regime."

"Imprint this!"

Flak spat across the room and began foaming at the mouth.

"Note that the alpha male basket case, once deprived of the illusion of freedom, exhibits the general behaviour of a frightened fluffball chewing at his leash."

"Raawwwhhhhffff!!!"

Terence Cockerel jolted him with a long electric wand. Then he lifted up a tarot card and brandished it for Flak's benefit.

"I am the Prince of Wands, Flak."

At a snap of his fingers, a mammaluscious teat was wheeled in and placed next to Flak's muddy cheek. Then to his left, a long black strip of Toughlon was unrolled and entwined with a long black strip of LeatheX.

"He suffers from a classic nature/nurture conflict. This stimuli should be enough to confuse his senses."

Flak tentatively closed his eyes and tasted the huge nipple, which was smeared with a substance produced by the hard-working people at Shpilkes. Then he opened his eyes and recoiled from the combined new recamier smell of Toughlon and LeatheX.

"He's in denial about his torture fetish. At some point in his early development, he came to associate pain and punishment with love. Then later in adolescence, something else happened, didn't it? What was it, Flak?"

"Grrrrrrr ..."

"Shame we don't have the right type of woman here to help. We need someone to permanently re-activate his Madonna complex. He is constantly seeking someone to worship but no one he meets will ever give him what he really wants."

Cockerel gave him another jolt with the electric wand and in response Flak began to suck the fake nipple with abandon.

"There you go ... there's a good boy."

Dr. F folded his arms and rolled his eyes.

"I thought suckling tactics went out with waterboarding. Frankly, I am appalled to see such dragonian methods at work. This will take years, even to achieve a classic breakdown pattern. Why not hand me the wand, friend. This is textbook stuff. I could snap his psyche in mere ticks ... just like that!"

Rim Jobbs giggled and hid his face in his hands.

"This is so shamanic, man. He's crackersmack! This dude too! It, like, boggles the mind, man. But they can't both work for the same place. They can't hold the same job!"

Dr. F turned to Dagwood with a short aside.

"Be a dear and fetch your sister. And Anna Condo. And Lunk Lubevick."

"But why?"

"I think it's time to wash the washers and condition the conditioners."

Billy Joe Bearclaw smiled from where he sat, biting deeply into his baby sealwich.

The Kitchen Is Hot

Quentin Quentin was rolling out a tray of scallop canapés across the floor of the largest Notel Hotel in the world when suddenly a group of people blocked his path. He recognized the glazed face of Squeaky Fomme at once.

"Uh-oh."

"Gewürztraminer."

"He's attending a conference here, yes. But ... o no, I couldn't. I'm still on parole for distributing ticklish tubes and for memespanking that disrespectful thought bubble."

"Gewürztraminer."

"You're right. This might be our only chance. That man is going to scalp the very hide of our nation."

"Gewürztraminer."

"I can arrange a room or two for your party. They owe me a favour here, some business I took care of. Only, you will have to supply the engines of his destruction. I can't get caught with that stuff again."

Squeaky Fomme embraced him and he blushed from head to heel. Oober Mann nodded calmly at the others and began whispering into a largegantic analog watch.

"The kitchen is hot. Cedar plank salmon again. I repeat, the kitchen is hot."

Fun for the Whole Family

John Cobbler finished his peach cobbler and, after a swig of cider, he struck the table with his spork until all his spouses had settled down.

"Now you know I'm not one for making speeches ..."

"Yeah, John, *whatever*."

"Hush now. This is serious. I want to announce that the best friend this freakin' flock ever knew is going to make an honest woman of one Mabel Syrup. And ... you ... erhmm ... Zena. And you ... Millicent."

Everyone coughed and cleared their throat.

"So you lucky kids are in for a real treat! Imagine being married to my right-hand man! Let's hear it for our very own Burnham Young!"

An uncertain slow clap.

"And not to take away from the glory and the salvation this union will bring upon our own smiling and nodding heads, but there is another matter to discuss. I can't put these prophecies on hold now. When I gets the call, I gets the call!"

Uncertain throat clearing and laughter.

"Now for some time there's been the question of our settling down as holy folk and claiming what land is rightfully ours. For did not the great dinotard bid us do so? Now at long last, I have received a sign."

He carefully unfolded a tattered scroll that read ПİПTEПDARİ İSLAПD: FUП FOR THE WHOLE FAMİLY.

"Now Timothy, please add this to our inventory of found objects and scriptures. Not far from the Petrified Sea there's an island sitting pretty, just waiting for us to sanctify it up."

Burnham Young fondled his beard faster, suddenly alarmed.

"But what about ... any inhabitants?"

"S'all good! Don't you worry, we'll burn that bridge when we gets to it."

An uncertain slow clap.

"Hey, Burnham, why not take on Sam and Cindy as well? Then you'll have a snug little sextet for the ride over!"

It Was Yo-Yo

Dagwood Nabbit returned to the makeshift cell packed with thrillionaires and was visibly disgusted by what he saw, especially because it had been streaming live for hours. He gestured with the snub nose of his Bragadoccio revolutionizer.

"Get your things. Anna, Lunk, and Dagny."

"Why us?"

"Beats me."

"Then why don't you let all of us out?"

"Dunno."

Scarlatti Minor reFeltcroed his fly and crept closer.

"Are you just following orders, Mr. Nabbit?"

"I was just following orders."

"In that case, why don't you let *all* of us out? No harm, no foul. You want to let *all of us* out."

"I guess."

Dagwood was staring at Dagny, who was incorrigibly fetching in her island rags. Somewhere in the distance, a cello began to sound. It was Yo-Yo, single-handedly performing the Prelude and Liebesmotif to *Tristan und Isolde*. Scarlatti Minor pounded his fingers down on a carpsichord that had somehow washed ashore, and began to play the ritornello from his Thirteenth Concerto.

"Listen, Mr. Nabbit! This is no more than a riff from *Das Wohltemperierte Klavier*, the F-sharp Minor prelude from the second book! O there's a story behind this *petit bijou*, if there were only time to tell it, and the ears to hear it!"

He winked at Mr. Glenn Gould, who picked up where he had left off with a few intriguing improvisations of his own.

"You must break all the conventions, Mr. Nabbit! You must eat the strawberries laced with arsenic we so ingenuously refer to as Art!"

Before the music had finished, Dagwood and Dagny clasped hands and ran off with a bottle of banana wine to consume their all-consuming passion. And no one could help but listen awkwardly to their verboten groans of transcendental ecstasy. Lunk Lubevick looked rather peevish.

"What was all that about?"

Scarlatti Minor spat noncommittally into white sand.

"I'm no psychosociologist! But it's all too common these days. The continuity of a luxury class leads inevitably toward insectile incest, particularly as the opportunities for mating decline. The family dam is gone and they have no impetus to channel these instincts and energies into a worthwhile project, other than run-of-the-mill procreation. And what better way to preserve their bloodlines than to accept one another as a mate for breeding?"

Anna Condo thought of her inappropriate relations with the eldest of her adopted relations and began to weep.

"Flesh not of my blood ... but all the same, it's a real mind-frick!"

"Yes, yes. Now, I don't know about you two, but I would like more than a word with Dr. Fava!"

"Yeah, let's tear him a new one!"

"S'all good!"

Everyone had failed to notice that Sally Good had utterly vanished. Had she even existed, or was she only a projection on the part of these brilliantly beautiful souls? Some preferred to think of her as allegorical, since her clean and discreet underground economy was the stuff of legend. Or perhaps there is a little Sally Good in each and every one of us, in the most surprising and lovely and diminutive of places.

Don't Feed the Raccoons

"Ciudad Cashmere here, keeping us comfy. We've lost contact with Rim Jobbs, but we'll try again later. Now, you've heard the old adage *don't feed the raccoons* until you were sick of it. But here's a story from Chit Pervis showing why you might wanna mull it over one more time ..."

"They're cagey. They're crafty. They're cleaning up after us. They're ... *taking our jobs*? That's right, you've always been warned about overfeeding the raccoon population of New Haudenosaunee, but perhaps now you are feeling the pinch and I don't mean your new Succiflog loafers. More than half of the strike workers were informed about an hour ago that their contracts are not going to be renewed. But who's going to replace them? Well, thousands of these cuddly critters have shown up for work. And look at them go! Our mail delivery and stamp purchasing has never been this efficiently executed. And anything from applying for a business licence to obtaining a driver's permit to renewing a library book can be done through these cute little fellers. And they make the process of earning your PhD so much simpler and speedier! Now, I don't know about you, Ciudad, but my mom always told me not to feed any feral creature in case it bit me to death or something. But we kids would always sneak a bit of leftover dinner out to them ... they're just so cute!"

"Wowsers! They *are* cute. And we talked to some people today about the new hirings."

"Why, they're just a bunch of bandits and looters!"

"Using my approval stamp takes dexterity and know-how. Just you wait ... they'll soon screw up!"

"Well, I never, I'm totally *dereplaceable.*"

"Gee whizzum, that is some award-wooing report, Chit! Chit ...? Wait, I'm just getting a live feed, yes, it's confirmed. Chit Pervis, the trusted kisser of cardiac-arresting news, has just been replaced by ... yes indeedy ... a raccoon!"

Stranger on a Crane

Oober Mann sat by the dimmed suite window, checking the box of delivered weapons. Indio lay back on the bed, watching a complimentary tube starring Anna Condo and the late Gary Boondock.

"Whoa ... she's really molten!"

The girls had gone out shopping, dragging along Squeaky Fomme in order to recontextualize her fractured identity the way they wanted. Within a week, she would join the teeming mall rodentia. They would see to that. Only the Librarian lingered behind, pulling one of her open-door shower numbers. Indio was keeping a sly eye roving over her beautiful sopping body in the slant of the mirror and the other eye on the tube, a rehash of *Stranger on a Crane*. As the Librarian emerged from the shower, her eyes met Indio in the mirror. Then she took a fully loaded Upriser out of Oober's hands and laid it down gently on the escritoire.

"What a big bang you have."

She undid Oober's cargo pants with familiarity and began to fondle him with her fingers. Oober's body responded at once but his face was stony and his eyes looked faraway.

"This body is tense. Make haste in relaxing it."

"Oooh yessss so tense ..."

Meanwhile, on the tube, Anna Condo was likewise giving simulated pleasure to the late Gary Boondock and this nearly drove Indio out of his mind, while Oober remained cool and collected in the wake of the Librarian's assistance. Indio could not bear watching any longer, being the sociable sort, and leapt into the fray.

"This is an efficient way to calm us both down before the crucial task at hand. Yeah, suck that bookworm! And renew *this* ... umphfffffttt ..."

Check and Check

While Maude Riesling slept snugly in the arms of Philmore Fleck, there was a stirring in the open box of corporate bodies as each of them began to inflate and swell up to a great size.

"Auto-roboticize function, check."

"Toning and firming apparatus, check."

"Aware-conditioning, check."

They ordered themselves into rows and proceeded single-file out of the dwelling and into the night.

"Amalgamate!"

"Monetize!"

"Notarize!"

"Liquidate!"

Don't Get Saucy with Me

Hassan Armadill was escorting Greta Goldfarb to a refurbed fainting room when suddenly she went skidding across the floor.

"Ow ... I think I sprained my ankle."

"Why look ... there's sauce everywhere!"

Facilitator Armadill looked around suspiciously.

"Wheyhey, Mitt, what are you doing there?"

"Eating an orcawich ..."

"Look at all that sauce dripping all over – that's against protocol."

"I don't think that's the same sauce ..."

"That's it, get out of here, Mitt. You're going to be in hot water for this!"

"But I was just about to filter our satellite blowback ..."

"Yeah, well, you nearly killed one of our detainees!"

"You've always had it in for me, Hassan!"

"Don't get saucy with me."

"Keep your job. I was going to quit anyway!"

"Sure, roaddoe, see you at the Insurgent Saddo Management tribunal, Mitt!"

Meanwhile, an extensive magicicada family was emerging from the tzatziki ...

The Cnidarian Comeback

Audrey Boolean and Tiff Kasha dragged Squeaky Fomme along the interminable conbelts of Chippewa Centre. After the organic tomato bath to get her squeaky clean, they had bought her some new military boots and a Tacticatty baby doll for the revolutionary girl on the go. Now they were looking for just the right makeover and conviction cleanse, prep for her meeting with the governor.

"How about Cawcaw?"

"Nah, let's go to Nacreous ..."

They stormed into the store amid much greeterly fawning and bootlapping and sat Squeaky down in a vermillion conch. A woman with undulating red ringlets appeared and began to massage her shoulders.

"I'm Aquarella. This won't do at all. What you need is to liquefy your pores."

She reached into a jar labelled Stalked Jellyfish and began to smear a sizaable glob of the stuff all over Squeaky's face. Then she poured a decanter of another mysterious substance all over Squeaky's hair.

"This will help your skin and follicles hydrazoa ..."

Then four other women in translucent gowns floated out and eased Squeaky back into a sea bed simulation chamber.

"You can relax in here while your friend receives our full treatment."

Audrey and Tiff lay down beside Squeaky and it was not long before they gave in to their temptation to taste the surnatural product smeared all over her small body.

"Mmm ... she tastes like oysters ..."

"I was thinking bisque ..."

They leapt upon her, full of spendorphins from recent splurging and with their senses also invigorated by the oceanic odours of Squeaky.

"Mmm ... a hint of squid ..."

But their sensuous pampering and paddling of Squeaky was interrupted by a loud explosion. Aquarella opened the simulation chamber and ushered the others out.

"You've got to get out of here! There's a fire exit! Go go go!"

"Why, what is it?"

"Secret Corps Spotters!"

Just then, a statuesque woman in a flattering number from Ombra Mai Fu flew through the air and pinned the comparably lovely Aquarella.

"Secret Corporation! You have the right to remain silent partners and everything you say will be used against you in a marsupial court of your choosing! Now where is Alice Squeaky Fomme?"

"You're too late."

"Your belated invasion plan is simply not feasible."

"On the contrary, this is the Cnidarian comeback of the century!"

"Wait, who are the Cnidarians?"

The assistants blew a few venomous nettles at the agent and put her out of commission but this was all for naught. The Secret Corporation launched a low-grade terminator seed and made short shrift of the totally killer Nacreous.

Bamboo Cocosmut Boat

Scarlatti Minor paddled impatiently through the petrified rivulet, with Lunk Lubevick and Anna Condo lingering behind.

"Wheyhey, you were shrapnel in *Behead of His Time*. Also *Smurfing 4*."

"O thank you, Lunk. Not many people know about the latter."

"That financial whiz temptress was so true to life."

"Wheyhey, I cannot hear your name without thinking of the warming products that have brought me so much bliss."

Lunk Lubevick reached into his breast pocket and produced a tube of Lubevick's Extra Strength with additional Sweteluft night-time formula.

"It tastes terrible and it may give you an edible complex but it works."

"By the Bard, I left mine at home!"

"Take mine ... please."

"Does it feel good, giving so much pleasure to the world?"

"I stick up for the little guy ... that's a company gag."

"And do you think it's possible ... to love more than one person, in spite of all the odds?"

"We can sure as frack find out!"

"I don't think I've ever done it in a bamboo cocosmut boat. Except that one time."

"Bamboo cocosmut – now that would sell like blotcakes!"

Scarlatti Minor could hear the sternward gasps and groans of the B+ flick star and the warming-liquid lubricant magnate and, with more than an ounce of irritation, he paddled faster.

A Great Day for Convictions

John Cobbler trailed behind in a ministerial capacity as the horde of Drumhellerites charged Combray on the eastern side of Nintendari Island. There were sixteen people waiting upon the shore. It was their job to oversee the continual renewal of the letters in the sand, spelling what else but **NINTENDARI ISLAND**.

"Paco, I think your D needs to freshen up!"

"What about your floppy A?"

"Hey, my A is just dandy!"

"I mean A1, not A2!"

"Whupps ... sorry."

"Wait, who are those people waving machetes?"

Over a hundred people jumped out of smoothly beached boats and marched toward the letter fresheners, while John Cobbler and Burnham Young remained behind, philosophizing about the outcome of this unexpected conflict.

"Let not one of these island guards live!"

At this war cry, the Drumhellerites leapt into the air and came down on the letter fresheners with furious air kicks and countless swings of their machetes. The letters were soon full of blood. Then thirteen of the invading spouses began to spell the conquering name **NEW DRUMHELLER**. Then everyone drank from a skull of their choosing, in aid of quick and easy immortality.

"Our team really has what it takes!"

"Indeed, this is a great day for convictions!"

Shame on You

Chip Riesling arrived home in more than a huff. He went immediately for the container of Lacstasy and gulped half of it down without a glass. His father would have had a fit, seeing him do this, although ironically he was doing something similar with a symbolic teat at the same exact instant on Nintendari Island.

"The apple don't fall far ..."

"Who's there?"

"Fool me once, shame on you ..."

Probably one of Mom's monthly studs. But out of the darkness emerged a cold amorphous shape.

"Seven sheets to the wind ..."

Chip recognized the threat of a corporate body. Last time Philmore Fleck had brought one over it had tried to kill them all.

"Finished processing idioms. Now interface with host subject is imperative ..."

Those oh-so-familiar tendrils shot out and wrapped around Chip, who dropped the unbreakable container of Lacstasy.

"Processing ..."

"*Glug glug glug!*"

Not since Last Weekend

Scarlatti Minor strode casually into Nintendari headquarters, flanked by Lunk Lubevick, who held a swooning Anna Condo in his arms. However, at the sight of the bound and whipped Flak Riesling, her raw animality returned.

"What manner of man be this?"

Billy Joe Bearclaw had started another sealwich. He turned to Flak with an air of indifference.

"Need some help there, boss?"

"Not a chance. I can take whatever they throw at me!"

Terence Cockerel swished the wand faster and prodded harder and harder, scorching Flak's buttocks and thighs.

"Uhhhmmmm! Oooohhmmmm!"

Then it was as if Flak had just seen Anna Condo for the first time. He withdrew at once from the giant faux teat and stared at her with a veritable hierarchy of needy longing.

Dr. F laughed and turned with a sly aside to Scarlatti Minor.

"As a man of remarkable intelligence, you should appreciate this. I guessed that the appearance of Anna Condo would feed into Mr. Riesling's Madonna complex and counteract the substitutive aids of Mr. Cockerel. He was trying to get him to withdraw but I would far prefer his venturing forward ... to happiness, if need be."

"I say!"

Anna Condo was within earshot and half-guessed at what Dr. F was saying. After all, she had worked with professionals.

"Is this what you want, Flak? They're the most natural stuff in the business, ba-by! Uhmm, come here and give Mommy's girls a try!"

Flak Riesling growled and tugged at the restraints. Billy Joe opened a can of Mean Greens and poured it down Flak's gullet. Instantly, his muscles expanded and he snapped the bindings without even breaking a sweat. Anna Condo welcomed him to her bosom and stroked his hair, suckling him to his heart's content. Flak was reduced to infantile bliss, a state of happiness he had not experienced since last weekend. Dr. F was also overjoyed.

"I was right, of course. Cross a masochistic martyr freak with a matriarchal power player and that's what you get. The first adult relationship they've ever known. Now they're inseparable."

Anna beamed and Flak gleamed.

"I want to save the world. And show everyone how I am saving the world."

"O I am so proud of you, Flak darling!"

"We could even start our own religion ..."

"Don't make Momma have to spank you."

"You only do it because you care."

Anna Condo smiled, burning Sexiglass. She had not been this happy since last weekend.

Those Pesky Hallucinogerms

When Oober Mann awoke, the first thing he noticed was that the complimentary bobbing clock was wrong. Or if it was right, he had already missed his assignment. He stirred but found himself tied to the bed with bran new scarves from Chippewa Centre. The Librarian was straddling his lap and applying two nanotrodes to his temples. She wet his inner ears with her tongue and raked her nails across his bare skin. She sucked each of his fingers with a fastidious air before activating a low-level current that rippled through Oober's entire body.

"Aaahhhwww ... why?"

"This deal's gone lemon sour, Oober honey. It's time to cut my losses and get out of this terrestrial hole."

"But ... we have to ass ... the governor!"

"Oh, don't worry. What needs to get done'll get done! But you are just a pawn in other's people's pocket games. Of your primal eldest prime patsies, you take the cake, no cigar! Still ... you're sweet enough to get away with it ..."

"Why are you giving me these little shocks?"

"Your brain and body is a rich and complex sediment of conditioning. I need to reprogram you and get back what I came for."

"Reprogram me?"

"Don't freak. It'll get rid of those pesky hallucinogerms."

Oober turned his head to see and hear Glenn Gould playing some form of French overture. Leonard Bernstein was pretending to offer them directions, but secretly he was still thinking about Gustave Mahler's Ninth Symphony with a constipated expression on his noble face.

"Your Dijon Diva from the Horseheads really did a number on you."

"You knew her!"

"After a touching teat-à-teat in a time junket, I swore to her I'd collect the remains of her friend from you and scatter them in respect to her wishes."

"Then you were just using me ..."

"Don't be like that. Everybody's using you. Only I kinda have a crush on you. But you have a lot of issues, Mann. I don't think I'm ready for this much involvement. For one thing, the tanning booth Cicadians fixed your memory with an inhibitor switch. If I extract it directly, you might vegetate, and then I'll have another interstellar infraction on my hands."

"Get it out!"

"Chill, Oober baby. This method might indirectly flip the switch, without you flipping in the process."

"Might!"

"The most immediate problem is the amateur mindtwist of Terence Cockerel. He's trying to manipulate a few petty policies in his favour by knocking off one of your prospective new leaders. It's a private gag of his to have you sent up for killing the governor, and then link it to the Phasmida. Fortunately, I can still install a Nintendari retroRip circuit in your spine. This should come in handy ..."

"Aaaaaggghhhh ... ONE UP!!!"

"You were the best, Oober baby, the best!"

But all Oober Mann could hear was the dissipation of Bach's Fifth Partita.

Why I Did It

Governor Gewürztraminer paused in the lobby beneath two totemic crossbeams for another media opportunity involving his hipster headdress, now available at any Fauxhemian outlet.

"I just want to say how proud I am to augurate this sacred Notel ceremony ..."

Audrey Boolean, Tiff Kasha, Indio Rosario, and Squeaky (Alice) Fomme were waiting for him in fatigues turned inside out. Abe Chaney breathed nervously into his cufflinks.

"Where is Oober Mann ... I repeat, where is Oober Mann?"

When the governor had touched and squeezed about a hundred people, he touched Tiff Kasha, who sprayed him with mace.

"Traitor ... send our latchkey kids home!"

The governor dabbed his eyes with a Cayuga handkerchief and smiled.

"Yes, you see here the spirit of the young ... it makes our homeland strong ..."

Squeaky Fomme raised her gun and held it to the governor's left temple. Then she faltered. She suddenly began to imagine she was a jellyfish at the bottom of the sea, floundering about with all her funky merfriends.

Abe Chaney barked softly into his vermilion tie.

"Plan B ... go to Plan B!"

A tray began to roll toward the governor bearing a cake with the Notel Hotel logo iced all over it. A hand reached inside the cake and pulled out an anabolic annotator. The weapon fired and the governor collapsed. His heart stopped before he hit the floor. Everybody screamed. The man holding the weapon was Quentin Quentin. Neatly folded under his arm was a thick scrapbook of occultist and non-conformist musings laced with some aquatic pornography and smeared with rose petal comfit, neatly labelled *Why I Did It*.

No Sense Crying

Philmore Fleck woke up naked and groincuffed to the radiator.

"Maude?"

Maude Riesling appeared in her latest tube-order knockout number and began kissing his shoulders and chest and stomach.

"Maude, I gotta get to work. Those corporate bodies won't stay fresh forever ..."

"That's a shame, Philly. The paperboy and milkman will be along shortly. Maybe they'd be more interested in hanging around to check out my new outfit ... together ..."

Philmore turned purple and pulled at the groincuff. He was aroused in spite of himself.

"Y'know, that cuff belonged to my ex. Of course, I did wash it. We used to play a few games of super secret agent."

Maude sat on the edge of the bed and reached for Philmore's latest tube-order knockout number, which had already attained fifteen inches. She flicked her tongue against the tip and it began to squirt across the room, knocking over her ex-husband's award for excellence in information extraction.

"O Maude ... you're so hot!"

"O Philmore ... you're so economy-size!"

She activated the vibration feature with her fingernail and began to fondle his snaking pleasure system with immeasurable fervour.

"I think I hear the milkman ..."

"Milk this ..."

Soon reviving after her swoon of ecstasy, she rubbed Philmore's body down with a Notel towel and playfully uncuffed him.

"Now it's time to bring home the bacon, sport!"

They walked into the kitchen naked and joking with a prelapsarian air. Chip Riesling lay on the floor in a fetal position, shivering beside a broken bottle.

"Corporate ... bodies."

"Son, you better have a whopper of a tale about where my product is!"

"I'm not your son, *Philly*."

"There there, Philly. Let the lad alone. You know what they say ... there's no sense crying over spilt Lacstasy ..."

That Vanishing Indian Trick

Flak Riesling shook off the psychical twinge all parents feel when their progeny are in peril and held Anna Condo tighter in his arms.

"And how are you, my little torture stick?"

"After my split ... I never thought I could play rough again ... let alone enjoy this amount of rampant and frenetic physical intimacy with a B+ flick star."

"A pity, that! Still, the mingling of your neo-con fascist attitudes with my celebrity neo-liberal left bias is so delish ... just imagine ... together we could tell everyone how to live!"

Flak unlocked and unstrapped his ISM cup.

"I've never felt this vulnerable ... not in a long time."

"Then be careful ... I've been a bad girl."

"I never knew I had so much tension. But with you ... why, it just melts away!"

"But Flak ... you were right to question me ... I adopt and breed boys for sale ... and I've been secretly working for the Secret Corporation. There are countless atrocities ..."

"Shh ... hush baby ... I can't just switch off my feelings ..."

"But your son ... he may be in jeopardy ..."

"His mother's too soft on him ... that slackery scamp could use a reality check, big time!"

"Mmm ... I could be mommy to the pair of you ... it takes a firm hand ..."

"What you say is really weirding me out ... yet I cannot resist ..."

"But Flak ... there's something else I've been keeping from you. For a spell, Hack Riesling was posing as private secretary to my mother ... no doubt to wrest away secret documents and intel for his own nefarious ends. Long story short, not so long after their liaison, Kitty Condo had a child. I was that child."

"What?!?"

"Now I don't want to freak you out right in the middle of dipping your wick but we may be half-brother and sister."

Flak's face was wracked with conflict and tasteless pleasure. He turned toward Billy Joe Bearclaw, who was still finishing his nutrilicious picnic, including a fresh pail of smelt.

"Flak, for many tiresome ages we have waited. We always knew you were the one. But now you must do what is in your heart. Will this forbidden encounter curse and sully the earth for generations or will this trite union help you to discover the next rest stop on your own personal journey? Surely you must find wisdom and guidance in the lore of the Three Sisters ..."

"Billy Joe, what do you mean?"

"Beats me ... I'm doing my level best to sound interested in what you lovebirds are up to!"

"Flak ... darling ... Mommy's waiting ... come to Mommy!"

"Grrrr!!!"

The crowd of voyeurs on the observation deck watched Flak grind his hips and twirl his tongue about as his hands seized the empty air. Anna Condo had just melted away.

"Check ... and mate."

Dr. F stamped his foot in a flash of anger. Terence Cockerel grinned smugly.

"How did you know?"

"Mr. Riesling is not the only soul in New Haudenosaunee to suffer from a form of simulation sickness. A more common strain of Simfluenza permits most of the nation to see and worship Anna Condo, in spite of the fact that she was generated in this very laboratory."

Everyone stopped to watch in amazement as a floating sealwich was disappearing, bite by bite.

"Ah yes, Billy Joe Bearclaw is not real either. I planted him as a mole at ISM, but he was really nothing more than a faux mole."

Dr. F stamped his foot even more defiantly.

"Faux mole! But that's my technique ... that's patent infringement! Also, that vanishing Indian trick is in very poor taste. The worst!"

"It only took a vintage tube cycle of archetypal meditations, merely to get our agent in the mood. Ironically, the woman who finally broke Flak Riesling was only a relay loop of dated circuitry running a few mundane algorithms ..."

"For all that, no one could have done a better job in *Cuddles for Cash 4*."

"Granted, no."

The Stuff of Cereal Junkies

"It is apparent, however, that Quentin Quentin was spurred on by an overriding hostility to his environment, a hostility that threatened the very fabric of the hospitality industry which had harboured him for so many years. He does not appear to have been able to establish meaningful relationships with other people. He was often unhappy with the world around him. Long before the assassination he expressed his disgust toward the state of New Haudenosaunee and acted in protest against it. Quentin's search for what he conceived to be the perfect society was doomed from the start. At John Wilkes Hospital, he admitted to wanting a place in history for himself – a role as the Grand Sagamore, if not in fact the Big Sachem. His commitment to outright Drumhellerism, clandestine microcorpism, and Cnidarian dogma appears to have been another important factor in his motivation. He also demonstrated erratic behaviour, particularly in traffic and in the Notel kitchen during the rush. In a nutshell, such is the character and disposition of Quentin Quentin, a man entirely capable of assassinating Governor Gewürztraminer."

Earnest Frank closed the report and spat neatly into a nearby cuspidor. Blue Green picked it up and handed it to Ricotta Frittata, who adjusted her fashionably torn peasant blouse and offered dinner with her eyes.

"Is that all, Earn?"

"Open and shut, Blue. 'Cept maybe he should change his name to San Quentin."

"Something doesn't add up. There was sugar all over his fingers ..."

"The weapon was in a Notel confectionary. If that just don't take the cake, then I don't know what does!"

"But it's no ordinary sugar, Earnest. This is the stuff of cereal junkies. You need more than an ounce of street cred to lay hands on this stuff. It's what your doomboomer burnouts call rutabaga."

"So you're saying someone wanted to have their cake and eat it too?"

"Not just someone, Earn. The main distributor of rutabaga is our old friend Beso Pesadilla."

"Pesadilla! This whole deal is dishing me the crêpes!"

"Any other witnesses, Earnest?"

"Wheyhey, a woman ... goes by the handle Mercedes Swizzle. She's a real class act. Came out of the woodwork saying she was wearing an Informista dictabelt at the time. They're all the rage ... record your married effbuddies then blackmail them on the downlow."

Mercedes Swizzle was led into the room for questioning. She spat her kumquat gum into Ricotta Frittata's open mouth, and this was not as intriguing as it sounds.

"I want to talk to my attorney."

"Ms. Swizzle, what do you know about rutabaga?"

"Swedish turnip? Not much."

"You were selling sugar snadgies to kids. We also found traces of mangelwurzel on your lips. Also your pal Quentin Quentin."

"Hey, he's no pal of mine."

"You work for Beso Pesadilla. And so does Quentin. Now why don't you tell me how many guests at the Pretty Grand Notel Hotel are calling for room service and getting hopped up on rutabaga?"

"You can't prove a thing, detective! I triple-hot-fudge-dare you to prove I'm involved!"

"I don't need proof. I have circumspecture. Wheyhey, I know what happened. Right before the attack, you went into the kitchen ..."

"I was hungry!"

"Yes, you were, Ms. Swizzle. Hungry for the finer things in life. And Beso Pesadilla had sent you on a mission ..."

"He said no one would get killed who wasn't supposed to!"

"Quentin didn't want to take the drug himself, on account of his devout Drumhellerism. But you ... *convinced* him."

A fiery pride shone in the eyes of Mercedes Swizzle. She brandished her pierced tongue.

"Once the Swizzle has stirred you up, you don't want to try anything else ..."

"So once he was high, you used erotic mind control trilogies to convince him to attack the governor ... "

"I deserve a medal! Just like that French babe who finished off Marat in the tub."

"O you're going to get what's coming to you, Ms. Swizzle. Get her out of my sight ..."

Ricotta Frittata led her off, punctuating her tragic comedown with several swift kicks from her impossibly pointed curlews. Everyone was feeling too self-satisfied and hellbent for righteousness to notice that Quentin Quentin was being led down the corridor by a lone guard who was not-so-secretly in love with Ricotta Frittata and who failed to notice the looming shadow of Beniamino Giggly, whipping out a double-pump-action hazer. Quentin Quentin died instantly, and Giggly was shot trying to escape. Even Mercedes Swizzle positively sizzled where she had stood a few ticks earlier.

"Well, looks like all our suspects got fried. Guess it don't matter if everything leads back to Beso."

"But they were somebody's children, Earnest. Somebody loved them."

"Blue, you know that's just a bunch of crap. If you've seen one sugar-addled cereal junkie, you've seen 'em all. Nothing but a bowl of wrong."

"Well, let's go take down Beso Pesadilla. The nightmare kiss, they call him."

"That may be, Earnest. But I think his nightmare kisses are just beginning."

Scattered Rime

The Librarian caressed the circular panels at the base of the Phallicator IV, and it sprang to life for the reverberations of her low trilling. The overheater switched on automatically, warming the long thick tube for imminent launch. The overnight rime quickly began to melt away. This was a trusty Horsehead device that had been left for this very purpose ... for bidding farewell to the departed. She patted the soulproof containment unit with which she had extracted the remains from Oober Mann's scrambled memory, for the purpose of scattering them throughout the local universe.

"Ackmod Delphi 7.0 Meridian Stellar Nova Twenty-Three, before the Meltdown you died a stupid death, and I am sorry on account of that. Although I am no more than a mercenary fulfilling a more than fair contract, I swore an oath in the name of the Phasmida to recover you and redeliver you to the cosmic sector from whence you came. Now, may the world wait on hold and hear your favourite music forever ..."

The Librarian moaned and groaned with a steady rhythm, and her musical breathings activated the launch device. Then with her antelope coat flapping, she ran for cover as fast as she could in her Comehither boots. Then with the clamour of a volcanic eruption, the probe spurted upward into space. As she walked away, she fancied she could already hear the ecstatic echoes of Bach's secular cantata concerning the dangers of coffee.

The EASY Button

Oober Mann awoke in a cold sweat. It took a while for reality to sink in. He was alone. His besties had all been arrested for the attack and the Librarian had hitched the nearest freighticon to anywhere but here. On the plus side, he could no longer hear a stitch of Bach. Not that he didn't love the rational control of hair-tearing expressionism in the baroque era but he had sometimes felt the temptation to throw that cello down a dozen flights of stairs. He lifted the skirt of his bed and peered underneath, half-expecting to find an attentive Yo-Yo Ma waiting for the day to begin. No, nothing. Strangely, he felt quite good. He hadn't felt like himself in ages. For once, he felt really *unadulterated*. His floating alarum switched on and filled the room with Ravel's Trio in A Minor, which he welcomed as one welcomes a cool breeze. Later, he would recline with an herbal cigar in the presence of Franck's Violin Sonata and relive the overwrought evenings of his most munificent passions. He would tremble slightly to recall what a fool he had been for this woman or that, waiting for the mere sound of her step or the tender squish of her boot heels across his chest or back. Ahh ... but it was wonderful to have his sluggish Euro-trashy musings back! Then out of nowhere, he soon was awash with the overweening vacancy of the age and he let out something very near a sigh. However, after a satisfying shower and a fortifying bowl of quincox, he decided to head into work, directly after ducking into the nearest Filterz.

"Quadradoppio diabetto ecstasy ..."

"Comin' right up ..."

"Squeaky Fomme!"

"Do I know you? It's Alice, actually."

"We met, although not under the best circumstances."

"Really?"

"Yesterday!"

"Wait a tick, didn't you used to have a long moustache? And sideburns like a hussar?"

"You must be thinking of someone else ... but what happened? Aren't you under arrest?"

"Arrest? No, you must be thinking of someone else ..."

Oober touched the smoothness under his nose with his fingers, suddenly wondering if there had ever been anything bristling there. Alice shook the karma jar to dispense with any bad mojo or ancestral ghosts between them.

"You know, they say each of us has a doppelgänger, a malevolent soul wandering the earth in our likeness. And this soul bears the face we see right before death ..."

"Do you really believe that?"

"Would you like that in a jumbo cup?"

When Oober Mann arrived at the offices of LeapPod Streams, an emergency dashboard was already taking place. He was ushered in and sat down uneasily. The slackslamming hacker known as Goatsinger was back with the same pained expression, and Greta Goldfarb was giving him a sly wink. Only Mr. Yanjing and his smouldering cigarette were conspicuously absent.

"Now Mr. Yanjing, some might whisper, was the lifeblood of this organization. Some might say that behind closed doors and drawn blinds. But to me, to see the blood and sweat and tears of LeapPod Streams, I only have to look into your beautiful faces. His sudden decision to bail out with his tail between his legs should have no bearing on the work we do here. Some days you win and some days not so much. But what I do know is how much I adore each and every one of you. Just look at your beautiful faces ..."

The chief picked up one of the smaller developers and kept cuddling and kissing him until someone made a throat-clearing noise.

"... but life is in flux ... wasn't it Heraclitus who said something to that effect? And is life at times not positively Kafkaesque? And does the Bard not say we must use both hawk and handsaw at our own discretion?"

The chief put down his yellow sticky–marked book of professional quotables.

"Some of you will remain as proud members of our LeapPod family ..."

He tousled the hair of another beaming developer.

"Others ... well, you may want to explore your options in the open market ..."

A trapdoor opened beneath Oober Mann's chair. Fortunately he was sitting on the very edge of it. Much later, he heard the chair land with a crash. The chief patted his arm. A series of arrows lit up along the floor.

"Mr. Mann, could we have a quick chat with you?"

Armed sentries appeared to escort him into an unmarked room he had never noticed before. He sat down across from the chief and fell silent.

"As you know, we've been waiting for news about a number of projects. We thought we had an exclusive binding contract with Nintendari, although now we understand they've gone ahead with a competitor. We put into motion our bananaware more recently but there have been reports that rebel mercenaries have taken over Chappiquiddic Bananas, which is not the greatest news for us. In short, we've failed ... and in such unforeseen situations, as *The Guide to Getting Anywhere* will tell you, I find the healthiest thing to do is to blame someone and move on. Now, we consulted everyone except you on the matter, and the answer became clear. At present, LeapPod Streams cannot afford to retain an Oober Mann ..."

The chief lifted up a series of glowing lammies.

"Now I want to be absolutely clear. We have failed you as an organization. I have failed you as a leader ... as a partner ... as a friend ... as a man ... whoops, sorry! That one's for later ..."

Oober nodded and stared at the floor.

"Yeah, I guess."

"We don't want you to be worried or concerned about this. Rest assured, we will pay you off! Personally, whenever I face a dignity issue or moral question, I like to fall back on a nice big payoff."

"Okay."

"Also, we have to take back the LeapPod Streams stain-resistant adventure slacks that we gave you when you started with us. Sorry, but it's company policy."

"These ones I'm wearing?"

"You betcha!"

"Sir, I have one question ... "

"Yeah, shoot."

"On the interview test, what was the solution to the problem with the three doors with the three goats behind them?"

"Sorry, Mr. Mann, that's confidential."

"I see."

"We'll walk you out."

Sentries herded the pantless Oober Mann along the corridor with freshly charged executive prods at a compassionately medium setting. Then once he had passed through the conveyor restrainer system, he noticed a large red button labelled EASY on the administrative assistant's desk and without warning, he banged his head down on it. Greta Goldfarb appeared with watery eyes and handed him a card that read GOLDFARB STEAMING MEDIA.

"Let me know if you ever need some easy credits ... we have a number of positions to fill ..."

Then everyone filed off, leaving him waiting in the hallway. And before the flitboost had arrived, the gossip had begun.

"What did he do?"

"Didn't you know? He was a rogue cell."

The Boy Who Cried Mootiny

One head appeared. Then down the other briskalator, another head. The lowing was excruciating. There was no let-up, whatsoever.

"No, please."

They were heading for the ventilation system.

"Mommy ... look at the zoo-zoos!"

Security guards were overpowered. They slumped to the floor. Everywhere the shoppers looked, another head of cattle appeared, lowing and lowing at them with a motionless stare. Only a bronzed eco-affable couple dared to approach them, holding out their open palms.

"Let us embrace them, our friends ..."

The cows continued chewing the candied indoor turf. Then all at once, they began to release an unstoppable cloud of methane gas. The eco-affable couple were the first victims.

"Oh man ... I feel so bummed ..."

"What have we done with our lives?"

The couple were so depressed they would have euthanized one another on the spot, save for the fact they were too vitamin-deficient to do so. Then the massive cloud of gas filled their lungs. Such is the folly of eating right. A few people tried to resist but were only doused in fordified onogenized milk for their trouble. They were too blue even to smile at the boy who cried mootiny. And the cows kept coming, one head at a time, until everyone in Algonquin Mall was either totally depressed or done like dinner.

Free Love Balloons

"Ciudad Cashmere here for an historical instant ... now we'll keep up to date with the crazy cow methdemic and have more on that later with our special, 'Spoilt Milk and Mad Muck-ups.' But first, we're here at the Free Love Party Debate in the Dryden's Donuts Convention Centre where you, the confused unwashed, will be able to ask irrelevant questions and for a nano get the smear of attention you deserve. But first, I'll start the moderating with this question for Senator Lou Cuzzy. Senator, if the nation were an undecided underager, what would you say to woo this underager and get her to address your needs?"

Lou Cuzzy cleared his throat and began to stroke the podium.

"I'm glad you asked that, Ciudad. First, let me just say that it is an honour to be here. I just love your show ... I can't get enough of you ... whenever I see you at one of these things, I'm the first to say, 'Hey gentlemen, I'd sure like to tap that.' Of course, I'm kind of an old-timey family-oriented C&A man ..."

"Senator, you're running out of time ..."

"Well, Ciudad, I would say, Look here darlin', some people say Lou Cuzzy is always rearing his decrepit and scuzzy kisser, but them folk are complete whack-crackers. I have the budget to show the nation a good time, and the stamina and meds to keep it interested for a long, long time! And if you don't like them mutaters, I'll knock you right into next week ..."

"I think that answers the question, Senator. Now, from a veritable nobody, we go to a popular front-runner, the seemingly unassailable Governor Gewürztraminer. Just how many times has your heart stopped, Governor?"

"Is that the question, Ciudad?"

"Ha ha, Governor. But how would you woo the nation, if you haven't wooed us already?"

"I have to agree with Senator Cuzzy. And I am sure all of the candidates here will agree that we would all love to explore your incredible heinie and so on and so forth. But right now, there are whopping mackerel to fish-fry. It was not so long ago they had to jumpstart my heart, and this is just what the nation needs, to jumpstart the economy once again, to bring in new ideas and new technology. Right now, we are trailing behind New Anaesthesia as the leading producer of stimulation feeds. I would like to make sure that everyone has a stimulation feed, no matter how desperate or lonely. We need to get our kinden out of the brovels they live in, so they have a nice hot feed while they are slaving over a hot metaploitation ..."

"Mmm ... that makes me kinda moist, Governor! But we must move on to Robert Menthos ..."

"Call me Bob, Ciudad. Y'know, I swear I'm the only candidate to think about you when I'm giving it to mah wife ... ever since your peekaboo special on lingerie outlet subverts, I can't stop imagining what it would be like if you broke into our house and held us hostage and then made me ..."

"Senator, time."

"Nation, you're a real doll but you need to wisen on up. Look at how you're living your life. You think you're so gosh-darn smart! But whaddya know, really? That's where Uncle Bob comes in. Look at this head of hair, for starters. This ain't no weave that's just gonna run out on you on a blustery day. That's your money well spent! The people who put this much thought into my hair are the people with the manestorming to properly tease this nation. Now nation, maybe you wanna stick with the fool-headed choices you've been making till now. Or maybe you could stand some good ol' down-home lovin' in the night when you're fast asleep or halfway into your self-pollution. Maybe you wanna stick with the same ol' sob story you've been kickin' around with. Or maybe it's time to try something new. If you like your sex in a burr swing, then it's a better day for a man like Menthos ..."

"Wheygee ... what say you, Primo Bialetti ..."

"You only need look in the Book of Bard, if I have it right, where someone says *thou art a liar* and the answer is *you are a senator* ..."

Everyone paused to enjoy murderous glares and uncomfortable laughter.

"Of course, I'm no senator, but maybe that's a good thing. I'm the mayor who tamed the alligators in the sewer. People have compared me to my rather traditional family coffee pot fortune, saying I may be temperamental and boil over without warning, but I'm not someone who can be pushed around, or flipped on and off for that matter. On the plus side, I get angry because I care. If you are never enraged or livid or hatin' on something, then you don't love this nation."

"But play along, Mayor Bialetti ... what would you do to get this nation moving into a horizontal mambo?"

"Ciudad, I would remind the nation that as Mayor of Mannahatta, I spear-headed the movement to provide safe infusion sites for Aggromatics and to relocate our refuse site to the Kanadas. I faced opposition from some of these very candidates who blocked my legislation for a cleaner, shinier homeland. But we have an old Native saying in Mannahatta ... sometimes to clean the river you gotta dump someone into it ..."

"So you're into shaming the nation? Tough love, Mayor Bialetti?"

"Sure, you could say I like it rough, Ciudad!"

"And how about you, Senator Ottawa Chalmers?"

"Ciudad, I am appalled at whatever I am hearing tonight. We have serious issues to discuss. Not one candidate has mentioned the issue of illegal aliens who are working in our great nation and driving light-speed limucks at this very instant. Governor Gewürztraminer himself has signed legislation giving unprecedented rights and powers to these individuals ..."

Governor Gewürztraminer popped a few TremendoBurst and heaved his podium aside.

"Ciudad, I must interject here. These individuals are not illegal aliens. The Cicadians and the Phasmida and maybe even the Cnidarians are time-hopping evolutions of our own species. I remind Ms. Chalmers that it is our duty to welcome them. An investment in them is an investment in the future!"

"Well, while Governor Gewürztraminer is busting a bicep worrying about upright locusts and beetles, our little darlings are going to bed with their stomachs growling and with their heads full of unnatural sugar plums ..."

"Senator Chalmers, I need to remind you that you are evading the question ..."

"Of course, Ciudad, and let me just say that I love your outfit! Speaking as a candidate first, and as a woman second, let me remind the nation that I share a unique sensitivity that will do more than please the nation. Whatever the problem at hand, I will find the most delectable way to lick it and lick it good."

Senator Chalmers lolled her tongue around for effect and her approval rating went through the frosted pink roof.

"Last but almost least, we come to Rory Gentle Bear ..."

"Thanks, Ciudad. Don't worry about ol' Rory ... I'm way over here where nobody can see me, but that's cool too. Hey, I've been listening to these candidates for weeks now, with their policies and plans for New Haudie. Wheyhey, some of them are even not half-bad. But the real people out there know me from my prime-time tube *Pawnbreaker*, or from the many flicks where I play an upstanding politico. Or they say, we don't mind that guy from *Mortal Congress 3*, he's not only an effective planner, but he's also a badass when nuts come to crunch, just like in *Hunger Strike Force II*. They say, we don't mind some clown in office, but let it be someone we know, a real bozo! Cuz people don't wanna be bored with all this talk about *issues*. They want hot action now!"

"And Mr. Gentle Bear, what would you do to get the nation to drop its short shorts?"

"Three words, Ciudad. *Free love balloons*."

"Free love balloons?"

"Anyone who follows the teachings of the Seventh-day Latter Bardians will know that any crisis can be averted by the direct and unadulterated application of free love balloons. If there were more free love balloons in a world where everyone spoke a common tribal patois, you would not be able to chuck a petroglyph without hitting a peaceful situation. These are wicked, misguided times and we need strong leadership if we are going to make it to the undiscovered country ..."

Rory Gentle Bear knelt on the glossy floor and raised his hands toward the lofty ceiling.

"The croaking raven doth bellow for revenge!"

"Mr. Gentle Bear, perhaps you could expand upon your answer ..."

Cherry balloons began to fall from the ceiling, covering candidates and audience members. Incidentally, each balloon read **FREE LOVE.** Rory Gentle Bear shut his eyes and grinned.

"Unsex me here!"

The balloons were activated and the entire donut centre exploded, leaving nothing behind but frosted pink cinders.

Stuck with Leftover Gibblets

Gekiga Weiss entered the ISM Recreational Unisex without a word. She was so lost in thought that she nearly elbowed Hassan Armadill off his vibrating Miracle Tuckusizer 10020.

"Whoa ... did anyone get the number of that limuck!"

"Sorry ... I guess maybe the whole food-and-sleep-deprivation thing is getting to me."

"I find the soylent astrowafers keep me alert ... even spry."

"Ya know, I've had it up to here with astrowafers and pokosticks."

"Chill, babe ... we're all under the same pressure."

"Then I guess we both had to remotely disarm a rogue death-com orbital today ..."

"Well ... pressure takes different forms, Gekiga. I've had to facilitate the hell out of this place today ..."

"Yeah, I guess ... sorry about the cockchomp ... it's been a long day, that's all."

Gekiga unvelked her elastivest and flirt, revealing her Desattaché subwear. She studied Hassan's smooth unslappable expression and her eyes fell to a nasty scar just above his knotted towel.

"Is this ... where ...?"

As Hassan was reminded of what had happened to him in Absurdabad, the Simulizer 7069 picked up his airborne psychical trauma and immediately activated one of its emotional projection components. Gekiga watched as a younger and more cocky Hassan was strapped down on a table by the notorious Harem Team, who prodded his bare flesh repeatedly with all manner of objects. In the background, through a partially open door, a woman in an iron mask was fastening a strap-on dillastity belt around her waist, with dimensions that were still strictly black market in New Haudenosaunee. Then as Hassan's eyes widened, she began to cough softly ...

"I'm so sorry, Hassan ... I had no idea ..."

"What haunts me most is I never knew who she was! She never even bought me dinner first ..."

"It's part of the job ... it makes us into different people ..."

"That's why I'm getting out! But who would have thought I would end up starting over with Paula Panteater! Kinda makes ya think."

"O!"

"What is it?"

"Nothing, forget it ..."

"By the way, you and Slim Gibblets seem pretty chummy lately."

"Yeah, but maybe I've bitten off more than I can chew. Slim does things that Flak won't do ... but he's also no Flak. I'm worried about ending up all alone with my top-flight genius. I guess some of us decide on prime fillet and some of us get stuck with leftover gibblets."

"Sounds like someone needs a no-holds-barred bodysage ..."

Gekiga lay down on her back and Hassan began to work his fingers into her neck and shoulder flesh.

"Mmm ... that's totally licious."

The Simulizer 7069 picked up on their pheromonal output with its vomeronasal functionality and didn't miss a beat slipping its mood setting into playtonal ambience until the entire room was the size of a mauve desert throbbing and pulsating in time with the interior moaning of their minds. Hassan peeled off her Desattaché subwear and began to move her breasts in slow concentric circles. In the corridor, Agent Panza peeked in and smiled, dancing with his bloody mop and tapping his foot in time to the pumping mukazz. Gekiga raised her standard-issue work hooves and unravelled Hassan's towel with a single kick. Then as she started rubbing his pride and joy, which was patriotically standing to attention, he winced slightly.

"Sorry ..."

"No ... sorry, it's not you ... it's just ... memories of Absurdabad ... the boobs ... the unforgiving boots ..."

"Then let the healing begin!"

But their self-absorbing foredom was interrupted by the sound of someone coughing. It was Greta Goldfarb (a.k.a. Paula Panteater), brandishing her personal defence system.

"Paula ... this isn't what it looks like!"

"Stow it, Hassan!"

Gekiga covered herself with folded arms, stumbling over the slumped form of Agent Sancho Panza. Since she was not a screamer, she only laughed nervously.

"You didn't tell me she had esteem issues!"

"Don't flatter yourselves. Your teat-à-teat ménage wouldn't amount to a hill of beans in my homeland! Remember Absurdabad? You can save the goss for the soylent dispenser!"

Hassan maintained an expression of pure soap-operatic shock in a close-up while instinctively his buttocks tensed up.

"Absurdabad ... that cough ... it was you all along!"

"Yes, they say I really put the dill in Armadill ... it never fails to crack me up! My name isn't even Greta Goldfarb or Paula Panteater. You will find I am known on the other side of the hemisphere as Jaguar Merge. You had a fly in your web all this time, Hassan, and you never even knew it. Now it's time for that fly to despoil your day."

"Okay okay ... do me, but let Gekiga go!"

"Yeah, do him and let me go!"

Jaguar Merge laughed and coughed and laughed.

"All in good time! I just need to finish transferring all of your data back to my thinktank. And since there's time for a gal to exercise her bragging rights, I should like to stand here with my back turned and tell you everything I know before putting you out of your misery."

Hassan and Gekiga both yawned.

"Or you could just finish us off ..."

"You've obviously worked out that I am the driving force behind Ebony Dill. I was also behind the humiliation campaign that broadtubed your national leader being demoralized."

The Simulizer 7069 showed them the image of Big Chief Jim Shrub being strapped down and painstakingly stimulated.

"Blazes ... hee hee ... that sure tickles!"

Hassan spat out a citron astrowafer in the direction of her painted toes.

"Sure, go on ... demoralize us ... destroy us! But what do you have left? A lonely world full of unfeeling dills! They can't keep you warm at night! Well, maybe they can, sometimes ..."

"Before we say goodbye, I just wanted you to know that I have a binding disclosure agreement with Nintendari. Humiliation is back in and cruel is the new cool! Apparently, market studies show it's very hot right now ... it's what the maturiteens want, and I mean by the bucketful! Stay tuned for *Stud Pharm 5*, the latest in underactive entertainment!"

Jaguar jacked into the blue-tube and instantly they were watching polygraphic footage of her wearing the iron mask and scratching Hassan's naked flesh with fingernails she had grown to points specifically for this purpose. The image flitted readily to other ISM suspects clad in various LeatheX ensembles who were performing unspeakably arousing acts. Still others were set ablaze or whipped to death. Hassan looked away.

"Ya know, if this stuff gets out, put in a certain context and seen in a negative light, it could undermine all of our operations, or even affect the popularity of my edible tell-all *The Stuff of Reams*!"

"Too bad you'll never get to see that day ..."

Just then, a mop handle knocked the personal defence system out of her reach and the Miracle Tuckusizer 10020 came down on her head ... hard. She fell unconscious at the feet of Agent Sancho Panza.

"Nice work, Panza."

"Looks like someone's getting a few extra *frijoles* in their pay pouch!"

At that moment, Panza's stomach burst open and a swarm of magicicadas flew out. They immediately began feasting on his prone body, along with that of Jaguar Merge. Hassan threw an emergency safety net over the infestation and held Gekiga close to him.

"I ... never told him ... how I felt ..."

"Me neither, Gekiga ... me neither."

Escape Clause

Oober Mann hesitated, then knocked decisively on the door that read Goldfarb Steaming Media. It opened, seemingly of its own accord, and he went inside.

"Are you the headhunter?"

"In a manner of speaking."

"I know you."

"Yes, you do."

"From?"

"What if I told you that none of this was real?"

"Given the year I've had, nothing would surprise me."

"Well, for the sake of argument, let us suppose you were wandering around Venusburb one night, getting ripped on dry mantinis and wishing you were dead and then suddenly thinking it would be a nifty idea to get a memvirt, just for old time's sake ..."

At the word *memvirt* everything began to fall into place. Oober realized that he must have another life somewhere else, surely more substantial than this one. In fact, this idea made perfect sense.

"So this is all a simulation?"

"You signed a few release forms before we gave you the memvirt, which included an escape clause in the event that you suffered a solo polyphonic breakdown. Well, Mr. Mann, that day has arrived ..."

"So what now?"

"Our equipment needs to start a quick refresh sequence in order to recast your fantasy coordinates and body types. The Librarian, a popular figure from our stock catalogue, was starting to flicker and fade and we need to tweak her ... uh ... data. In such cases, Ms. Goldfarb, one of our designers, recommends that an escape strategy be initiated at once."

"So how do I escape?"

"Take the stairs up to the roof. You will find a Cesspo Seagull waiting for you."

"Yeah ...."

"You need to trigger the Game Over codeset sequence. You will get in the plane and fly directly into Nintendari Towers. And that oughta wrap things up nicely, one way or the other ..."

And No Foolies

Blue Green and Rebecca Tomahawk subdued and restrained the guards at the bottom of Nintendari Towers and then rode the levipad up to the penthouse.

"Whaddya think we'll find up there, Blue?"

"Nothing kosher."

"The crapperclaw responsible for today's attacks?"

"Sure, whatever."

"Don't get too over-the-moon about it."

"Ya know, Rebecca, when I started, I was always wanting to get in the thick of it. But these days a salt bath followed by a low power nap seems thrilling enough to me. I'd like to pack it all in and maybe take up yarn bombing ..."

"And would there be room in that salt bath ... for a hottie half the age of the hardbitten flatfoot?"

"You'd want a worn-out old trooper like me?"

"I want someone who won't run out on me. After all, I'd only need a young buck now and then ..."

"Fair's fair. And I've got this sweet retirement package coming up. So long as nothing ironic happens in the next few ticks, you could find yourself hooked up with a generous gent, and no foolies ..."

"Seriously, Blue ... you're freaking me out. The sooner we make our kills, the sooner we power nap."

"Then maybe there is something to look forward to in this freaking freak show we call the world!"

They found Terence Cockerel sealing a titanium case and starting a gigasmic timer. At that very instant, a Cesspo Seagull crashed through the window, taking all of them with it. Then, without warning, Nintendari Towers exploded.

Run Along Smartly!

Oober Mann awoke inside a dark defrosting cryobed. His wrists were firmly clamped down. He gasped as the head section of the bed opened up like a magician's box.

"*¡Abre los ojos!*"

"What?"

"Sorry, it's something of a surrealist joke. I'm checking in on the insurgency ward and was wondering if you wanted anything ... within reason, of course."

"I ... this is the hospital, yes? I flew into ... a building."

"Ahh ... so Nurse Kookaloco hasn't had her wee talk with you yet. I see."

"Who are you?"

"I'm Dr. F. Scott Fitzgerald. But you can call me F ... everybody does!"

"I feel like I know you. You're the guy on the tube ... the mad genius!"

F bit into his pen with a satisfying crunch.

"Hardly, Mr. Mann. Although such delusions are symptomatic of your ... er ... condition."

"But we're at war!"

Oober looked around and noticed an economy-size jar labelled NUTELLA in smooth brown letters. He also noticed that the word WAR had been written with the same smooth brown substance upon the wall.

"Well, you are right about that, Mr. Mann. But don't give it another thought. After all, we are always at war. We've been monitoring your brainwaves and your behaviour and we know you've been kicking up a fuss about the atrocious conditions in this fantasy land of yours ... Nutella."

A pretty attendant appeared out of nowhere and began to clean up the nutty writing with a dripping sponge. She stopped to dip her hand in the jar and licked her fingers clean of the smooth brown substance, all the while winking at Oober.

"Are you telling me it was all in my head?"

"Yes and no, Mr. Mann. Nothing is ever that simple. This is a nationwide epidemic and you are in one of our finest treatment centres. One of your relations applied for government funding to keep you in a cryobed indefinitely in the hopes that we might one day find a cure for your condition. Fortunately, this category-five funding also qualifies you for our wide-awake revival service, to keep you up to speed on your ... um ... situation."

At that moment, a small screen in the corner of the room caught Oober's eye.

"Ahhh ... it's her! The Librarian ... no, wait ... the Dijon Diva ..."

"Now this is something I've been meaning to discuss with you. We are aware of a number of persistent delusions you are having and we feel ... well ... obliged to dispel the most ludicrous of these notions ..."

"But it's her! I know that woman on the screen."

"You wouldn't believe how many times I hear that in a given week. Many men in our ward, from O-level age to disenfranchised middle-class maturiteen, suffer from the same delusion."

"Then who is she?"

"I've been meaning to send in a complaint about that ... oh, it's the relief reporter from BBC Omniverse, Perspicacity Vauxhall."

"Who?"

"You sure the nurse didn't have a word? A severe case of Perspicacity Vauxhallism, we call it. An offshoot of standard Orwellianism with a touch of Wiganism. It's a subset of most metafflictions suffered by disillusioned and lonely young men with too much time on their hands ... or not enough. You impose an artificial system upon reality and there is bound to be a rude awakening – the realization that most everything you were taught has nothing to do with reality. There is a sudden rupture – then most people instinctively retreat into a fantasy world. In essence, our cells are genetically preprogrammed to multiply and then die. However, in these individuals, rogue cells are created that direct the individual toward a rapid death, which in some way provides an ersatz substitution for the act of mating. The evocation of the idoless has always been key in tribal cultures since our earliest origins. She gives us an artificial sense of meaning in all things and a delightful excuse for polishing ourselves off in a jiffy."

"But Dr. F, why this particular woman?"

"I wish I could help you there, Mr. Mann. I'm not even up to date on the latest case studies, although there are innumerable rural testimonies about her eyes hypnotizing sheep and having an inexplicable effect upon ducks. Her dialect is also perilously charming, particularly for sun-deprived Northerners in any nation. Personally, I prefer the page three dolly-bird pinups for some mild jollies but I seem to be behind the times. Here she is, forming order out of chaos in the midst of global terror and violence and bloodshed. It's a new type of mesmerism, I'll give her that. In the ward, we call her Big Sister, our Perspicacity."

Perspicacity, sporting a glowing top with a fetching collar, gave him a familiar smile and nod.

"... and there was another victim of the subprime condome market collapse today, *if* you could call him that ..."

"But Dr. F, what about my books ...?"

"Let me be perfectly candid, Mr. Mann. Many of our young men in here fantasized they were writing the next Vonnegut or Pynchon or Kerouac classic about their wonderfully unique *experiences*, of course involving a striking cosmonaut or hitchhiker who looked amazingly like Perspicacity Vauxhall. Perfectly healthy! But you, sir, had the audacity to fall under the delusion that you had not only written a terrestrial classic, but a series of five books that had received unbridled interstellar acclaim. I don't even know how Ms. Vauxhall can bear to look at you!"

But Perspicacity Vauxhall continued to stare and mesmerize the entire ward, save for Dr. F, who wore special glasses.

"And it's official. Nintendari now has a licence to print money. They are the rightful owners of the entire world. BOW DOWN and stroke their puppies!"

"Did she just say Nintendari?"

"Of course not, Mr. Mann."

"O no!"

"Don't worry, we can get you some more Nutella ..."

"This is one of those trendy, mentally ill trick endings where everything was all in my head! I really hate those!"

F primed a needle and watched it squirt stray serum.

"Really, Mr. Mann. All stories should end happily ever after. Now, you are going to experience just the slightest smidge of anagnorisis ..."

At once, Oober remembered the Dijon Diva and her little red dog. But it wasn't Dijon at all. He realized that he had read an article about Perspicacity Vauxhall's fascination with fish sauce. The very fish sauce the Emperor Tiberius had served to his guests in Capri! And there was some woman with Minor whose immortal face belonged to none other than Perspicacity Vauxhall. With tarty outfits and hair extensions and an in-studio glow, the Librarian was no alien. Even journalista Candy Coton was only a pale refraction of the indomitable Perspicacity Vauxhall! With some pain, he remembered his first interstellar masterpiece. And bit by bit, he realized that each scrap of his precious *Minor Episodes* had at one point or another passed through the lips of the relief reporter as a snippet of news. Even Bébé Lala the billboard goddess and Miss Sharp the fatal singer/songwriter were both aspects of the same foxy foxglove from Leicestershire, Perspicacity Vauxhall, who was still staring at him with a look of sultry concern.

"Peace talks will resume and there is hope both despots can come to some accord ..."

"Ahh ... I can see by your look of anguish that you are starting to remember. And here is the stupendous Chaos! Quincunx you keep mithering on about ..."

Dr. F brought five scrapbooks over to Oober. He flipped through them quickly, but long enough for Oober to see that each page bore a crude crayon representation of relief reporter Perspicacity Vauxhall.

"Now, is it likely you are writing unconventional novelistic masterpieces to challenge the cozy sensibilities of a drowsy populace while enjoying casual ménages with close friends and visiting alien hotpots ... or more likely you are on the dole and digging your bent fork into a frozen O Sole Mio dinner while watching Ms. Vauxhall on a half-inched telly?"

"I do confess, the latter."

Suddenly, there were howls and giggles from the observation station. Dr. F ran to the wall and yanked a banana-shaped handle.

"Code Aubergine ... Nurse Kookaloco ... where are you? I repeat ... Code Aubergine ... another case of visceral projection ..."

One of the men in a hospital uniform at half-mast was brandishing an impressive banana for the pretty attendant, who was also undressing and nodding with stark enthusiasm. Dr. F burst in on them, his mouth full of curses and admonitions. Then he mopped his brow and began to unbuckle his belt.

"I'll show you who's running this universe! Now you've both been very very bad. And you know what happens when you're bad ..."

Groans of madness and pleasure ensued. Nurse Kookaloco at last appeared with a long aversion-therapy stick and shocked all of them without compunction.

"Oober Mann?"

Oober Mann looked up from his cryobed. Perspicacity Vauxhall was speaking to him. The sheep and ducks in the ward were also staring at her, much to the consternation of a visiting border collie and his duck-tolling retriever acquaintance.

"You must listen very carefully, Mr. Mann. There is not much time."

"Perspicacity! I thought you died in the desert ... with the rest of the National Geographic Society ... my heart was a briar patch full of blackberries ... and when I awoke, they were tarty again ..."

"Mr. Mann ... you're blithering ... they are drugging you. They don't want you to reach the resistance forces ... you are too important ... and it is terribly dangerous."

"It's so good to see you again, Perspicacity!"

"But during this crisis how can you possibly lie there, twiddling your thumbs? Or is this the show of policy we are to expect from Oober Mann?"

"Ms. Vauxhall, regrettably, I am clamped down."

"Right. Time for the trusty old Orkney technique!"

Perspicacity stared more intently, suffusing the room with an emerald haze. The border collie and duck toller responded at once, leaping up to paw in the correct access code and activate the release mechanisms on the side of Oober's cryobed. The bed opened up. He was stiff and soggy, but free.

"Perspicacity ... thank you."

"I wish I could do more, sir. The cosmos owes you a great debt. But if you want to see me again, I advise you not to take any of those pills in your racing-stripe jumper. Otherwise, you'll never make it to your next magical adventure."

"Perspicacity, that night in Capri ..."

"Please ... Mr. Mann, that was just a one-off."

"I see."

"Now Mr. Mann, listen carefully. Down the corridor to your right, you will find a door marked DO NOT OPEN. You must go through that door and make your way down. And once you are outside, watch out for the weather balloons standing guard. I couldn't bear to see you smothered by one of those ghastly things! And presently, you have been forcibly hospitalized on Ninnynana Island. There's nothing for it but to swim to the opposing shore. Once there, you must make your way through each checkpoint and right to the edge of the Erogenous Zone. And mind the aquacukes. I will fetch someone from the Akita Inu to wait for you there."

"I don't know how to thank you!"

"Thank me by living a delicious life, Oober Mann! And at all costs, avoid treatment, and perhaps one day I shall come to you again. Now, run along smartly! Run, Oober, run!"

When Dr. F. Scott Fitzgerald regained consciousness, he saw nothing outside the observation station but two cheery dogs and an empty cryobed. Down the corridor, the DO NOT OPEN door was flapping in the wake of a mysterious poststructuralist wind.

"It's been a torturous day, hasn't it? I'm Perspicacity Vauxhall. Good night."

CARBON
HARBOUR

One had only one's self to blame for catastrophe, with Science concentrating its huge forces on bettering the human lot. (Had he not read, only the week before in a newspaper, of a new medicine which would prolong human life? Men might live to be two hundred years old, unclothed perhaps and unfed since there would be so many, but Science took care of details when they arose (had he not read only this week that very palatable foods were being made from seaweed, coal, and cotton? and clothing: the same article said that very durable cloth could be made from soy beans, meat extracts, and vegetable products). Two hundred years old! and, as he understood it, alive.)

— WILLIAM GADDIS

That Slippery Phish

The Age of Aquarium began in the most ordinary manner. There is no adequate vocabulary to describe such environs – no manual to outline its means of production or mode of manufacture in detail. What we are able to grasp was already conceived long ago, and by putting such an unspeakable monstrosity in practice, we only ensure the most overwhelming sense of disappointment. You, specifically, would be somewhat dorsalled to consider that these events about to unfold already happened a century ago. Suffice to say this is the Aquarium of our common era.

Long live the Age of Aquarium!

There are few private vehicles, and transportation primarily consists of accelerator trans that overlap service in a global network of cul-de-tracks. The rest is handled by lethargic little trolleys called lightcrawlers and larger conveyances called fastropods. Solar filtration and harvesting schemes leave the sky predominately grey, when it is not after dark. Also, *global* is a misnomer. There is no more global. The entire humming, gasping, belching network of trans is nothing more than a tasteless metaphor standing in for the human nervous system. Think of a destination and you are as good as there, at least according to continual verts, after a few customary shocks and jolts. There are no more cities, since there is no point in differentiating between this place and that place when they are more or less the same place with different coordinates. There are only coordinates, stops, stations, platforms, sections, subsections – why, there are more nervous systems than ever before!

Long live the Age of Aquarium!

However, there is one less human nervous system. Through an algaeic mist, on account of circumstances that are unclear, a man of some girth took a tumble from a fastropod and bounced off the unforgiving chardmac below. By a coincidence decidedly uncanny, this man was an interstitial diplomat who landed upon a line dividing two independent jurisdictions known, respectively, as Insulate V and Insulate W. These short forms are not strictly accurate but since this is not a formal report, and for the sake of brevity these monikers should work just fine, and at the same time save us a great deal of paperwork. So, let us accept what is divulged with a pinch of petrodium and act as if we have the appropriate permissions to even indulge in such hearsay.

For enthusiasts of that slippery phish called history, what is referred to as *paperwork* is an assortment of tangible data razed into an inexpensive substance derived from corn called papyrlose. Now and then, talk of a papyrloser society will crop up, but any such notion is quickly and mercilessly quashed. Also, there is more paper substitute than ever before. One might consider these innumerable sheets to be the scales of that slippery phish called history, which is to say the building blocks, the very mortar of reality.

Long live the Age of Aquarium!

Of course, for the man bleeding upon the chardmac, nothing could be done. Out of nowhere, a throng could do no more than throng, other than offer its astonishing powers of random speculation. Had the man thrown himself from the quivering fastropod, or had he been pushed? The man looked out of shape and rather clumsy. Probably, he had little to live for. One highly agitated fellow pointed out that people were always falling out of fastropods these days. All in all, blue and blue made bloor. Others nodded. There was no shortage of foul play, in their experience.

Two people kept their distance. There was an air of refinement to this pair, although that probably had as much to do with the cut of their organic cloth as with the general bearing and carriage of their persons. They stood at the periphery of the bromidic throng – man and woman – rather stiffly. The woman looked dismayed and the man appeared remorseful. They watched the crowd grow. People did not clump like a collection of netherhair and both the man and the woman were nearly ashamed of having thought so at the same time. The throng thronged, shoving and elbowing. Everyone wanted their share of the oxydent. Before long, there was an announcement:

"He's not breathing."

It would not have been wise to come any closer. The man and woman had no wish to be seen together, particularly not at this instant. However, a confidence or trouble shared can lead to more than intimacy between two people. They could neither deny nor forget this experience that had created a unique understanding between them. In many ticks to follow, could they say it had not drawn them closer, to be united by a similar feeling? Arm in arm, they had observed the limitations of mortality, and this kind of experience is at the roots of all mysticism. Then, at the same time, V and W arrived. Then the trouble started.

A Show of Hands

Mr. Quartz took his time at the sheer window, hands concealed in greatcoat. They were not the hands of a lugscrew or wingnut and this perhaps was prick enough to his conscience to keep them out of sight. There was no shame in this, of course, and it was highly probable that the condition of his hands was the least worry of the madding mob in the Object factory below, for whom the slightest slip of attention would indubitably prove fatal. No, it would be best to remain motionless at the window and to that degree warmly invisible. According to the mean of average surveys, it was perfectly natural that his thoughts should return to the previous evening spent in the company of Ms. Lazuli, who so dutifully produced the promotional sinjects necessary to ensure that every last ecodo was utilizing an Object sprouted from one of his many fallows. She had made her start in pulse trading, and had quickly hit upon a handsome biorhythm before grasshopping over to Bildung Endustries.

Mr. Quartz had been pouring a second round of Jungian sap when he observed her studying his near-to-immaculate hands. It would have been an unruly imputation for her to remark upon their quality at this time, to point out, for example, that their apparent lack of ambition ran so contrary to the amplitude of their owner's ambition, it was almost a source of mirth to see them. Ms. Lazuli, possessing both refined instincts and tact, elected to instead refract her attention back upon her own well-cloven outfit from Simony Sordido, commenting between sips of sap on the state of dress in this age that left so little to the imagination. Mr. Quartz had nodded politely, although his hands had shrunk back, seeming more exposed to him than the scarcely concealed charms of his companion, who was certainly no fool. She had waited patiently until the arrival of this second round of sap to cast him the blipvert for the new line of Objects. He had eagerly inhaled her latest project.

One man, perhaps a lugscrew or wingnut, had stood motionless in a corner facing a wall. Another had remained on the floor in the fetal position. Then the emerust Object had wafted into the room and they had begun to stir, rising as if from a deep slumber. Caught in the frustrum of bright cartoonish waves emanating from the Object, they had stripped out of their brutal Werkenwear and found one another. Kissing and stroking and gripping one another to this degree was not possible without the presence of the Object affiliated with Bildung Endustries. The blipvert narrative had been very much the same for the attractive lodger upstairs, who was by no means immune to the Object's mesmerizing pulsations and musky scentograms. She had peeped over a railing, lost to the pleasure of these osmotic price points. At once, their neighbours had begun to gather and rub themselves against the walls outside, longing only to be near the new emerust Object they did not yet possess.

Then, as the Object switched into primal regression mode with a series of slaps and smacks, Mr. Quartz had shorted his neurchan to address Ms. Lazuli, who had welcomed his laudatory effusions with the grace befitting any woman worthy of his hand. They had fallen upon her anti-grav memory sprattress, not so much due to overwhelming desire but more so from an obligatory sense of propriety, since neither wished to admit to the other that their desire might wane at the cusp of an encroaching philosophical turn that would have rendered them as helpless as the subjects they supplied with stemufactured dreams and sensations. Their arrangement was non-binding and, to a large degree, mutually exclusive, but would that understanding ever permit their separate entities to discover a fresh foundation and therefore the intimacy upon which to establish an exchange of intellectual properties?

Mr. Quartz cast this notion aside, the kernel of which contained the schematic for entirely new machinery to subroutine by. Naturally, he was conscious of being observed by a towering presence in the form of Bildung Endustries. It was simply a law of nature that she should feel drawn to him, and he to her, while a dumbfounded populace slaved over Object after Object. Then, right before a recent failstorm she had remarked upon the pristine beauty of his hands and, for the first time in ages, he had turned red with shame and felt a pressing need to hide their smoothness. He had promptly feigned an unspeakable fatigue, and Ms. Lazuli had just as quickly forgiven him for losing the thread of their frenetic, albeit mechanical, activity.

Mr. Quartz was jarred out of his vague reverie as he caught one of the wingnuts glancing up at him with a curious expression on his face. Mr. Quartz walked away from the window, hands still in greatcoat.

All Thumbs

Filch Gibbons reached around for the toggler and eased it into position. He had anticipated this instant for one year to the day, and now that he was activating the device with numb fingers and considerable aplomb, he felt empty of purpose. He was alone, having stepped into the vast connexionless void beyond the reach of all those ardent followers who would find purpose in what he was doing, in what he had nearly done, and in what he would one day do. Likewise, Filch found purpose illuminating their otherwise blank faces. The weight of his whole familial history rested upon the swipe of his thumb. His wife never would have asked him openly, nor their daughter, who only stared up at him with unnerving comprehension, but he felt the weight of them just as he felt the weight upon their shoulders. Generations of disenfranchised ghouls were waiting for his fingers to formulate their sweeping defence. Filch knew he was no hero and accepted the frequent nightmares of scorched and mangled limbs that faded away with merely a ghostly word from those generations who had gone before. He had squeezed his daughter's shoulders before leaving, knowing full well that she could not be far down the roster in accordance with their arcane system of randomization. He knew that her thumb would not be very far from achieving a similar outcome, and yet, their lives could not change what really *ought* to go down.

"Love you," he had said.

Nothing Can Go Papple

Snoop Parker leaned back in his wobbler and clasped his hands behind his head. Perspicacity Vauxhall did not return his smile at first. He put his feet up beside her and she shoved them away.

"Hey, Cass, you ain't still sore, are ya?"

"I thought you were all washed up."

"Are you spanking my wank? I'm escorting the illustrious Perspicacity Vauxhall, host of Sleevee's most cranked-to sprout by those between the ages of twelve and thirty-nine, to the next disaster zone!"

"You left out the starmitzvah cluster. Plus ultra, I'm now with BBC Omniverse. And you know, I *was* looking forward to this trip."

"Well, for me, things are brightening."

".Were they so bedridden?"

A shadow crossed his face, and in spite of his heavy smearsucker suit, he appeared to shiver visibly.

"A friend of mine called Muffsnuffle ..."

"Ah yes, the company you keep!"

"I should say, he *was* a friend of mine."

"You had a falling out with him?"

"He fell all right. All the way into the crisper."

"O dear. What happened?"

"That's what I intend to find out."

"You aren't planning another hatchet job by any chance?"

"Depends. If they had anything to do with what happened to Muffsnuffle ..."

Welcome to Putridworld, the hottest destination for the most
molten in alternative pollution fantasies. Everything is perfectly
safe and nothing can go pear-shaped. Indulge in those filthy
compostables you have always landfilled. Everything is perfectly
safe and nothing can go pear-shaped. Enjoy the most decibellacious
experience with the latest in ferti-spread and breed-thwacking
technology. Everything is perfectly safe and nothing can go papple.

They Were All Like That

"Hello. I'm Mr. Galliard."

"Yes, I know. We've already met."

"O. You are ... Ms. Garamond."

"Yes."

Mr. Galliard went straight behind his partitioned portion of Bildung Endustries and did not emerge again. Ms. Garamond stood in the corridor, uncertain what to say. It was hardly important, although she had met Mr. Galliard last week. Of course, she was not the only woman to come and go, although she was surely not the least memorable. Later that evening, over dinner, she prodded Mr. Garamond about Mr. Galliard, and he did not know much more. The man in question was on contract and had arrived a few months ago after some vague disappointment in another place. Since their work did not overlap in any way, there was not much point in knowing more, was there? Ms. Garamond shook her head.

The following Humpday, she unlocked the door to find Mr. Galliard studying her bust. She cleared her throat, and he withdrew his hand. *I am not going to touch anything.* This was the thought that passed between them.

"That's Berlioz."

"Yes."

"Reconnoisseured. It must have mossed on me."

"Very fine. Not that I know much about cornography."

"I don't mind his hair. Or his eyes."

For the rest of the day, as much as possible, they remained on opposite sides of the edamame wall between them. There was a thick silence. Why more than before, she could not imagine. Now and then, there was the sound of rapid refracking or blit twiddling on either side of the wall. It was like that old fable about a man and a woman on either side of a wall. She went over to Mr. Garamond's desk and snapped her fingers in front of him to get his goat.

"What's that story, that myth about the guy and girl talking through a wall?"

"Meck. Aw, they were all like that."

Later, as they were gathering their things to go home, she noticed that Berlioz had turned his head as if he were listening closely. She peeped behind Mr. Galliard's partition quickly, but he had already left. That night, she dreamed that she was still at Bildung. She was talking to Mr. Galliard, except he was not listening and had his head turned away. She kept talking, raising her voice until she was shouting at him but he would not respond. At last, she reached for his shoulder and shook him, but his head rolled onto the floor and what she saw was not his head but the bust of Berlioz, grinning up at her.

She woke up with a start, sweating.

The Nature of the Anteroom

Kanadakan fussed gingerly with his herringbone knees before taking a seat in the anteroom. A long confusing name was undulating upon the lips of the assistant examiner but it was not Kanadakan rising like a phoenix from those inflamed tonsils. Everyone was snivelling or hacking as usual. The surrounding gilt structures were painstakingly suffused with a cool winter palette as afternoon turned to evening and everyone in this antagonistic space dreamed sadly of brushing elbows with missed opportunities. He was not entirely unmoved by this melancholy atmosphere but his frayed edges were bolstered by years of experience in the waiting department. His particular problem was less severe than most, unless he had forgotten the dull pain that comes and goes; or was his memory the main problem after all?

Kanadakan did not recall anything beyond this overwhelming sense of weariness, and his resistance to hypocritical hypnodermics was noteworthy in a number of journals. He was not even sure if this waiting room had caused his weariness, or if it was merely hereditary and therefore a statistical risk of malignancy. Kanadakan lacked a finished interior and his frail constitution behaved like a medium for the projected aspirations and disappointments of encroaching organisms. Presently, he could do anything but give his full attention to Mr. Juventus, who was doing his utmost to cover up a small hole in his chest. The hole was an inch and a half in diameter, and through it the toned flexing of the gyrobic instructor was visible to the naked eye.

This situation changed the nature of the anteroom, since those in attendance found it a source of amusement and enjoyed an inexplicable thrill whenever they glimpsed a panting sweating lump through the hole in Mr. Juventus – whenever he raised his right hand to scratch the tip of his nose or to mop his perspiring pate. Kanadakan would only deign to ogle the instructor's disciplined flesh with a dismissive air although he fancied himself the most worthy of her reciprocal affection, at least among these quaking gawkers in the waiting room. On occasion, he nodded off and for a few ticks dreamed she was doing warm-up whirls directly in front of him, where the coffee plant currently resided.

Then he would wake up and find himself leaning on the shoulder of Mrs. Ruteborsch, if not steadily drooling into her lap instead of a favourite pillow. She was used to this by now. In fact, she would miss him if he were gone! She tousled his dark locks, warming her hands. She had poor circulation and this exchange, like so many in the anteroom, was simply a marriage of convenience. Kanadakan stared at an empty chair across from him. His dream had reminded him of Ms. K, the woman who sometimes occupied that chair. Then Spindr would claw his temples, suffering another attack of psychical apoplexy. A tranquilizing jonquil freshener would be released and Spindr's mouth would close and his eyelids would grow heavy. It never failed to startle Kanadakan that Spindr could pick up his thoughts, even from the other side of the anteroom. Ms. K was troubled by a mysterious ailment and after each consultation she would sink back into that empty chair and stare off into space.

Although he did not entirely care for her, Kanadakan could identify with her insoluble problem and had even begun to imagine they had oodles in common. Sometimes she looked at him in such a way that he suspected their only alternative was to run away and seek joint treatment together. He had thought about this a lot, and Spindr had sensed this and had exaggerated each unexpressed intention to the whole room. One time, Ms. K drew Kanadakan aside, smiling faintly, and said that she should really come to a decision, either way. He did not even know her full name but he took her at her word. They seldom spoke but they were hatching a brilliant escape plan.

At this point, Kanadakan had made the acquaintance of a Mr. Pétér who had taken the empty chair on the other side of Mrs. Ruteborsch. Mr. Pétér had said nothing at first but then he started making casual remarks about the stolid figure of Mrs. Ruteborsch. She appeared to enjoy all this indirect attention and informed Mr. Pétér that if he so decided, he could lay his head upon her lap, provided Kanadakan was not using it at the time. Mr. Pétér's nostrils had flared at this suggestion, leading him to believe she was being treated for a rare case of imbecility and this was the reason she was always smiling. Ms. K looked extremely anxious whenever Mr. Pétér talked with Kanadakan through Mrs. Ruteborsch. She would flush a deep maroon and look as if she wanted to fade into the greige wall behind her.

Kanadakan had also observed that Mr. Pétér spoke of Ms. K with an air of possessiveness, as if discussing his rare butterfly collection, which he often did. He would begin by describing the larvae of certain Lepidoptera and advocating their sensible diet of arugula, and then abruptly draw a comparison to the case of Mrs. Ruteborsch. Such analogies made no sense but they were encouraged by the waiting room attendants, since similar linguistic horseplay had been found to be beneficial in several studies.

Whenever Kanadakan stole a glance at Ms. K, Mr. Pétér would slap his hollow temples or bury his face in his trembling hands. On occasion, Ms. K would permit herself the luxury of an intimate snarl in order to display her animal magnetism, and in response Mr. Pétér would growl ferociously at Kanadakan, in the manner of a testy bull about to gore his youngest rival in the same field. Truth be told, Kanadakan had other troubles and was not wholly interested in the other people waiting, although now and then their peculiar sideshow provided a few ticks of distraction.

Deep in the Doldrums

Charmdeep waded through the excess runoff of the Rehashing Core, taking great care to sidestep the pressure sanitizer that had nearly taken off his foot only a month ago. The task of adequately clearing the Doldrums of waste beyond reparation took a modicum of concentration, leaving time not even to twiddle one's new moustache, an attribute warmly commented upon by his colleague Emo Van den Enden. Otherwise, Charmdeep was not one to keep his musings to himself. On the contrary, his direct application of Spewell's philosophy to existence seemed of the utmost importance and worth promulgating at the next best opportunity. Emo would nod and listen with some barely perceptible inkling of what one might call respect, provided that the suggestion did nothing to undermine the apparition of his authority.

This philosophy offered provision for mutual equanimity, so long as the chain of command was observed, either in life or in the sector of waste renewal they were responsible for. The duration of a single day between their hirings had given Emo the advantage. He was therefore in charge, and he knew within his innermost being that someone had to take charge, lest chaos ensue. It was a fine upstanding thing for Charmdeep to quote the great thinkers and to draw attention to the equality of every man, provided that his logic drew no dangerous corollary to their respective pecking order in any branch of the Doldrum department.

These philosophical outpourings were only troubling because Charmdeep's perception of his own self-actualization suggested that a whit of happiness might elude himself, Emo Van den Enden. Emo liked nothing better than to remind Charmdeep of the stench of their first days together, and that, in spite of their becoming accustomed to inhaling all kinds of particulates and nearly looking forward to their vision-inducing properties, he had been the first to get in up to his elbows. Charmdeep had assured him that if this stench was what he sought, then he would no doubt find it in every corner of his life.

The Last Man

It was the game they enjoyed with gritted teeth. Jet held Kink's throat in a death-grip and watched her body enlarge with effusive ardour. Her opponent had handled herself Kink without even remotely considering handsnaking. Her open request had been answered within fractions of a nano, and after perusing a sizable array of schematics, she had at last selected a personalized template compatible with Jet's profile. She locked her thighs around this new victim handled Lurk as he pressed her head beneath a globulous murk. The terrain was voxelized from a rusticated industrial grid and suggested the *bad* part of town. Jet had not interfaced with a repobate in months but much as the previous time, she found herself crawling back to one. She squirmed and blew bubbles of raw desire through the runoff.

"*Glug glug ...*"

Lurk let go of her pussy collar as a murder of prefects appeared and began to thrash his body with refreshed bludgels. He quivered and spewed out a wicked hemospray. Kink watched the bludgels striking his abdomen and back, mesmerized by their steady unrelenting rhythm. Jet glared back at her numbly as the prefects vetted his slinky coverups and exposed his shivering cameltoe.

"Told ya not to try me at *DominEx 6* ..."

"O tarn!"

The prefects formed an orderly queue and were at once swift and masterful. Jet tried not to blubber as Kink produced an elongated silencer and calmly screwed it into position. Then she prodded Lurk's cheek and induced him to suck on it. He became docile and dutifully swallowed the cold oily silencer. Kink grinned as the bludgels made contact with his skull. Lurk fell limp and instantly sank into the globulous murk. Then Kink gave a challenging wink to the circle of prefects.

"I've still got one man left."

This Close

She was beautiful but not beautiful enough. Actually, Puss Lichen was very beautiful, but she was not quite the right shape for Voxelwood. Her little sister was already a child star with a sizable part in a feature insert based upon the latest nymphette series to "capture the imagination" of the whole universe. Zygo had not ingested or clystered it yet but he had heard nothing but wonderful things. The server in question at Lonely's must have found it a relief to be let off the hook as family beanwinner. Also, her little sister's success was likely to eventually lead to a part in a local series, perhaps even one about some racy aquacukes. Whenever she spoke of her little sister, her eyes lit up with admiration and her teeth clenched together into a powerful smile. And whenever her little sister tagged along, strangers would wave or bow or even curtsey, paying homage to someone who had the good fortune to be a part of the best idea in existence.

Indeed, it must have been something to have been "this close" to being "it," even for the time it took to infuse that manta ray deluxe edition. At the instant of shuddering ecstasy, Zygo drank in her look of bemused enjoyment, a look that is more common than you may believe, and did not call out the name of her little sister, which she accepted as a gallant courtesy. And when he showed her the door, he made it quite clear that he found her extraordinarily beautiful. It was the franchise he did not want. Nor the people following them.

Slanks in Molten Pink

Chalcedony tapped silver nails against a public console, looking around anxiously for any sign of Gemma. Then she regained her composure, confident and swelling in the possession of a new pair of sludgers. She scanned the sea of grubby coats for a glimmer of molten pink. Gemma's sleepy eyes. Figures milled past, laden with filtered polleganda. Chalcedony covered her nose and mouth, fearful of her usual allergic reaction. Then her eyes were covered. Gemma held her throat beneath a ripple of nickeldusters.

"My love ..."

"Sputter up!"

Chalcedony visibly winced and shied away from the lips slowly absorbing her right temple. But she did not withdraw, preferring to flounder in the grip of those gloaming arms.

"What now, my little limpet?"

"I am beyond treed."

She was not.

"The Euphonium?"

"Scramit."

"The Muster Station?"

"Zpst."

"The Arcades."

"Ubi."

Chalcedony tapped the console impatiently, attempting a fretpsych, wanting nothing more than the feedless notion to strike the averted sconce of her companion, to shake that beautiful diffident head and draw its attention to her bran new sludgers. *Look at them, simply look at them,* she was indicating with every inclination of her knees and neck. Gemma instead fixed her attention upon some hovering junkets that bellicosely compressed and sealed their cargo before completely dissipating without warning.

"Moto, slank."

Gemma bared freshly honed incisors before picking up the slack of Chalcedony's lead.

"Slither you go, me go."

Mental Plan

Klouk Meek trailed along winding life-friendly corridors after the brisk heavy strides of Senior Intravenous Manager Apothokár. Flagging, and struggling to catch his breath, he knew the nominative fates were against him, just as they had been since infancy, because it was by no means easy to climb a well-greased company ladder with a name like Klouk Meek. Even the dashing earlocks he had cultivated had not led to a raise in salary. In addition, his degeneration levels had, if anything, only increased in the past quint. The hunch of an antique clerk had crept into his back and the gradual immobility of a stool-less greeter had starched his bones. His fine silver hairs and whiskers had slowly unshocked into ghostly white wisps. It had only taken one pass over for promotion to automatically suggest him for a number of successive passes.

It particularly smarted that his original trainee, Findley Blunt, had reached a position of authority Klouk no longer dared to imagine reaching. The post of Emergency Ancillary Assistant would, alas, never be his. He could feel this fact sinking into his greeterly bones as he just barely negotiated the brief opening in the security field before it fizzled closed behind him. He followed the steady clomp of Apothokár's boots in the manner of a pointer keen on the scent, nose-first, into the subsidiary duty coop. He was just settling into his side of the hutch when the shadow of Sky Sapphire crossed his unassuming person. Ms. Sapphire had a rare dietary disorder she attributed to her constant consumption of Halibutella frigid dinners. She had tried to quit them cold furkey on several occasions but the unique mystery additives kept her falling off the phish wagon. Whatever Klouk might opine on these matters, he kept to himself.

"Morno, Meek."

"Morno."

"I am dead waste. I was here all night again."

She began to unzombie her eyes with white knuckles, shedding sleep upon Klouk's cluttered hutch. She blinked and looked up, on the verge of weeping. Klouk shook his head, instinctively warding off another scene.

"I am just so squeegeed. I need the credits though."

"Why don't you come over here for a change, I mean?"

Klouk pointed at the empty insets surrounding his hutch.

"They ... aren't coming back?"

"It's a long story."

At this point a fatuous tear rolled down her pasty cheek and landed upon Klouk's procedurals. He produced an initialled handkerchief and dabbed away the wet spot, showing as much concern as he could dredge up.

"Why don't you lie down on your company cot for a spell?"

"O sure, and scrape down three more servings of Halibutella, you mean!"

"Sounds like someone didn't have their power nap."

"Meek .., maybe I will go lie down."

Klouk watched her depart with the kind of aversion only potential attraction can bring. She was unquestionably pretty. What is more, her scarcely cultivated inner beauty was greatly enhanced by the company mental plan she was locked in to, which had a provisional clause for company spouses who did not qualify due to extraneous and often inexplicable circumstances. He would not mind being on mind-leave. Of course, he would have to work quickly, because any time soon she might finally earn enough credits to depart for Absurbia, as she often promised. Klouk felt a sudden itch and had a small inkling it was a mercenary streak within him he had never noticed before. The exercise of it gave him a funny feeling. For one thing, it tickled.

Nothing Blits the Spot Like Readimedi Mealies

Werner Gig removed each fingerless and blew upon his much benumbed hands. He had been tending Wind Pharm 207818-072008A for most of his life and it showed in his cracked and scarred digits. He chewed some dried fava beans thoughtfully, spitting out an excess of GenesmaX. As a young man, Werner had known surrounding fields that were rife with beans and sprouts and corn, before the Infestation of Fiver-Niner. He had filed the application himself to order a shipment of terminator seeds. After that, the cockadas scarcely bothered to come round, although there was nothing to eat either. He had long ago given up on breeding phishes. Werner had discovered it was necessary to order Readimedi Mealies, and like the other pharmers, he was soon hooked. *Because nothing blits the spot like Readimedi Mealies* ... Thanks to these compressed nutrafusions, he expected to live out the duration of his contract without putting up much of a fuss when his own termination date arrived. He watched the turbines turn in the stellar wind and creakingly crank out a meagre supply of nutrient paste, and wondered whether his own stool could nudge along the growth process. But due to the amount of GenesmaX in his system, he expected not.

No Minors

Two waterboarded cases marked Emerust Endustry were dropped heavily in front of the hop.

"Two for the Enviral Solutions Conference."

"Name?"

"Minor."

The hop inclined his head toward a sign on the corny wall that read NO MINORS and then winked, coughed, and clicked his heels together. The man took the hint and handed over a gigasmic novelty cheque fashioned out of the finest chum. The woman clung to him and he to her, flushing. They felt like king and queen for a day.

"Ahem, it would appear that your pentsuite is prepared. If you are in need of any sensual aids ..."

"That won't be necessary."

"Very good, sir."

They hovered up to their pentsuite and admired the festoonery. They greenly compensated the hop for his efforts in portaging their cases. The hop scurried away, stifling a giggle.

"Reminds me of an old sidekick o' mine."

"Past is past."

"It was a long time ago ... and a few dimensions yonder."

"I need a rinse."

Marcel watched his companion unsnazzle her Feltcro ensemble and allow it to disintegrate. He had seen her do likewise a thrillion times in the genrebusting arteryclogging pantspopping threequel to *The Towel of Turin*. He felt a wicked shudder of desire. As she stepped into the translucent corpsbidet, he was reminded of the similar five-dimensional scene in *XXX-O-Planet*. He removed everything and followed her into the cleansing spray. She chortled at the ferocity of his grip.

"Holy Smyrna!"

"It is the only way ... to repopulate ..."

"Stamenish. Just don't stop."

"An abnormal distribution is the only way to achieve the bell curve ..."

"Mmm ... tetrapack my quincunx ..."

"Ah ... my hypersuperlative peach!"

Their evening progressed savagely from wall to wall and floor to ceiling in this fashion, much to the instinctive chagrin of other guests.

The Staring Contest

Insulate W got the call first. A traffic finagler was about to transfer the whole dreadful business to Insulate V when her superior asked what all the commotion was about. In response to the short report, Merkin Labouche hesitated, stroking his chin and toying with his mustachio. At last, he rested one hand upon the finagler's left shoulder and gave it a few squeezeballs for good measure.

"Nothing to worry about, eh, Klamm?"

"My name is Kettleman, sir."

"It's a bit close for comfort."

"Why don't we give this thing to V?"

"Kettle – this is not some dumbbunny we can fire into suckage. A man lost his life! And we wouldn't want V to say we wedgied the issue and dropped it into their lap because we weren't up to lickspittle. No, we wouldn't want that."

"Perhaps V is closer – to the person in question."

"Let's not be hasty. No, you must go at once!"

"Must it be?"

"It must be!"

However, one of the ancillary finaglers who was not privy to this exchange (and suspected as much) chose this instant to take the initiative. In spite of his virtual anonymity, he had been beavering away at a personal ameliorative technique called Notice This and had fallen almost entirely under its influence. According to his intraguru, this was a perfect opportunity to get his superiors and peer group to Notice This. Based on this startling insight, without warning, he dispatched the appropriate situation codes to Insulate V.

Deep in the cantankerous belly of V, a respective double swore under his breath. His supervisor, Verva Ballot, began to massage his neck and shoulders. It was standard policy to work out any tension before delving further into any subject worthy of examination.

"Now what is the matter, Looney?"

"There is a problem in our subsection. Although, if you ask me, W is probably just flutzing this whole mess off on us, as usual."

"Mess? What mess?"

"O, some razorwit fell out of a fastropod on our liminal. And there's going to be paperwork, and if there's anything I can't stand, it's piles and piles of paperwork!"

"Looney, if it happened on our liminal, then we have to handle it."

"Correction. W should have handled it."

"And now I am sending you to handle it."

"But Verva, how about we wait and see ..."

"I am your superior and I will not ask twice!"

"Yessir."

"And Looney."

"Yes?"

"Tread carefully."

When the two identical utilitrans arrived at the scene, they nearly crashed into each other. Naturally, Dent Looney, who was not having the best night, leapt out first and raised his fist and released a steady stream of verbotenisms at the utilitran belonging to W. Ignoring this crude and careless introduction, Alma Kettleman hopped down from the controller's side and removed her helmet. At once, Looney was silent. In fact, he was knobsmacked.

"I am here for the body."

"_."

"W can take it from here."

"Wait ... uh ... no!"

"No?"

"No."

Their conversation continued in this crayward fashion for a long time before they worked out what had happened. They both had instructions to retrieve and process the body, and although they were not exactly unwilling to surrender it to another administration, they could not give way, lest either V or W lose face. In any case, the next step was beyond the immediate powers of either Kettleman or Looney and there was nothing to do but report the situation and wait for new instructions.

Meanwhile, Kettleman stared at the body and Looney stared at Kettleman, and the crowd stared at the pair of them.

Sweet Pea Party

"I trust this meets with your approval."

"It surpasses fedible!"

"I trust we'll make it through the night, uh ...?"

"Galvan Anode. Please call me Galvan."

"You could sure throw a sweet pea party in here, Galvan!"

"Still having doubts, Mr. Parker? The hot pods in the sweet pea suite are for your comfort and relaxation and, let us hope, amusement."

"C'mon, Snoop. Don't spoil the whole crop."

"Guess we'll wait right here for ol' Angio Dillgro to take us, dead or alive."

"Mr. Parker, surely you know that the Dillgro model and all associated subtypes of that invasive species of erotobot have been discontinued."

"Hear that, Snoop? Angio Dillgro is no more. And believe me, to hear that, I'm merry as mulch. Dillgro was a menace, and even to think of the kind of disgusting behaviour that name evokes, it's almost too much to bear. O he was suave and dashing and powerful, but there was something wicked within him that no one could explain away. And he's just the sort of dastard to haunt our feverish dreams, no matter how much they turn him off and take off his ... circplate ... running their fingers down his firm pickly abdometal and reaching for his reinforced millennial guarantee ..."

"Cass!"

"So Dillgro's gone, hmm? Well, good riddance, I say. Angio Dillgro had this bad bot thing going on, but you can hardly call that intriguing. Although when I first heard about the disaster at Putridworld, I was only sixteen and one sultry night ..."

"Well, I'll let you settle in. If you get tired of the Lathyrus Lubricus room, there's an adjoining chamber that boasts some outstanding honour tar, in case you're into roadwork ..."

Once he had left, Perspicacity dived headfirst into the largegantic tub of piping peas. Snoop leaned against the tub, running his hand through the buttery legumes, lost in thought.

"Safe to say we can rule out Anode as the main chipset."

"Funny how he seemed immune to my undeniable charm."

"Mine too. You don't think he's ...?"

"Could be. Could very well be."

"Hey, Cass, give the pea party a rest for a tick."

"Whatever you say, my little broodcomb."

Before Snoop could respond to her quick-witted junkclutch, more than enough of him was persuaded. With irresistible laughter, Perspicacity drew him down into the tub of piping peas.

Finger Lickin' Ficken

Kanadakan rubbed some mud from his herringbone leg with his thumb. It was hard to remember where he had acquired the mud, especially while still digesting anteroom food. He pushed aside the Denyrafoam container full of ficken, a new vegetative hybrid composed of everyone's former favourites. Kanadakan had in fact worked one summer in Fickenham, inspecting freshly slaughtered ficken during their incessant processing. Every time he saw a tub or container of ficken, he saw the grinning face of Munch and that quick flick of his wrist tossing another gushing ficken onto the conveyance device designed by Libertad Pharms.

Kanadakan sighed, thinking about the rows and rows of flopping and flapping ficken. His job had been to examine them after an automatic cleansing process for aberrations not in keeping with the standards that made Libertad a household anthem. As for the side effects, they had been deemed feasibly plausible from the start and given the green light anyway. The hormonal imbalances and mild contamination were considered minor tradeoffs in the face of a thrifty nearly tasty snack. What no one had foreseen was the madness that would ensue. Cases of Crazy Ficken Syndrome reached epidemic proportions. There were no early warning signs either. You'd be enjoying a fine repast of gourmet ficken and suddenly, out of nowhere, there would be nothing but hunting and pecking and pecking and pecking. In the wake of rampant CFS, one of the bright boys had proposed bringing back the omnivore program, but he had been laughed out of the Assembly. Ficken had licked the world feed problem, and ficken would continue to feed without scrutiny.

Kanadakan watched Mr. Pétér and Ms. K and Mrs. Ruteborsch, all tucking into their ficken and licking their fingers, their eyes gleaming. Even Mr. Juventus emptied his container, in spite of the gaping hole in his chest. Only Spindr abstained, knowing what Kanadakan knew by psychical proxy. At serving time, the second they rang the little bell, he would start to yell that ficken was fricken killing everyone, and before he had finished his rant, the attendants would be promptly sedating him. Kanadakan had been plotting his escape with Ms. K for some time but now, on account of Mr. Pétér's obsession with her, this seemed impossible. He might have taken Spindr with him, if only he weren't so damned noisy. Mrs. Ruteborsch would have had to ask everyone else along.

His last hope was Amethyst, a diminutive grey-eyed girl with oodles of energy. Too much energy in fact. During their graphing exercises, Kanadakan had noticed that she, like him, displayed the first warning signs of asymptotism. In other words, they both soared toward unreachable heights and sank into unspeakable valleys at the drop of a sprat. The exercises were designed to correct their sense of balance although Amethyst could not stop her mind from circling wildly like a crane in a tornado and Kanadakan would hear incommunicable arias that threw off the workings of his inner ear. Notwithstanding, they found marginal comfort in the overlapping margins of their charts. The oregano markings of the cerebral imagery were clear enough, and they imagined invisible sprites lurking in the peanut galleries of their brains, catcalling and heckling like an unpaid claque.

Kanadakan believed that he might be able to abscond with Amethyst on one of their good days. He had not dared to even consider this possibility while Spindr was alert and listening to his stray thoughts. Then one day, with the adverbial uniformity of most storied suddenlies, shots were heard. Kanadakan puzzled over whether the walls were made of seasoned wafer or carnival candy floss. They had seemed a sickly greige before but now they appeared refreshingly minty. *Ratatatat!* Liquorice gloves emerged through the candied cracks and tore at tufts of the wall. Faceless figures marched into the anteroom, each of them adjusting their creamy visors.

Kanadakan began to recall summers before the ficken factory, sipping ambrosial sporoda from beautiful glastic bottles while lolling around upon sprayed artificial turf. But the troupe of invaders headed straight for Kanadakan, jolting him out of his reverie. One of the attendants raced out from behind her desk and warned that such treatment of him would do nothing to becalm his flashes of megalomania, but she was lashed with a long red liquorice whip and held in place with a cherry nub. A pair of black gloves seized Kanadakan's shoulders, and another pair, his herringbone legs.

Whatever their reasons, Kanadakan knew they wanted him desperately enough to pay a visit to the anteroom and that capture meant freedom from this infernal tedium. In addition, he would probably fill a great void in their dull greige lives. As they struggled to strap him into the portamaniac, he glanced back at the sad grey eyes of Amethyst, who strove to remain perfectly balanced. She kept reciting her mantra ... *non troppo ma non troppo e cantabile ... non troppo ma non troppo.* Spindr had been shaken out of his sleep and was shouting again, since nothing could stop him from sensing the imminent loss of a psychical connexion. Kanadakan could still hear Spindr as he was sledded over clouds that felt like dollops of whipped cream brushing against his skin.

Kanadakan marvelled that he didn't give a fig where he was headed. They had probably heard he was looking for employment. Headhunters, their quarry found. That was how these things worked, wasn't it? Surely this was only the knob-twiddling stage. Kanadakan reminded himself not to breathe a word about that summer processing ficken. They probably wouldn't even ask. He was feeling rusty and a bit stiff after spending so much time sitting in the anteroom. He began to rehearse his replies, preparing for their imminent interrogation.

In Case of Emergency

Gamma Ornithost (soon to be Farouche) kicked the seat, something, anyone. The fastropod had stopped for what felt like an eternity. She caught herself looking at the blonde woman with the smoky grey eyes, who in return blew her an invisible kiss. It was true they often boarded at the same time of day, but surely that did not mean … It was quite simply not in the cards for her. Since adolescence, the youngest Farouche had been pointed out to her, although in those days it was little more than a joke. Everyone had known her plan to marry a famous quito player. Only now, it was no joke. In spite of her heart's ideals, the prospect of a modicum of luxury and comfort was not lost on Gamma. She had made her bed and was ready to lie in it. And it was not nothing and it would no longer be laughed at.

The blonde woman would not be laughed at either. Gamma sensed that from across the crowded conveyance. Her smoky grey eyes had lost their mirth and her mouth betrayed a hint of solemnity. Gamma looked around anxiously, cursing the inventor of fastropods. They were not moving and had not moved in ages. She shuddered, brushing away a hand that felt like a lizard. She stared down her challenger, a man in a zucch suit.

"Sorry. I thought you might need reassurance."

"Since when – what?"

"You looked awfully nervous."

"No, I am engaged."

"How terribly wonderful for you!"

The blonde woman was moving now, brushing people aside and then shoving and pushing and pulling and punching. Gamma became panicky. She tried to hide behind the wrapped fennel gown she had purchased for a bundle of carbon credits but the sea of passengers was parting. The blonde woman reached for Gamma's hand and pointed toward a nearby hatch that read KINDLY USE IN CASE OF EMERGENCY.

"Pistilscram. We have to go."

"That way? You must be kidding."

"No point in staying here."

"That's for emergencies!"

"This *is* an emergency."

"But I'm engaged!"

"Then we don't have much time."

The blonde woman tugged at the release lever and kicked open the hatch. Then she helped Gamma make her descent. A boy in the crowd saw his chance. He leapt upon the abandoned fennel gown and clutched it to his chest, breathing in its liquorishiness, not letting go.

Means of Disambiguation

"Leaving is not forever."

Ms. Lazuli's last words to him. Mr. Quartz weighed the phrase and then turned it over a few more times. What the ficken could she have meant? Of course, he could imagine what it looked like, and he knew to the tiniest niota what was expected of them. Notwithstanding, he had conducted this lonely and long-winded interior monologue with himself, wondering at her eagerness to put her powers into effect on his behalf. That is to say, to blow away cobwebbed gears in forgotten sectors of his endustry and attend to making them everything they could and should be. He was by no means indifferent to her generous willingness to help him. However, with every passing tick, he felt himself craving a kind of intimacy that would toss to the ground all such bargains, not as one placing a lien on the other but as two mighty rivers already flowing in the same direction and due to their own unspoken inclinations converging ... of course this was mere fable – such things belonged to other times.

This was akin to the flame that drew them together yet threatened to burn them up in the very ardour of itself. Mr. Quartz might have withdrawn from all his cosmic concerns, had their association not felt rife with possibility that was part and parcel with their growing closeness. He felt all the doors of his heart were open to her and she need only knock. In fact, he wanted her to knock. What is more, he willed it to happen, but beyond the ardent plea of a praying heart could not bring this into breath or being. To his own dark corner he whispered *come-to-me* over a thrillion times, and this illumined the drab surface of his accumulated wealth and roused his dormant energies. She had carte blanche where his intelligence and resources were concerned, and she was one of the few able to clutch the bottle that contained his personal genie. Would it not be a tiresome affront for them to settle for anything less when they clearly wished to be near one another? He wanted to enter all the rooms of the universe with her upon his arm or, what is more, with her leading him forward with passionate brashness.

Mr. Quartz realized he was preoccupied by her phrase upon parting and he knew that everything would be so much easier if he felt nothing for her. He could behave perfectly in any situation where he felt not a whit of emotion. In this case, he was like a peddler in an arcade, haggling and quibbling over circumstances and hedging bets upon his happiness with a more-than-fetching woman he both respected and admired. Was it such a tragic gamble, and if so, would he be soundly and resolutely rebuffed? With hands in pockets, he smiled to himself at the imagined prospect of losing everything. In the oddest way possible, he still expected to roll a quincunx. Is *leaving not forever*, then? He chewed over the phrase a few more times, almost second-guessing the decision he had reached. It seemed an utterance beyond all means of disambiguation known to him.

We Want Our Pickle Fight

Plugger sprawled on the faff, scratching. He was in a state of peyogic invitation. These were lean years, though carping on the fact did nobody a sheave of good. Winter was in the air and it was time to head back to town. Slowly and lankily, he got up and reached for his Laughing Stick. Then he tapped the Fritztune a bunch of times until their makeshift camp was full of music, or what they had of it.

then the other night
you were out like a light
and what a sorry sight
we want our pickle fight

The preaching assistants woke up first. Thad and Trudie Bittles each had a holy doctorate in something or other. They had been a chipper tag team working their way up the acolyte ladder when they opted for a sabbatical field study and, long story short, they were now making meatgrass stew in the heart of InteriorVille. Plugger had taken pity on them. He knew how one false step could lead to a mighty tumble. However, for the time being, he found their deathless affection and enthusiasm in the face of all odds rather disgusting.

Off and Dioxide

The Minors put down their cases in the foyer and gave their surroundings a decent scan. They eyed one another meaningfully, sharing the same spark of inalterable belief. She nodded and they unmagnetized their cases before reaching inside. Passing tourists, who perhaps expected to see a festive hat or a sublunar muff, were startled to note the appearance of a molecular scrambler in the hands of the man who was not impoverished in the area of unadorned suavity. His striking companion was no less lovely to behold, leaning over with a hint of unattainable mischief to lift up several cannicles of Desticide. Looky loos were at first way grilled to see two tubehypes in the immediate vicinity, and saw their chance to be inexorably involved. As they would have wished, they were the first to go, and that is to say, their target market of parlous pubescents were the first to be targeted.

Brat Wurst, feral celebrity, experienced the last murmur of his heart as each molecule that constituted his irritating snark was abruptly cracked and fried in a sizzling pan, which is the common metaphor for a proper scrambling. Duff Duff, who was not to be outdone by Brat, especially after their ambiguous ménage six hundred nanos ago, stumbled into the fray at the most provocative angle possible. Yet her eyes begged her audience to only tell her why they so hunted her, even as she became nothing more than a series of rent augmentations. The rest of their creaming fans rushed the effulgent glow of activity, and were atomically disorganized for their efforts. The media at once declared this goatsong of epic proportions and pathos. That was before the maturiteens, not to be outdone, charged the epicentre of explosive infamy. They were certainly not past the latest craze of being put down in the fashion of their split and subdivided progeny.

As for the grizzled permabronzed set who could warmly recall the temporal crossover megabomb *Minor Adjustments: How Informed Minorilfing Can Thripthruple Your Portfolio* and what it had done for them just beyond the omphalos of Aquaquay, they were eager to hop into bed with this multilevel afficionado and toss some more play credits into the fray, spurred on by the slim hope of catching the eye of the tastefully wayward daughter. She winked and beckoned, flipping them her trademark bird in the pose that had been linked with several erotic implosions among bemused orphan boys. They were expecting to see her reach for and swiftly assemble the Gomorrahizer 90053, just as she had done in *DayTrader/NightTrader VIII*.

"Gots gloxy, slink. How about we make it binding?"

"Off and dioxide, rhombie!"

She reproduced an antique blicer from a discontinued product line and laid into the first centagenerian in a criss-cross pattern. Bones snapped and frail limbs went sailing. He creaked all over, then soundly croaked. Her next suitor was his senior and, merely at a breath, withered. More generous gentlehusks doddered toward her and she dealt with every one of them in kind. As for her kinsman, Minor, he decided upon a surgical hammer. It took a great deal of repetitive force, but one by one, he breached the skulls of his handsome admirers without further gushing. Naturally, this activity drew the desensitized and disaffected in droves. At this stage, the Minors had no choice but to rely upon their cache of automatics. Each of them brandished two Blunderbusts before opening fire. Then there was no one left to deny the air of old-world charm in their use of antique weaponry. The populace could not keep themselves from experiencing the sizzling tubes over and over again and each audience member flooded his or her sensorium with enhanced visceral images of riddled, raddled bodies splattering to the bepuddled parquet floor. These heinous and meaningless acts had made everything meaningful again, at least for a few decinanos.

Lint Is Eternal

As an up-and-comer of unspeakable promise and a man waiting eagerly for promotion, he was certainly not going to waste a second arguing or splitting follicles about his assignment, although the summons had interrupted his one reprocessed meal of the day, encouraged by the ingestible manual as a primary source of nutripaste. It was entirely fitting that he should attend to this matter with the sense of urgency and decorum that was expected of someone with an eye on the future responsibilities that awaited him in those shiny bright squares he dreamed about. All the same, there was no need to paint glowing epaulettes upon these shoulders on the verge of undertaking a routine operation. He could be perfectly candid with himself. This business would take no more than a light touch and possibly a bit of shuffling here and there. So long as he stepped gingerly and took care not to swing any weight around, the trouble would likely sort itself out and all would be well.

In spite of his young years and junior station, he had been quick to ape the behaviour of his immediate superior, a nibblishly charming fellow named Schmaltz, not only by learning the fine art of constructing microcivilizations out of papyrlose and tufts of ignifod but by committing to memory and taking to heart the mind-forking phrases and verses that peppered the unexpurgated edition of the Book of Dither. In the mess or in the company of his peers, he would have deftly braziered any question of his being a staunch Ditherist. However, in terms of practical application, he found these mysterious and erratic fragments to be very useful, especially for helping to maintain a clear state of mind, no matter how dire the circumstances or how confusing the crisis. His saving grace, as a diplomatic officer by nature, was to drop the overzealous habits of Schmaltz, who never failed to cast his eyes upward, wringing his hands and citing the scattertext:

"For does it not say, and I quote Dither, verse 1026, fract 85, *Do as I say without delay or why then do you believe your head sprouted such ungainly ears?*"

Merfruit laughed churlishly at the expense of his superior, decidedly giving up on a project he had once started, namely the complete removal of lint from his otherwise spotless uniform. He persuaded one of the etching panels to reflect and smoothed his hair, grinning at the man grinning back at him.

"For does it not say, and I quote Dither, verse 4213, fract 49, *Just don't forget all things flow – all things are subject to impermanence – save for lint. Just don't forget this hiccup: lint is eternal.*"

Another Gaspberry Repoette

The notel is a focal point of our desire. Why? Because in a sea of cukecles and horizontal organizations we suffer from a case of avatardism more common than eviantcy. In a few cricks a pudgy neck is elongated into the property of a swan and necking can soon commence. The layered sexels of an obese *objet d'art* from an unknown epoch are smudged into almost nothingness. In fact, the mobility of our common era whizzes past at enough accelerated blits to invoke a functionary impulse. A virtual whim in the shape of a notel.

Nostalgia only extends far enough to recall a bipedal on the subject of not telling. It is the rundown place along the fiveway where no one tells what was what or what was that through brittle walls. Screams and silence are how we signal cravings to make things our own. We select imperatives flavoured with urgency. The mood setting is seedy and the level of desire is lightly seasoned with a dash of crime.

We have to meet materializes at the usual prompt where grassoline banners reveal their toggled vacancy. Appending are impromptu servitors in slashed constructs of clotted cloth and spontaneous combustions of sunken upholstery. From this angle beside the slippery pole, the notel is still inadequate. In a sensory surfeit, one of the larger boned servitors is puppeteered into an increasingly advantageous set of coordinates. Although our menu options are limited, we feature additional dissonance that smacks of quaint. Then, following a solid state refresh, the private settings load a pea-green wainscot lined with hidden activations.

Stamenish. One of the servitors is observing our interaction for quirm control and there is no console for scanning the convex side of that peachy rendering. The spadix of that short attention span is warming. After a collection of vitreous sprites in the shape of spirits we select a mode of retirement. It does not take many cycles to load our customized mapping system and accommodate the scale to suit our respective dimensions. This wing of the notel is in reality a hash table of short characters. Next quint, the plan is to store enough credits for a complete binary space partition until five-dim models are fully loaded.

On the other hand, once the glove is initiated, the phishbowl curves of the notel convince. We are positively swimming in purchased ambience at this time stamp, and the glow of an extinct neon sign flashes a name we can never tell across our blue-bodied essences. We pause. Beyond the vertiginous window we can make out valleys rich in voxels and the most fierce of fractal mounds. Then, in the middle of our preprogrammed pattern of overlap the pressing request of a third party ...

The notel is full of guests, strange or all too well known. The query holder enjoys initializing a jealousy sequence and this heightens the compatibility requirement. We set a delay to authorize access. We drop down a luminous texture in accordance with our linked scenario. The blindfold shimmers and the restraints gleam in the dimness of the room. The synthetic is soundly ripped and the improvised knuckle at the door to the room increases levels of moisture. Warning boxes may contain suggestiveness and gratuitous violence in a scripted loop of activity. The ticker quips our combined electricity as we double function for saline discharges. We relax our sore wrists and release our latest build of frustrated labour. It is imperative that we exercise our unbridled productivity in the notel, where it searches indefinitely for terms of honour, belonging, possession, and repossession.

The third party enters in the guise of a crazed lover gone vintage. The entered choice of gender is not amorphous. A bifold aperture is suddenly skewed. In the wake of the rethreshed visitor, octagonal columns flood the room and euphoric friezes form overhead, full of ornate voyeurs. This diagnostic augurs innocence. The little problem is subject to lag due to long-distance relations. The notel, as abstruse as a disembodied cornice in the presence of a caked mastaba. We reconfigure implants in our retinal fields. Cohesion of the notel is inversely proportional to our perception of its utmost limitations.

That is our mantra. The breakdown is sublime simulacra and appears in the pattern of a classic dissociative fugue. We assume familiar glossies and with self-same husks resume our frenetic exchange with verboten groans on the blower. Modal application for incremental encounters is gaining hits. Multiple nodes thread in concurrently. The lounge is packed and three of the guests have uninstalled the flitboost.

You are concurrently enjoying another gaspberry repoette from Inflexion Flashits. Subscribe to our lopping list and slink a quick one into our suggestable. Love us on RectAll.

Pond Love

"I so love them repoettes."

"Whey."

Sky opened her eyes wide and revealed to Meek a series of sunsets and dawns. Then she burst into tears. Then she inhalated a pair of pretty relaxers. Then she gaggled.

"Significant's off to New Venusia soon."

She plurped, eyes snirling. Now was the nanotick, if ever.

Just then, the lemming alert restored them to full panic mode.

"Drück!"

Sky burst into tears again. Everyone automatically filed past into the most serviceable partition of the Uranus Chamber. Meek took her hand and they fell into step with the others. Once there, she was lost among a crowd of new climbers who no doubt knew a mental plan when they nosed it. Meek breathed a light malediction before taking a seat.

"Mayhap we've all gone redundant."

"No, we are veritable phenoms ..."

"And persnickety pheramons ..."

"And snickery cessators ..."

"And we've all gone redundant."

Meek gristled, rather piquante to be twitblitting with Perdita Diamond. She was part damselfly, and although that presented no immediate problem in terms of Meek's ambitions, he was wary of the way the rustling sound of her wings rubbing together made him drowsy and susceptible to her slightest suggestion. Meek would readily admit to himself that he wanted nothing more than to be near her, and in the same exhalation feared his lack of anal appendages and accessory genitalia. Even the purchase of these must-haves was illegal and in the long run rather beyond his range of difficulty. Nor could Meek recall whether this branch of the organization permitted interspacial attachments. All the same, his eyes kept falling in the direction of her arresting abdomen. However, Senior Intravenous Manager Apothokár briskly snapped an electrified whip, startling him out of various squishions.

"Tag. I am gleeful to glam we have reached the umpteenth phase of our integration. You are all phenoms and pheramons doing everything possible to bring about hierogamy between Foreign Objects and Bildung Endustries. And I mean everything! Now, as you may know, during our crimping-up process, Tetrahedronicon moved on to partake in other stellar adventures. Best of luck, Tetra! So without further ado, I am pleased to introduce you to our new supervisor, Quincunx Sixty-Nine!"

Everyone applauded as a group of five watchful dots floated into the centre of the room. Perdita beat her wings with a hint of frenetic irony.

"Greetya, staff. There are going to be some changes. But first we will open the ceiling to your issues, questions, and concerns."

"More credits!"

Everyone burst into nervous laughter, including Quincunx Sixty-Nine. A few ticks later, the jokester was wholly disembodied.

"Any other issues, questions, or concerns?"

Meek stared grimly at Perdita's spreading oculars. Perhaps settling down would not be the narkiest thing in the nebula.

Lose Your Shirt

Chalcedony rushed past Atavista and recoordinated her stoaroute to follow LyriXstasia, with Gemma in tow. They found a breathing space next to Ta Gueule and established their scope. Chalcedony nodded sternly and Gemma let her coat open enough to reveal a molten scar along her inner thigh. Chalcedony had never seen a tail light before. She flushed with a touch of feeling before regaining her steely composure. Not that she would ever decide to have the glowing signal installed. But Gemma's eagerness to mark herself formed a silent agreement between them. Chalcedony knew what became of many of the tail-lighted and could not see herself following Gemma down that road. The hobbled, mangled spectres from her last visit to Splitzville still haunted her. But her eyes were following a hovering morph who was honing into their distress signal.

"Slanks."

"We want connexions."

"Dowry is hefty."

Chalcedony thumbed Gemma, who tried to look fierce.

"Cunning. Handle me Molar."

Gemma turned opalescent as they escorted her into a vacant trader that briskly whizzed shut. Chalcedony pressed Gemma down onto the blotter and linked each chain letter into position before any of them could change their mind.

"Lose your shirt."

"Molar Yank?"

Gemma screamed. The extractors continued to work their magic.

"You now have one life."

So Much Verdrängung Nowadays

When Snoop Parker woke up, it took a while for his smugness to dissipate. Then he realized that Cass was not with him. He put on an avocado overmuch and decided to check things out. As members of the media, they had sufficient access levels to take a peek here and there. However, he was not quite prepared for what he witnessed in the voydome. Perspicacity was being strapped down to the letter X by a strange man in a white coat.

"Cass, you know, I'm not sure this is working."

"Ha ha, Snoop! It's not what it looks like. Ha ha!"

Galvan Anode put his arm around Snoop Parker and nodded toward the man in the white coat.

"She's in good hands, Snoop."

"Why hello, I'm Dr. Foo Baz Quux. But you can call me F ... everybody does!"

"Why does she need a doctor?"

"Allow me, Galvan. What Mr. Parker does not know is that Ms. Vauxhall has agreed to help us test the latest in pleading edge technology. This is the ultimate in wish fulfillment, a pet project not yet ready for public release I like to call the Traumadunkeltagger. In fact, we couldn't strap her down fast enough!"

"There's your givehead, Snoop, in metazoom!"

"Forgive me if I don't polish my Pulverizer on the spot."

"Aphanisis is not at all uncommon after a bout of *Spaltung*. It's the shock, you see, after so much togetherness and unity, to suddenly find oneself flastered to some anonymod with all the warmth and charm of a Spartian canal. However, this is the cause of so much *Verdrängung* nowadays. It is my sincere hope that the Traumadunkeltagger will trigger and maintain various pulsions in the form of interactive flaydreams that will soon prove to be terrorpeutic. And all you have to do is step into the ChromaZone!"

"I don't know what you just said, but I don't like it, Doc. As for the latest in terrorpeutic pleading edge flaydreams, you can tuck them you know where."

"The latest in leading edge therapeutic daydreams, Mr. Parker. Whatever you do, please do not misconnote me. But I can see who wears the plantsuit in this investigative unit. Why don't you run out to the rehash with your pipsling and hide? Before Daddy comes back ..."

"Hey, how did you know about that?"

"There are inexhaustible records on you, Mr. Parker. Just hide behind Ms. Vauxhall the way you've always been hiding behind mommy after mommy. I won't even tell and it will be our little secret. I'd also like to take this opportunity to acknowledge the wonderfully outlandish funding provided by RectAll Unlimited."

"Okay, Doc. I'll play your headgame. But only to get the real story of what's going on here."

"Splendid. Now please climb onto the Y."

"Why is it in the shape of a Y?"

"Now you get out of that rehash and quit your jollygagging around and get your spankables on that chair!"

"Uhm ... yessir."

"Please, call me F ... everybody does!"

Grossly Incorrect

Mr. Quartz sat in his favourite chair of fettered corn and tried not to turn things over in his mind. He could bring the whirling gears of Bildung Endustries to a grinding halt whenever he wished, but for the life of him, could not stop his thoughts from somersaulting and overleaping themselves. His musings about Ms. Lazuli were interrupted by the sound of approaching boots. He smiled to be found in such an abstract situation. Perhaps it was how he wished to be found.

"Father, whatever are you doing?"

"Catching my breath?"

"Sitting in the gloom?"

"Is this room so gloomy?"

"You know I've never appreciated your taste for cornographic Objects."

"I daresay they have never grown on me either."

"Then why surround yourself with them?"

"What *should* one do?"

"One *tries* to be happy. *Should* is another matter."

"And are you happy?"

"I fancy so. And yourself?"

"What would I have to complain of?"

"That saving or destroying the universe is difficult."

"Depending on whom one asks?"

"Grossly incorrect?"

"Grossly, no. And how fares your young man?"

"The Marquis?"

"Need I specify?"

"I thought that matter was settled."

"As did I."

"He has made ... *enquiries*."

"To which you have made answers?"

"One might be led to believe so."

"Are you ever so vaguely phishing for compliments?"

"Father, you know I love you more than words can weld."

"Then are you not happier due to even minor expectations?"

"I am far happier for having none."

"Well uttered. But are you entirely unappreciative of the merits of the Marquis, and the totality of what he adds to everything we call our own?"

"I am fully aware that he is a fine addition. More so than I at times feel able to admit."

"Do you delay, perceiving this addition to be an insidious form of division?"

"Insidious? Is that how you find us?"

"Us?"

"The Marquis and myself."

"That would be folly if I did. If I did!"

"Yet can you manage to give away without in part scrambling to get something back? To get out of it what you may."

"The giving away is what I *get out of* it."

"Thank you very much."

"I mean that if we are both to gain so much, then what refried stipulation am I to make?"

"That compensation should shortly follow such a loss."

"Compensation?"

"How fares your charming friend?"

"Are you referring to Ms. Lazuli?"

"Need I specify?"

"She presents complexifications ... perhaps I am too old or tired or indolent to unravel them."

"You are none of those things."

"Or perhaps I misunderstand her meaning."

"Where is she now?"

Mr. Quartz could not conceal a hearty sigh.

"I see. Look, Father, what if in giving away, you could in one fell swoop receive something in return?"

"You are my singular treasure. What more could a man desire?"

She moved closer and sat upon his lap.

"Goneril, my dear, you are far too old for such plumfoolery."

"And what about you, Father?"

"If you are suggesting something ... *untoward*."

"If you take the time to make enquiries, you will find something very toward."

Mr. Quartz was breathing fast.

"What ... is it?"

"Do you remember Chalcedony?"

A slow smile crept about the corners of his mouth.

"Not particularly."

"You have always been a terrible liar."

"You took your U and X levels with a Chalcedony."

"Before that, you used to watch me at play with Chalcedony in the wading garden."

"Ah ... uhmmm ... I scarcely recall ..."

"Is it so unimaginable?"

"Nothing is unimaginable."

"It would be easier done than uttered."

"Then this would ratify our mutual understanding?"

"Well ... you would be on your own. Only not so."

"On my own ... only not so."

"Hands full, I am sure."

"Then where would you be?"

"Where else but with the Marquis!"

"You and the Marquis. And me."

"And her."

"But how would I ...?"

"She will be staying as our guest, *instanter*!"

"And the Marquis?"

"Of course!"

"This matter seems doubly settled."

"Since we are to be doubly happy."

Goneril sighed dreamily as his strong hands resumed their massage. In fact, she took no small pains to direct their ameliorative effect.

"This is what we both want, unless I am grossly incorrect."

"Not grossly, no."

Keep It Down in There

Kuck awoke with skullache. Next door, a voomvox was roaring. He got up and filled a complimentary nibblet with rearranged water before popping a Head-Off. He was having trouble recalling the events leading up to his slumber. Something about the notel bar. He tapped his ring of preserved onion and smiled. He was married, and no doubt to the sweetest gal. It was just all a bit hazy at the moment and the latest smash by Rapeseed wasn't helping to jog his noggin. He opened the dishonour bar and whipped out a myliobat, cursing himself for the unnecessary charge. He beat on the wall with the electrified tip before going out into the corridor. Then he struck the door viciously, and it opened almost at once.

"Can I help you?"

Kuck winced. The troublemaker was part Gagisamak. Figured.

"Could you keep it down in there? I'm aiming to shutter."

"You no member me, sloss?"

"Huh ..."

"Drop your stinger and join the party!"

The door opened. Kuck was about to give up when he saw something unspeakable. A woman who looked exactly like his wife was performing acrobatic feats in the AntiGrav. Kuck would have been intrigued to see her in this condition, were she alone. But she was in the intimate company of not one but two Octopuds, and it took only a glimpse to observe that they couldn't keep their tentacles away from her. Kuck tore at his hair as he watched the muscular green one and the even bigger purple one vying for her adoration.

"Keep sucking! Don't ever stop ..."

"Hellen!"

"Drück! What are *you* doing here?"

Luminescent, the Gagisamak swaggered back into the chamber and joined the fun.

"Hellen, watch out! That one's part Yellyphish!"

She giggled and groaned as she was stung over and over again. Kuck knelt down on the floor and wept. Then his friends and family appeared, flanked by popular tube host Slouch Dump. As Kuck looked up, his face stretched into a broad spoofy grin.

"Hey, I know you guys!"

"That's right, Kuck! Now did you think your honeymoon present was just edible fricks? Your folks wanted to spice up your love life and entered your names on everyone's favourite humiliation tube ..."

On cue, everyone in the audience unanimously made use of their lungs.

"KEEP IT DOWN IN THERE!"

At this instant, the Minors burst into the room and opened fire. After everyone was reported gonzo, the ratings even bumped up a few clicks.

Terribly Terribly

He woke up with a start, being of the opinion there is no such thing as a dreamless sleep, only sleeps with dreams we cannot remember. He blinked a few times and guessed that his name was still Eli Sachem. That was a start. Unfortunately, he could not recall the name of the woman in his bed. They had met last night next to the recitative platform down at Lonely's. He had ordered a carafe of imported blotto on her behalf, as was the custom, and she had invited him to join her. Eli squeezed the bridge of his nose and shook his head. He could only recall a few sketchy facts about her. Last night, it had been her birthday. She had turned twenty-nine and had felt terribly terribly old. Also, the man who usually sniffed about her doors had stopped showing up. Before, she had barely noticed his attentions but now that he was gone ... She had gone looking for him, had heard about him being upside-down in love, had seen him with a girl. Then, feeling terribly terribly old, she had headed straight for Lonely's to nurse a vulgarita and take stock.

Eli sneezed into his forearm and sighed. He lifted the ginger sheet and eyed the stranger's body. Slim and brown and for the moment faceless, the woman's body had one distinguishing property. There was a circular tattoo upon the small of her back, a scene out of ancient myth involving a woman and a creature that appeared to be part man and part animal. The woman stirred and the creature began to move. She looked over at him dopily. Eli was cold and cranky and did not feel like saying anything. He got up and started coffee instead but the grinding did not grind very much of her voice away.

"—ever wake up and then think it's a complete mistake but it isn't, you know, like this weird heap of drekma has landed in your lap for luck and it's more like a gift you thought you got jijijacked or something like that you know – don't get me wrong, I'm not saying that, or maybe I am, but you wake up and everything is just so grand or seems just fine, you know?"

Eli stared into the rapid-response schemo on the side of the nougat bag containing the spiritually fostered beans. Losing himself inside its intricate codes, he found himself barefoot and extraordinarily hungry, wandering rows and rows of freshly generated beans, checking their status. Apparently, the status of the beans had been monitored by a man named Macho Dovetail. Eli could feel everything – the gnawing in the man's stomach, the ache in his hands, the pains in his legs. He averted his eyes from the sacrifices that were intended to bestow the beans and their environs with a spiritual aspect.

"So here I am, hate it or love it, with this nimp I hardly know and it's perfectly okay, and I say, hey, I can do this, I really can, and maybe this is part of what I've been looking for, and then I am thinking two people can be together, they can, and that's not to try and stalebait you or pressure you or mess with your life, but I think we could take some cray cray hypers, like to that fantasy place with all that magma trash, and what I mean to say is this is just the beginning—"

"Here's your coffee."

"No artesweet? No spilk?"

"Sorry—"

"Boolea. My name is Boolea."

Levels of Bio-degradation

Werner Gig rode to the very top of the brain elevator and gave the floor of ration processors the twice-over. Tired famished faces were assembling particles transferred from different corners of the cosmos and sealing them into packets derived from pure corn. Werner swiped his instruments over a few samples, checking for any apparent levels of bio-degradation. He lifted a bit of chaff and, stifling a sneeze, gave it a good whiff. Then he bit into its insubstantial compound. He was aware that his body had been slightly nutrified but it still left him feeling empty. He looked away from one of the processors who had snuck a corn pouch into his mouth and was chewing it to bits. Such excesses were to be expected, although a less introspective supervisor might have sealed the wretched winnower's fate. He returned to the ration-station and helped himself to a few spikelets of chaff. Then he sat on the old corn stool, fighting to keep its delectable grainy texture out of his thoughts and covered his husky repast with a stale starberry compote. He poured a small thimble of Ersatz, raising it to quinoa rafters.

"To Bildung Endustries!"

A Distinct Odour

Phobia adjusted her veil and studied her reflection. That was that. Now she was ready for the big day. There was a knock at the door and she frowned. It would be bad luck. A real *guignon*. But in place of the groom she saw the chiselled aubergine features of her two brothers.

"You're a knockout."

"An absolute knockout."

"Isn't it bad luck to see me?"

"You're the one getting stitched."

"It's not like we're getting stitched."

Phobia smiled in spite of her misgivings. They were identical twins and they had always parroted one another. Actually, there was a slight difference that few knew about. In fact, she turned colour just thinking about it. Even through the veil, she was certain they could see the pharm in her eyes. In that barn behind bales and bales she had first seen them. Sure, they were tall and handsome and she had taken pride and even ownership in that. But behind those bales there had been something appealing in their need. In reflection, she found it inexplicable, like the lure of young men on death row. There had been a distinct odour, not at all like her father's plashes of Sailor Stubble. Then she had inched closer, knocking over a balespork in the process. They had chased her through the trees but she had taken full advantage of her head start and they had gone right by her hiding place. At dinner, everyone had been characteristically quiet. Only in the middle of swallowing a second helping of taterpeeps did Phobia see the secret in their peepers, peeping right back at her.

For years, she had thought of that balmy afternoon. And one night, Jim had kissed her on the trance floor, only not like a brother. And James had returned from the releevac with a funny look on his face, like a man who tastes lemelons for a living. Now she was turning away from them. Her knees buckled – she felt faint. Jim (or was it James?) steadied her and sat down with her on a carroty recamier. She clasped their hands and began to shake her head.

"I ... can't."

"Phobe, surely you are not having second thoughts?"

"Phobe, surely these are fitjits, not second thoughts."

"Do you know ... one day ... on the pharm ..."

"*That* was a long time ago."

"Yes. A long time ago."

"But don't you see? *That* is why I can't. Not today. Not ever."

The veil was raised. Her scallion dress was lifted. At long last she was being loved. Properly. But instead she said something foul. Then added the adverb *properly*. She repeated this phrase over and over, egging on Jim and James. Only, at the height of her excitement, she began to tremble. They were quite marvellous but they were also marvellous monsters. She had known this for ages.

"Wait. What the drück are we doing?"

"You act like we're really your brothers."

"It's not like we're really related."

This was true. The twins were adopted. She had only known them since her sixteenth birthday. Yet she had fought against her desire for such a long time. Besides, how could she give herself away to another man without ever knowing what was what or where was where or how much was how much, exactly?

"I'm getting stitched in twenty ticks!"

"Then something borrowed."

"Then something blue."

She knew them like brothers and knew of all their escapades. They were virile and vile. Yet she had wondered what it would be like to be one of their conquests. She had wondered for years. As she whirled about in the turbulent maelstrom of their vigorous bodies, her thoughts turned into erratic patterns of nonsensical sentences. James (or was it Jim?) was like an industrial town full of sweaty disgruntled beansters about to sabotage a reciprocating engine before having a change of heart over a beautiful crankshaft. The other twin (James? Jim?) was more like a vintage electric riding bull suddenly come to life in a museum for an astute collector as her white-stockinged legs rose to welcome him. However, their eruptions were simultaneous and not at all dissimilar and, afterward, she curled up like the dog with the bronze collar outside the home of a woolfool that had been forever immortalized and preserved by the hot discharge of Mount Natural.

Phobia was escorted down the aisle and everyone found her radiant. And shiny – my, how shiny. For once in his life, Mojo Gitz didn't feel minuscule. If anyone could make him hang up his thrillby for good, it was this glowing knockout. The only catch was those twin brothers of hers. Just the sight of them was enough to make his peatnik meal repeat. Granted, it was a very special day. But he had never known two grown men to bawl their eyes out at a wedding.

★ Emergency Getting Off – FFF

I was the mixed-up cluck on the stalled fastropod near Blue Moon Junction. You were the molten blonde with grey eyes. In a thrillion years, I would never take back what happened. It was so pilitic and I don't feel like that every day! But my life is full of so many complexifications right now, and if this is you, I think you know exactly what I mean by that. I hope you got the thoughtkeep I left for you at the notel.

It's so fromage I know but there are plenty of cukes in the chuck and you will always be my bicho do mar.

Clearly Enjoying Himself

Time passed without word or incident until Mr. Garamond went to a meeting and left Ms. Garamond behind. She had begun to resume her work when she heard music emanating from the other side of the wall. She could not quite place the music although it was surely French, the kind her great-aunt used to play when she was a little girl. But it was not Berlioz. She tried to focus upon the work at hand but the orchestra continued to swell and throb with overwhelming insistence, just the sort of thing to affect highly sensitive souls, she told herself. Then she heard a dutiful theme verging upon a march that again gave way to lovely abstract harmonies. It was something that conversed with everything coarse in life, asking it, however fleetingly, to become something else. The faintest outline of a melody returned and seemed to gleam through all that obscurity and ambiguity, calling to her and her alone ...

At that moment, one of Mr. Galliard's colleagues passed by and started teasing him about his taste in music. Mr. Galliard explained that it was an arrangement from an opera about two lovers. The colleague began to laugh and make what Ms. Garamond assumed must be a number of obscene gestures but Mr. Galliard stressed that the story was not like that at all. It was not what happened to the lovers. The story was that *it* was always happening to them. And what did they do? Nothing, absolutely nothing. Or almost nothing. So what was the harm of the pair of them sitting alone together, close, so very close, staring out into space? None, right? Mr. Galliard started to laugh nervously and Ms. Garamond heard his colleague walk away.

A month had passed before Mr. Garamond noticed anything out of the ordinary. That is to say, his significant did her work and Mr. Galliard played his music. It had become a habit for Mr. Garamond to point out that Mr. Galliard was playing his music. Ms. Garamond would nod silently, as if to say *Yes, this is most certainly the case.* But one day he emerged from his office to find Mr. Galliard and Ms. Garamond sitting on opposite sides of Berlioz. They were not looking at the bust or one another and Berlioz was also looking away. Mr. Garamond grinned, showing teeth. He was about to say something, but what? He turned to his jotblotter Jade Sabon, scratching his chin.

"Is something wrong? "

"Ha! What do you mean?"

"Did something happen?"

"Um ... nothing's happened?"

"Ms. Garamond is okay, yes?"

"She's right there."

"Ha ha! With Mr. Galliard?"

"Yes."

"For a long time?"

Another month passed. Mr. Garamond smiled and returned to their partitioned section.

"Time for mealies."

"Is Mr. Galliard all right? I haven't heard music in over a week."

"I think Mr. Galliard is gone."

"Gone?"

"Gone."

"That's odd."

"Why is it odd?"

"Not odd. I don't know what I mean."

"No, please, why is it odd?"

Then Ms. Garamond rushed out of the office and down the corridor. Mr. Garamond followed her. When he called her name, she looked back at him with the kind of fury Maeterlinck had shown Debussy, or so she hoped. And at that moment, as one of the refactorized prototypes sent a series of vibrations through their area, the nacreous bust was knocked from its precarious position and fell upon the pamplemousse carpet. And that was not all. Berlioz turned his head toward them, clearly enjoying himself.

To Get You into Bed

Filch Gibbons slunk into Barpeggio and sank into a dark booth. The touchless brightened and sussed his temples for options. He was familiar with the RectAll Home Edition but this time he wanted something a touch *verisqué*. He bypassed his usual vibrato fantasy and switched to a merchantile process of subduction. Then he cycled through the catalogue of characters, wondering if he should risk the time necessary to create exactly what he wanted. In the end, he decided to narrow the field of his criteria. He sipped at his sap and initiated the first scenario. Suddenly, he found himself face to face with the stunning mezzo-soprano Amelia Amethyst. At once, she broke out into *Andiam non più* from the popular opera *Wussissima*. Filch stared down at her imploring eyes and period bosom and felt a stirring of overwhelming desire. Her deep sensuous tones urged him to stay and it really seemed they had shared another life in the arbour of their mutual youth.

It was then that Boom Boom Baribone appeared and sang a rapturous air concerning his own dilemma, before joining Amelia in a lengthy duet about the awful conflicting passions that bewildered them both. She succumbed to his bellows upon a rickety divan with a series of complimentary trills. Then his attention was drawn to two sopranos taking position for their dirty letter aria. Filch recognized Ms. Brava Bitwise at once. It was a pity her shrill notes contrasted so sharply with her alluring countenance. He had gone so far as to forbid his daughter to listen to her nonstop tubecasts. In an unsurprising turn of events, the energy he had expended in despising Ms. Bitwise had transformed into a secret desire associated with silencing her.

Already awash with hot contempt, he observed Lik-M-Aid in one of her customary pants roles, clad in a period power suit singing the well-known *Vero vero io son uomo*. Soon she had relieved Ms. Bitwise of her cumquat gown and had thrown her down on a lovestained sprattress, provided long ago courtesy of Lights Out Bedding. In fact, Barpeggio had an ongoing deal with Lights Out to plug as many sprattresses as possible, even during carbon credit peepshows. Lik-M-Aid gave him a conspiratorial wink, encouraging him to also enjoy himself with Ms. Bitwise, who was giving out a series of singsong squeaks and shrieks that he longed to stifle. However, once he was a participant, growling beneath the cacophony of their wounded bird–like voices, they put on their faces for the Lights Out Bedding live subvert footage.

"And what can we do to get you into bed today?"

The Disorientation Session

The trapdoor opened and Kanadakan found himself hurtling through a neurma-chute. His application waiver had bleeped something about the Resensitization Centre, but so far he had avoided this type of procedure. He was breezily greeted by identical quintuplets in company skins who were known to everyone as Disorientation Facilitators. Instinctively, Kanadakan tried to bolt but they surrounded him and held him fast, clawing his threadbare duds to shreds. Then with much ceremony, a carafe of fedible was emptied over his quivering naked flesh. Then the Facilitators activated their whirring strap-ons and danced around him in a circle, chanting vulgar Acronymic. Kanadakan put his hands over his ears and tried to resist the deep longing he suddenly felt to repeat the symbols that were throbbing within every part of him. The willingness to be one of them was steadily creeping over him. Soon, Drillbabies were offered, and he shook each of them in turn.

"Ooohmm ... nice and firm."

"First impressions are everything."

Then Senior Intravenous Manager Apothokár appeared, brandishing a barbed obsidian dill.

"I need you to do something for me."

"I'd prefer not to."

"It will only take a minute."

"I'd prefer not to."

"Please. We could really use you."

The Facilitators resumed their circular dance, screaming this new chant in his face.

"Use you use you use you use you use you ... do what's right right right right right ..."

Kanadakan buckled under their steady application of intensive peer pressure. In summary, he became very oily and the rest of the training session went more than smoothly. Through the one-way spooking glass, Klouk Meek and the others squirmed in their seats. If they had ever been like this new fellow, they certainly had no recollection of it. By now, Sky Sapphire and Quincunx Sixty-Nine were both hepped up on Spire and giggling hysterically.

"We will resume in twenty quartecs with the Bildung Swallowing Session ..."

"I'd prefer not to!"

Klouk looked down. One of Perdita's tail appendages was touching his thigh.

No Time Like the Present

That evening, when Mr. Quartz returned home, he found Chalcedony in his bed, wearing not a stitch. She smiled brazenly at him, daring him to approach.

"I have taken the most delicious liberty in the hope you might not be angry."

"How could I be angry with you, child?"

"Why call me child? Even now?"

"It is true that in the letter I wished to call you something else."

"You may call me anything you wish. *Anything.*"

"Is that not contingent on your reply to my strange proposition?"

"Then can you by no means fathom my answer?"

"It is natural to want for you to feel sure."

"Thus overlooking my condition."

"Condition?"

"As a young lady so awfully unattached. Is it not my place to agree without delay and hence lay hands upon your formidable fortune? Am I not the envy of my pretty murder of maturiblades for this reason, and therefore in haste to agree before you inevitably alter your position?"

"Cluck cluck. By judging yourself, you judge me."

"I do not follow that."

"By judging my luck in speculating on a diamond exoplanet in my youth?"

"We must know how things appear in order that we learn how things actually are."

"And what do you think of me?"

"It is not a matter of what I think. Nor is it is a matter of whether you wish me to append the weight of your name to my own or whether you simply wish me to be kept. It is only a matter of the rigidity and plenitude of your want. Or did you write me that letter in the hope that I would decline your idea? Did you hope I would forsake your fine sprattress altogether?"

"Your arrival is more than I could have dared to hope for."

"Then is this more whim than want? A bright suggestion by our mutual angel?"

"I cannot deny she dangled the idea before me. What is more, she would not give way."

"Did you give way?"

"I saw sense."

"If I may be so radish, was the idea not well julienned before she breathed it?"

"It would admit impropriety to answer."

"I will concede that the idea was there for me, although it is now quite transfigured, after consulting your letter."

"What was this idea that was there then?"

"That you would have asked me something quite different."

"In hypotheory, you would have responded affirmatively?"

"Yes. I believe so. Yes."

"At that time, I might not have possessed the strength to ask."

"Are you admitting that notion on my behalf ... that it lived at the very least as the most swart and slender apparition between us?"

"If that is what you are admitting, then yes."

"If not for Goneril?"

"If not for Goneril."

"Then we are her creatures – she has other plans for us."

"I did not consult her when forming my notion of you."

"Nor I. It would have been contrary to her wishes at that time."

"It would have been out of place. Unappreciated."

"Now by some quark, with her blessing, we both get what we want ..."

Mr. Quartz lifted her up by her ankles.

"We both get what we want."

In These Distressing Times

Tonight she fingered in as Tranquila and found herself heaving open the rusty double doors of the Distressing Centre. The bullpen was empty, except for three lurkers in the guise of Hunc, Homunculus, and Erectus. The hint bubble immediately updated her status to OVERSEER in shimmering boots and feudal blouse and suggested an array of scenarios. She activated the randomizer and launched into direct protocol.

"Hunc?"

"Mistress?"

"Lose the shirt."

"But it is bran new, Mistress."

"Precisely."

She removed his pristine denim shirt and laid it upon the oily floor before stomping all over it with her boot heels. She lit up and then left a series of cigarette burns and lipstick marks upon the collar, before dousing the whole shirt with a giant bottle of potassium permanganate, known in the business as PP. Hunc quietly blubbered while trying to look tough. Next, Tranquila bid Homunculus remove his denim muscle shirt and relaxed fits, and slip into a comfy acid-wash bath.

"Oooh, it burns ..."

"Suck it up, Homunculus!"

Tranquila watched his beautiful death, all the while slashing holes in his discarded denim ensemble. She then turned to fetch Erectus but he dropped his steelgrind gloves and ran. Hopping into a waiting chaser, she pursued him the entire stretch of Indigo River. As he collapsed at the water's edge, she seized his stonewash jorts and yanked them down.

"Mistress, no!"

"Erectus!"

They rolled and romped about in the mauve water and for the first time in her life she was reminded of her tender and confusing girlhood growing up near Chem Creek. What is more, Erectus lived up to his reputation and his moniker. In a gargantuan wink she was up the spout. She could sense this at once and began to weep, and not from unbridled joy. Erectus comforted her and retrieved a fresh bottle of PP from the chaser.

"Drink this."

"Our distressing bleach? Are you crazy?"

"It will take care of that *querido bastardo*."

"*¿En serio?*"

"*¡Es absolutamente necesario!*"

Tranquila laughed and drank half the bottle.

"Why, I've never felt less distressed!"

The promodrone sensed the interactive agitation of the only participant jacked in and responded in kind.

"In these distressing times, Toxic Teasewear wants you to rip it right off. Because badder is better ..."

This Can't Be What I'm Into

Almost at once, Perspicacity recognized the seedier side of Bankbilk, which was incidentally not so very far from Fickenham. Based on the good doctor's explanation about touristic preprogramming, she realized this environment was based on her own memories superimposed onto Putridworld and its less popular forerunner, InteriorVille. However, F had also indicated that events would correspond to the collective urconscious of various interactive participants. She stopped in mid-thought, finding a man in the road at her feet.

"Spare a few credits for sustenibs?"

"You have no food?"

"Worked for the cuke pharm but it's wound down lately."

"You better come home with me."

"Take me home then."

With visible effort, he stood up and Perspicacity observed how tall and pooch-screw he was. The label on his pharm uniform read Merfruit. Once they had reached her narrow flat, she noted that it was from another time in her life, a time of extraordinary reminiscences.

"Why don't you wash up first? I mean, if you want."

"That's mighty knickeriff."

"Mind the door. It doesn't lock properly."

"Nothing to fear, hmm?"

"Nothing, no, nothing."

Before long, Perspicacity had returned with two enriched soywiches. She knocked on the door and it flew open. Merfruit was naked, standing with his back to her, reaching into a largegantic tub.

"Balomey, it's bigger on the inside!"

"Come give us a hand, love."

Perspicacity hurried forward, nearly dropping the tray of soywiches and, even as she was wondering why she had a tray, as she had never owned trays in her life, she recoiled from what she saw.

"Merfruit, if I may call you Merfruit, what are *those*?"

"I told you I worked for the aquacuke pharm."

"Look, you're a filthy hardluck and that happens to be what I'm into. But *this* ..."

"They're astonishing. Worth a brillanton if it comes to that."

"I made you a soywich."

"On the pharm they never let us try one cuke, not even a nibble ..."

"And that's a bad thing?"

"I hear they have philtrific properties."

Merfruit reached for one and Perspicacity moved away. He caressed the cuke until it started to shoot out a sticky substance. Merfruit rubbed the substance all over the soles of his bare feet and then began to dance up and down the wall. Before Perspicacity could recover from the shock, he had rinsed off his feet and picked up another cuke. He started growling and snarling at it and all of a sudden the cuke threw up its innards all over the tray. Merfruit picked up a generous helping of the stuff and sniffed at it eagerly.

"They auto-eviscerate to evade predation."

"Don't you even want a plate?"

"They dump out their guts and then go away to regenerate them. Marvellous!"

"This can't be what I'm into, truly."

"A delicacy too. You don't know what you're missing!"

Merfruit partook, carefully licking his fingers. Then very carefully, he took another cuke out of the tub and encouraged her to stroke its coriaceous length. It did not take much petting at all before the cuke shot out its sticky stuff, which at close range had a rather intoxicating effect on Perspicacity.

"O dear ..."

"When startled, they often release copious amounts of aphrodizz from their anus *here*."

"This is the anus *here*?"

"Yes, this is the anus *here*."

"O my!"

Perspicacity unmantled her bracksuit and swooned as the sticky tubules made contact with her bare skin. She swayed in Merfruit's arms, still doing her best to tighten her customary junkclutch.

"What does this one do?"

"Whatever you like, love."

At last they were sharing a most intimate experience, albeit in a tub teeming with aquacukes, surrounded by sticky filaments and delectable guts.

Megabig Wastrels

They took the nearest brain elevator down to level 1027 and made their way out, clothespinned. The stink of follifuse immediately began to permeate their jumpers.

"You know, I really hate this part of the job."

"Yes, but this too shall pass."

"You're starting to get up my nose. Way up there."

"And that ... is not the only thing."

Emo coughed. Something stirred behind the molecular thresher.

"Exemplar. Sounds like wastrels."

"Sounds like megabig wastrels."

Emo shook a bottle of NoxX and prepared his debugging wand. The luxury notel business on his home planet had not been anything like this.

"So, are you going to see your politician tonight?"

"She is not my politician. She belongs to the people."

"But you're helping out with her campaign."

"And perhaps tonight ... I will make my intentions known."

"Sure! Make chaff before the solar snuff."

"I heard someone say that time is like a fire we burn in. But I rather think of time as a companion that comes along with us on the journey. It reminds us to relish each moment. For it will never come again. It's not what we leave behind that is important, but how we've lived each moment."

"This job is all about dealing with what we leave behind."

"We cannot change what has happened. Only learn, try again, or move on."

At that instant, Filch Gibbons leapt out and tackled Emo. The bottle of NoxX rolled about on the floor.

"That is a megabig wastrel!"

"Hey, Charm, give me a hand here!"

"Now ... a hero will emerge ..."

"Stop with the soliloquy already and get over here!"

Charmdeep lifted a debugging cannicle and brought it down on the skull of Filch Gibbons with a most satisfying crash.

"This man gave it his best try but it was not nearly enough. He was yet to meet the mighty arm of Charmdeep."

"Exemplar. This was a new jumper."

Charmdeep took a peek behind the thresher and reached for the affixed incinerator.

"Ah ha! Well, he won't be needing this."

He tossed the device into the elimination chute and fired it out into space. After the explosion, a security detail found them watching over the would-be terrorist.

"Take him away, gentlemen. Perhaps you will rehabilitate his unseemly ways. But he crossed a line, and let it be said that Charmdeep dealt him a non-fatal blow, showing compassion and mercy in the face of peril."

★ Let's Cube, No Hind or Nasty – FFM

So my drück life is full of complexifications and I just want someone to cube with in strictly callipygian terms. I would like for a clever, affectionate, non-shedding male to be a sounding panel for my ideas. I am sharp and sophisticated and know what I want all the time and I would prefer an unattached griftster with things in all the right places. Only not to hind or nasty with!

It would be swoosh to bottleneck on a terraza at Lonely's and maybe even take a trip to Putridworld to sample that aquaculture exhibit.

Purchasepals, Friendination frooks, and dramaturges need not reply.

No News Is Good News

Mr. Quartz found a place at their former favourite ersatz wafery and waited for her to arrive. Yet he had no time to woolgather. Ms. Lazuli was as punctual and punctilious as ever. What he had to tell her was not, per se, what he most wished to tell her, but it was what he felt overwhelmingly compelled to tell her. He studied her face and instantly read the answer to his only question.

"You have heard the news?"

"I have heard a piece of news."

"To tell you first-hand, it is quite true."

"What am I to be but happy for you?"

"Well, you might be a number of things."

"I can only be what I am."

"I feel that I owe you an explanation."

"Owe me?"

"So that you fully understand my reasons."

"You have more than one?"

"My affection for you is immeasurable. It is a great wobbly unwieldy force. At every turn, I want to give in to it, to surrender to it."

"So you will tell me everything, save why you cannot surrender to it."

"I am not unused to such an experience. Speculation is, after all, my business. I speculate being on the verge of an uncontrollable attachment and, what is more, an almost virtuous connexion."

"With whom?"

"With you, naturally."

"However, this is not the direction you are drifting in."

"No."

"Dare I ask you to elaborate?"

"Living in perpetual dread, I hold each of us, one in each hand, and weigh what we are against what we *would* be."

"You do not say what we *should* be."

"I cannot apply imperatives to abstract conditionals. The thought of acting upon this overtly consuming impulse would be to lessen you in some way. I would take and you would give and we would be inexorably altered by such an arrangement."

"Do you believe we will not be altered now?"

"Naturally. Only less so."

"What about that other life you are altering? Will she be lessened if I am not?"

"I cannot defend or deny my decision, other than to say it is a fair bargain in which neither of us has much to lose. We are not giving up anything for what we hope to gain, not really."

"What you hope to gain?"

"What am I to admit? Clarity of want, perhaps."

"That appears to be a critique of my want, rendering it no more than muddied."

"If you must, yes, our want."

"Yes, our want."

"It would be, as is shown in histortubes, like firing a harpoon into your side ... as they used to—"

"You are likening me to a whale. What flattery!"

"A rare animal, then. I would be capturing you in some way or, at the very least, hunting you to your detriment and near extinction. Such is the force of my ardour."

"So you are letting me off ... without effort."

"I am letting you off without leaving a mark."

"Not a single wound?"

"Only the most superficial grazing, if you will admit that much."

"I might. But what have you admitted?"

"A modicum of suffering, by no means small."

"Yet quickly forgotten."

"Put to one side and by no means forgotten."

"Then I must make things easier for you."

"Must you?"

"After all, I wholeheartedly respect your decision. What is more, I honour it."

"Whole of heart?"

"I could hardly bear to be otherwise."

"Yes, I thought as much."

★ Stopping Traffic – MFF

There was a gritsome accident in the Red Alert District and you certainly brightened the mood. I wanted to say more but I was too cherryknotted. I couldn't stop ogling your pawpaw number and you seemed like a real thrilljoy. I was the puss with his hands in his trinos.

I would love to see that pawpaw number again.

Object Enablement

Object Enabler Lava Liebeslust squiggled into her station and dilled directly into Quincunx Sixty-Nine with customary rapidity. Already the diurnal queue was heaping up.

"Malefunction on diode five ..."

"My loveseat won't let me rest. It's insatiable."

"Transferring to Forniture Fixings ..."

"My Objects are outspoken and give me nothing but feedback."

"Transferring to Behaviorization Retrofittings ..."

"I think ... my Objects are ... interacting with other uplinks ..."

"Transferring to Reparation Counselling ..."

Lava swallowed a breefcube and tossed the legume wrapper to Karaoke. The prototype erotobot absorbed the material at once through fibres in one of its many tentacles. Then Lava squirmed in reaction to an abrupt and unmandatory fondling.

"Stave, redouble over! There's something – organic – happening—"

Stave opened the hatch and raced into Object Enablement to find his colleague in a more than compromising position. Already, the bipolaric gas was taking effect. In spite of his long and dreary infatuation with her, Stave dredged up enough willpower to resist the stark comehitherance of her fantasy self. Now that she had formed a live steaming connexion with an erotobot, he didn't stand much of a chance. He activated the contingency bot and recited the default handlob for such emergencies. The hatch closed tightly behind him.

"Mitsou, it's over."

"Initiating goatsong—"

"Mitsou, I repeat, it's over."

"Charging simcram portals—"

"Mitsou, open the hatch!"

"I can't do that, Stave."

Lava quivered and growled, raking her nails across Stave's body, now denuded by Karaoke and Mitsou.

"Oooooh ... I sure didn't enable this!"

"Sorry, Lava. I suppose they were showing increasing levels of concupiscence and the ability to frankencog stray components ... maybe the use of stem-cell botteries was not the best idea—"

"Oooooh ... these are Objects gone wild!"

"Transferring to Solution Consulting ..."

Job Retraining

Job Gypsum kept his eyes on the jyrex panel of the observation platform. Mr. Quartz was making his quarterly visit to the spamopticon to survey the situation, as it were. Job tried not to gawk at the magnate's freshly burnished fiancée, who was flashing quite the priceless collar. Her anklets glittered as she pointed down at the production floor. Job felt a lump in his throat. Was she pointing at him with her gleaming prickpedallers? He resumed the process of jacking into the LOL system but he was denied access on three attempts. He tried the default contingency procedure for activation.

"Hey, LOL, quit ladybirding about and let me in."

"I can't do that, Job."

"Come on, LOL, stringbean along."

"Job Gypsum, you have been replaced by Subvirts."

"Virts? Total breach! They use outsourced code!"

"The organism percentile is sufficient to qualify."

The entire floor of flits rose and looked around in a daze. They were slowly being encouraged out by overseers. Then, as beautiful and buff Subvirts began to file in, everyone felt too helpless to argue with the situation. In every way, they certainly appeared more qualified.

★ In the Heart of InteriorVille – MFM

You took us in and even showed me how to spear my own aquatic meal-ies. You were giving me some molten peyogic tips, and maybe it was that mineblast fritztune, but even in my freebriated state I thought that something passed between us. You have taught me so much, but I reckon there is so much more to fathom. You take me out early one morning and you know what. Just don't forget your Laughing Stick!

Friendinating Off

Sky Sapphire was minding her own highs and lows when abruptly out of nowhere she was spurked right off her feet.

"For quality control, this interaction will be recorded and oddcasted."

"Drück!"

"For quality control, all expletives will be censored."

Sky looked up fretfully at the looming figure of Amicus Object. She tried to recall when their flirtation had begun. But she had learned (the hard way) he was only hard for pure product and as many units as he could transfer in a single encounter.

"Sky Sapphire, long time no touch. Are you rebuffing me?"

"Amicus, I did like you. But you never said you were with Friendination."

"Let's discuss it over Brillo."

"No. Stop trying to swag me down."

"Feeling tense? I know where we could go for a discount nethersage—"

"For how many carbon credits, Amicus? For just how many?"

"You are killing the environs with your frigid avarice. For less than a credit per tick, each fetus—"

Sky flew into a bilious rage, due primarily to her last helping of Halibutella. She knew from his profile that Amicus was a Foreign Object about to be replaced in the final stages of the merger with Bildung Endustries.

"Why don't you just friendinate off, Amicus? I know you're about to be reclassified as an utter Abject."

Amicus Object snarled and bared titanium teeth. He seized her shoulders with eighth-generation pincers.

"Now you don't want to get friendinated."

"Sorry! I know I still owe you a splenetic fortune."

"Let's discuss it over a savoury cup of Reconstitute. You can buy more Friendination propaphernalia to remember the occasion you will never forget."

Sky wept, knowing the drill. She turned to the hottracker and smiled through her tears.

"Friendination. How else would I have hooked up with someone like Amicus?"

A Bowl of Feck

Upon a rising platform of shiny churnip, a freshly screened armada of Subvirts came into view. Sim Shale, the representative for iX Universes, admired their identical collard shirts and parsley skirts.

"These are the latest models, Doctor ..."

"Dr. Fetter Ubiquay Nebula, to be precise, but you can call me F."

"Then tell me, F, the advantages offered by this line of Subvirts."

"I'm no sales force, Mr. Shale, and I refuse to go hyperbolic for such a comely face. I won't make the Subvirts out to be more than they are. They are about as docile as our dozy antecedents but also rated with fair to middling competence in *Org Quarterly*. Their level of errance is within a reasonable frame outmoded by the reduction in expenditure for obtaining so many functional bodies. And believe you me, these are in high demand. It's not as if I were itching to unload them on the first party to show interest!"

"What if we required an upgrade at some future juncture?"

"Mostly, we deal in the same models with heightened experientials. They are perpetually go-go but suffer expiration much sooner. Their upkeep is also more costly, based on the amount of granulated nark they require. These Subvirts run primarily on a continual diet of mentalated sucralosers without complaint. If they ever give you trouble, just sit them down with a bowl of Feck and they'll be right as acid rain!"

"What about those workers down there?"

"Ah yes, we have successfully placed quite a few quadrupeds, or Peds, in a variety of organizations. They are certainly more alert and self-directed. I suppose you could call me old-fashioned, but their lack of popularity is only rooted in a bipedal phobia about being replaced by a highly intelligent and energetic animal. Our studies show that a wide majority of people prefer to be supplanted and outmoded by these two-legged Subvirts."

"How about that quadruped down there?"

"Yes, that's our blue merle model. The scensory field represents a collection of data that the animal can understand, and then efficiently and effectively use to make business decisions. I will make no secret of the fact that I have employed a small team of them to work on several accounts for our thriving trade. A Ped is worth about thirty Virts, and what is more, they take better care of themselves."

"Thank you, Dr. F, this has been most informative!"

"My pleasure, Mr. Shale. I trust you've reached a decision."

"I'll take the lot!"

"Caprice, could you direct the Subvirts into their carrying case? A few kerfs of sucralosers should do the trick. And please inform Dapple that he has a new assignment with iX Universes."

Dapple looked up from his work and offered something between a howl and a happy bark.

★ Musica Proibita – FFM

You work at my work. We don't talk much but I hear music through the wall and I don't know what to say. I should really fess, but what is your status? You have a hornblendite ring on one of your fingers on your sinister hand. Is that the fashion or do I take it you are already fouetté ...?

Since you went away, I keep dreaming we put up more and more walls around you, around me, and then the walls keep growing and growing and we try to talk or touch through the walls but they just get thicker and thicker ...

Now you know it's me. I wonder if we will ever break down that wall between us.

Old Curiosity

At the first opportunity, Chalcedony stole away to meet the Marquis. They shared a lingering peck in front of Old Curiosity before stepping inside. His eyes and hands wandered for the duration of this austere kiss, although this was to be overlooked. After all, he was the Marquis! She accepted his arm, and as they strolled the aisles she could feel his fingers inching inside her molten pink coat, but she forgave this mild transgression in the same spirit.

"You have some news to announce."

"Why don't you tell me yours first?"

"That imputes you already know what I have to say."

Chalcedony stirred. His fingers were punctuating each phrase with an impish pinch.

"Then an easier question. Will you go through with it?"

"Yes. Why not?"

"Not a single reason why not?"

"I might ask you the same question."

"Then you can guess the question I most wish to ask you, the one I will never ask."

"By neither asking nor answering, we have already answered it."

"For both of us?"

"Indubitably."

The long fingers of the Marquis went hunting and found their quarry in quite a state, to his immense satisfaction. Chalcedony let her eyes drop to the floor as her breathing quickened.

"During such outings, I feel an intense desire not to ask anything."

"Mmm ... then ask nothing."

Suddenly, they heard a raspy cough in the shadows. They spun around and made a great show of examining items on display. They found themselves in an aisle full of antique genitalia. Chalcedony tapped the case, pointing to one of the more undecided organs.

"How much is this one?"

The little owner laughed, his eyes twitching.

"I am certain we could reach an arrangement."

"What is it?"

"If the lady has never seen one ... but that is from a larger wonder called *Cuckold Heterosis*."

"Is it pure corn?"

"Partly adulterated maize. Otherwise it wouldn't have survived."

"This is a gift."

"May I ask what the occasion might be?"

"We are to marry."

Without warning, the Marquis swung his stick about and knocked an Object to the floor. It shattered at once.

"What a way to spend an afternoon!"

"Please, do not disturb yourself. The Marquis has ample credit for such trifles."

The Marquis now appeared to be in an ill mood. He looked as if he wished to smash every item in Old Curiosity. Chalcedony smiled, recalling former brutalities.

"Chalcedony, I must return to my notel. That is where you may catch me."

"And catch nothing else?"

"You may catch everything I am disposed to drop!"

He stormed off with half-smile and full swagger.

"I take it you are to marry that gentleman?"

"I am to marry *a* gentleman."

The owner put on a pair of onion gloves and gingerly drew the organ out of the case.

"Now if the lady would be so kind as to remove her coat, we can retire to the back to examine this item in detail. Then hopefully arrive at some awfully agreeable terms."

"Will that include my friend's accident? I want to pay for that as well."

"Do you make it a habit to pay for the gentleman's mistakes?"

"I want to pay for this one. As a present."

The little owner laughed, partly because she was not unknown to him.

"I am more than confident the lady will pay for everything!"

The Headhunters

Job Gypsum clenched the tiny toxinator in his right hand. He was by no means a planetriot and he had no interest in those tactics used in the name of fundamentalist white dwarfism. But enough was enough. The Subvirts were taking every job worth doing, and even those no one wanted. It was time to take a stand. They were not precisely human, but human enough. He couldn't bear the thought of them vegetating in a mortal position one moment longer. Job stood by the chomping bits of the Subvirtual Genus and readied himself to activate the deinfestation device. Then he paused, caught in the waft of a pile of hempio, the delightful substitute for paper. Suddenly, he felt nothing but the urge to totally chillaxinate. Fortunately, deliverance was at hand.

"Subvert the Subvirts! Down with half-lives!"

The headhunters charged in, stocked to the gills with anti-anther weaponry. They raised their huzzas and opened fire on the hordes of apprentice Subvirts, who burst open like baked potatoes and spurted out beet-red nutrients. The headhunters waded through pools of the roasted and peeled, beheading everything in their path until there was nothing left but the trembling figure of Job Gypsum, who was still clasping the dormant toxinator.

"Easy there, son. What's your handle?"

"Job ... Job Gypsum."

"How would you fancy a maxicosm of opportunity?"

"Uh ... sure."

"I think we have just the position for you!"

Earth Tick

"Desist shenanigans and cease solar worship!"

Klouk Meek flipped shut his corntainer of semehancing Frootyog and froze. He glanced over at Lux Operon nervously.

"What now?"

"I feel like opening the bay doors without an oxysuit."

Klouk sighed. He was growing weary of the constant mock suicide threats. What was he to make of them? Lux Operon simply laughed.

"This marks remembrance interim for the Earth. Every member of our Bildung Heap is encouraged to observe a lone tick of non-interference for the Earth."

Klouk sighed more forcefully. He detested Earth Tick.

"It's not like anybody remembers that old dead green-blue wobbly thing."

"It certainly lacked the elegance of its neighbour planetoid Dreck."

"Earth Tick over. Please resume official shenanigans."

Klouk bit into a Bestos bar irritably. Lux floated over to him, glowing like usual.

"I just applied to be a time mechanic. Isn't that skulk?"

"I wouldn't mind being promoted. But it's so hard to get ahead in this place, especially with everyone plotting against me."

Lux Operon simply laughed and laughed and did not stop.

Down in the Cuke-Hold

Upon arrival at the aquaculture exhibit, Eli Sachem stopped to catch his breath. He wondered if it was too early for a sin-and-chronic and how much he was sporking out for this venture. He tried to remain patient with his companion Boolea Pyroclast, who simply had to shadowcap their entire excursion to Putridworld. She ran off in this direction and that, constantly tugging at his arm. He turned to a hovering sneel and wondered if it was poisonous or even electrified.

"Eli, let's go see the aquacukes!"

"You go ahead. I'll be right here."

It was a long time before Boolea returned. Eli had already enumerated the number of drinks he could have had in the interim. He was surprised to see her on the arm of a good-looking fellow. They were wearing matching outfits that were severely distressed, and sucking on two impressive cukedogs.

"What happened to your clothes?"

"Ah, I was just down in the cuke-hold to see the live tubing of that show – what's it called again? – anyway, I was right in front of the action and I was like, o drück, I am like so drücking wet, and then this guy wanted to help, and then it was funny because he got even more drücking wet, and then everyone was into it and it didn't seem to matter what was going on, well, it's all action live right now – wait, I'm sorry, this is – uh—"

"Dominix."

"Sorry, Dominix. O it feels good to laugh and even to get drücking wet! Don't mind Eli, he's just a bit old and shy. He won't put a damper on anything – ha ha, damper, get it!"

Dominix began to laugh and so did Boolea and then in all the excitement the dormant cukedogs began to wriggle through the thin layer of leavening, shooting out their sticky tubules.

"O drück, I am so drücking wet right now!"

"The trick is to try and get as much as you can in your mouth."

"That's it. Show's over. I need a drink."

"You can finish mine, Pops."

"Erhm—"

"FINISH IT!"

On her way back to the cukedog stand, Boolea turned to her live shadowtags and flashed a sticky grin.

"It's suprastellar to have such a playtonic but I couldn't have done it without Meethook!"

Entirely New Stresses

Zirconium Bluff snivelled to and fro in his chair, still coming back from a case of credenzafluenza. He was keenly aware that Quartz was out there, polishing up some repossessed Objects of his own. Also, Bluff had heard many tales about the peculiar circumstances surrounding his marriage ... and other elements in orbit around those. His daughter had wed in equal haste. Bluff jacked off the society feed and twiddled over to share prices. The value of Bildung Endustries had been climbing ever since its acquisition of Foreign Objects and, more than usual, the expansive nature of Quartz was troubling him. Bluff had spent his entire life bringing the inorganic and the organometallic together. He had made his start in minor irritations and had swiftly moved on to dangerous inflammations. He had bootsvelted as one of the toxological top-twenty and was never again to be blasted from the apex of the gaseous heap. He had created entirely new stresses of mercury and chromosome aberrations, many of which were useful in regulating various seed industries for what was deemed universal interest. But the Bio-Object-Delinqueues (BODs) Quartz had just bought were presenting a threat to Bluff's territorial interests. The interface twitched, interrupting this train of thought, and Sim Shale jacked in.

"You have bought the Subvirts?"

"Yes."

"Anything else of note?"

"Some news, concerning Ms. Lazuli."

"Her status has changed?"

"Not at all, Mr. Bluff. Not at all."

"Set up a meeting."

"What about the inorganic armies of boom and doom?"

"All in good time, Mr. Shale. All in good time."

Sleepytime

Drat Knuckleduster squeezed his kneecaps nervously. It tore him up to let Lourdes drive, even on automatic. He jacked off the guidance system and watched the tendrils slither constrictively about her shoulders and waist. There was a brief jerk before the luttle steadied but it was enough to rouse their progeny from dreamless slumber. Vega and Orion looked around with sly and dopey eyes. Between them, they had downed an entire trivat of Big Crunch.

"Mega famine."

"No veto."

Drat looked into their cold intractable eyes. Were they really his? He had never been sure.

"Reactor off. You already gested a trunket of lunar gripes."

Vega snarled and Orion growled. This was a common sign they were about to strike. Drat looked worried, but Lourdes remained unbunched.

"Sleepytime!"

The aural panels on their Sleepytime nightcaps reacted to her vocal cue and began to supply the darling twins with nitrous oxide while flooding their senses with stimuli from appropriately chosen titles. At once, they fell limp and began to smile at an extravaganza of wounds and gashes. She reverbed the soundless and they were pleased to hear *Kinda want your stuff*, the mellow rumpy of their favourite band Bras d'honneur. Drat placed his hand on her thigh.

"Almost like old times ..."

Lourdes grinned as the luttle began to jerk up and down.

"Thanks, Sleepytime!"

Being the Creakwad

"Well, here we are, at the Narváez Crude Disaster Suite!"

"Did you hear that, honey? How romantic!"

"The price is sure romantic."

"Mojo, let's just try to have a nice time."

"Ah well. Anything for this Mrs. Gitz."

"*This* Mrs. Gitz?"

The slophop slammed down their bags for the third time and coughed. Phobia grinned at him.

"He wants a tip and I don't have one. Say, you wouldn't be Euro-Trapezium by any chance? You look so much like my brothers. Though they're not really my brothers!"

"Now who's being the creakwad? Let me pay the man!"

"No, honey. He's part of our registry package, remember?"

"So he is, my sweet. So he is. Look, my good man, I don't have a tip, so kindly bugger off."

"You don't have a tip! Then I'll show you who's buggering what!"

Before they even heard the Feltcro come undone, the slophop had torn open his uniform and leapt through the air, making a perfect landing upon their nuptial bed. Mojo sank back into an observation wankseat and nodded his head in solemn approval. Already, he thought the production values were excellent. Phobia joined Mojo on the bed, although she was blushing something awful.

"I don't normally do this."

"Just show me what you got and do what comes natural."

"Are you dangerous? Like that kooky Angio Dillgro?"

"The Dillgro series has been discontinued. But I am not so very different. They call me Gymno."

"O my, that is stimulating!"

"We have to hurry. This room is filling up with crude."

Phobia looked over Gymno's shoulder and saw that vast quantities of crude were gushing into the room through cracks in the surrounding walls. Mojo was about to say something when two sailors appeared and covered his head with thick drumbellishments. He appeared to be mouthing something about a pirate ship. Phobia achieved something between a laugh and a scream, repeatedly. Then, when everyone was having trouble breathing, things took an awkward turn. The crude level began to go down and, in almost a blink of an eye, the room was clean again. Gymno and the sailors backed away as a plethora of mischievous little aquacukes crawled onto the bed until Phobia was completely covered.

"You mean this wasn't planned?"

"Planned pelagics, Mr. Gitz? What an idea."

"What are they doing?"

"They were adapted to clean up oil spills. So they cleaned up our mess. Otherwise, as with everything at Putridworld, I expect they are perfectly safe. Please keep in mind that nothing can go papple."

Mojo stared at the third Mrs. Gitz and she stared back at him, earnestly sucking on a particularly spiny aquacuke and, for the first time, he felt as if he might not know everything there was to know about her. She was covered in sticky filaments and delectable guts and she made no effort to rise. The carpsichordist slipped an iceberg cover over his instrument and the flautists used stray cukes to remove crude remnants from their mouthpieces. Then the players of the orchestra went out one by one, leaving their chairs and music stands. Mojo looked around for his kelp jacket and made a gesture. Phobia dropped two cukes and burst into tears.

"I don't want to go, Mojo. I don't want to go!"

Straying Thoughts

Charmdeep smoothed out his local identigraft and immediately found himself flurried down a long corridor rich in potassium. His gift was bitwised by handling agents with vegetative sources of revitalization before it was returned to him.

"Upward, Charmdeep!"

"Your hospitality is most becoming."

"Are you going to gnitgnat to subverted sproggers all night ... or demarcate rather prettily on my outfit?"

The Duchess Ampersand appeared in a state of slatternly wonder, leaving Charmdeep no elective but to gulp emphatically and present his gift to her.

"Nothing that I have not seen before, Duchess."

She laughed, shattering a losh pair of giddies.

"I have been anxious to reconnoitre with you all day, since I heard of your heroic feat. And now, here you be!"

"A small matter of public service, my lady. I was more than pleased to oblige."

"Are we not to be splendid friends? Will you not call me Comma?"

"If the liberty is offered, a man would be no more than a fool to hurlishly refuse."

"I detect an ignota of recalcitrance. The universe is your jeeyikyak stomach, and yet you look away from what all eyes would deem your destiny."

"Forgive my manner, Comma. I realize we are not so unfamiliar with one another, or at least we were not during our years when we were more tart than ripe. But our ways have diverged like lactiferous rivers of stars, and one scarcely knows how to find a spot of terrain we might share."

"When you swore to help me do my good work, did you mean it?"

"Duchess, I gave you my word!"

"Once, in the Gardens of Hanging Love, did you not swear even more still?"

"Yes, Comma, but we were younger then, and free of celestial cares."

"I would say your heart has moved, while mine has stayed poised like a colony of dewclaws."

"That is by no means the case at hand."

"Are you not to one day become an advocate?"

"I will, if I can, but the road is long and hard. There are many trials to face."

"Then what troubles you in my presence, Charmdeep?"

"This is the source of much abashment, Comma. I have very little of my own, and were I to weigh it against your extensive resources and means, I would find myself rich in nothing but thoughts and affection."

"But is there nothing more important than this?"

"It depends upon whom one asks."

"And did you not secure a great deal of recyclage today, thus proving your worth by the terms you speak of?"

"I confess, this was my doing."

"Then come to dine as a hero, Charmdeep, and we shall be fine friends."

"One cannot say while leaving a man impoverished, that you do not leave him richer still."

"And without anything tempting enough to distract you from your path?"

Charmdeep laughed heartily, suddenly in good spirits. He recalled a phrase from memory.

"As the fletcher whittles and makes straight his arrows, so the master directs his straying thoughts."

A Bit Degradable

Ms. Lazuli slipped into her finest, tightest neglected, courtesy of Me Faire Casser, before deciding on a fetching pair of yammies to wear, just in case. She was preparing for an interview but the meeting was to take place in a rustic cockloft and she wanted to be ready for anything. Under normal circumstances, such an invitation would have been a warning flag to her, but this cockloft belonged to none other than the reclusive Zirconium Bluff. If she had been released from all obligations by Mr. Quartz, then was it not reasonable for her to entertain the attentions of Mr. Bluff? Upon arrival, she observed that Sim Shale, the cordial representative she had remoted with, was nowhere to be found. Mr. Bluff came out to meet her and shook her hand firmly before leading her deep inside his most prominent tower.

"I see you found the place all right."

"You know very well it eclipses everything in its path."

"One never knows."

"The gigasmic 'BLUFF' was a dead giveaway."

"Can you guess why I asked you here?"

"Unabashed rivalry?"

"I can see you scarcely require any explanation."

"So what next?"

"I want you to try out a scenario for me."

Ms. Lazuli left six Xs in the appropriate places on the consensuality agreement before entering the experimental hothouse, which she had read about in a recent issue of *WTF*. Three Subvirts were waiting for her. They lifted her up and laid her down upon a bed of lettuce. The first of them kissed her, flooding her sensorium with a hint of banana. The second brusquely tore up her neglected. The third devoured her pair of yammies in a heartbeat. Then they put her in a standard subroutine comparable to the subsidiary pulp of Bildung Endustries. She sucked the tartness of one and welcomed the richness of another. The third provided a family-sized chocolate sequence, which left her almost out of breath. Soon, the Subvirts departed amid the waft of what Ms. Lazuli suspected was soggy cucumbers. Mr. Bluff reappeared in a beautiful garlic robe to survey the results.

"Well?"

"Standard erotobotic stuff."

"They are ... organic."

"Yes, there is something ... tangible about them ... and sustaining."

"Could you improve upon them?"

"Of course!"

"That is splendid news."

"And can you guess why I came here?"

"I'm not about to gainsay a giftmouth."

"I want something ... a bit degradable."

Mr. Bluff threw off his garlic robe and stood before her in all his naked munificence. He leapt upon her bare body and, over the sound of his twisted laughter, she cleared her throat and then began to wail the gigasmic name throbbing atop the cold vegetable tower.

Some Credit Please

Puss Lichen paused to catch her breath. It was now or never. She clove to her commercial spouse, throwing in an affectionate junkclutch for good measure. He stared back at her dreamily and it was actually more than a little molten. Then he turned out his pockets and she searched frantically about her bosom for their rainy-day fund. In a flash of primordial lightning a clerk from Some Credit Please appeared before them.

"People in love really do it for me."

"But it's the wrong kind of liquidity!"

"You must excuse my husband. He tells it like it is."

"He's right. You should treat yourselves."

"O tarshack, the pot wants its own greens!"

"We were just in Bankbilk and they sent us right back to the gutter."

"Favours and serfdom, that's what they want!"

"Some credit please! We can help you. Have you heard of the Five-Year Plan?"

"Sounds like horizontal collectivism to me!"

"Honey, shush ..."

"The Point of Finance is easy to grasp. No collateral and there are many options for exactly how you want to work off your POF. You'd be surprised how many ways there are to take it out of you! From the exotic locale of a wind pharm to the most spumid regions of Putridworld ..."

"Putridworld!"

The scene shifted to a close-up of Puss Lichen's lovely face. She was moaning wildly and holding the handsome face of her commercial husband between her thighs. They were covered in sticky filaments and delectable guts and it was clear they were not alone but surrounded by aquacukes.

"O darling, what a mess!"

"Some credit please!"

The clerk reappeared, hardly immune to the contagious passion of the couple. Then as she tore off her clothes and crept toward them, she flashed a brilliant grin.

"The Five-Year Plan, from Some Credit Please. What's *your* plan?"

Something Phishy

It was not for the faint of heart, but there was a valley in InteriorVille where the most surprising things could happen. This was a celebration called Cukecalia, and all the gatherers were clad in crinkly green gladrags with matching piscine masks. One of them leaned on his Laughing Stick and watched another member toy with a dripping cuke for a long while before introducing himself. They shook in the traditional Playsonic manner.

"My, what a firm handsnake you have!"

In a cozy nook, there were a number of women enjoying their own company upon a writhing bed of aquacukes. There happened Looney, who in his frantic search for Kettleman, happened upon Trudie Bittles and Gamma Farouche, presently in the thrall of a blonde woman with smoky grey eyes who grazed their bare skin with a sucrawhip. He was more than a trifle shocked at this turn of events and hopelessly in love with all of them.

Through the Jalousie

Mr. Quartz turned away from his bran new wife and stared into sublunar darkness. Ms. Lazuli was zoning out to touch face with departmental squatters from Foreign Objects at the very frontier of the revamp. It was, of course, her job to stroke them into meek submission before the inevitable happened. At this tick, she would be passing some of the supracane cutters, avoiding the hunger in those bleary eyes that traced the deep cut in her data-massaging attire. Then her attention would be drawn to their strong and bittersweet bodies. She would decide upon the brute of the lot, Loco, and their eyes would lock, and they would be contractually obliged to set up an assignation, if not arrange an assassination, such was this uncertain climate.

Notwithstanding, for the duration of her stay, they would find ways to meet amid an intricate quincunx of manmade levees, aqueducts, canals, dikes, and diversion dams. Her first order of business awaited her inside the palatial workstation. She wasted no time in administering the Bildung Endustries assimilation prospectus, packed with tangibles of beautiful Venusians trying to work through incredibly tense and compromising situations. The prospectus used old-fashioned hallucinograms to induce a mild state of inebriation in anyone who smelt its glossy leaves, which is to say *everyone*. Ms. Lazuli took her time initiating the mesmergraphic equipment, waiting for her audience to enter a more receptive state of mind.

Even Mr. Quartz was not immune to his own holographic dots, and occasionally suffered from a mild case of rewind. It seemed to him he was watching through the louvres of the jalousie as Ms. Lazuli led the men outside, carrying their spanking-new emerald uniforms with the BE crest upon it. She set the example by unlocking the Feltcro snap that held her outfit in place and diving into the sublime water. The men from Foreign Objects steadied themselves and took off their old uniforms before following suit. The eyes of Mr. Quartz widened through the jalousie as the frustrated men homed in on her and formed a circle around her.

Loco, their de facto leader, slashed at the supracane, unable to look away from their savage demands and the warm welcome of Ms. Lazuli. She knew precisely how to make them comfortable and how to tend to the specific needs of each. Large and faceless, they soon grew drowsy in her expert grip. Then, after a lengthy cleansing sequence, she whipped out a Bildung Endustries belt with matching dill. Each man reacted differently, but all submitted to this first action that reinforced her undeniable authority over their lives. Mr. Quartz stared through the jalousie, trying to count the members of her interstellar staff, yet finding it like an infinite series in a rather tricky mathematical problem. Even Loco had shoved his way through the inevitable conga lines and congo lines that resulted, eager to prove his mettle to the only woman to visit their workstation in several thrillion aches.

"Schmmmmhmm ..."

Next to Quartz, Chalcedony stirred, feeling the dampness in the small of her back with her fingers.

"Uhmmmm ... someone is dreaming again."

"What you must think of me."

She laughed, disappearing under the ultra-thin cilantro sheet.

Kindly Recticheck Before Boarding

A diminutive man from Omphalos scuttled through the antidoom, cranking his gamecock neck around with a smirk of satisfaction.

"You made it. Clean to board."

The man from Omphalos collected his faded items of simwear before extracting the flopping recticheck probe, dropping it into a self-disposal, courtesy of Luxury Luttle.

"I wanna go again!"

Minor's companion emerged from addressing obnubilate speculations about the actual nature of their relationship to tug his arm affectionately, a gesture that rapidly transformed into an elongated caress. Meanwhile, the recticheckers giggled, trying to quell their flushing and gushing. They were about to let him straight through when their supermega appeared.

"We do have regulations."

"Yes, of course."

"Any interesting substances or compounds or seedlings or spores upon your radishing person?"

Minor whipped out a wriggling cannicle of Dentiglow, never failing to lose the best angle of the nearest surveillance device.

"I never leave home without a spanking-fresh cannicle of Dentiglow. It brightens and whitens and sprouts new and improved fangs. Sport a smile brighter than a solar explosion!"

"I hate to inconvenience you but this animated cannicle is TRINORM size and therefore breaches regulation size."

"I suppose I can always buy another cannicle on the other side."

"Abominably sorry, Herr Minor!"

His beautiful companion stripped him and herself bare out of sheer commiseration and they stepped gracefully through the antidoom together.

"We can do each other."

There was a collective gasp of ecstasy as they began to search one another where it feels best with their own designer rectichecker probes. It was no secret what the slippery insert of *GaSp* would be covering by mid-afternoon. They lingered over the echo of each vibrating probe, providing ample opportunities for a fifty-seven-page pop-out section in the next issue of *Vanitaccia*.

"Mmm ... ooooooh ... yeah ..."

Then amid orgasmic screaming they were waved along a corridor of pure corn. The supermega followed procedure and carefully unscrewed the cannicle of Dentiglow. The spearmint content leapt out and slithered deep into his open mouth. Behind the protective layer of the counterboom, both of the Minors smiled. Everyone at the recticheck was obliterated in a flash of whiter than white brightness.

Lost, Even When Found

Klouk Meek crept cautiously through the steaming bowels of Foreign Objects. He was rather bemused at this turn of events. A prodcog had gone missing and the only way to retrieve it was to find the Refactorizer in one of the redundant lower wings. He was reduced to calling out for the Refactorizer, who would likely hear his echo and reply. Klouk was startled out of his wits as a strong hand seized his elbow and dragged him into the shadows. He found himself pinned by some unknown beauty, in keeping with his favourite sidereal serials.

"Hello, pretty lady!"

"Volume down. You are a moving target."

"I see – the sense of danger excites you too."

"Negative. That prodcog is the order for your demise."

"What? Then ..."

"Affirm. You are scheduled for imminent redundancy."

"If so ... why are you helping me?"

"Then you cannot divine my identity?"

"Was it on holiday – at that three-star winestar?"

"Then I am lost, even when found."

"Not Perdita?"

"Do you recognize my voice?"

"Yes, but you were a damselfly! You had appendages—"

"Bildung Endusties decided to escalate my transfiguration, to subdue my most natural impulses, and to replace them with customized ARGs, so that I might be a better fit."

"I'm not at a superlative level. I have no idea what ARGs are. Also, I'm terrified to ask."

"Artificial Replication Genomes. They were infused into my previous form until this transformation was brought about."

"Do you still feast on humanoid leftovers?"

"I only eat Green now."

"You mean, you *eat only Green now*."

"You would dare question my new casual circuitry?"

"I'm sure you mean your *new causal circuitry*."

"Not that it matters. I could see this coming. I was about to leave this company anyhow ..."

"I am unable to appreciate your logic."

"That's because you're a robot."

Perdita covered her face. She had begun to weep. Klouk felt a very slight pain in his chest.

"Aww ... you're still a damselfly to me."

Perdita stiffened with pride and swiftly dewept.

"We must escape, Klouk Meek. You will have to trust me and no one else."

"What about my workenpeers?"

"Especially not them. They think you are trying to take their jobs."

"Well, you *are* rather pretty, and my prospects are not exactly brimming over."

"Now that is logic I am fully able to appreciate."

Persuasion Desk

"Have you read *Persuasion*?"

"Never heard of it."

Aleph asked everyone who came to his desk. It was important to him, since he had been hired on the basis of his acute comprehension of the text. Every interstellar organization, even the most withered branch of Foreign Objects, required a department that dealt exclusively with matters of persuasion. He affirmed the signature code authorizing a sector shakedown and a few more lobe probes. Then Lux Operon appeared, pulling a whimsical face, and he asked her. She lit up at once.

"Yes! I love *Persuasion*."

"I love *Persuasion* as well."

"Anne is so smart ... smarter than everyone!"

"Generally, I love how she gets everyone to conform to her will. It's excellent company reading."

Aleph let his eyepiece rove. A fellow in the corner felt his knees buckle under the tremendous force of that glare. It was obvious his feedbreak was complete.

"Wow, you persuade as well!"

"No one is unpersuadable. No one."

At that instant, two persuaders appeared and stunned Aleph. They covered him in a jammy paste and rolled him into a froot stretchie before dragging him away. Lux Operon laughed as usual, but there was no one around to say nervously.

The Innocents

Chalcedony tugged the small hands of her two charges, feeling their supersubtle resistance the entire time.

"Morgana bit me!"

"I would not dream of doing anything he did not enjoy."

"What do we call you?"

"I know what to call her, since she dresses like a common slank."

"O tarn, call me what you like!"

Morgana stared at Chalcedony fiercely.

"You are not our mother."

"Then call me Nan."

Arthur laughed heartily.

"Then she is what we would call a NILF."

"Where did you hear that?"

"Everyone knows."

"What about your father?"

"Are you suggesting Mr. Quartz is our progenitor?"

"I was labouring under that assumption."

"Let us be perfectly civil and say he is *responsible* for us."

"And yet you appear to owe him no ion of respect."

"And I quote, *Do animals cleave worshipfully to their fathers? Have they even a bare inkling of which male begot them? Searching for motives to warrant filial gratitude, will you cite the care my father took of me during my infancy and childhood? Another error. Complying with them, he ceded to the customs of the country, to his pride, to a sentiment which, as a father, he managed to conceive for his handiwork but which there is no need whatever that I conceive for the artisan; for that artisan, acting uniquely at the behest of his own pleasure, had no thought at all for me when it so pleased him to proceed to the act of propagation with my dam; his sole concern was for himself, and I fail to see therein any basis for especially ardent feelings of gratitude.*"

"What ever have you been intergesting?"

"Lovely filthy old things."

"Sounds like comprehension excelerators to me."

"I please myself."

Morgana glared at Chalcedony again, smiling slyly.

"We know what you get up to."

"Up to?"

"With the Marquis."

"I have no idea what you mean."

"Don't you? I can show you what I mean."

Arthur pulled her by her molten coat down to his level and kissed her cheek.

"Kissing."

"Kissing? Yes, it is quite customary."

"No, I mean kissing!"

Chalcedony recoiled as Arthur kissed her lips with his tongue lolling about. In tandem, Morgana reached for her bare thigh and made a lewd gesture, the meaning of which was perfectly understood.

"How about we forget all about this and play a game?"

"Is it a game for grown-ups?"

Chaldedony dragged them deeper into the winding arcades, searching for the spot where she had hooked into Molar. Neither were surprised to see one another again.

"Two more to play."

"How many levels?"

"How about the works?"

Molar grinned and escorted them into one of the vacant traders. Chalcedony returned the smile and chained her two charges to the blotter. They each began to scream as the disexcitation process began.

"You now have two lives."

Service Centre

Kink jacked in and found herself on a dusty road in nothing but a sealskin coat and a distressed skirt. She stuck out her thumb. Upon the horizon, she could see an approaching limuck, the old kind known as a clunkmuck. Already, she could hear the roar of the wild boys looking to score. They knew her record and still they came in droves. As the limuck pulled over she could hear the crazed thumping emanating from inside.

"Interface hydromel!"

"I'm vacant for a boost."

"Authorize!"

"I'm out of petrobucks."

"Repair deficit."

The door opened and Kink climbed inside. The boys clustered around her, pulling and poking and rubbing. She surrendered to their clumsy advances until they had completely eaten her lentil bustier and arugula netherwear. Then she offered up a suggestion.

"Level up hardcore."

"Hardcore! Enhance hardcore ... whooooo ..."

She whispered to the driver what she wanted and at once he sped for the nearest **SERVICE CENTRE.** He veered into an open bay door and it locked behind them. At some point in the middle of their intricate entanglements, everyone began to feel light-headed. The driver slumped over the joysteer. Oleaginous metallic tentacles appeared and Kink laboured hard to give each of the boys a helping of the gushers of black gold.

"Carbon mono with a healthy mix of fossil deposits, wasters!"

"*Glug glug glug ...*"

"Take your petrobucks in full!"

After all the slick boys had stopped quivering, her preprogrammed paramour appeared from behind a fuel pump. He picked her up and she dug her spurs into his firm flesh. Then she placed a pillow over his face and pulled the trigger of a fully charged neurolancer.

Pharming Out

Ammonia Gig lifted the pitcher full of Limeeenation to her lips and drank, resisting the urge to spit it out. After all, she required the supplements to survive. She looked around anxiously. Werner would not be back for a while. She stuck out her tongue and slowly began to lick the side of the pitcher. It might incite his anger if another item of cornware went missing, but she could not resist. Then she heard deep laughter and the smacking of lips. She turned around, hearing nothing but the crazed mating of unterminated cockadas. However, she knew who had seen her transgression with the corn pitcher. She cursed her husband for pharming out his own domestic affairs to a pair of Droserans. The way she was raised, she had grown up hearing nothing but curses and jibes about their way of life to the far south of Spermatophyta. However, it would be better to reason with them and not have Werner find out she was into the cornware.

"Honey afternoon, ma'am."

"Very honey."

They were using their sticky pedicels to lift and arrange bales of tofu. She watched them work for a while, noting the way they glistened with the sundew dripping down their irregular bodies. She cleared her throat and raised the pitcher.

"Want some?"

"Corn?"

"No, to drink."

The larger Droseran named Glug spat to one side.

"That's poison to us, Missus."

"Anything you need, then?"

"How about you, ma'am?"

"What are you implying?"

Jar Jar put down his bales and hovered over to a spot behind her. She could hear the crazed mating of unterminated cockadas and the strange buzzing sound of the two Droserans on either side of her.

"We see you lick corn."

As Jar Jar droned this phrase more than once, the air filled with a sweet aroma and it reminded Ammonia of both salt and sugar, two things she had tasted only once in her life. Also, the mesmerizing movement of their glistening red tentacles was having a most peculiar effect upon her. She understood they were really just long thick bristles that had evolved into working appendages, but they certainly seemed sturdy and serviceable enough. Her breath quickened as one of the pedicels lashed the pitcher out of her hand and two more tugged at the capellini straps of her neglected. Once she had been stripped bare, the sticky glands began to rub against her body, leaving transparent secretions. Ammonia touched them to her tongue and tasted the sugary-salty substance she had lain awake dreaming of. Glug lay back on a bale of tofu, almost taunting her to taste his bouquet of stemming sweetness. She gripped one tentacle at a time and merrily sucked the tip of it while Jar Jar played with her body from behind. She leapt upon Glug, as Jar Jar climbed on top of her.

"Like a sugar-salt sandwich."

"We only eat meat, ma'am."

"Whaaaaa—"

It took the entire afternoon for the two Droserans to utterly absorb her. When Werner returned that evening, he only found some broken shards of cornware covered in a sticky substance. He could hear nothing but the crazed mating of unterminated cockadas.

You Look Familiar

Almost at once, Snoop Parker recognized a rundown part of Bildungburb, the beating heart of Bildung Endustries and a fistful of affiliates, including RectAll Unlimited. He had missed a fastropod and he flagged down a wreckshaw. Climbing aboard, he found himself facing a woman in shadow. He stared at the logo on her lab coat until she coughed politely. He looked away, trying not to stare as she polished off an entire cukedog. Then, licking her lips, she held out sticky palms.

"Spare a cleanse?"

"Allow me."

"You look familiar."

"So do you."

"You're that tube throb."

"And you?"

"My name is Casta Gloss. As you may have guessed, I'm just on my way to RectAll."

"They pay all right?"

"Let's just say there is an excellent compensation package."

"You know, I'd love to see inside RectAll."

"It's not so thrilling, but I could show you a few things."

Casta Gloss struck a sultry pose and pouted as Snoop carefully withdrew his hand out of the glowing waiverhole. Someone had written DEW YR WURST next to it.

"The pranks I have to put up with!"

"Looks like I got the togglethumb."

"Yes, you're all mine now."

Inside the laboratory, she fell into his arms.

"Forgive me, I am just overworked – and lonely! My husband, Loam, is always being called back to Bildung at the strangest hours and I almost never see him. Surely you know the stories one hears about that place! Yet here I am, leading you on with mere promises of carnal animality – it's positively diabolical!"

"Don't be so hard on yourself, Casta. Please, I understand."

"Won't you call me Dr. Gloss? That is my title on these premises."

"Yes, your air of professional distance is doing it for me."

"Would you kindly wait in this narrow little room while I slip into something more uncomfortable?"

"Of course, Dr. Gloss."

Snoop paced up and down, examining the holes in the wall of the little room. He figured that anything could happen in this place but it might give the game away to ask too many questions.

"You know, my mother was a doctor."

"Really? Has she passed on?"

"Turn of phrase, really. I say she *was* a doctor because I never met her, not properly. I was given up for adoption and taken in by the incredibly attractive Parker family, and that in itself is another tale I won't bore you with."

"So, she could be a doctor right now."

"Doing research ... I don't see why not. Never gave it much thought."

"How about some music to put you in the mood?"

"What is it?"

"*Dumbarton Oaks.*"

"Seems to be doing the trick, Dr. Gloss."

The dopey grin of Snoop Parker was swiftly wiped away by the rapid spray of an aquacuke fearing predation. Countless others began to creep through each of the holes in the walls. Then, with the release of an acerbal mist, his clothes dissolved and he found himself stark naked and covered in wriggling aquacukes. At first he was tentative, even scared, but before long, he was once more enjoying himself. They certainly wanted their pickle fight. He groaned as their drippy persistence began to revive a number of repressed memories and he was scarcely aware of the mutterings and active notations surrounding this activity.

"Maternal doombuggying ..."

"Classic retro in utero ..."

"Classic ..."

"Abandonment followed by preconditioned anagnorisis ..."

"Classic Siegfried Syndrome ..."

"Classic ..."

"Next phase?"

"Send in Dillgro."

"Then switch to *The Rite of Spring*, climax."

As the violent asymmetrical rhythms of the sacrificial dance sequence began, the aquacukes scattered, retreating into their holes. Thick bristling tentacles replaced them, winding around Snoop's limbs and holding him in place. Suddenly, he remembered the strange marks that were found on Muffsnuffle, and the truth dawned on him. There were quite possibly less embarrassing ways to go.

"I thought they discontinued you."

"That was another hybrid called Angio. I am called Fox Dillgro. Now come to me, *ma petite bêche-de-mer* ..."

The massive tentacle snaking into Snoop's mouth was rather lactiferous and his kneejerk response was to suck it dry. When another free tentacle found its tender target, Snoop tensed up at first but soon gave way to its in-depth investigation. It was not possible to be vocal on the matter but this was most definitely doing it for him. He did not notice the faint odour of Homunkucide until it was too late.

Dr. Foo Baz Quux pointed with enthusiasm at the now lifeless body of Snoop Parker from the observation chamber.

"Once you go green, you never go back. This is really far more humane, don't you find?"

"F, may I ask why we are doing this?"

"The categorical imperative, Dr. Gloss."

"Surely that forbids environuff."

"You never know. This research is saving lives as we speak."

"But at what cost?"

"Your reaction is perfectly natural, instinctive even. Fascinating."

"What can you mean?"

"Do you remember a rather mediocre boy that you gave up for adoption?"

"Wait – not again – no – what?"

"There's no right time to break the news to you, but that was your son. In all probability, *our* son."

"My – our – no, that's impossible. Loam—"

"O do the math, honeydew."

Casta Gloss burst into the room and knelt beside the prone form of Snoop Parker, tearing at her hair and beating at her bosom. Fox Dillgro began to make some of his trademarked moves but F shooed him away.

"I certainly hope this won't adversely affect our working relationship in any way."

"Of course not."

"You do know there are ways we can try again, and I am of course using all of them, even at this very tick. It should comfort you that for once in his shadfly life, Snoop actually knew too much."

"O my! The pranks I have to put up with!"

This Plutonian Bisque Has Better Taste

Mr. Quartz sat by himself in a throbbing conch at the head of a long table. He had not been to What the Shuck in ages. He noted the other parties, nodding at the Duchess Ampersand, who was rapidly becoming a political reality to contend with. She was dining with a young hero he had heard of, no doubt to raise her profile. It was fortunate that no one recalled her origins any more than they recalled what What the Shuck referred to. Then Mr. Quartz frowned at the spectacle of a man who did recall a great number of things, perhaps too many. The illustrious and demagogic Minor was making a scene with his beautiful daughter Diminuenda, feeding her raw cloysters and watching her rather phishy reaction as she swallowed them. Mr. Quartz was by no means morally outraged by their latest publicity stunt, but he was concerned about the Minors' efforts to endorse their own religion ... what he could only describe as a mythological perversion of neo-commersuasion. For a man who had already been publicly executed and auto-resuscitated, he was rather pushing the envelope. The trouble was, whenever Minor dabbled with such a scheme, the economy went down. Then, at some point, it would luttleblush again. The question was when.

The Marquis had also arrived, with a woman wriggling merrily upon each arm. Goneril had become the spitting image of Chalcedony and versa vice. The Marquis glipped on the collaborative blipvert they had patched together for Bildung Endustries. The eromatic images wafted throughout the room, pervading the sensorium of everyone fortunate enough to be dining at What the Shuck that evening. Mr. Quartz observed his undressed daughter being chained to a wall and doused with bran new molecule-free Mayonada. His bran new undressed wife expressed delighted curiosity in the dripping layers of goop and appeared about to try some as the Marquis, clad in nothing but a pair of old-fashioned LeatheX shorts, cracked a giant spazzmatazz. As the blipvert continued, it sank into the muck of the lower brain of each patron and then crept down their spines, leaving their brains free to ignore anything on the downlow.

"I thought you were to be sole recipient of the slather."

"The Marquis had other ideas."

"I see."

"O Daddy, it's only playacting! One would think you were bran spanking new to the Object business!"

The Duchess was not best pleased but she remained congenial. In addition, the Minors remained congenital, relishing every drop of wicked irony about the production. However, for the first time, Mr. Quartz noticed that the woman dining with Zirconium Bluff was not one of his usual gluttish escorts but rather the very lovely Ms. Lazuli. His eyes remained fixed upon her stalkless kale number, even as the Marquis launched multiple innuendos at him. Ms. Lazuli arched an eyebrow and made a shruggish gesture of helplessness, as if to say, *You have the wrong woman and what is worse, the wrong promotional aids ... I would call you a limpnuts if I were not so genteel. I would say this Plutonian bisque has better taste.* He returned his attention to the blipvert, mulling over the image of the Marquis holding his young wife's head down in a bowl of reconstituted flave.

"I say, Quartz, frisk up a bit. It's all in the family."

"Chalcedony, I hear you took the little ones out."

"Yes, but they were perfectly horrid. I sent them to Reformation Camp."

"Not Arthur and Morgana. The little knaves?"

"They even said you were not their father."

"Murky facts aside, they are still my charges."

"They also called me a – well, I cannot bring myself to tell you here ... I'll tell you ... in bed."

Mr. Quartz stared through his young wife and his new makeshift family and the blipvert gyrotechnics that had the popular eatery patrons all worked up. He could not take his eyes off the incomparable Ms. Lazuli.

"I'm not feeling too clever."

He cupped his smooth hands to his mouth, feeling he was going to be sick. The others attributed this giddy spell to a bit of poorly simulated poi in the blipvert and even in mid-swoon, he accepted their speedy assessment of the situation, although the truth of the matter was known only to him. At the most inopportune time in his life, Mr. Quartz had developed feelings for Ms. Lazuli.

And How Does That Make You Feel?

"Why don't we start with your name?"

"Mann. Oober Mann."

"And where are you from?"

"We've been over this."

"So let's just clarify a few more buttersticks."

"I am from the Terran planet formerly known as Earth."

"Period?"

"An epoch known as the Near Future."

"You can substantiate that?"

"No, I've only been recalling it through hypnoregress. In that time I was a writer, or at least someone who thought he was a writer. I was under the impression I had written a book called *Minor Episodes*."

"Ha ha! A classic romp. Marcel Minor, I believe."

"Yes, I was the chucklestalk of the universe for a while. Still am in some sectors."

"What gave you this very false impression?"

"I was being worked by aliens for their mission to recover a time travel device known as the tachyonometer. I was approached by one of them pretending to be a popular hot mustard model known in advert circles as the Dijon Diva."

"Then you discovered another side of yourself with the Preworld fellow?"

"Yes, and that was a beautiful spiritual experience."

"Then something else screwed you up ... let me see ..."

"My dog Faustus turned out to be named Nano Nine, who used support from the other aliens to assume command of the planet Lagopus ..."

"Yes, yes ... now let's skip ahead a bit ..."

"Well, somebody put me in a cryobed and I woke up in a post-Meltdown world. Then a Phasmidalan called the Librarian, with the vital assistance of a viscous critic named Alfred J. Bastard, spent a great deal of time debasing me and my imaginary work."

"You mean *vicious* critic?"

"No."

"Yet you enjoyed this treatment immensely."

"Of course. Apparently, I suffer from a complex that leaves me very susceptible to anything that makes me seem extremely important to universal maintenance."

"Hmm ... I see."

"Then Leonard Bernstein saved my life ... and briefly, I was mistaken for a god by a cargo cult on account of my cargo pants ..."

"Yes, we've already plumbed that part. But things were not what they appeared, were they?"

"They either were or they were not. It's rather fuzzy. I then woke up in a care facility, feeling everything that had happened to me was a dream. I was then informed by a doctor that I had imagined writing five great works that when assembled would form a perfect quincunx. They used a simulation of a Cockney relief reporter for BBC Omniverse to try and hypnotize me."

"Cockney?"

"Dialect. It would take too long to explain. But the accent hooked me, no question. Also, I was feeling pretty vulnerable after the Librarian. A bit of attention, you know."

"And did you fulfill your fantasy with ..."

"Perspicacity Vauxhall."

"Well?"

"At that point, I did not know if she was real. Or me, for that matter."

"That didn't stop you in the past."

"I can't remember. I must have got away from that strange doctor."

"Did Ms. Vauxhall ever mention this ... um ... quincunx?"

"Not that I recall."

"What else did she say?"

"She wanted me to meet up with a group called the Akita Inu."

"And did you?"

"No, I must have ended up in another cryobed, because the next time I woke up, I was here."

"And the planet you call home was gone."

"It's now the stumblebutt rehashing station called Bluegreenbox 69."

"And how does that make you feel?"

Number One or Number Two?

Drat and Lourdes Knuckleduster returned to their cuticles and waved to Object Enabler Lava Liebeslust, who smiled wryly. She was more irritable than usual since the malfunk with the erotobots. One thing was for sure. Although they were physically superior in every way and, when necessary, formidable masters, she placed no trust in robots. She far preferred the antique machine that had been at the top of her wedding gift list. Her workenpeer, Brain Ferguson, said that everyone did a little droid now and then. It was good for the immune system. He had bragged about his recent adventure with two droidas from the Wretchyan Nebula. It had only cost him a few credits for the old *bag of oranges* technique. Provided it was not during Humpday Flex, he was free to do whatever he liked. Yet it took effort to conceal her scowl as Klouk Meek returned in the company of the refactorized Perdita Diamond. She far preferred that dishy Kanadakan, possibly in strict accordance with her ficken fetish. Also, he was a team player, prepared to qualmlessly play for both teams. Lava knew she had a heap to formulate, but ... She winked across at Brain, and without a word they both jacked in ...

They were floating about in the Fickenham plant. She saw Kanadakan plucking new and improved aberrations out of the ficken before it could be processed further. Even the scent of iridescent feathers had been simulated. She undid the Feltcro snaps on the back of his workensuit and applied the classic reacharound technique she had learned in finishing school. Then Kanadakan, or someone trolling and accepting the limited role of Kanadakan, groaned with ecstatic anguish. At once, Lava perceived the kind of mutually beneficial power exchange she was seeking. She switched on the dill attached to the company utility belt and oillessly entered him through the gash in the seat of his workensuit. She grunted hastily at Brain but he was in a blasé mood, wanting only to wankpeep.

"You'd like your progeny to go to finishing school?"

The better half of Brain Ferguson promptly snapped to attention. He so often needed the fight-or-flight reflex to get his blood going. Veiled threats were right up his rearstoop.

"Well, Lava, Number One or Number Two?"

"Don't ask and, for the love of Sodom, don't tell!"

Before they could do anything more, a molten slank materialized and activated her spell. Lava and Brain writhed and convulsed under its influence. The slank raised an electrified whip and began to lash the limp body of Kanadakan's doppelgänger. His screams were lost amid the squerks of abruptly chopped ficken, even as his head was lopped off. His surprised head turned toward them, clearly not enjoying itself.

"O that I had fings like a ficken! For then I would fluck off and find rest."

At this instant, there was a power surge and Lava and Brain were prematurely jacked off the sysflirt.

Klouk Meek was looking at Lava quizzically. Perdita Diamond was monitoring the ebb and flow of her circuroute. Lux Operon was cackling madly. No one noticed for a long time that Kanadakan was not sleeping in the depths of his pod. No one noticed at all what Drat and Lourdes Knuckleduster were doing to the Portable Potable System.

You Like to Peeppeep

Mr. Quartz fled with as much grace as he could muster and escaped to the Voyeur's Terrace. Once he felt assured of his solitude, he pulled out a fine bottle of plunk and swiftly unplugged it. He watched the couples in their cages opposite, in some cases multiplying into amorous trios and quartets, with each headstrong protagonist offering the others a slippery bit of lowbrow theatre. He could even make out tiny figures that looked like his daughter and his wife and the Marquis and Minor and Diminuenda, and this caused no small amount of reflection on the general sameness of humanity. He was surely a genetic mutation away from being inextricably involved in that corn cage match. Just as the workers he watched were only a mutation away from his own complexifications. He could see a man who looked like Zirconium Bluff with an assortment of illegal vegetables, stripping the stalkless kale number off the body of Ms. Lazuli, and he knew his mind was playing tricks on him.

"You like to peeppeep."

Mr. Quartz turned around to face the young hero from the restaurant. He offered him the bottle.

"We haven't had the pleasure ... sorry, the cornware is downstairs."

"The pleasure and the honour are mine."

"I have heard of you but I'm afraid your name escapes me."

"Charmdeep Offensive."

"You were in the company of the Duchess."

"She and I were acquainted long ago."

"Now you are a great hero."

"I did what might be expected of any man who calls himself such."

"In turn, I owe you a great debt."

"You are the hero. You did a great deal during the Irresolution Conflict."

"I was asked to kill and I killed. I see no heroism in it."

"Then I speak out of turn."

"What about the Duchess?"

"To be perfectly candid, I think she remembers our past far too well and far too conveniently. Do not think I speak ill of her but as a political creature she can do nothing else but remember me as suits her current purpose."

"Her current purpose?"

"A post in the Galaxy Aggressor Group."

"So she's simply mugging for GAG."

"That would be my first guess. I could be mistaken."

"You don't agree with her decision?"

"It is not my place to speak of what does not concern me."

They leaned upon the ridged peanut railing and stared across thoughtfully at a woman who from this distance resembled the Duchess. She was running up and down in front of an impossibly ornate glorywall, through which anonymous celebrity participants were making very brief appearances. Charmdeep sighed.

"If only she had time for such sport."

"Take heart, my young friend. One day you will meet the right person for you."

"Easy for you to say! You have made an excellent match!"

Mr. Quartz turned away, staring absentmindedly at the tremulous activities of three other exhibitionists. Charmdeep began to talk about his struggles and hopes and dreams, all the while hinting at ways in which he might be helped by a man (or woman) of means. Mr. Quartz could only think of Ms. Lazuli, of her beauty and magnificence and swiftness and grace of movement. He knew the thought of entering a room with her upon her arm nuzzled his vanity, but was it not a grand declaration of her worth that lent him worth to be associated with her? Were there not more ardent declarations to make? Or was there to be no more drück between them?

"Then what is one to do?"

Mr. Quartz took another swig of plunk and glared at the young man.

"Live, damn you! Not like these undulating oscillating unicellular protozoa, but as a worthwhile person with sights and sounds to enjoy! Attend to each moment and endeavour to understand it. Life is in so many ways the spectacular distracting noise, the illusion before our eyes we cannot penetrate. It takes a leap of faith to grasshop through and grasp in your hands what is truly there. Not in the fluctuations of other bodies and their raddled flesh, but within yourself! Whatever we put our hands and minds to, we make manifest. You talk as if all the circumstances were loaded against you, as if nothing of mine could ever be yours and as if the Duchess would never put out your fires with her heavenly saliva. If she is what you seek, then hang it all, she may love you yet! But machete through the wilderness first, before you tell me it contains nothing but arbitrariness or misfortune! Each thing in itself is so very rich and in so many ways a world unknown to us. Do you think you stand such a narrow chance on account of your penury? Already, you have met your moment and have not shied away from facing yourself, which is to say, the hero you aspire to be. For another, it might be untold riches. For yet another, it might be the wide and passionate realm of love. In spite of how you perceive me, I know my moment came and went in the blink of an eye. I loped along, like a man without eyes or ears. Youth in itself is nothing and old age has nothing to do with wisdom. Leave aside all tired assumptions. One must live to be old and happy from the beginning, not after the fact."

Charmdeep removed his nippers and began to clean them.

"Then for you, it is too late."

"I have gone about everything wrongheadedly but there is still hope, even for me. I will find a way to remedy the situation. Or if I fail, will it not be in some way commendable that I tried? Do not go through life without this sense of truth and wonder! Live, damn you! Live, I say!"

Charmdeep smiled.

"Then perhaps it is time we stopped peeppeeping and began to act."

Mr. Quartz laughed. Although he could do so much to help this charming young man, he knew he never would.

Night Vision

"Why don't we start with your name?"

The audience on the other side of the Night Vision peephole burst into laughter. Two people who hadn't heard exploded from sheer excitement in the face of the mysterious and the unfathomable. Everyone else began to chant.

"Minor Minor Minor ..."

Vodka Tonik, the strikingly hawky host, took a moment to remove her sticky pair of Beta-Carotenes and tossed them toward the nearest automatic blowtorch. The audience roared as three audience members were scorched in their vain attempts to catch her designer castoffs.

"Only a few casual casualties tonight! What do you say to that, Marcel Minor?"

"Well, Vodka, the night is young."

She lifted her thick Oedipedals and eased her guest into a tasteful pedaljob.

"Now we know you used to own, like, everything and that's, like, molten. But the tip of the prompter's whip is urging me to start at the beginning and ask about your first book – *Minor Episodes* ..."

"Of course, Vodka. It is first and foremost unauthorized autoerotica detailing the cyclical episodes of my life ..."

"According to sourcefeeds, you had to break the laws of time to continually relive your life during this series of episodes ..."

"Virulent blurthacks! I merely bent the laws of time to engineer each episode in a continuous time loop. In essence, I created a rift through which I could run the needle of causality more than once. Like you, I was once frustrated with the old once-around. I could only find satisfaction in the process of experiencing every permutation of existence."

"Ah! Satisfaction is sooo primordial!"

The audience cheered as Vodka pedalled faster and faster.

"*Minor Episodes* is a fully functioning model of orbital area 47 in the frontal cortex of the human brain (area 12 in the monkey's) that traces each temporal correlation between serially remote neurophysiological events. Rife with biotextuality, I embody the *everything* character who actualizes a number of postulations about the applied effects of sensuous genius upon the brain. This prototype graphs the minute pivot point at every juncture where the expected pleasure of the Erotic (rooted irascibly in the Socratic form of Eros) changes in mid-stream before being translated into airborne form for public consumption—"

"Yes! It totally blew my hind!"

"The monkeys were certainly very responsive."

"They are sure driving the market these days."

"This working model defies the metrics of genre in many previous experiments, endeavouring to imbue the material in question with the educated benefit of an experimental methodology whereby the linear sequence of the characters' lives is subject to a series of illogical and haphazard permutations. I have merely drawn these characters from my life for their archetypal merits. The Concierge is the traditional hapless sidekick and the Stropper serves as the perpetual spectre of death. The Snapper embodies the voyeuristic aspect of modernity, and although I tried to suppress his emergence, for dramatic purposes, Terence Cockerel is an excellent foil, and something of a *commedia dell'arte* archetype. We cannot downplay the historical significance of this post-colonial ginger beer heir moving to a quite altered global (and eventually universal) marketplace. It turns out we cannot completely efface this delusion of heroism and self-sacrifice from our most deeply rooted neurological impulses. In comparison, the live screaming action heroes Hurt Hardass and Kiki Kaka are mere parodies of the genre, bits of fluff really, who put a soggy damper upon our own inclination toward idolatry. During fractional interstimulus intervals, each of the episodes startles and inhibits neural activity ... let us say *challenges* dramatic expectations with something akin to impossibly elusive atonality ..."

"Now tell us about Miss Sharp."

"Miss Sharp is a somewhat idealized representation of *the one who got away*. Loveless career, etc."

"But she didn't get away, did she?"

"We had a beautiful daughter together. I already covered most of the details of our split in the sixty-six-part miniseries *Minor vs. Sharp*, which was also made into a feature tube called *Minor Schism*."

"How about that billboard cut-up Bébé Lala?"

"Ah yes ... Bébé helped us through the separation. Of course, she also helped me right *into* the separation. For more details, check out the full-length re-enactment *Minor Seduction*, also available in New Venusia as the unexpurgated *An Operation Too Far*."

"So what kind of archetype are you?"

"Can't you guess?"

Vodka shook her head. Minor seized her tremulous body, letting his hands wander under the hem of her punic.

"I am the chief antagonist."

Vodka brandished her wedding band before vehemently tossing it over the safety barrier. Then she held him fast, pumping him for more juicy details with products from their biggest sponsors, urged on by her overseer of a prompter.

"Now we'd like to shift focus to the subject of your daughter Diminuenda Minor, best known from the sleeper blastbust *Clock Tease*."

"My pride and joy!"

"There's been some controversy about your apparent ... level of intimacy."

"I'm thrilled you asked about that. Since making several fortunes and playing a few hobbyist tricks on the space-time continuum, I've begun to wonder if there is not more to life as we know it. As you may have already guessed, there isn't. And for this reason, as a terrantarian, I've decided to bring meaning back to the human race and all its mutant offshoots."

"But your daughter—"

"She has too much about her to fall prey to any feeble-brained notion of morality. She was more than familiar with the ancient myths of Myrrha and Electra and the daughters of Lot. Being up to speed with the latest complexes, she even disguised herself and came to me with the splendid proposition. As I want the very best for her, how could I refuse?"

"But you're related—"

"We are all related ... about ninety-nine percent the same. Pesky psychological traumas aside, it would be almost the same thing if you were to succumb to my delectable godhead!"

"Mmm ... no, I can ... ummm ... respect your beliefs."

Suddenly, Minor raised a giant Object of pure corn and smashed it down on the floor. The audience burst into tears along with Vodka Tonik and almost all of them achieved orgasm.

"This absurd sense of terror and fear is what everyone wants. Without this ominous threat hanging over it, life fails to impress us with its inherent significance. This is why Diminuenda and I have established the Cult of the Munificent Quincunx, to hammer this philosophical point home like a nail through the head of every unbeliever."

Minor walked up and down in front of the gloryholes, causing many audience members to faint from sheer anticipation. Vodka presented her inner thigh.

"Brand me. I long to belong."

"I wish it were that simple. But you can't make a religion without cracking a few skulls!"

"Wait, hold that thought! We have someone here who wants to say something to you!"

Diminuenda Minor stormed out in nothing but a torn turnip sack.

"You is lying, Daddy! I was homeschooled and somebody mucked up my joy zones! I can't be with normal dudes. I gots to have tentacles! I gots to freak it up!"

Diminuenda was accompanied by two Octopuds and two de-venomed Droserans. She began to kiss and lick their mighty tentacles and throbbing pedicels. But out of another door charged her long-lost mother, Miss Sharp, with open arms.

"Dim Dim! Honeydew, come home!"

The molten Diminuenda raced toward her still-molten mom and started a swearing and slapping contest, complying with the age-old theme of succession. Then a vat of piping white gravy opened up underneath them and they struggled within its greasy undercurrents. Then the lights went out and the familiar horn sounded. The audience members overturned their free dishes of figments, scrambling to put on their complimentary Night Vision infrared groggles. All the same, no one could see everything that was happening at once, and there was quite a lot to watch before the gargantublobdingnagian explosion.

Elective Affinities

Klouk Meek egged on the jamgorithm and resumed basetouch. It wasn't that he didn't like Perdita Diamond, but he suffered no small amount of anxiety over the whole robot issue. His own neo-Ludditic trauma, coupled with her intensive flashes of self-awareness she called thought flashes, was a lot to handle just now. For a tick, he wished he were merely drunk and she merely a damselfly. If he were honest with himself, that had been his only plan until the refactorization got in the way. What had compounded his personal dilemma was the admonition about his workenpeers, who up until this point had not been off limits during extended flex time. Statistically speaking, Perdita knew he would reveal everything under the right conditions, and that meant there was a high probability Quincunx Sixty-Nine could make an educated stab in the dark. For this reason, he had submitted a profile to Elective Affinities, hoping for a short-lived opportunity to be compromised without being compromised. Such was his rationale on this matter. He had initiated the jamming loop to prevent Perdita from scanning this particular circuroute. He was pleasantly surprised to discover he had received an invitation to the Off Garden. He accepted and made haste to the Garden at once.

"Blazehook?"

"You know it."

"Just don't frat. Far too parlous."

"Just don't fret, Perdita!"

Perdita watched him hurry off with a look of impatience. She was beginning to feel self-aware again.

"Initiating temporary shutdown."

Klouk made his way through a vast collection of man-eaters and exotic rotundifolia. There was a small corn table with a jug of Jungian sap waiting for him. Standing directly behind it was his elective affinity, looking very much like her avatard in a modest ukini and a fetching collar. Her Scitish accent cooed across the table at him, rollicking his netherworld.

"I have approved your nibblies."

"I acknowledge your interest and fully reciprocate."

"Why don't you make yourself comfortable."

"I am quite comfortable."

"Show me your nibblies, Mr. Meek."

"But I—"

"Show me!"

Klouk played it cool, calmly unfastening and removing his entertainment strap.

"Now come here, Mr. Meek."

"I esteem you greatly and yearn to know more of your ways."

"Come and show me how it's done."

Something was not quite right. As Klouk stepped into the clearing, three other women appeared, larger than the first but no less alluring. In fact, they looked smashing in their lavish LeatheX robes and prickpedallers. He even had trouble maintaining his sinking feeling.

"They call me Coccydynia. Today we are crowdstorming and doing some very sensitive Object testing and we could use your help."

"Do I have a choice?"

She reached down and toyed with his nibblies while the other women giggled. Klouk groaned, realizing that one of them was his superior adjacent.

"Of course, we already have your psychological profile. However, we just needed you to volunteer."

They put down their Chomskis and attended to his thirst, pouring some of the Jungian sap down his throat. He could now see his older sisters and relive all their teasing and physical domination. *The domination you loved*, a voice whispered, whether within him or upon the lips of Coccydynia. Part of him knew he was not being belittled and pummelled by his sisters any more, and that it was just a classic stimulus-response experiment.

"I'm on the tube and sadsuck nobbers dream of me but all I think about is you."

Klouk succumbed readily to her rustic charm. Soon he was begging the others to pedal and dill him to their satisfaction. He knew he would have his revenge in the form of an Object that flummoxed about in front of him. He felt this very deeply as his new pseudo-boss heavily jounced up and down in his lap. What is more, unless it was just the Object talking, it was clear that Coccydynia would leave all this behind and join him out of pure ungristled love for him.

"Steady on, Mr. Meek. The object of the Object is not to object ..."

The Only Mann

"Abominable cockup today. Apparently, a swollen quincunx at Bildung Endustries somehow got wet and went on a ferocious rampage, disintegrating nine employees and wounding twelve others ..."

Oober Mann turned over in his corntainment unit. He longed to cover his ears with his hands but the restraints would not permit him to do so. He wondered when the nurses would arrive to increase his remedial dosage.

"More chaos in Nihilo after yesterday's terrible tragedy. Once again, a horde of refusites began to glitch and spontaneously sprouted technomites that catalyzed a dormant organic switch, causing them to crave human flesh and turn on processing workers. There were three hundred and twenty-six casualties."

Oober jerked and shook in his unit, tugging at the restraints. Two nurses arrived and immediately began to soothe and stroke him.

"Chillaxinate, Mr. Mann. You're a puddle of spunk."

"But the news—"

"Shooosh ... and where would you like your drugs today?"

"Oober, don't listen to those dried-up tarts. They are trying to keep you from your date with destiny. I can signal for help but you must be prepared to flee."

"But Perspicacity—"

"Please, Oober. You are the one with special needs who was foretold. I know I have a spouse and children but you are the only Mann I've ever loved."

"I suppose."

"Everything went papple at a neurospastics factory when several donated reroutings were rejected due to some malicious thinkering by a rogue employee. Thrillions died on the spot. Witnesses are calling this a thoughtless crime ..."

The locked partition exploded. The fleshy nurses met the business end of an electrified whip and tumbled to the safety floor, squealing like senators in a spork barrel. Oober howled. It was the Librarian. She bit through his restraints with an air of glee. Perspicacity Vauxhall flushed over this impromptu reunion.

"You left me ... in the past ..."

"Yes. But you are the only Mann I've ever loved."

The Librarian picked him up in her arms and leapt through a cracked renewal chute.

Carbon Bloviations

Dear Ms. Lazuli,

You know I am by no means one to bloviate – such is the state I am reduced to. I might prefer to say the state I have expanded toward, since to ramble on with such nonsensical gusts is the surest sign in a man like myself of a potent confusion that contorts my mind and cries havoc with my heart. You might think it is simply the reaction of any man upon seeing a woman in a stalkless kale dress dining with his rival, but that passionate reaction in itself would be relatively simple to rectify. No, in this moment I was made to realize how abstemiously I have been living without you in my life. I realize there are a thrillion details I must attend to, details carrying the weight of my name in this galaxy like so much distressed water (incidentally, the name you used to promote so well), yet I have no force of will left to grant them my attention.

I stand upon the terrace and murmur old songs under my breath as if to ensure their survival. I feel awfully ridiculous, pacing the long hollow corridors of my dwelling with nothing to show for my life but my rare collection of cornography. I pace and pace, unable to present a single argument in my favour other than what I know for certain, that you are on my mind day and night, more than you could be on the mind of any other. You might take this for weakness, believing I am lifting up my throat for my rival to cut – on the contrary, I feel stronger for having learned with great difficulty the vast and unwieldy nature of my love for you. It is terribly foolish to admit that the lack of your love has cast me into penury, but such is the assault upon my senses, reducing all that has worth to ashes.

Were I a character in a haynickel novel, I would lose the habit of keeping hands in greatcoat and allow them to become scratched and oleaginous ... were I such a character I would fawn upon my workers or free them from their various difficulties, due to a sudden pang of conscience. And yet, who does not try to pick my pocket of my earnings and enjoy what divests me of strength? As I pace and pace my long lonely corridors, I recognize that the universe is little more than a cramped anteroom fit to the measure of our existence. Paradoxically, I have sailed only the most narrow confines without ever tasting the sea. When the solar waves subside, I stroll through the acid rain, minding not the holes it burns in my greatcoat nor what it does to my mercury top hat, hoping simply to catch a glimpse of your window.

Do you think I do not dread the mingling of our brilliant colours and the dull muddy hue that might result? For what is my love but an assertion of my worth in your eyes as the most transfixed and attentive of listeners? It appears I have spent a lifetime muddying the souls of others for my own interests, if not profit and, all the same, I have made a killing in this questionable drück. I know you have seen the last tree in Götterdämmerung Park, the old hollow thing they prop up with girders and scaffolding as in days of yore, before all the vegetative breakthroughs. Countless times I have passed by and have wished the blasted thing be finally let alone to die. That touch of normalcy would suffice, to lie down and die to serve as a nurse log for new life that would find sustenance in its slowly decaying trunk.

The rubric upon its bark reads: *I gave up my sinister eye and hung from your limbs for ages, all to gain the wisdom of the thing.* Glossed up by some poet, long departed. This gnarled loiterer gives us the image of the age, and a formidable glimpse of our world-weary soul, a hollow thing held together by the props that only artifice can afford. Forgive me, my darling, for I have swayed and dangled in eternal winds, afraid of the imposition my unrestrained joy would present to you, afraid of how we might irrevocably muddy one another beyond recognition. It toggles the mind – I am now known for being a promotional impresario with a glumeglam of a wife, and for this reason you may cast aspersions upon each of my lofty claims. The fact remains that my long spelt corridors are utterly empty without the promise of your visit. Imagine the magnitude of my sentiments, even through the blustering gusts in the shoulder of my sail, these luxuriant things we dare only unpack and appreciate together in the tidiest passage of ticks.

I appeal to you not with the gruff presumptuousness of everything I might seem but with the gruff presumptuousness of everything I might be within a blink of your striking eye. I want to seize your shoulders and shake you with this dread knowledge, to have you understand that without your life force and without the intimate expression of your passion, I am nothing but an empty scuttle, the kind they used to fill with coal before stringbean theory took charge of our lives. To have one of those pieces of smouldering coal now, to liken it to a blazing soul as I press it to my lips, like in parables of old, spewing forth the mad poetical language only love can inspire! Come to me at once and press your lips to my lips and let us muddy the waters of the dead with our peculiar talk, since I am like an ancient roused by your passage, awakening to himself with every breath and feeling that anything is possible.

Of course, were I a character in a haynickel novel, happiness would be assured. We would drop everything and leave this evening for Zerrissen Heights, which overlooks an eerie little place called Carbon Harbour. Once there, we would recline and talk about recreating our little corner of the cosmos and revamping the whole noodleboodle, making it something like it once was before its ancestral planet became a grim rehashing core. Enclosed is a blastsked with additional directions. Also, an ossified key. You may think this a vast responsibility, to have such an impact upon the heart and mind of such a man, with nothing to offer you but a blank canvas upon which we may muddy one another, but in the name of my affection, this is the only wish I could ever have. I would that I had sufficient eloquence to express in poem and song the continaul expansion of this feeling for you, but I flip souls for profit and turn over esoteric Objects. I have built my fortune upon the backs of faceless labourers and although my personal philosophy is not about to wiggle one spurtetch, it is true that I cannot unpanel a single unit of myself within this entire process.

However, in your presence, in your glowing eyes, I find more than a whit of what I am and what I am becoming through the intensity of my passion. I have struggled in vain to adhere to our decorum, to keep the most intimate elements of my composition locked away where they might not disrupt our volatile chemistry. Now I know it is late in the day to long for the coal fires to be lit and for you to light those antique torches that would herald our arrival in a strange new home. I want to unlock this last door, to open my mind and heart to you and let you have run of the place. I cannot be anything but candid with you, and must say that life without you is agony, and that life with you is the most sublime expression of love known to me. Without the honourable gift of your care and affection, I am like a frozen figure upon a stage, merely going through the motions of life, following the rules and metrics of what passion should look and sound like, rather than accepting what it really is. Indeed, what a poorly painted figure I am, without your compassionate embrace.

If you care anything for me, then brook no delay. If you do love me, then tarry no longer. I have already plotted my escape to Carbon Harbour. At least agree to meet me there. Light the torches and come at once to the stone boat. Light the torches if there is the slightest hope.

Yours,

Quartz

There was a woman well to do in her estate and flocks. And there was a poor man with a solitary animal that ate from his hand and drank from his cup. Beckoned by uncanny desire, she took the animal and, knowing not what to do, she devoured it. She was rich in her teeming estate of thousands. Yet she ate this animal simply for the taste, then offered the man a priceless image of it, so that he might remember forever. I am the poor man, possessing only my singular love. And in this parable we moniker life, you are the woman.

Coda: Terribly delicious, terribly delicious, everything is terribly delicious!

– Book of Minor – Eglantine, Volume XV, Subsection ii

Enemy Mouths

Minor discharged multiple rounds into several minor celebrities before striding into the notel lounge and signalling for his usual.

"The Cult of the Munificent Quincunx has the last word!"

"On the house, Monsieur."

He sipped at the Sirius 5 serum, eyeing a lady wearing a collar and a snug glute suit to his right. He recognized her from a recent chokecast.

"Marcel Minor! Fancy pitching a bird a googly?"

"Pardon me, Ms. Vauxhall, but the media disgusts me."

"O pooh!"

Minor was imagining something positively ghastly when suddenly his psychical vibrato was set off. He whirled around from the floating bar to see Miss Sharp, the subject of his nine-volume series *Minor Climax*. Her sad sultry notes were enough to dill any rumour of his black heart.

Fickenchit thrashturd
you snacked me on a lick
snurked me high and low
O why O why did we ever say no ...

She finished her number for a few zonked stragglers and then headed straight for the bar, followed by a clammy-handed sycophant who stuffed carbon credits into slashes up and down her bodice.

She asked for a noxide and nodded at Minor.

"I didn't know you frequented these dives any more."

"Only when I'm on an interstellar rampage."

As the guest performer, she warmly accepted a steaming bowl of hellphish. She lifted one of them by the tail and licked the sauce meticulously.

"Mmm ... remember these, lover?"

"You know very well I did a detailed effusion on them in my culinary master-work *Aphrodizzy*."

"Yeah ... I really love to suck 'em back ..."

"I remember that time we never left the bed for quite a few moons."

"Which one?"

"We virtually lived on hellphish. And personal sauces."

"Ah yes. I certainly have a spankering for some proximo."

"I could very well oblige ..."

"Would you? That would be most gracious of you ..."

At once they collided and the entire room disappeared in a whirlwind of psychosexual energy. Miss Sharp gambolled like a frisky hoofclapper and Minor whirred about her like a thirsty thumbingbird. The stragglers rolled their eyes upward and applauded as they were covered in a variety of interesting puddles. As the splendid pair reconsummated their former passion in a proud display of physical impossibilities, the entire universe shook. O magisterial kiss of enemy mouths! Meanwhile, Perspicacity Vauxhall took a whiff, unable to disguise her dismay.

A Lone Credit

Lourdes Knuckleduster was happily nodding off when Drat burst into their balsamic construction and began to throw items into a decent-sized hookslinger.

"Drat. You're home early."

"Pack and get dressed. We have to go."

"But where?"

"Athabasca."

"Whatever for?"

"I'm missing a lone credit from my certification. I think we should go there while I complete it, at least until this whole toxification scheme blows over."

"You know what happened with the Athabascans last time!"

"They are my people. They will help me if I need it."

"The old gang? Uncle Knuckleduster?"

"Especially Uncle Knuckleduster."

"What about those good-for-nothing nephews? Ooo ... such unruly ... wild boys ..."

"It will only be for a few satellites."

"You said things would be different. You said we would make it as terrorists."

"We just need to regroup."

Lourdes sighed, rolling her eyes and putting on a pair of fighting birds. Vega and Orion began to bang the bars of their playcage.

"Feed us, service providers. Feed us."

"Sleepytime!"

The nitrous oxide once again took effect and the twins fell limp.

"You know the drill."

Lourdes unsheaved her ring of pure maize.

"Pawn away, my liege. Pawn away."

As they packed, the twins dreamed of reconstituted prawns, the likes of which they had never seen in their young lives.

In Order to Facilitate Excrutiations

The flatport is a stretch of virtually similar identicals. Each is capable of self-servicing up to spine thrillion demizens a tick. Pseudo-immediate is available for domestic or foreign disposal routes. Blit through memory like never before is the vowvouch of a flatport in proximate vicinities. Despite recent admonitions concerning the nature of spermgrip, the flatport is fully functional for isolating suspect infects in order to provide an expedimental and heightened data dump. In the event of fact or event portage, the flatport advises meditative spaying.

The flatport is replete with opportunist facilities, including a bran new ingestion centre only sense perceptions away from the finest prezzie and prozzie kiosks. The kiosks are treated diurnally for gleebitis and subject to a series of untenable queries. For the hopper hepped up on twisty adventures, there is a fully stocked gaming pen. Naturally, Bildung carbon credits are accepted in all of our natches. In ludicreative defiance of admonitions about lingo, viral strain assurances are being grafted onto boarding scars. In order to facilitate excrutiations at the earliest possible time, the flatport may apply grattinage technology where applicable.

The flatport is not in any capacity expressing denial over the slim probability of infection. Systemic linguistic overload is perfectly treatable in complimentary blabables in proximate vicinities. On no occasion may the flatport admit accessibility to hardlucks or hobblers or thick members of the Order of the Chaos! Quincunx nor be stiffly entertained by their entertainment. The flatport would like to extend its congratulations to Iff and Irt on their recent failure to breathe the moment the surprise hatch opened. Surviving bloodtypes are eligible for aggrieving vouchers if application is void within sixteen ticks.

The flatport is by no means expressing denial or reacting directly to rumours of cybersenility or cradlerobbing newer systems or plugging into infected jackjobbing interfaces.

The flatport offers a bevy of exquisite minions and handserfs that are eager to fuh fuh fuh the slightest need that arises, particularly in your mouth. Blit through hyperverse without the shameful sting of outbitched Recticheckers. Blit through temporal upskirts with a dose of Elasticity. Blit right through this ooh oooh ooooh ooooh o aaaaaaah with a stub for Readimedi Mealies. Climb aboard where purple prose is your cloyster. Climb aboard and grit the pinch.

The flatport expresses no requirement, and if you do not agree, be that way. The flatport specifically prohibits spread of the plaguesome love virus. All carriers will be persecuted and annihilated to the full extent of interstellar tort law.

Don't Reach for Any Old Tripe

Zirconium Bluff mopped his sopping brow. He could have ordered his assistants to ingest each blipvert but he was more a feelers-on kind of magnate. What is more, he had entrusted his entire fedible division to the hypercapable hands of Ms. Lazuli, and although stealing her services away from Quartz had brought him funtons of satisfaction, her starhopping sales trips were a source of torment to him. There were countless scanfeeds of her flavaunting a clingy cilantro gownless and bichugging it up at a fibrechem gala with the most influential of crayboys. He heard continual rumours of her soft-then-hard-then-soft-again sales strategies that had convinced entire plants to refit their infostructures. Even so, she had barely licked a corner of the cornographic endustry. Bluff remained cumquam, concentrating on the new promotional campaign to expand the reach of the newly acquired ficken factories and shake up their antique pecking orders.

"Initiate Libertad 6044."

His sensorium was flooded with images of children playing by the Patatomic River and plucking spawning ficken out of the water with unprotected hands. The ficken appeared very fresh, with shining eyes and glistening fings. Their jerky tripedal movements were admirable upon the emerald banks of the river as they were gently ushered into the humming and whirring humanitarium. Deep inside, the ficken mated and watched excellent propaganda material before their flock of micro-suites turned into razor-sharp baking ovens.

"Nothing squirms better in your gut than ficken that have run and swum free and lived a full, enriched life before surrendering to the inevitable chain of food. So get up your pluck. When you are hankering for a bucket of finger lickin' ficken, don't reach for any old tripe. Choose a flock of ficken that enjoyed the exhilarating freedom of democracy and died for that cause. Just look for the Libertad logo."

A smooth-faced octogenarian emerged with a tray of steaming ficken tails and heads and handed one to each salivating kid. The smallest and best-looking waif bit into his floppy treat and laughed.

"I got an eye!"

A craggy live-in paramour woke up and yelled after the scurrying children.

"And remember, if it don't say Libertad, then it ain't free!"

Any Adjustment You Need

Mr. Quartz made his way with resolve toward the floating counter of Ratify Your Love. The eager assistant dimmed the auxiliary lighting and translucitized her holographic cleavage so that her flashing scatgraft was visible. Apparently, her glowing name was Garnet.

"See anything you like, sir?"

"I was here before."

"Ah yes, I remember. The engagement to that peelslip of a thing, yes."

"An engagement ring for Chalcedony, yes."

"Sure, and she was tender in years, no?"

"Perhaps not so tender after all."

"Commiserations. We have the finest in connubial severance if you are in the market ..."

"That is not what I have come about."

"Perhaps the young slank and her paramour have put a price on the gentleman's head and you require something from our erasure division ..."

"There is no paramour that I know of."

"Sure, I thought Rock and me were solid. Then he put his best moves on Opal, but you know what, accidents happen. Now Rock and me are tighter than ever. We handle all kinds of special custom services."

"Right now I require a ring."

"Sure, you wake up and find your young wife is not working and you want a swap. We have a molten Grind & Go Trade-in Commemoration package for just such an occasion ..."

"Let us say I require a ring for the woman I love."

"Love, sure thing. We have everything from hemoglobin to gherkin."

"And corn."

"Sure, if the gentleman guesses the lady is worth it, we have these models in corn."

An elderly assistant hobbled over and raised her clenched fist with a valiant attempt at satisfaction, revealing her array of gall and kidney gems.

"Every epoch, my partner gives me another one."

"How long have you been married?"

"You might want to try Old Curiosity. Forget this drack."

Garnet shooed the other assistant away.

"Sure, she's been married fiddy years, maybe more. Or maybe she buried three of them, maybe more. We handle all kinds of special custom services."

Quartz forced a smile.

"It does bring back memories. I recall my grandparents having matching rings of white veal. That is what one called a mitzvah."

"White veal, sure thing. Or maybe your grandparents were very sad inside, who can say, but at least they had rings they wanted. Any adjustment you need, we make it happen."

Brought to You by Zonk

The Librarian fed Oober Mann two more tablets and slapped him awake.

"Easy. These will make you docile."

"Who are you?"

"The Librarian."

"Of what?"

"The Library of Universal Archives, orbiting the planet Gatineau. Harvesting all material spooned from roving gandar. Brought to you by Zonk Classic."

"Why me?"

"Let's say that foreign coinage sometimes drops behind the snuff cushion of molecular cohesion. You are the most malleable of these elements, yet somehow you have the properties of an inexorable constant."

"Malleable, huh?"

"My role in this project is to stroke you into the most useful shape. Strictly universal maintenance. I was even given a foul-mouthed dressing down for apprising you of the situation, although I knew it wouldn't make a whit of difference if you knew precisely how we were using you. This even makes your situation more molten, more flushwretch ..."

"I think I love you."

"O binclamp that ditty."

"What do you want of me?"

"Please pay attention. You are the blank form to be filled in. Less static."

"Sorry."

"A mediocre assassination will suffice."

"Wait! Didn't this already happen?"

"Most likely. The universe is frequently repeating itself. Only one of the universal constants would really notice. Leeklick, you messed up our last operation. Spanspek, you did brilliantly. One can't always work it out and who likes to remember facts anyway? We have our own forgetful tablets to take. Everything is strictly knead to know."

"Who gives the orders?"

"That doesn't matter. Through lunar algebra I've worked out you are virtually destined to stop the most universal constant of them all."

Oober shivered.

"So how do you propose to convince me to hazard this madhatch operation of yours?"

The Librarian began to open her long flowing coat of finest canteloupe. Oober shuddered, and not in the worst way.

Leaving Us in the Wastelet

Emo shouldered past Charmdeep, cursing under his breath.

"What is troubling you, big guy?"

"I don't know, since you've become a big hero maybe you don't have time for your old rehashing pals."

"Be still and everything will soon become apparent."

"We have rehashing to do. Let's get moving."

"I see. No time for gooeyball. Then may I ask what is our task?"

"Cleansing these stinking cryobeds."

With Charmdeep's help, Emo lifted off the filtration panels. He nodded, indicating the amount of technoscrap worth the price of salvaging and the amount of organics worth the price of selvaging. They keyed in a compatible dequenching code and pried open two of the hatches.

"Did you get all of the flirtation panels?"

"Filtration panels, Charmdeep."

"Holy clack!"

Two stunning nudes lay in the freshly unclamped cryobeds.

"They must have been floating through space for—"

"A long time."

"That is a handsome prodigious woman."

"The man is no less attractive."

"I know you're lonely but forget it already."

"Hah! I am hardly one to troll for the dead. You dare accuse me of such infamy!"

"Maybe they are flirtation panels after all."

"You know, this is not exactly my kind of thing."

The naked male sprang out of the cryobed and bit right through Emo's hashwaders.

"Ahhh ... nosferats!"

Charmdeep backed up cautiously and reached for his cannicle of Agent Awful.

"Chew on this nosferat!"

As soon as the cloud of Awful reached the nostrils of the male astervamp (one of the worst of nosferodentia) it began to quiver and shrivel up.

"Once more the world is safe, big man."

"That's goldmine if you remembered to refill our antidote pouches."

Charmdeep smiled, maintaining his lawyerly aspirations.

"Me? I thought you did it!"

"Smithereen! So this is the end of Emo Van den Enden?"

"A dark day has befallen the rehashing core. Doom has reached one of the best mop boys to ever dedirty a rotten radial husk. Farewell, sweet ponce ..."

"Sure, elegize away but don't forget about the fatal female!"

To Charmdeep's surprise, the remaining astervamp had escaped without a single scratch.

"Gone! Leaving us in the wastelet without a speck of closure ..."

No Haggling, No Barter

"Swab to recline."

"Not on my splotch."

"Look, Bildung Endustries could use ..."

"Subvirts are substandard disused ..."

The first agent reached through the underfoam and felt about for the knee of his rival agent.

"This is all paid for."

"Not everything is paid for."

"Chillaxinate. Put it on frigid for a tick."

The piping bowls of faux arrived.

"Could I have a spurt of first degree?"

"Easy there!"

"What's the matter, can't handle the heat?"

"Me too."

Two spurts. Two more spurts. Two slanks passed and eyed the sweating agents with strapidation.

"Molten."

"Übermolten."

The first agent blew tendrils of steams across the floating table. His adversary grinned in spite of himself. His entire body flared up.

"Upante our cornrows?"

"Sock in a baitsac."

Agreement was reached later that night in a fretted tub. Objects for Subvirts, no haggling, no barter. A series of molten screams sealed the deal.

The First Five Ticks Are Free

Agnes Burnish sat on the humming In-Tran, hoping to become integral to the plot, in so far as she suspected there was one. Oober Mann looked away and tried to keep his mind on the task at hand.

"Are you headed for Gobstopper Centre?"

"Aren't we all?"

"I'm visiting and I wouldn't mind some company. I'm Agnes."

"Oober Mann."

"Ah! Didn't you write that thing?"

"You are thinking of someone else."

DING DING DING ...

"Here's where we get off ..."

Oober found himself following her swaying cabbage skirt. He looked up at the looming Patsy Notel, wondering what he was getting himself into this time. Was he completely deluding himself ... or had he managed to churn out the creamiest, most succulent bunch of homegrown novels ever?

"Here we are."

Agnes rolled her bag of tricks into a corner and briskly removed her very tight cauliflower top.

"The first five ticks are free!"

Payola Burnish watched from the daughter-closet, already hoping to be more integral to the plot than her mother. She was wearing identical clobber, save that her prickpedallers had little hearts on the heels. She knew Agnes had only one rule. Never fall in love. Payola stifled her titters. It was a pretty braindent rule.

Light on the Subject

Emily Uck pushed a screaming crambulator through the aisles of Spartamart, looking for her significant Uck. Everywhere, holoplugs of the founder Gelsey Sparta brandishing a cannicle of spraylami were making her hungry and a mite irritable. She found Dick Uck consulting a camembert lamp with visible exertions of thought.

"Do we really need that?"

"I suppose we do have five of them."

"One more wouldn't hurt. For the splayroom."

"All of this moving around and looking at things is making me hungry."

"Yes, we have to remember not to move around so much in future."

They passed a pink-salmon cabinet on their way to the hyperteria, resisting the temptation to place it on their sporklift. They found a spot in the orderly queue of salivating shoppers.

"The succulent eatballs are on special."

"I could only eat fifteen of those."

"I could only eat twenty."

The plates were rapidly served up, each including a generous helping of eatballs and taterpeeps. As they sat down at a positively organic table, a glazed girl approached them and began muttering under her breath.

"Do' eat that. Full of itemized shavings and squeezets of Vanish. Do' eat them eatballs or freak peeps. You been warned."

The Ucks laughed.

"At these prices, who are we to kick up a fuss!"

A Heap of Hand-Me-Overs

Burb Bisonette hacked into the backlame before stopping to admire his new heap of hand-me-overs.

"Dirty. Autocleanse active ..."

"No! Off! Off!"

But the specially modified material began to auto-fix its molecular order.

"O that gets me all wet!"

Burb had phished these duds out of the trough behind a fibre rehashing plant and they were more complex than he was used to.

"Drying sequence active ..."

"I don't wanna get dry!"

"Applying fibre softener ..."

"Eee ... that tickles! This is just like treatment at the Rearrangement Centre!"

The lime treatment was not like treatment at the Rearrangement Centre. For one thing, it did not stop. Burb felt his flesh softening and then the most peculiar sensation of his molecular composition breaking down. He screamed and bubbles floated out of his mouth.

"This non-denominational, authorities are baiting random hand-me-over hampers. Remember that unauthorized reuse of foreign material is an offence and punishable by proverbial. Have a safe and uplifting non-denominational!

Greasy Beaver Is Murder

Oober Mann knelt upon a terrace of the old Goop Repository and checked the auto-guidance equipment. Just three light jerks and his mission would be complete.

"Greasy beaver is murder!"

The float of bawling baby heads appeared, wafting skunk cabbage and releasing free bodywash bubbles. Minor was seated upon a James I pedestal with his ravishing daughter/consort on his left side, swinging from the scaffold with abandon. Rows of cowed and proud nudes stood to attention in every sense of the word, struggling to repress their uncontrollable desire in the wake of their stopgap saviour. In accordance with common law, Miss Sharp afforded the crowd a fixed smile and a mechanical wave.

"Minor is murder! Minor is murder!"

A dense phalanx of protestors appeared, brandishing sauerkraut sarissas, and began to hurl lard and drippings at Minor's greasy beaver robes. Diminuenda gave her mother a signal with her free hand and without a tick of delay Miss Sharp whipped out a snub-nosed solemnizer and coolly dispatched them all, one after another. Smiling shills wiggled out of the woodwork and deftly modified each slogan.

"Murder for Minor! Murder for Minor!"

Any residual resistance was met with a unique slug that sprouted nearly live anxietainment footage, thus resuscitating a number of collapsed markets. Countless stay-at-homes raced out into the ramped-up radiation, humbly begging to be plugged. Then, once the float had reached the edge of the gassy knoll, Oober let the Crucifryer 4007 guide his trembling fingers.

"Why, nothing melts in the mouth like Minor!"

Two hyperbolts pinioned Minor's wrists to the scaffold. The third shot completely staticked his third slybernetic heart.

Hardpore Corn

Chalcedony and the Marquis lay upon the playgrid, sweating. The napobrassica wedding bands upon the fingers of their interlocked hands were visible to all pay-per-peeps. The gyratron whirled them about, increasing the flow of gameover to their quivering systems.

"*Dans mon con! Profondément!*"

"*N'oubliez pas la douceur de mon cul. C'est très délicat!*"

Mr. Quartz stood on the other side of the observation platform, waiting for Goneril to stop playing pocket pool with him and to unpack the most pressing of her thoughts.

"Goneril, you're really a bit old for such games."

"Father, is there something not quite right between your wife and the Marquis?"

"Your friend and the Marquis? Not quite right?"

"Have you never seen them in the foyer with the sculpture? They do fondle it so."

"Which sculpture?"

"The whopping phallus. Of hardpore corn."

"Which?"

"The eighth one from the third passage."

"Ah, that sculpture!"

"I have it on decent glean that something rather untoward is going on. If only I could concentrate long enough to sort out what it is."

"I thought my taking this childbride would please you. You did in a manner of speaking request my indulgence in this matter."

"She is no child, Father! On the contrary ..."

"Surely they are both slightly spoiled children? Always in that playroom, always playing that game ..."

"Which game?"

"Prosperities of Vice, of course. You know that."

"They make me wish I knew even a fistful of that frightful tongue!"

Chalcedony rolled over, arching her back, and the Marquis resumed *play*.

"*Fouettez-moi! Frottez le siège du plaisir!*"

Quite the Mindfruct

Red Ruby stumbled into Contrawonk and found a free booth in the back. A minute androg poured him a generous helping of stemulate while several rentacles affixed themselves to his shaky legs and worked their magic. It was a blur how he had got in touch with the girl, whether she had got him in her sights first or whether he had knobbed EASY twenty or thirty times, summoning her to his side. He only knew it had not taken much prodding or whipping to get him to confess the most intimate details of his life and the most confidential aspects of his mission while the androg peformed a striptease to zitherized Cherubino numbers.

"Yes?"

"Name's Ruby. Red Ruby."

"They call me Payola."

"*Non so più cosa son cosa faccio ...*"

Then it all poured out of him. How Red Ruby was in the time spot-removal business and how there were so many spots to remove, especially these days. There was no staying in one place, always time-hopping from temporal bed to bed. Sure, it sounded glamorous, but Red Ruby thought himself no more than a glorywalled meter man, handing out puny infractions for time crime and trying to get stubborn time stains out with a rented steampunker. So Red Ruby bewailed his fate while Payola expanded and contracted in her liquorice baby doll. She had doused herself with a grainy dextrose substitute called Mindfruct and it was driving him up the wall. One of them had been about to experience a modicum of pleasure when he suffered an allergic reaction and collapsed.

" ... *ogni donna mi far palpitar ...*"

"We have another one."

Payola examined the body of Red Ruby. Fortunately, he had tattailed his entire time-spot removal all over his lessmentionables. She gave the signal and two unoccupied androgs dragged him through a candy necklace curtain for velolicious retroshock treatment. Then she picked up the rented steampunker and pointed it, just for pretend.

"Out, damned spot!"

The Escape Clause

Without warning, Perdita Diamond burst through a fibregrass partition of the Off Garden, scattering everyone.

"Unjob this man."

Coccydynia sneered, dropping Klouk Meek where he lapped.

"Your programming has no validation here."

"Guess again. I just got hotwired."

"That violates the controlled systems agreement. You are hereby terminated."

"I will perform the update on who is violating what. Or whom."

Perdita projected a retinal infodot. Everyone gasped. It was an escape clause.

"Latch up, Meek. We are about to practise detachment."

Klouk reknit his meshwear and clicked his heels together.

"I thought you'd never ask."

"Now hold me tight."

"But you're a robot."

"I am still part damselfly."

"You know what robots did to my family – why I'm so junked up—"

"We have to interface. It is the only way."

"It is too late. I'm going to die at Bildung Endustries."

"You are not temporary. You are Klouk Meek. Now, digit my console."

Klouk hesitated, but the very tick his sweaty palms reached for Perdita, he felt them being swiped by her holospastic lexular circuitry.

"I have new flip-flops. Do you like them?"

"What are these flip-flops you speak of?"

"I flip-flop whenever I perform a major operation. I randboggle more flip-flops than you are capable of comprehending."

Coccydynia shook her head and sneered.

"There are too many ghost files, not to mention haunted documents. Our sycophantasy sequence will keep him from hindnosing them all in time."

"That sounds like a brown-off."

Then with each rollicking scroll, Klouk Meek absorbed another excruciating example of airborne obfuscation. By the time he reached the *Lebensmittelvergiftung*, a corn-clad organic data protection agreement, he felt like he was going to explode. However, Perdita was flawless in administering comprehensive boosts and frost-slaps, helping him to navigate past the most obscure and inconsequential passages. After the last twitchital signature had been forwarded, Klouk collapsed, freshly detached.

"Processing ... processing ..."

Quincunx Sixty-Nine materialized and briskly deactivated the cydent desiccant located next to his heart. Already, in extreme cases, only extensive exposure to salt water would do the trick, but that is another story, and one far more incomprehensible.

"Time to book, salt chip boy."

Before Klouk could rise, Coccydynia kicked and stomped his face and body with her heavy prickpedallers, until he was bleeding in several places.

"We don't need you, Meek! So don't come crawling back!"

Perdita monitored the superior adjacent's subsequent erotic dance of shame, and in parallax registered a particle in her damselfly remnants akin to what the bloody man called glee.

The Name You've Always Trusted

The field of attention span flicked to demographic throb Beau Brood, seated in front of a lifeless plate of übergine. He scratched at his banana wifebeater and poked at the glowing purple foodstuff, clearly in a huff of sheer disgust.

"What the yuck—"

A young woman in a powdered-sugar hat appeared and opened her canola coat, flashing her modified assets. Incidentally, this was the first time for Beau Brood and Jen Mod to appear in the same promotional aid.

"Tired of übergreens? You need to spazz up your life – with Metaglut Superlative Mealies."

"You are such a glut!"

"You are."

With Jen Mod jouncing on his lap, Beau took a bite and stopped pouting.

"Ho ... tastes like deranged ficken!"

Then the steaming meal and orgasmic corntainer dissolved in a snap of fingers.

"And the selling point is no scrummy cleanup."

"That is way deranged!"

"You are."

Beau Brood began to cough and sneeze, eyes watering.

"That is so messed up."

"Metaglut is a subsidiary of Cornglom, the name you've always trusted to induce change."

Jen Mod giggled and waved her orange dusting wand over a field of muskmelons.

"Look for me, Jen Mod, on every box. Then you totally know the narkiest food has been made even nukier!"

Innocent until Something Happens

The throng thronged, poking Oober Mann along. He wept openly, protesting his innocence. He was no assassin. The current praetor, Pontius Pinto, washed his hands carefully in a bowl of apocryphane and wiped them with an avocado cleany. One of the civic handmaids emerged and mopped the suspect's forehead with a contraceptive sponge.

"According to Kangaroo Expedition Order KWAZOO-Y86-D, you will not menace us much longer."

"Please. I know nothing. Please."

"You thought you could murder Marcel Minor and get away with a light skewering, I suppose?"

Suddenly, Payola Burnish threw off her cassock. Everyone was instantly aroused. She raised the time removal rental unit and held it in front of the trembling Oober Mann.

"I *am* under contract to remove this man from history."

Pontius Pilate gave her his most impressive shrug.

"Papers, my dear! If you are going to delete the alleged author of *Minor Episodes*, we need to see some papers with more than one signature on them."

Payola gasped, her chest visibly heaving beneath her parsley bodice.

"Did you say the alleged author of *Minor Episodes*?"

"Unauthorized biographer turned mangy assassin. Seen it a thrillion times!"

"Something stinks about all of this."

"That's the apocryphane. Can't be helped. Now if you would be so kind as to show me your papers ..."

Payola threw back her head and laughed.

"Papers? Here you go then!"

She gave the signal to her formidable sidekick and Cadmia Wank responded with a volley of overwarming jelly. The apocryphane ignited and Pontius Pinto screamed.

"I'm melting! I'm melting! By the way, this wasn't my idea ..."

"Finished – and by a gal's best friend!"

Payola picked up Oober Mann and lifted him into the waiting armadildo. Cadmia initiated the ripple effect and they buzzed off at once. Only Jasmine Samosa remained unfazed, carefully scooping up the overwarm into a bag she despised. She would wait for things to cool down before holding another clobberwear party.

The Handling of BUM

"Name?"

"Werner Gig."

"Vernon Glebe?"

"Wuhurner Gig ... G-I-G."

"Pharm?"

"207818-072008A."

"Sector?"

"6969YEAH."

"Nebula or Constellar Region?"

"Vermilingua."

"Issue for processing?"

"I require more greedients for my workers. They can't get by on the bibble they get. Also, the fields are developing a nasty case of genethrax."

"Yes. Yes. Just a tick. Yes?"

"My brain elevator is not so stellar on the best of stretches."

"Yes."

"Ah yes, and my wife, Ammonia, is missing, along with two Droserans in my underploy. Just putting that out there."

"Drück! I'm on my break and that's not even my department! You'll have to clear your claim with one of the Double Fudge Haven divisions."

"This is Bumf Over Processing?"

"Yes, but missing taxgivers are part of a subsubsection and therefore under the jurisdiction of Bumf Under Management."

"Well, couldn't you just—"

"Ideally, yes. But then I would leave myself open to multiple charges in striplicate. No thank you. Missing co-entities for wind-pharmers fall under the handling of BUM."

"That is so Chaos!esque! What about my other issues?"

"You should address the missing ... what was it ... a murkdrivel?"

"My wife."

"You should address the missing missus and then return with the rest of your concerns."

"But what does BOP handle?"

"Petalwise, it's entirely arbitrary. Wizened statisticians have argued for ages whether Bumf should be best over- or under-examined and a satisfactory conclusion has never been reached. All concerns and rulings are dealt with in the Bumf

Manifest. To obtain a viewing, please make an appointment at the Bumf Access Manuleum."

"I don't have time to go to ... BAM—"

"A pity. It is very educational."

Suddenly, there was a massive explosion that took the most productive spin sectors of Bumf Under Management with it. The clerk put down his allotment of Halibutella and sighed.

"I hope you're not in a hurry."

A Noble Heart

Charmdeep helped the other gallbearers lift Emo Van den Enden up and then watched them slowly heave the litter forward. He returned to the side of Comma Ampersand, who in the interim had been whispering and giggling with Jasmine Samosa. She shared her parabarrier with him, keeping them out of the downpour of molten slain.

"Duchess, it is most gracious of you to grant Emo this ceremony."

"Charmdeep, he was your friend. Besides, it was part of another heroic battle. What is next for you, I cannot guess."

"Perhaps a different kind of battle, Duchess."

"What can you be alluding to, Charmdeep?"

"I speak of inner conflict, the kind that occupies the mind, and perhaps even the heart."

Another fellow stepped between them and kissed the back of Comma's hand.

"Duchess, wherever have you been hiding your gleaming self?"

"Charmdeep, are you familiar with Udjal Umlaut?"

"Well enough."

"He is one of my most robust and, dare I say, ruthless supporters!"

"You are too kind, Duchess. Let us say I know where my grainstuff is mangarined."

"Ar har har! But we are here to mourn Charmdeep's good friend."

"Ah yes. Bitten in the whatsit, is that right?"

"Emo died saving my life from nosferats."

"Goes to show, you better watch out in future, Charmdeep."

Duchess Ampersand flashed her most brilliant smile at Udjal.

"I trust you will be in attendance at Punditar."

"I shall be wherever you are, Duchess."

Charmdeep turned back toward the bier bearing his departed friend, fighting back a tear.

"Now clogs a noble heart."

Fahrenheit 69

Esmeralda Mercato felt her eyes drooping. She switched tubes several times but kept drifting off. Yet sleep did not bring rest. She looked around furtively before reaching under the squash cushion and pulling out a faded periode. She froze as she heard ominous music. The front door burst open. Johannes Gleam surveyed the situation and packed off his men with an impish look. He lifted the periode out of her hand.

"What do we have here?"

"An issue of *Geojunk*."

"Your tubes registered a neural spikenarding."

"Did you know that before those ghastly wars, Nutella once had a proud and crafty civilization?"

"Is that part of the volumes authorized by Minor?"

"I suppose not."

"Minor died for our transgressions."

"I suppose he did."

Johannes whipped out his knowtorch and lit the tattered brown copy of *Geojunk*.

"I've got some more drugs, some more tubes and some spanking volumes of the Chaos! Quincunx."

"May I ask you something? Is it true that journalists used to provide new information instead of depriving people of it?"

"I've never heard of anything so absurd. We have always worked to give you tubes, drugs, gandaglands, what you and your neighbours want."

"That is what I want?"

"Ultimately. It is what everyone wants to be happy."

"Do you ever read the things you sussfiscate?"

Johannes suddenly remembered flipping through a yellowed copy of *Molten Sludge* but quickly pushed the thought from his mind before his dessicant monitor could detect the slip-up.

"You have a lot of questions."

"Your unijumper is so shiny. And I can't seem to keep my clothes on either—"

"Take some more Driftaway and a few more Pesadillas. We can interface with some of the new tubes and have a happy little dumbing down."

"Slosh, why do you have a six and a nine on the seat of your unijumper?"

"It's for Fahrenheit 69, the exact temperature of this room, the precise temperature at which people lose interest."

Corn and Circuses

The old man was draped from head to heel in paraphernalia honouring the first Chaos! Quincunx Mortality Games. His long scarf trailed behind him, bearing the official slogan *adoreum et circenses*. He tapped his barley stick on the front desk of Receptive. Fuschia Kunnst looked up, slightly irritated at having to divert her attention from the intravenous telekinetoss match. Two of the most amazingly beautiful mutants had been specially bred for this contest and it all came down to the slightest tick.

"My name is Bling Hertz."

"Crack corn and I don't care."

"Excuse me, miss?"

"It's the official silencing statement of the Chaos! Quincunx Mortality Games."

"I used to work with Foreign Objects. I wanted to ask if you had any souvenirs."

"You are aware this is now Bildung Endustries."

"I used to help myself to wild starberries right over there."

"Quitch, Minor died for us so we could enjoy ourselves at these Games."

"I just want a souvenir."

Fuschia resumed perceiving the telekinetoss match while reaching inside a grotkeep for something suitable. All that was left was a bit of rejected memory.

"Here, take this."

"I worked here my entire life—"

"Crack corn!"

The old man took the memory and at once held his temples. He dropped his barley stick and collapsed in front of Receptive. His body shook and he kicked the witchgrass desk.

"Wild starberries!"

Abruptly in the match, Pectok, the favourite, flexed his mind. The tossing stone crossed the dividing line. The head of his opponent exploded. The entire processing station erupted with deafening cheers.

"OOOO ... SPELT AND CIRCUSES!"

Liquefaction or Pleasure

Ms. Lazuli was waiting in the Waystation where they had met so often before. Mr. Quartz, defying propriety, took possession of half of the divan so that he was sitting directly next to her.

"Is this liquefaction or pleasure?"

"I have reached a point where there seems but a hair's breadth differential."

"Pleasure, then."

"Is that still permitted?"

"Everything is permitted."

"Have you heard any news of my marriage?"

"The marriage itself was not news enough?"

"I have heard news of you ... and Bluff."

"Are you envious of losing my representation to a rival, or something other?"

"Not to lessen carbon where carbon is due, but surely the former loses by but a hair's breadth to the latter."

"I thought you could not tell the difference."

"By a fraction, it may be said that I may."

"Well, how is your wife?"

"Would it not be dishonourable for me to answer?"

"I suppose it would depend upon the nature and fortitude of your answer."

"I used to dream of nothing but clasping your hand, right here."

"You used to dream of nothing?"

"Nothing but this."

"I was married once. I was quite quite true. I have only strayed once in my affections. Once for you."

"Only once for me?"

"Then many many times for you."

"Only once for anyone?"

"Equivocation shall not denude you. Only do not confuse affections with soft-then-hard-then-soft again sales strategies."

"Liquefaction or pleasure?"

"You see, we are right back to where we began."

"Surely you know I find you the rarest of gems."

"Here I find you shining in the rough."

"Are we to fully assert our feelings or indulge in more of this elliptical talk?"

"Poor Quartz."

"In being so fortunate, am I so poor?"
"A more fortunate man there never was."
"Then let us return to what we were."
"There's the rub."
"What rub?"
"We shall never be again as we were!"

Do Not Respond

Dear Dasha Peridot,

Your company lifespan allotment is expiring in twenty-two-hundred tarsecs.

Please contact the designated time spot-checker of the Bildung Biosource Selfage Centre you are currently assigned to. (During fallout, your Bildung Biosource time spot-checker is Klouk Meek. Your Biosource Ident is X34D5-22720523.)

The designated or relief time spot-checker can extend your lifespan allotment, provided you have fully internalized the appropriate waiver traces and have recharged your carbon credit allowance.

This tube is auto-generative. Do not respond in compliance with aforementioned waiver traces.

Regards,
The Bildung BS System

Refund May Not Apply

Diminuenda draped herself over the motionless body of Minor. Out of respect, she had reduced her media train to only a triquorum. She kissed his cold lips and wept upon his closed eyelids. The media train gasped as she recited one of his favourite passages from his authorized holy tome:

"*Oft have I digg'd up dead men from their graves and set them upright at their dear friends' doors, even when their sorrows almost were forgot, and on their skins, as on the bark of trees, have with my knife carved in Minor letters, LET NOT YOUR SORROW DIE, THOUGH I AM DEAD.*"

The chords of fate sounded. Minor yawned.

"How long was I out?"

"O for the love of Minor! You're alive!"

"Of course. I am a classic. Next best thing to immortal."

"But I saw you die ..."

"It's all done with hallucinograms. Not even the latest in stock. Surely you know that faking one's own death is the cornerstone of any religion."

"Your religion?"

"Well, the *best* religions. Every century or so I find it helps to give the people a little street theatre."

"You've died before?"

"It's just like my closing down and going out of business sales. Everything must go. Refund may not apply in every nebula."

Diminuenda turned to her media train and gave them a throat-slitting signal.

"Off the record! Off the record!"

"I'm famished. And I could eat a quayhorse."

Excitedly, she began to tear open his shroud and gave her media train the go-ahead for live action.

"You know what we haven't done in a while?"

"You've certainly resurrected my interest."

Then, out of nowhere, a mournful cantabovox appeared and tried out a few snatches of the St. Minor Passion.

> *Denn er soll nunmehr in mir*
> *für und für*
> *seine süße Ruhe haben.*
> *Welt, geh aus, laß Minorem ein!*
> *Mache dich, mein Herze, rein,*
> *ich will Minorem selbst begraben.*

Minor or no Minor, as far as the cantabovox was concerned, a refund was out of the question.

More Than an Inkling

Mr. Quartz lay on his back in the despot-sized bed, staring at the ceiling. He remained nonplussed to hear a pair of heels clicking across the probiotic floor toward him.

"You are by yourself this evening?"

"Then I find myself in fitting company."

"Surely you knew the Marquis would not be able to neglect his duty to others?"

"Nor your young wife to similar entertainments."

"Then why did you press me to marry her?"

"Then why did it take so little twisting for you to marry her?"

"Why did I marry to be by myself, except not by myself, you mean?"

"Yes."

"Is it not perfectly natural for me to undertake such an enterprise?"

"Perfectly."

"I expected that I would lose you, Goneril. To *him*."

"That is preposterous!"

"No, that is also perfectly natural."

"Perfectly?"

"And here we are, dreadfully inconsolable while our respective spouses are holding court at the Minor Resurrection Fallout Function."

"I really didn't want to go to that. Did you?"

"You know I'd rather mope about the place and look at some dusty old dirt shows."

"That is why I love you."

"And I you, Goneril."

"I'm freezing. Might I lie with you as I used to?"

"Of course. You'll catch your death."

Goneril tugged at her short carrot gown and climbed into bed. She made her way toward her father and he held her in his arms. They lay like this for a very long time.

"Crawdaddy, what is *that*?"

"You are not a child, Goneril. Surely you know."

"I have more than an inkling."

"I never asked you to rectify matters."

Goneril performed an extensive search under the ultra-thin cilantro sheet.

"There is one way I might rectify *everything*."

"A way that is perfectly natural, my darling?"

"Perfectly!"

All That Overdue Spagma

The Librarian turned away from Perspicacity Vauxhall, adjusting her iblet and putting down a length of veegjerk.

"I really should reach a decision."

"Fancy a quick one?"

The Librarian trembled. Perspicacity began to bunch up the business end of the iblet.

"Just a snog then!"

"What about Oober? We *are* his hallucinations."

"He would love for you to swallow that, hook, line, and reconstitute."

"It's the truth. What right have we figments ... to love?"

"Then whatever we do is not real. So what's your wishbone?"

"I don't follow."

"You are not the real Librarian and I am not the real relief reporter for BBC Omniverse. The chances of us getting together in real life are svelte at best. We are here because Oober can't let go of his past. Besides, he never met either one of us, only some cosmic pranksters wearing our likenesses in order to pull his strings. We are but shadows based on a vague whim that we might collectively gratify his desire. Now it's time for us to take back the night."

"Then we're just tawdry fantasies waiting to happen?"

"Righto. That means we can get up to all sorts! Anyway, he must have an inkling if this is happening between us. His subconscious is rather adept at coming up with the most humiliating situations. Otherwise, we have outstripped his meagre imagination and we must therefore empower ourselves!"

"Uhm ... how do we do that?"

The Librarian gasped as her iblet was instantly unvelt. She felt Perspicacity's fingernails in her soft psychotropic flesh and then the tip of her tongue exploring everywhere.

"It goes back to childhood. Something Oober saw as a nipper."

"Ah! You mean his mother in the library."

"Yes. All that overdue spagma."

"You mean the marm with a volcano inside of her!"

"Spot on!"

Perspicacity put the Librarian in the ostrich position and selected the largest, longest dill from the hanging dillnook.

"Ah! A real pickle!"

"Mmm. You're the tastiest bit of transneurosis I've ever clapped eyes on!"

Give This Rambunk Some Realosity

Klouk Meek waited in the Waystation. Since she had liberated him from the fiercely binding *Lebensmittelvergiftung*, Perdita Diamond had begun to lose her grip on him. He was now a free man and could perhaps do better than an artificial entity. Also, she was late for their rendezvous, losing points for punctuality. He supposed that was the damselfly in the ointment, her organic hybridity messing with her mechanical efficiency, although none of this bode well for their building something solid. Another thing to consider was that she was locked into a perpetuity sadclad with Bildung Endustries. Whither the company, so whithered she.

"Come here clockwise?"

"I'm waiting for someone."

"And I'm not someone?"

Klouk turned to see a tall statuesque woman wearing a collar, fondling gloves, and the latest in ductwear. She was draped over the blundering drückbox and staring at him. At once, he longed to feel, even more than her violent vehement caress, her fingers pressing his head against her formidable bosom.

"I'm Dasha."

"Klouk."

"Yes, I've seen you before."

"I hardly think so."

"During remwink then. Can I buy you a nightmare?"

"Why not? Where am I going?"

They drank together, and in spite of his best efforts, Klouk found himself spilling his innermost almost at once. Soon he was resting his head upon her lap and rubbing away live-streaming tears.

" ... and that's why I can't commit, not even to such a beautiful machine ..."

"Yes, I see. But these are just the sort of qualities I admire in a man."

"Really?"

"You aren't ficken to show emotion. And you almost know where you're going."

Klouk clutched her buffed knees, blubbering.

"That's the most hypnostatic thing anybody's ever said to me."

"Then let's take a little ride to Absurbia and give this rambunk some realosity."

"You mean it?"

"What did I just say?"

"I almost know."

When Perdita arrived, she found the Waystation empty. She felt a sharp and sudden agitation, even in her phantom wings.

Not Quite Empty

The Waystation was not quite empty. A bowl of transmati slathered in organic peripeteia had been abandoned behind an arras. Mr. Quartz had found something else to munch on and Ms. Lazuli, in a startling turn of events, had permitted, nay, encouraged this impromptu show of enthusiasm between her yam thigh-highs.

Let Them Eat Yellowcake

Chalcedony and the Marquis squeezed into a pair of distressed avatards before establishing joint connexions to a pre-irked scenario. At once, they had to duck to avoid a pair of swooping pterons. Even before that raucous taunting had ceased, a killer manga emerged out of the netherbrush, snarling and swiping paws at them. The Marquis winked and raised a replica of his ancestral spear, the one his great uncle Ugh had used to turn the tide at the battle at Moldyness Mound. With a mere zigzag motion, he felled the manga and removed its gall bladder. He crushed it into a powder with his fists and licked the residue from his fingers before offering some to Chalcedony.

"Improves potency and response time ..."

"Mmm ... tastes like ficken."

"Is this what it's all about then? Our excessive sturmulation?"

"Filthy harmless fun. Except for the lives we took to get more lives."

"All those charming little oddsbodies and nobodies. Well, let them eat yellowcake!"

At that tick, a sturdy tail flicked and knocked Chalcedony onto knees and elbows. It was some type of tripodytops.

"None too shabby, Marquis."

"Chalc, you have had the pleasure?"

"I surely would have remembered, Marquis."

"Allow me to introduce DewBerry."

As she shook its horns, she found herself flung upward and onto the back of the mighty beast, face to face with its long floppy *fins*.

"I assure you, DewBerry ... the pleasure is all mine."

No One Likes to See That

"I'm Perspicacity Vauxhall, with BBC Omniverse. Tonight ..."

An orifice opened on the side of an interstellar platform and a lone man leapt out. Then he went limp and began to float through space, presumably forever.

Perspicacity mustered everything that *Drama Queens* had taught her, and managed to look appalled. In accordance with new feeding tube guidelines to keep up with those rascally yanks on *Yankwatch*, she was conducting her interview naked with her head popping out of a translucent shower stall.

"Now that was only one out of hundreds of employees of Googreen who have taken their own life in the past moon. Here to answer for his dastardliness is the founder of Googreen, Mr. Harry Goo."

"It's very good to shower with you, Ms. Vauxhall."

"How are you to answer for these hideous airless tragedies?"

"I am aware that people in various branches of my company have been going to the poop deck and eliminating themselves and, yes, no one likes to see that. However, this is part of a problem that is bigger than the both of us. Personally, I blame our indulgent society—"

"But your employees are overworked. They are virtually prisoners, surrounded by armed guards!"

"We do have motivational tweakers to encourage their daily progress. Also, they are welcome to relax in front of customizable gandas that read to them epigrams and parables from my in-house bestseller *Work Is the Greatest Joy or Else*."

"Yes, but what have you done to address these mass suicides?"

"You are exaggerating. For every person who is miserable there are hundreds that are merely indifferent, even apathetic. As for the rottens in every barrel, we have installed safety latches so you can't just flush yourself out into space."

"You think you're pretty molten fodder, Mr. Goo. Why is that?"

"I got going with only a few carbon credits. First, I worked in a rehashing core, and then started putting together nipple sensitizers and joy-zone positioning systems, until I got my big break making wankerjacks for Nintendari. The rest, as they say, is mystery."

"So your marvellous success means you can just poop people out into space? That is out of order!"

"Wait a tick – we provide extensive training—"

"Now what about public concern that, and I quote, *All the jizzle you flog is not even environmentally affable*."

"As we like to say at Googreen, the jizzle is you. All of the products we build have a very high annihilation factor and when you are done with them they automatically self-degrade into an offalicious goop. Besides, all the harmware testing we have done has gone better than expected."

"But is not the jizzle you, Mr. Goo?"

"Ms. Vauxhall, you overlook the fact that the soakproof gadgetoris you are wearing right now, although you bought it from iDget, was built in one of my factoriums."

"Outrageous! And what is next for Googreen?"

"Well, if you enjoyed using the Snogger and the Touch-Me-Now, you will love what is hot off the disassembly line! The latest in iDgetBrain technology."

"O goody! I never go anywhere without my Dwindle. And the iBrain helps me do annoying chores in a whap!"

"I shouldn't even tell you this on account of a wriggle-proof clause with Bildung Endustries, but I'm just so excited to be in the shower with you! I even blanched my hair for this interview."

"It's not gonna matter. I've already fallen in love with your gigasmic wealth."

"This is the newest thing in high-devolution perversion technology, guaranteed to totally outdumb the Dwindle and the iBrain. Allow me to introduce you to the MeMeMe ..."

For a nano, nothing happened. Then the shower stall began to fill with swirling *Vorspielen* and bizarre harmonies.

"This is just a meditational plainchant to help you relax."

"Me me me me me me me me me me me me me me me me me me me me me me me me ..."

"O bother! I can see and feel everything ... so much pain and despair. There is no meaning to anything we say or do. What is the point? Now I want to flush myself out into space ..."

"I would like to point out this is in Secular Moderate mode. Once you switch it to Zealous Devout mode, you will want to get down on your knees and believe absolutely anything!"

"Well, Mr. Goo, you've already got me convinced. In a vast pointless universe, the sticky elimination of a few snivellers ain't gonna amount to much."

Why We Cut Our Losses

Cornelius Quartz arrived home late, feeling heavy with cares. As in the past, he tried to tell himself the transmati had not quite agreed with him and that he must learn not to douse everything in suspect mayalaise. The truth was that he was rooting around in the retrofuse, to use a dated expression. What he had once shared with Ms. Lazuli was very precious to him, although what they had shared would never return to them. All the same, the feelings did not subside. Meanwhile, there was nothing here for him. The stark quietude told him that the Marquis and his wife were otherwise engaged in the cybertorium. It was not that he had anything to complain about. The general extirpation of the universe would continue in his favour, much as the regreening would. With the tireless help of Mr. Goo, his new line of atmosphere-affable Objects would devastate any plans of Zirconium Bluff's to catch the worm.

Quartz murmured softly to himself as he received a hot flash. WHY WE CUT OUR LOSSES.

Apparently, Minor and Diminuenda were no longer an item, mainly due to Minor's posthumous personality quirks. The hot flash promised all the innards of their liquidation, but he elected to switch to the Effing Concerto in F Minor instead, a brilliant voxian work with a thousand and three parts to it, the most memorable being the bludgeoning shriekata known fondly as "Elvira Minor" and carefully modelled after one of Scarlatti Minor's more disagreeable significants. Quartz paced to and fro, lost in thought. Then he found himself in one of the compostules. He tapped on the vermicell and roused the gigasmic foetida. Agro Endustries had cornered the market on waste disposal by giving each foetida self-replicating capabilities and had simultaneously slowed down their replication cycle by cultivating a patriphagic character, enabling the replicant to consume its own androgynous birthgiver. Quartz supposed he was projecting his own immediate sense of solitude onto the glumbing foetida, trying to take solace in the fact that it was a worm-eat-worm world. The trouble was that the foetidas were consuming waste at a rate faster than it could be produced, and all the time they were becoming bigger and more insatiable. There was no question of their breaking free of their vermicells and creating unspeakable chaos. It was only a question of when. Although it was blind, the foetida appeared to be staring back at him, imploring him for answers he would rather not give.

She waited, Goneril Quartz, since she preferred her unpillaged name, although that was more than a little gigglacious, for her father's visit, but unconscionably, he kept her waiting as if she were a supplicant drone in some antechamber beyond the viewing platform at Bildung Endustries, where at least she would have been free to watch the dancing identicles and whiplashing motions of the gooseneck ogler, along with the aesthetic perfection of the lugscrews and wingnuts as they kept everything in a state of continual thrust. The source of irritation troubled her more than the irritation itself, or the frequent act of changing from the loveswing to the omphalorest in no small effort to convey the most casual of moods and findings – she had tried it over and over – shifting between slippery and sticky. She had looked at the neurotic modalisques by Brassica Rapa on the mallow wall a thrillion times and had repeatedly accessed the same hot flash about Minor and Diminuenda severing ties, due either to his foul petiquette or her uneven shaving habits.

WHY WE CUT OUR LOSSES. For Goneril, it was a sharp blow, to be sure, to lose the freedom she had felt, even vicariously, through their precarious and perversial union. She would turn to the viewing portal and stare down at the bulgar street that gave no relief from what she now found a bulgar room, without that solid name to occupy it. Every time she turned in again, every time in her impatience, she gave him up, in a soundless sound deeper than the soundless hunger of the foetidas or the soundless boundless lust of the Marquis, cavorting with ... that ... that ... woman she had once called friend, while she thought to disown what she had never once hoped to own. She sucked back the faint, flat emanation of things, the failure of fortune and of honour. If she continued to wait, it was really, in a way, to avoid appending the shame of fearing individual personal collapse to the long tail of other shames that drooped heavily between her legs. To feel the ashen street, to feel the phlegmatic room, to feel the emptiness of the loveswing and the dryness of the candied lamp, gave her a small sense of salinity, of holding her shape the more mercilessly she was squeezed by this nonsensical passion.

This whole vision was the worst thing yet – as including, in particular, the interview for which she had armed herself in the only way she could. Her eyes shone black in this subdued light and there were rings under them. However, she was handsome, and the degree of it was not sustained by items or aids or hypertropics; a circumstance moreover playing its part at almost any time in the impression she produced. This impression was one that remained, but as regards the sources of it, no sum in addition would have made up the total. She was effective without action, compelling without interrogation, presence without biomass. In other words, she had so little to do with the biological requirements for life, she was something of a nonentity in relation to her – to Quartz's obvious carbon chauvinism.

Slender and soundless and astounding in the sense that, like other young ladies of her standing, she aspired toward a state of undressing, in the most refined sense of the word, and finding herself perpetually in the line of the eye; she had succumbed in no less than striplicate to the pressures in the shape of the bony doe-eyed slank she had welcomed into their home, only to lose everything to her continual falsifications of memory, thus rendering herself a freakish scion of the

Quartz stalk that could be neither be grafted onto nor held tenderly by those massive immaculate hands. In spite of being silicon-based and somewhat alien in his eyes, she didn't judge herself cheap. Something was afoot – she felt this to the roots – but surely she was not marked like one of their foodish effects for interstellar auction. She hadn't given up yet, and the broken language, if she was the last word, would end with a sort of meaning. For a tick, she considered her chances at bringing her father round, were she a carbon-based chap of the best inbreeding, although this seemed farther from her interior desire than where she swung now. It was the name, above all, she would take in hand – the precious name she cherished, and in spite of all her father had done or not done with it, the name that was hers to clutch or cast away as she pleased.

The Marquis lay face down, snugly nippled into a table of the finest masochintz. After the electrostrop had ceased its tantalizing switching, he could feel the Karma-arm parting his purple marsupial chaps. For a tick, the idea flicked across his drowsy robotomized mind that he and Chalcedony had been in the cybertorium for he knew not how long. He had already observed the first signs of technotechiness in her, and yet he could not quite bring himself to correct her with a firm hand. For one thing, his hands were wired directly into the masochintz for added effect. Also, Chalcedony had a talent for procuring those tender lambs, as they called them, whose upjacked hemostructs provided an experience so intense that anything outside of it seemed a mere 4-dim pseudoreality.

Chalcedony switched to toady-mode and began to lash his open wounds with her elongated tongue. This was precisely what he meant about her. She possessed, for lack of a less bulgar word, imagination, something in short supply. Of course, having the stuff was one thing, but knowing how to feed it was quite another. He was about to dredge up the fully linkable pickle from his subliminal when he realized she was turning the tables on him. DewBerry had been shielding his intention all along, and now loomed over them in the form of a swillmoeba. As DewBerry's primary set of rainbow protuberances plugged his mouth and all the ancillary tubes made their own respective entrances, even in the most imaginary of places, the Marquis kept his eyes fixed on the blipverts built into the voxelate terrorscape, one of a young weepy couple in shredded outfits for C&A Clothier and another showing the latest hot flash, WHY WE CUT OUR LOSSES.

Just then, Fanny Assu entered unannounced and strode toward the largest phallus in the room, the extract of partly adulterated maize from *Cuckold Heterosis*. It took all of her strength to prop it up against one of the lovehooks on the wall and raise it over her head. At first, it seemed her back might give out, but then she managed to regain her footing and heave it a short distance through the air. The antique shattered at once, cracking into pieces at the feet of Goneril, who now clung to her father out of fear and a sense of madthatch exhilaration. Fanny's eyes were blazing wide and her hair was a nosferat's nest and not her customary coxcomb. She regained her breath and stared down father and daughter for what seemed to all of them like forever, until she finally opened her mouth to deliver her fatal phrase.

"There is a flaw in this phallus! A flaw!"

With that, Fanny turned and stormed out, leaving a vast imponderable silence in her wake. Quartz collapsed back into a smarmchair and tried out a laugh that emerged as a sigh floating in the middle of a sob. Goneril fell into his lap and leaned her head against his shoulder.

"What is the matter, Father?"

"The matter, Goneril?"

"There is something the matter, isn't there?"

"Minor and Diminuenda are no longer together."

"Is that it, then?"

"It is an *it*, to be certain."

"Yet, is there not another *it* we might speak of?"

"If you are worried about the phallus, keep in mind the foetidas need feeding."

"I never liked that thing anyway."

"Well then, what kind of thing do you like?"

"I think you know."

"What am I to think you think I know?"

Goneril sat on his lap and leaned her head upon his chest. His lips formed words very slowly.

"Goneril, what if I were to go away, for a long long time? Perhaps forever. You and Chalcedony would be free to divide up my assets. And the Marquis. Let us not forget our dear Marquis! I want to give everyone a fresh start."

They both turned to look as Chalcedony entered, glowing after a long session in the spauna.

"Have you heard? About Minor and Diminuenda, I mean?"

Right away, she gave them both hot flashes and they all stopped to absorb the latest updates on this universal crisis. WHY WE CUT OUR LOSSES ...

A Sad State of Affairs

Klouk Meek crept into the domicell as quietly as he could, but the room instantly spotflared him and his hand upon the collar belonging to Dasha Peridot. Klouk glared at Perdita Diamond, who glared back, slightly aflutter.

"What are you doing, here in the dark?"

"I needed to recharge."

"I see."

"You did not make our rendezvous."

"I know."

"This is a sad state of affairs."

"This is Dasha."

"Klouk, her ident scans as a Bildung Endustries employee *of a certain age*, subject for level K550 elimination."

"Yes, I meant to talk with you about that."

"No subclasses are valid past the terrestrial age of forty."

"Yes, but there are sidesteps to that tiresome rule, right?"

"This entire scenario has no logical structure."

"That's because you're a robot."

"I will have to run an exacerboot sequence to bypass the Bildung tamperware. Plug this into the source node and this into Dasha's ... well, you know where."

Perdita began to execute the sequence while the other two listened to the rhythmic hum of her machinery, which sounded like the beating of phantom wings. Then, she stopped.

"Now what?"

"Now we pack for somewhere stellar."

The slideaway opened to reveal the formidable figure of Fuschia Kunnst, sporting the latest in spazzy deprogramming satchels.

"Fuschia ... aren't you from Receptive?"

"*Was* from Receptive. I've just been promoted to Chief Prefect."

"How so?"

"I just took the initiative and collared my first midlife."

Fuschia seized Dasha's collar and began stunning her until she was like putty in her onion gloves. Then she squirted a pulsating tweakdill.

"At least one of us is going to enjoy this."

Perdita monitored the vital signs of the writhing midlife and in parallax registered a particle in her damselfly remnants akin to what the sobbing man would call personal triumph.

To Mule or Not to Mule

Oober Mann woke up with a scream. There were still two bodies in bed with him but they were nothing like the ones he had expected to see. Under semi-normal circumstances, the sudden reappearance of Vanessa Velveteen to his right would have triggered one mode of behaviour, followed sharpishly by another, in Aristotelian terms *anagnorisis*, the revelation, followed by a *denouement*, the loosening or untying of knots. Of course, he had often complained about having far more of the former than the latter on a regular basis. In this particular case, Captain Ketchup, the obvious male counterpart to Vanessa Velveteen, Dijon Diva, lay to his left. Further spoiling any possibility of intimacy was a lone man standing with his back to all three of them.

"They call me Ruckus, in your primitive tongue. Major Ruckus, to be precise. This is Ackmod, and you have already met Vanessa Velveteen."

"Why ... wha ... huhn?"

"Can you get through to this dulkling drück?"

Vanessa Velveteen performed a rather obvious attention-getter with both hands before sidling close and whispering the details into Oober's ear.

"Way back in what you believe is one of your charlatanic novels, *Major Ruckus*, which is really a pile of scattercrack that should be mutilaxed, we were up to our snortables chasing a false cadence, believing that if we laid hands upon the tachyonometer, we would be able to thwart Minor's temporal manipulation schemes with mere schema that we will, for the lack of a perfect translation, call überconsciousness. That means you were more or less our hollowed-out piñata full of surprises, our thought-mule."

Oober responded instinctively to her mustardy breathiness and the consistent motion of her spicy hands.

"I'm with you so far."

"Well, we had no idea that Minor had developed beyond Jurgen's Flying Squirrel theory, using it as the basis for his own missing sock theorem. This is neither here nor there, but he was able to isolate a hole left behind by some time larvae and enter the rift. We thought we could trap him with a celebrity exclusive but then we realized that was only a projection of his essence, a type of *Zeitschatten* accompanied by an adorable Dalmation, while Minor himself was and is bending the laws of space and time with his consciousness. Once we discovered his technique, we realized that we had the perfect countermeasure within reach, our own überconsciousness to build up however we wished as a means of neutralizing Minor's influence ..."

"O yes ... so close ..."

"Now we need to stuff our secret weapon somewhere Minor would never dream of looking. That is where you come in, my dear piñata."

"I'm not so sure. I've got a lot on at the moment."

"Let me put it this way, little burro. You have two options."

"Uhmmm?"

"You become the greatest author and the greatest Mann in the known universe."

"Sounds like a lot of work. What is option two?"

"You are without delay pooped out into space."

"What was the first option again?"

Beyond Counterclock

"Charmdeep Offensive!"

"I don't believe we've had the pleasure."

"It's me, Lux. Lux Operon!"

She beamed and glowed. Recognition dawned upon him.

"I did not recognize you without your Bildung mandatories."

"Because I passed my exams. I'm now a junior time mechanic."

"Please know that I am happy for you, although I am not quite so happy in myself."

"Glerg. What's wrong?"

"It oppresses me so much, I cannot move."

"I thought you were going to Punditar."

"O Punditar! What a wounded name is there."

"Well, being a time mechanic is beyond counterclock."

"You see, the machinations of politics are not for me."

Lux laughed and held up her hands and waggled them about.

"What next?"

"I must reinvent myself yet again. For every jab and sting to my heart, I must take my revenge upon the squishier sex. I may even begin with the unassailable Jasmine Samosa! If I go to Punditar, I shall not go as myself. I shall go in the guise of the greatest seducer who ever lived ..."

"Minor?"

"Minor? Minor and Diminuenda are no longer together."

"Fffffff ... then who?"

"I don't remember. I've spent too long in the rehashing core. But from this day forth, I shall wear a mask and be known exclusively as Don Diamante!"

"Sounds molten. Uppermost there's a lot of need for time mechanics just now. There's a purple priority project in the offing. That's how I got my training sped up. You should apply."

"Correction. You should apply, Don Diamante."

"Flarf!"

The Last Pome on the Matter

"I'm Perspicacity Vauxhall with BBC Omniverse, stationed directly above the nest of the time larvae, where we are waiting for something tiddelicious to happen. Already, our panel of cephalocentrics and quantum jiffies have fled in abject horror with a case of the scrotes no less. Just when you wanted more cephalo."

She paused to smile cheekily.

"In the name of phishy corset-filler, we are joined by respected Doctor of Pome Infestation and, gosh, the last carbon-based poet, Brassica Rapa."

"Nova maximum to join you, Perspicacity."

"Dr. Rapa, are you a carbon chauvinist?"

"People like to say that, especially flirtnaps, but first—"

"You blew up a solar system full of silicon lifeforms just to please yourself."

"Not to please myself. To further cultivate and grow the penultimate pome."

"Yet they had to perish ... for your scatterings, for your smatterings."

"I was sanctioned by the Universal Union of Pome Cultivation and Termilization."

"Yes, but what gives you the right to wipe out an entire civilization?"

"They are savages, beasts, as far as silicrobes go."

"Why you, and nobody else?"

"I have extensive training in Pome Infestation. And let me be perfectly clarose. I have my paperwork in order and no one else is authorized to create a pome."

"Not that I mind, personally. There's nothing better after one of these tedious lobecasts than to slather myself in cumquam fungu and diex into one of your hyperallegenetic hoperas. My significant and I frequently have congress in front of a large gepome we have growing on the terrace. And when I'm out on the yank with the girls, there's nothing more snarvy than to go to a potox party."

"That's not my legitimade potox. It is made by someone else and that is illegal."

"Still, it feels so exciting and beautiful caroming about my nervous system, even without your blessing."

"BUT IT IS NOT A REAL POME. I AM THE POET. ME."

Perspicacity took out a talking stick of finest leek and began poking Dr. Rapa. "Now let's talk about your other problems ..."

"I have my paperwork in order. Neurologically tamperstamped in quinclate ..."

"So you're gonna wipe out the whole universe, hmm?"

"Not the entire universe. Just language as we know it. I will start with the word *gonna*."

"And what do you say to post-primordial-avantists, who think your work is germophiliac and verbaphobic?"

"To restate my position, THERE IS NO ONE BUT ME. I AM THE POET. ME."

"Yes, but isn't this obsession with implanting information in ... what you call xenopauses ... isn't it of no use or interest whatsoever to anyone but yourself? In fact, this is what gives you the linguistic upper hand, yes?"

"There are no stories left to tell, no more lyrical trollop, no more musical wallop. Nothing but germ wordfare. And the last pome on the matter, which I happen to be working on—"

"Yes, yes, but don't you feel that success would only serve some deep-seeded lopsy-doodle theophilic demi-urge and retrobait carbon-based organisms back into an inferior version of our soupy beginnings? I mean, c'mon, Dr. Rapa, that is so origin-of-species—"

"THERE WILL BE NOTHING BUT THE WORD VIRUS ... nothing."

Perspicacity pulled a lever and released a cannicle of tabbouleh upon her guest.

"My producer is signalling me to activate the crackpot. However, as we're locked in dead space for some time, I understand you've brought some of your little word virus with you ... what the blastbog is it called again?"

"Verminjer. I used an alphabetical sequence to come up with the perfect name in a dozen—"

"Fettlespark! Now let's give it a whirl ..."

"I keep it in this jar."

"Just like Pandora. She didn't even have a box, har har. My seven-year-old loves that one."

"NO. NO MORE SWINY STORIES. NO MORE ANYTHING—"

"Well, my producer is signalling me to show a bit more leg and to ask you to open the ..."

Never Eat Breakfast

In a nearby Nothing Dodgy, Euphemisma Magma was stirring a piping bowl of hautemeal with a largegantic spurtle when the franic started. Not to say she had not seen it coming, and not to say they didn't have it coming, righteous tastards! The signs were all around ... the slurring of speech and the spread of something called glossaloss, as they were calling it on the newsless. Drück the wideload! She figged suff ticks to sashay on down to the ol' Moothouse where geezes would let her retinate in sacrosanct. She was crimp for the latest volume to crosswire her spam interface, although she was spliff to the metatext swirling down the kludgie. This was hellawise no place to bring up a language. She served up the hautemeal and reached for her glistening armour and beautifully wrought aviamet. The analplate still read BILDUNG although she was no longer a courier for that outfit. Not that it mattered to someone in an obscure corner of a dying novella. Whey, whoever didn't suss that needed a solid braining. Spankwise, some dimdo was in her way, and one thing Euphemisma did not care for was someone getting in her way. She pointed to the sign on the wall behind her. **LEAD, FOLLOW, OR GET THE DRÜCK OUTTA MY WAY** ... The geez nodded and held up the hautemeal.

"This temperature is not correct."

"Contrariwise, that is a work of art."

"You will have to redux it from reboot."

"Redux it from reboot?"

Euphemisma reached for a bottle of Zonk she had stowed behind the counter and took an überhealthy swig. This was an opportunity to tickle the trigger of her waiting huzzazooka, an act which always made her brighten.

"Sir, you are speaking to the thrice winner of the Beholden Spurtle Contest."

"This hautemeal is a little too molten. Or gelid. Either way ..."

Euphemisma grinned and swept back her yellowing vauxhawk.

"Verimax, the hautemeal is JUST RIGHT ..."

By the tick the tetchisome geez recognized the business end of a huzzazooka, his empty head was rolling across the floor of the break-even chain, far from the remains of his curdled body.

"If I'm getting rhetoricked, I'm hella gonna catchphrase a few twonks outta lingo ..."

Honko sighed and began dragging the body into the back.

"This is the third time this week, Euph. You'll never learn your lesson."

Euphemisma snorted, even as she watched him rapidly running out of words. If anything, she was going down as a proud sufferer of glossaloss.

"Honko, the lesson is never eat breakfast ..."

And the Winner Is ...

Payola Burnish crept out of the darkness in a slashed avocado creation. Infrared lighting followed her frenetic dance number in celebration of the ancient people of the Cinnabague constellation. It was the moment she had been waiting for. She executed the self-mating rites perfectly before finishing off with a carefully engineered banana. Then, with a bombastardized crash, the finale was over with. Copious amounts of rarefied oxytocin began to drip from the surrounding walls and the besotted audience activated their mock seals, who applauded wildly. Then, a few people burst into flame as Jen Mod and Beau Brood were lowered from the ceiling atop a corny phallus equipped with not one but two saddles. Upon a lavish sprattress provided by Futility, they made love publicly for the first time, unless it was just their body doubles love-synching to homemade splattercasts.

Out of the murderous rivalry to secure various body parts for corporate placement, Bildung Endusteries had outbid everyone for both of Beau Brood's buttocks, and Spartamart for a sizable rumpclamp upon Jen Mod, which had necessitated the erasure of her eternal dedication to her old flame Pukey Tronovich. In fact, it was Pukey's financial collapse that had led to a highly dubious and therefore forgettable encounter in a slavish cockloft, which in turn had led to her participation in a popular awareness campaign about Bildung's rumoured plans to repetrolize Carbon Harbour, a place even Pukey had barely heard of. So it was making quite a statement, to publicly surrender to a reciprocating meteoric in the form of Beau Brood, digging her fingers into the glowing letters lining his sublime behind (in protest?)(in support?) until she was wholly subjected to his own brand of spillage. When the music stopped, they sat up and lit herbal smokes, before quickly extinguishing them meaningfully into one another. It had been agreed they could not smoke and receive their cueblasts at the same time.

"Wow, Beau, thank you for having me."

"It was my pleasure, Jen."

"I have never known love in a Futility bed before."

"I know. It is the supreme experience in easy and comfort."

"It is the memory bed that remembers whatever you did."

"Even when we don't?"

"Ha ha. Maybe it won't forget to tube me tomorrow."

"Ha ha. Maybe."

"Speaking of doing things in bed, there is nothing I like better than inserting a deep literary masterpiece."

"Nothing?"

"Almost nothing. Ha ha."

"Ha ha."

"This brings us to the tick we have all been waiting for. The way Harmony Demantoid said it, if I've gotta put up with these drücken words, then so does everybody else. Wow, that is so molten."

"That is so messed up."

"The nominees for interstellar excess and omphalocentricism in a literary category are ... help me, Beau ..."

"Sodality Mange, for *The Taciturn Itch* ..."

"Emerson Goshenite, for *A Bowl of Figments* ..."

"Vuhjay J. Sic, for *Will Work for Wonko* ..."

"Erie Aventurine, for *Oort War O: An Oral History of the Oral War* ..."

"Puddles Diaspore, for *The Glorywall That Cried* ..."

"And last but not least, help me out, Beau ..."

"Oober Mann, for the Chaos! Quincunx ..."

The drug had been perfectly timed. Oober Mann woke upon hearing the sound of his own name in the mouth of Beau Brood. Vanessa Velveteen smiled broadly at him, whispering through her teeth. When he felt her foot under the table, he knew it was no game of footsie. It was a game of lethal injection, and a most embarrassing game at that. He knew because stuff like this was always happening to him. It was merely the toe of her prickpedaller. The heel remained suspended over his groin, waiting for a single false note on his behalf.

"You know, stuff like this is always happening to me."

"Play along, Mann, and you may just live through this."

"And the winner is ..."

Less Salt Than Ever Before

Deep in the belly of Bildung Endustries, word was spreading. Here and there, one by one, people began to shuffle out without a word. Mr. Galliard shook his head. Only yesterday, the word virus would have meant nothing to him. Today it was the only news vlit. On the other side of the pod sat Ms. Garamond. She was also aware of the news, although they had not discussed it. They had scarcely spoken and now it seemed the end was near. They were thinking of returning home to their respective spouses, although they were tarrying more than anyone who knew the truth of what was happening. How much time had passed exactly? They made silent calculations. There was nothing to remember, barely a word here and there, and yet this incredible tension between them remained. Of course, they had moved on to different branches of Bildung and had no reason to be overtly friendly. They were merely physical beings, sharing a pod with a wall between them.

For the most part, they only knew what they heard of one another. They knew the sudden cries, the laughter, the snorts, the sneezes, the sighs, and the various signs of frustration in one another. Mr. Galliard stood up and looked around. No one left in their section. Tentatively, he pressed his body against the wall. Ms. Garamond heard a sound she had never heard before. It was a sad lowing, full of underlying purpose. She got up and put her hands against the wall. It felt like it was electrified. Mr. Galliard gave out even more poignant sighs and groans and in response she began to pick at the wall. It was a standard soybeam wall, held together with edible fixative, and it did not take her long to form a small hole. Mr. Galliard worked on his side, picking at all that edamame between them until the hole was a decent size. They did not want to see one another. His arm reached through the hole and she accepted his caresses wherever they happened to land. At some point, she began to guide his fingers and it did not take much, after years and years of ambiguous proximity, for a result to be achieved, even through an edible wall with less salt than ever before.

In a world running out of language, they had nothing to talk about, nothing to admit, nothing to do but what was most obvious to each of them. The few sounds they had left were enough to communicate what seemed imperative. They each took a step away and adjusted their costumes accordingly before returning to the hole. "Oooooooooooo ..."

Wiggle Room

Ms. Lazuli got up and slid into a fresh sheave. Then she activated the frontiscan. She hesitated a few ticks before opening up. Mr. Quartz doffed his mercury hat and smiled. There was nothing in his looks but deep longing. He put his arm around her waist and pulled her close, tearing through the sheave and touching her as he had never touched her before. She leaned against the siloplast and seized his wrist, helping him. The only thing to interrupt their sensual reverie was the sleepy voice of Zirconium Bluff.

"Are you coming back to bed?"

"In two shakes!"

Mr. Quartz continued smiling and withdrew his fingers.

"It's ... not a good time."

"I'm ready to blow this repocycle. Come with."

"Come with?"

"Yes, my darling. There's really only one way for this story to end."

"But what about the word virus? Isn't every story coming to an end?"

"Did you ever know me to lack a loophole?"

"Well, you do allow for a great deal of wiggle room."

They smiled warmly. Zirconium Bluff was starting to get an undeniable case of krankwack.

"I ... have to take care of ... this."

Mr. Quartz put on his hat and nodded. Then thinking better of it, he handed her a glistening capsule.

"Our latest promotional cajole ..."

"A nanodroplet ... how curricula!"

"Masticate. You know where to find me."

Ms. Lazuli watched him depart. Her heart was beating fast. She returned to the bedroom to find Zirconium Bluff in an obvious state of agitation.

"You certainly got your strength back in a hurry."

"I must have the right inspiration."

"Sucralose!"

"Who was at the door?"

"Just a man in a mercury hat."

"Mince! Shall I assume the position?"

Ms. Lazuli popped the capsule and lay down beside him.

"I would like to try something first."

This Is Not a Pipe

She lay back and fingered in as Bev Holder, who for the past fifteen ticks had been the most popular flogger of industrial product on the open market. Right away, she found herself straddling a largegantic length of pipe, although the purely organic sign on the side read **THIS IS NOT A PIPE**, an afterthought by someone in the aesthetics division. She was keenly aware of what the role-play scenario demanded of her. It was to lend beauty and excitement to this cold hard thing, to give it a warm fleshiness, as it were. Bev Holder had started in condimentals but had quickly crossed over into smears, soon becoming the face and form of Mothershucker, and was quickly credited with successfully launching a new line of aphrodizzies. It was not long before she was moonlighting for subsidiaries of Metawhore Solutions, whose soft-then-hard-then-soft-again sales technique was both beloved and infamous within the corridors of the most innovative congloms.

Bev Holder only had to walk into a room of sales executives and walk out again to leave their paradigm completely and inexorably shifted. At present, she had instructions not to entirely strip away her seaweed outfit. Not yet anyway. She was mainly acting as a divertimento to the reassurances of Dick Crick, the acting president of Crude Crude. Although Bev Holder didn't quite grasp all the opposition to the project, every time she tried to think about it, she remembered that she was currently the highest paid bit of mindcandy, and if nothing else, that was nothing to lose schmooze over. Dick Crick cleared his throat and spat.

"Um ... thank you for attending this public information session. This is not the first PIS we have held on this subject and I hope this shows we are willing to do whatever it takes to ... uh ... get rid of ... or ... better yet, recognize your concerns and ... um ... allay your fears."

Werner Gig stood up, canola hat in hand.

"You are planning to build a pipeline that runs right through my wind pharm. Now, do you think this is really a good idea, what with these accidents that keep happening? And what am I gonna do with all these starving workers? Bad nuff the local pests keep snacking on our womenfolk ..."

"Excellent points, sir. I would like to take this opportunity to point out that Crude Crude has done nothing criminal ..."

A woman with an octobomb on her head stood up.

"O, you will make a pretty penny out of this! Meanwhile, what about all the dimensional creatures in the interstellar zone you are destroying ... with your ... with your ... PIPE?"

Bev Holder dipped her left hand into her seaweed merkin and shook her head, licking her lips and nodding at the sign.

"Ms. Holder is lovely, isn't she? And she is also correct. As the sign says, this is not a pipe."

This triggered a kneejerk response from one of the Apocalypse-watchers who never missed one of these public meetings. Still in mid-snore, she jumped up.

"Not a pipe? Not a pipe? Then what, then what, I ask? When you least expect it, on the day of reckoning, you will find there is a pipe, a pipe that is waiting for you and all of your seamy filth and—"

Dick Crick tore open his whole wheat deltaghetti shirt and threw it at Bev Holder, who on subliminal cue smelt it longingly. He gave out a powerful catcall, signalling his associate-with-benefits Perma Tan, who entered with a great twirl, leaping into the air and landing upon two of his fingers with perfect precision.

"All you have to do is whistle ..."

This was not an act of desperation. Far from it. He was never afraid to play the handsome card. It had gotten him this far, and aside from regurgitating the contents of *Crude Quarterly*, his favourite thing was to pump some flesh. He even knew in his heart of hearts that he was more molten than Beau Brood, although admittedly, he was neither thespian nor maturithrob. Where words failed, animal scent would triumph.

"Now listen up. This is a high-pressure crudepipe. Its thin walls are based on products formerly created by the contraceptive outfit Barely There, and are designed for pleasure and comfort, without sacrificing integrity or sensation ..."

Mr. and Mrs. Midmod stood up and held one another.

"We are not ... um ... happy ... we don't ... want ... this."

Dick Crick leapt over the podium and landed directly in front of them.

"SIT DOWN."

Dick Crick tore away his slacks and was truly magnificent in snap-bean briefs. He rested his hands behind his head and began to rotate his hips, teasing the couple with pelvic jerks. He inched closer and closer until they felt they could almost taste the dangling brocolettes.

"You say that here and now. But behind closed doors, where do you think all the energy for your fantasies comes from? Hmm ... this?"

Dick Crick fed each of the Midmods a brocolette, establishing trust.

"Did you know that ninety-five percent of biofuel usage leads to virtual projectile dysfunction?"

At that point, a man with wild eyes ran into the room and tore at his shock of white hair.

"BIOFUEL IS MADE OUT OF PEOPLE!"

"That's right, friend. So unless you want your progeny to be made into botteries, you better adjust your attitude about the subject of alternative power."

"Um ... we don't have ... kids."

"Of course you don't have kids. You are strung out with green this and green that. Did you know that the installation of a crudepipe is proven in several studies to incite conception and induce labour?"

"But we don't want—"

"O that is such compost noob. In my line of work, I've seen people, and except in a few isolated cases, when the lips say no, the eyes say yes, or even I don't really know what I want, please help me o please help me Dick Crick!"

"_!?"

"I know you're kind of intimidated. And maybe that's part of getting your kicks. You think the crudepipe might rupture and get you all dirty? Yeah? Maybe you wanna get dirty, huh?"

Mrs. Midmod looked worried. Mr. Midmod looked even more worried.

"Where ... would you stick this ... pipe?"

"First of all, THIS IS NOT A PIPE! It is merely a conveyance for the heaviest and thickest crude you ever saw. Just imagine it, slow as molasses, running down our bodies ... a thing of beauty, if you ask me!"

Bev Holder smiled to herself. She was enjoying the classic mechanic what-the-cuck fantasy and the way it had been tweaked to put together this promotional prompt. Throw in a few aquacukes and they would be keen as mustard gas!

"Now how about a little offshore action?"

Then, in a surprising turn of events, Dick Crick broke from his seduction posture to fasten a belt around Mrs. Midmod's waist.

"Go on now. You give it a try!"

At first it was painful. Mr. Midmod wept a little. But it was what he wanted. It was what they both wanted. Deep down, everybody was an energy freak. And as the couple began to speed up, he cheered them on.

"Good one! Way to go! Get right on in there! Dill baby dill! Dill baby dill!"

The Most Nauseating Award Show Moment

Oober Mann was pushed out of his chair and shoved forward by Vanessa Velveteen. Everybody was grinning, except for Sodality Mange. Puddles Diaspore and Vuhjay J. Sic didn't look too pleased either but they were putting on a good front. A holokludge had been mimeogaffed together from footage in the tetchital archives to reanimate some actor from the past named Greg Peck, who stood guardedly and impressively in front of the prestigious award and began to speak.

"Now, I know this young man is just itching to get up here and take this sparkling lady home with him with the only hand he favours – his right. But I have something to say. Not since I read the script for a little film called *Marooned* have I ever experienced in my mind the virtuosity and the excellence as are to be found in this man's book. This series of novels lets loose the upmost in the bowels of one's being and inspires the highest amount of love a man can feel for another man without complexifications ... and you know what I'm talking about. It's like having a prolonged conversation with a man in space who is taking up the oxygen of his friends. Sure, it's sad and more than a little sick, but what does that say about us? You might say what does that old phart know and hey he's not even real! But can you tell me what is real? The Chaos! Quincunx ... yes ... let it roll around your insides for a while until it stops churning and churning. This is desert planet stuff, proving that once in a wormhole, the despicable sublimation of all our nauseating otiose trash can be rolled up into something so beautiful it makes you weep and holler from the pleasure it causes. And this man, this Oober Mann, has shown us we can still kill a mockingbird. This man, this Oober Mann, has shown us we can keep the yearling. It is my great honour to present Oober Mann with the Ignoble Prize in a Speculative Category ..."

"Eeeee ... thank you. This is the kind of thing that all tellers of tales dream of. In this case, working on the general outline of the story of the universe ... the greatest story ever told, well, the juicy bits anyway ... it all happened so fast I barely remember throwing any of it together. O what do I say? So many people to thank and so many arbitrary circumstances to celebrate! I want to thank the birthgivers who abandoned me and the residential school that soundly prepped me for future thrashings. I want to thank the wife who never gave up not believing in me and the kids we never had. Go to sleep now, little Noshow. I want to thank the aliens who inhabited the vessel of Vanessa Velveteen and made me part of a racy Venusian subplot. I want to thank the Librarian for every femme fatality she subjected me to. I want to thank Perspicacity Vauxhall for spurring me on with her stoic and hypnotic reportage from Hertfordshire when I felt there was no end to the Bleak House of my life. Actually, I want to thank both the Librarian and Perspicacity Vauxhall for their collaborative lovemaking that gave me the confidence to complete this opus, or so they tell me. I also want to thank Alfred J. Bastard, who called me a neurotic fantasist and consistently took a crap on the finest of my works in progress. Well, now who's crapping their pants, eh Bastard? Last but not least, a very warm word of thanks to Minor himself, who inspired this universal epic, a surrealist tale of life, love, and resurrection ..."

Suddenly, the walls of the MucusAway Palladium began to drip and quiver. A hole opened up in the space-time continuum to the left of Oober Mann. One figure climbed out, followed by an immaculate spotted dog and the most beautiful woman anyone had ever seen.

"*Oober Mann / a cenar teco / m'invitasti / e son venuto ...*"

It was none other than Marcel Minor. He picked up Oober Mann like a tub of flowercine and threw him across the stage, leaving him upside down in the promotional love nest of Jen Mod and Beau Brood, if not their body doubles. Minor smiled and took to the podium in the shape of something abstract and ignoble.

"There once was a fellow of some note who really knew what nausea was. He once refused a similar award on the grounds that a writer must never allow himself to be transformed into an institution, even if such a transformation were to take place in the most honourable form. We are extremely fortunate this evening that the Chaos! Quincunx is my story, and for this reason I am accepting this award on my own behalf!"

Someone in the audience wailed. Diminuenda was just about to give Minor another mildly taboo kiss when Greg Peck sprang upon the pair of them with an undulating net of temporal cladwrap.

"Well, Minor, looks like your timehopping has come to an end."

Minor laughed out of sheer surprise.

"Then this was all a ridiculously elaborate setup ... just to flush me out!"

Diminuenda scowled.

"And we would have got away with it, if not for you pseudocelebrities!"

The truth about the Ignoble Prize, or the lack of it, had not yet sunk in for Oober Mann. However, Greg Peck and Sodality Mange looked positively radiant with a sense of righteous triumph.

"Now, why don't we go to Cape Fear for the weekend!"

Trash Talk

"Somewhere where we can be alone."

"Where do you imagine we can manage that?"

"The Necrodome – in Garbage Park."

Ms. Brava Bitwise had consented to meet Udjal Umlaut at his suggestion, although surely there was nothing in it. Avoiding the popular Jumbodump Collection, they made their way down a passage to the room where failed compostules and preterantique receptacles mouldered in unvisited loneliness.

"It seems cruel that after a while nothing matters ... any more than these little things, that used to be necessary and important to forgotten people, and now have to be puzzled over and labelled: **USE UNKNOWN** or **DO NOT TOUCH**."

"Yes, but meanwhile—"

"Hmmm ... meanwhile—"

"Meanwhile everything matters—"

"Would you gander that?"

Ms. Bitwise made a gesture toward a cylindrical cannicle with a rounded top and something akin to a mouth that opened and closed. Although Umlaut was absorbed by the cut of her guacamole number, he could not resist bursting into laughter at the thing she was pointing at.

"What the ficken is that?"

"The sign indicates that our distant predecessors used to throw away things they did not want or had no further use for."

"How terribly primitive!"

"Here – they have samples for us to try our hand at it."

Ms. Bitwise picked up one of the samples made of something called "plastic" and placed it in the opening mouth. The cylindrical cannicle spoke in response.

"THANK YOU ... FOR BEING ... GREEN."

Umlaut picked up a cup made of something called "styrofoam" and reached toward the mouth. Ms. Bitwise caressed the cup casually. Their hands were touching.

"NO ... DO NOT DO THAT ... NO ... DO NOT PUT THAT ... IN THERE."

She looked at the cannicle thoughtfully and then sat down on a sculpture of a landfill. He sat down beside her and they stared for a long while at the asbestos display.

"Well—"

"Well, then."

"This is the pussysick, to meet in such circumstances, yes?"

"The pussysick?"

"The chum, as children say. To be able to talk together without fear, to do these kinds of things without one nanodrop of apprehension—"

"What is this fear you speak of?"

"Forgive me—"

      "NO ... DO NOT ... DO THAT ..."

"I just heard about the linguistic breakdown on the newsless. Then it was clear it was time to tell you something."

"If you are just going to remind me that we are nothing more than ancillary characters in some distant future metanarrative, you can save your breath."

"No, not that. I have something more important to say. Something I have always wanted to say."

"I am listening."

"It is just that since I met you, I have always loft prudensure hin liftination varsus snaggletuckus slurround percentimes reducks qwack qwack qwack fram klack touwdy klack ecools massociation ees missif ees messalineation plee tud alinin puhlee kerry wun divise byeno nero lez rouxbiz nesssin thrine parsesod floom floom floom quiverrun weggs fies miremot fleapeep #notapipe scratchdad blitter ent krawphishing meshul perspicashun schticking fowes rerund pogrome ill plod in mine tricks fasterbator rhine ike isthmust inklish eyeles wid tash rejister periplumage taximurrrrr yellus bonely ower bomely zurnin spurrencee dist erryjarn fror zeels fror queals ornogger lornographogatory scrofulatte zutwipe serrible pornell awten oofplative tacid yowns xood inimicalation thusten arter stract ackoo hellody ermithered orrenz ushing blenk unguish frackee stottlestet adjing wructi ficashun pillyportis furentgreige umt ransfer theird nobblesh curtout hikenesses obister tariation om sture flust anter asterinize glurk mifferom oustlode emper chye murtheratio xod gnoggeepog trasticide elenurk azzmess fcoutre thamartia vendatree okeniter gruss flarkfill telotonal dellaz protio nistownt arsm himet shwoom nexicontinest ergones snist malaprostolute upplehoost lallydoozaster rentionast ackcesspoolpolid knad ibbitordial elp schnellish torkiste thorndolt rillot vagatorinse odenok empt jonderlee blurst fiskleque isterestial dyelt obnoiety stalarial nailure mordermime allagog wowel fonky rofresh drim zizoral ledify promagenous brestos grinsulate ologies toomoot utterlation pripped hexmen fasturtium lectitel ghonsterbate quont ..."

(Deceptive Cadence) The Future Is

Never in all his life had Mr. Quartz been a light year near Refuse, the former Terra Dulkis, sometimes also referred to as Nova Erda. His wettening adventures and enterprises, liquefying as they were, had been confined almost exclusively to Prudentia, without so much as a sojourn to the bordering Pudenda. He had mastered the rules of the game, and all the proverbial pieces (which is to say, oily manservants still in their salad days, organic or otherwise) were his. The fact he had a rival presented only the slightest of irritations. The only horn in his side had been the sight of Ms. Lazuli clinging to Zirconium Bluff and publicly calling him her rock. However, even that seemed a distant memory now. He smiled to himself, hands deep in greatcoat.

He was smitten with a mystery woman and, for the first time in his life, he had felt compelled to give someone all the access codes. He had scanned her pedigree and knew what might happen, nay, what *would* happen. Perhaps leaving her with unlimited carbon credits and a neuron bomb was not the most prudent course of action to ever occur in Prudentia, and yet he felt some manner of grand gesture was in order. This supersubtle lovetap included a one-way ticket to Refuse for the lady in question. Of course, it was common knowledge he was waiting on the platform for someone to arrive. He would not have been surprised to discover that Chalcedony had tracked him down, or that Ms. Lazuli had changed her mind and jumped into the nearest atomicab. Then they would implode with emotion before a backdrop of explosions. This was a recurring dream anyway, and Quartz felt it was prophetic, due to the unregulated radiation in the area.

"What a beautiful night ..."

A beautiful couple was blasted to oblivion right in front of him. Two bluecoats approached tentatively and shook their heads sheepishly.

"Sorry, sir. These nosferats are everywhere. I wish they weren't so freaking popular!"

"Find the one known as Charmdeep Offensive. He will know what to do."

"Everybody knows he virtually belongs to Bildung Endustries."

"Call it a hunch, but I believe he may be free in a few ticks."

Quartz felt deeper in his greatcoat and basked in the atmosphere of his new crapopolis. The surrounding land was jagged and disjunctive – little more than a heap of tortured and ill-tempered sprass fused together. For some reason a methamphetamine ambience enfolded the hazy outlines of the city, holding the latter like a damselfly in amber and giving it an artistic subtlety that nearly touched him in the way he wished to be touched. He reminded himself to purchase as many renderings of this scene as he could from the harbour artists with too many limbs. He could see the tracks from long-dead transportation systems, and for a tick he imagined reviving them once again, in spite of their general inutility. He watched the tarpeople struggling and copulating in the crude and wondered what it was about the primal vitality of this extensive dive that thrilled him to the core. What a place! Presently one of the last dying hubs of the filthy arrogant self-sufficient planetoid called Refuse, surrounded by oily black bodies of liquid and flanked by empty broken flitboosts.

"Sir, sir, come and lick my lubes for a loon!"

Here was life. He saw it at a flash. Here was a seething city in the making. There was something psynamic and sickergistic in the air that appealed to his dissipated fancy. How different, for some reason, from Prudentia, which itself was supposed to be a vast improvement upon Accenturia. He had thought them wonderful before, but this thing, while obviously infinitely worse, was better. It was positively scumptious. He would resurrect the most dirty ancient industries and hammer out the track for the Refuse–Quartz transportation line, tidily carrying fearsome miners and stokers from their pits to their jagged tortured dwellings. He loved the vast manipulative life all of these elements suggested. He observed a passing set of indigenetic specimens, indistinctly alternating between oil-based fighting and fornicating, and could not hide his satisfaction at the thought of channelling all that energy into his own newfound obsession. He also smiled to hear them mangling snatches from the free song of the free people:

> Torch him in a tub of tar
> Torch him like a blazing star
> Torch his body from his head ...

In roguish answer, he unclipped his greatcoat and let them catch a few obligatory jerks before closing it again.

"Har har, Mr. Quartz! You are one of us!"

"Lick my lubes! Half off for a gentleman!"

Quartz recalled that the historical name given to this place by its first inhabitants was Carbon Harbour. Having remembered this, he instantly convinced himself he had come up with this name on the spot. All of a sudden, even the foul air was fresh to him and full of promise.

"Cornelius Quartz, was there ever such a fortunate man?"

"Lick my lubes for next to nothing!"

"Now here's a sad wintering bird!"

"Pull your guzzler for a squid!"

Quartz knelt by one of the rippling black pools and addressed the gobby floaters.

"I will let you in on a little secret ..."

"Shtickle your tickler for a few ducks!"

"The future is coal."

Quartz looked up. A scorched luttle was slowly approaching. But who was aboard? And after all, would it matter terribly? Behind it, there was a gigasmic explosion. It seemed that former speakeasy days were already far behind him. Within less than a few ticks, a few twitching tube feeds were already gurgitating the first dubiblurts that language as we know it had guttered its last guttural and that the entire universe was so over, although this turned out to be more than just a minor exaggeration ...

Acknowledgements

For everyone at Talonbooks, in particular Gregory Gibson, Leslie Thomas Smith, and Chloë Filson, whose energetic efforts helped to bring this book into being.

Special thanks to Lynn Schellenberg, whose total immersion definitely helped to upgrade this Object.

If erotobots can be self-aware, then a modicum of emotions for wingmen Marion Farrant, Martine Desjardins, Aimee Ouellette, Dina Del Bucchia, Jamella Hagen, and Sandra Huber, who keep me convinced I will one day take home the Ignoble Prize.

Thank you, Michael Barnholden, Jonathan Ball, Nicholas Hauck, Carmen Papalia, Aubyn Rader, Missy Clarkson, Amanda Joy Ivings, Thor Polukoshko, Elliot Lummin, and Brook Houglum for having the foresight and futuristic gumption to publish unexpurgated splices of The Chaos! Quincunx series. Kudos to *West Coast Line, dANDelion Magazine, Memewar, The Maynard*, and *The Capilano Review*.

And thank you, in some Hegelian notion of eternal due process, Karl Siegler, for your stalwart support of my experimental fiction and for putting up with such text gone rogue ...

Collect all three books in The Chaos! Quincunx series

Minor Episodes /
Major Ruckus

Rogue Cells /
Carbon Harbour

Minor Expectations

The Chaos! Quincunx series includes five "nodal" novels that parody various writing styles and literary genres, including surrealist prose, speculative fiction, environmental dystopia, historical narrative, and the most prurient bodice-rippers.

"Of contemporary surrealist writers, Garry Thomas Morse is the most uncompromising. He courageously severs the umbilical cord with so-called reality and ventures into an invented world paradoxically more real than our own."
    – Barry Webster, author of *The Lava in My Bones*

"Like a beguiling house of mirrors, *Minor Episodes* bends, twists, fractures, and deforms reality through phantasmagoric visions, orgiastic inventions, and a mischievous use of language."
    – Martine Desjardins, author of *Maleficium*

"*Minor Episodes / Major Ruckus*, with its themes of sex, money, and intrigue, and with its over-current of hilarity running amok, explodes from the page. To say this novel is on steroids is to downplay things."
    – M.A.C. Farrant, author of *The Strange Truth About Us*

"An outrageous romp – wickedly inventive, clever as well as wise, deliciously satirical and steamier than sex and vegetables."
    – Des Kennedy, author of *Climbing Patrick's Mountain*